Robert Ryan is an author, journalist
contrib——es to *GQ* and *The Sunday Times*
for s——— years. Ryan is currently work
of tele——on projects. Find out more a— www.robtryan.com and follow
him or ——witter @robtryan

Praise for *Dead Man's Land*:

'Deep —— the trenches of Flanders Fields, men are dying by their thousands
every ——— But when a body turns up with bizarre injuries Dr John Watson
is sus——ous. Soon more bodies appear – there is a killer who must be
stopp—— *The Sun*

'Vivid ——epicting the war at the front and the machinations of the casu-
alty c——ing process, and with some strong characters and an interesting
Chur——il cameo, this is a page-turning read from Robert Ryan' *Daily Mail*

'A vi—— account of life in the trenches . . . this is a genuinely fascinating
and —— ly researched piece of war fiction' *Daily Express*

'Ry—— reinvention of Holmes' amanuensis Dr John Watson in a striking
new ——ting is the richest the character has ever enjoyed' **Barry Forshaw**

—— wondered what Dr John Watson got up to before the other guy
t— —l up? This ambitious new novel (approved by Conan Doyle's estate)
s— ——ts he was patching up war heroes at the Front while hunting down a
sir—— r killer behind enemy lines' *Time Out*

—— vid account of life in the trenches . . . this is a genuinely fascinating
—— ́nely researched piece of war fiction' *Daily Express*

'A hugely powerful depiction of wartime horror, a cunning murder
mystery and a brilliant re-invention of Dr John Watson. Conan Doyle
would most definitely approve!' *Mark Billingham*

DEAD MAN'S LAND

ROBERT RYAN

**SIMON &
SCHUSTER**

London · New York · Sydney · Toronto · New Delhi

A CBS COMPANY

First published in Great Britain by Simon & Schuster UK Ltd, 2012
A CBS COMPANY
This paperback edition published 2013

Copyright © Robert Ryan 2012
First chapter of *The Dead Can Wait* copyright © Robert Ryan 2013

1 3 5 7 9 10 8 6 4 2

Simon & Schuster UK Ltd
1st Floor
222 Gray's Inn Road
London WC1X 8HB

www.simonandschuster.co.uk

Simon & Schuster Australia, Sydney
Simon & Schuster India, New Delhi

A CIP catalogue record for this book is available from the British Library

Paperback ISBN: 978-1-84983-957-0
Ebook ISBN: 978-1-84983-958-7

This book is a work of fiction. Names,
characters, places and incidents are either a product of the author's
imagination or are used fictitiously. Any resemblance to actual
people living or dead, events or locales is entirely coincidental.

Typeset by Hewer Text UK Ltd, Edinburgh
Printed and bound by CPI Group (UK) Ltd, Croydon CR0 4YY

NOTE FROM THE AUTHOR

To Bella

And for Clive Powell, a proper Leigh Pal

DEAD MAN'S LAND

TEMPORARY

GEORGE by the Grace of God, of the United Kingdom of Great Britain and Ireland and of the British Dominions beyond the Seas. King, Defender of the Faith, Emperor of India, etc. To our Trusty and well-beloved JOHN HAMISH WATSON, MD.

We, reposing especial Trust and Confidence in your Loyalty, Courage and Good Conduct, do by these Presents Constitute and Appoint you to be a Medical Officer in Our Land Forces from the twenty-second day of October 1914. You are therefore carefully and diligently to discharge your duty as such in the Rank of Major or in such higher rank as We from time hereafter be pleased to promote or appoint you to, of which notification will be made in the *London Gazette*.

Given at Our Court of Saint James's the twenty-second of October 1914 in the fifth year of our reign.

By His Majesty's Command

JOHN HAMISH WATSON, MD,

Major

Royal Army Medical Corps

Land Forces

SATURDAY

ONE

As the observation balloon cleared the spindly crowns of the surrounding trees, the major gripped the side of its wicker gondola tight enough for the blood to leach from his knuckles. He risked a quick glance at the rapidly receding forest floor. It was covered with the men of the 3rd British Field Balloon Company (Training), who were fussing over the arm-thick hawser that snaked from the nose of the rising inflatable to the winch on a flat-bed lorry, making sure it ran free and easy as the balloon gained height. Others were carefully folding the disconnected umbilicals that had fed the gas from the tanker truck into the greedy belly of the balloon. Forty-eight men to launch one balloon, so they had told him. He could well believe it.

The men of the ground crew were shrinking to insect-like proportions already and what had seemed a huge clearing in the forest was but a small hole in the great swathe of beech, larch and oak surrounding the launch site. Beyond the tree line was his car and Brindle, his driver, shading his eyes as he looked up at the strange apparition that had risen from within the forest. The driver waved and the major felt obliged to return the greeting, albeit rather self-consciously. It didn't seem at all like correct form to be waving at one's orderly.

Beyond Brindle was the village they had driven through in the semi-darkness of dawn, with its church now revealed to have a shell-damaged steeple, shocked out of the perpendicular. He could see the black ribbon of the main road stretching off back towards the hospital they had left before the sun had troubled the sky. To his right was the soft, cotton-wool plume of a steam train heading towards France and the coast, perhaps ferrying wounded to the hospitals at Bailleul or St Omer or the great tented encampments that stretched from Calais to Boulogne.

Elsewhere, the sky swallowed the puffs from the smaller locos, shifting men and munitions around this vast hinterland on their iron web of hastily laid rails. He could see the unwavering line of a distant canal, drawn across the landscape as if with a rule, its dark water thick with overloaded barges. Beyond it, a huge lorry park, a man-made crop of green and brown, metal and canvas, slab-sided vehicles sprung up where once wheat or oats had thrived. Over towards Wallonia, fields dense with hop poles, their regular patterns interrupted by deep depressions, as if a giant had pressed his monstrous thumb into the midst of them, scattering and flattening the delicate frames. Shell blasts, he assumed.

From his fresh aerial perspective he could see that the entire land, its fields and forests, ridges and marshes, was covered with a skein of footpaths and sunken roads, old drovers' paths and bridleways, cart-paths, towpaths, dykes and greenways, all the traditional ways and means of moving across the countryside, from farm to market, village to chapel, hamlet to city, birth to death. And all far too slow for modern warfare. A new grid of roads had been laid over this landscape, wide and brightly metalled, designed to echo to the sound of hobnail boots and the thrum of rubber tyres. Between these new seams stitched into the fabric of Flanders and Wallonia, he could count a dozen whitewashed farmhouses, with their brightly tiled roofs and cobbled courtyards, some filled with toy-sized livestock.

He had almost relaxed when a gusting breeze caught the flanks of the inflatable – 'Florrie', as the men had christened her. The cylinder bucked like a harpooned whale and the basket suspended beneath it twisted against its lines. The major gripped tight once more.

'You all right, sir?' asked Slattery, the lieutenant who was his companion in the flimsy gondola.

No, he wanted to reply to the young man with his glowing cheeks, wind-burned from many such ascents. I am not all right. The major had sworn after the accident that had changed his life that he would never ride in anything that tried to defy gravity, ever. Yet here he was, soaring above a forest clearing in Belgium, borne aloft by a tumescent sausage full of thirty thousand cubic feet of distilled coal product, enough of which had leaked to give the whole countryside the whiff of the gasometer, standing in a basket more suited to a picnic on Hampstead Heath. I am a doctor, he wanted to explain, not a . . . what did they call them? Balloonatics? Yes, that was it. A word that was far too close to lunatics for his liking.

Florrie gave a groan as she was buffeted again, but this time the wind filled the crescent-shaped pockets in the rear of her gutta-percha envelope and spun her to face into the breeze. The hanging basket began to pendulum and the major's stomach flipped in a queasy somersault.

'I must be mad,' he said under his breath, he thought, but loud enough for Slattery to hear.

'Not to worry. Worst part of the ascent as the tail stabilizers fill, I always think. She gets a bit twitchy for a minute. You get used to it after a few times.'

'I'm not intending to do this more than the once,' he said. 'I'm only here under protest.'

The major's request to move closer to the front had been met with much resistance within the Royal Army Medical Corps. There were those who thought a man of his vintage had no place crossing the Channel, let alone being put in harm's way. Strange, he had answered, that we insist on killing our young men, valuing their lives less than that of one who has put in a good portion of his three-score and ten. His passing would cause precious little anguish in the world, he thought, recognizing a kernel of sadness in the sentiment.

Eventually, his demand to be deployed at a forward station had landed on the desk of the Deputy Director of Army Medical Services in France and Belgium. Any senior medical officer who wanted to experience life at the front, the DDAMS had said, must go up and see for himself what he was letting himself in for.

The front. It had taken on the qualities of a mythical beast in the major's mind. He had seen its vicious handiwork in the beds at Charing Cross Hospital and on the stretchers at Victoria Station, Dover and Boulogne and in the overcrowded wards at Wimereux, Lille and Bailleul. Wounded men pleaded not to be sent back to face it again, others lamented friends still in its grip, some flinched at the mere mention of it and a brave few were eager to do battle with the front once more, as if it were some test of manhood they had somehow failed. In his mind, the front was a living creature capable of chewing up and spitting out thousands of men at a time. He had seen its sinuous shape marked on maps and talked of in hushed or awed tones, as if the cartographer's legend said: 'Here be Dragons'.

'Right,' said Slattery, peering upwards at *Florrie* and apparently satisfied with what he saw, 'it'll all be smooth riding from now on.'

The lieutenant busied himself with freeing two pieces of rope that had been tied to one of the gondola cables. Let loose, they dangled on either side of him and stretched all the way up to *Florrie* and over her flanks. 'Just in case, Major, you should know about these two pieces of kit. This one is the bleed valve. It takes us down slowly, with or without the winch. This one –' he tapped the cable that was marked with a red band 'is the panic panel.' He pointed up at *Florrie*. 'Whatever you do, don't touch it. It rips out a piece of the envelope and vents a large proportion of the gas. Gets us down fast if there is an enemy plane coming. Sometimes too fast. But don't worry. Nothing much happens at this time of day. Even wars stop for brekkers.'

As the balloon calmed, the major looked down once more at the Belgian soil they had recently vacated. How high were they? He stared over into France, trying to focus through hazy air, wondering if they would gain enough altitude to see England.

'Major?' He felt a tap on his shoulder. Slattery was handing him a heavy pair of binoculars and pointing to the east. 'The front is that way.' The major took the glasses, turned to face east, and pressed them to his eyes, his head swimming as a blurred world leaped closer. He adjusted the focus with the central ring. Through the binoculars, humanity was no longer a succession of indistinct blobs. He could see a farmer quite clearly, one foot on a gate, smoking a pipe contentedly as he watched a sow suckling her piglets; a few hundred yards away, a cluster of soldiers were brewing up tea in a three-sided farmhouse, and in a field, several cavalrymen were brushing their horses, the post-gallop steam rising from the animals' backs clearly visible. A young girl, white blouse, long woollen skirt, her hair tied with a yellow scarf, moved among a flock of belligerent geese, scattering feed, lashing out with a lazy foot at those who got in her way.

There was a field kitchen, the cooks ladling out food to grimy-looking Tommies and, nearby, outside a bell tent, two officers bracketing a rickety table, a breakfast of eggs and thick, crusty bread laid out between them. They smoked and chatted and supped from tin mugs of tea. One of the pair threw back his head in laughter at a remark, almost losing his seating as a chair leg sank into the soil, causing the other much mirth. Boys, he could see now as they joshed each other. Twenty if they were a day. Some hundred yards to the right of them, yet another alien feature: a cluster of wooden crosses, the bodies of the fallen waiting for the time when they could be exhumed and transported to a more permanent resting place. A solitary figure stood in front of one of them, head bowed, possibly in prayer, his steel helmet in his hands. The major moved his prying eyes on, feeling like an intruder on private grief.

Each and every subject his magnified gaze fell upon was acting as if they were a long, long way from any conflict. Just how close they were in reality was soon apparent as they continued their ascent. Foot by foot, yard by yard, the war was heaving into view.

'As we are a training unit we are a little further back than an operational company, so our perspective isn't quite as good, sir. But look to your left. North. That's the Ypres Salient, a bulge into the

Germans' territory. See the rise of hills? German positions. Poor blighters underneath that don't half take it. Those few shards sticking up? Used to be villages. See the artillery emplacements? They're ours, of course. Now look straight ahead. Believe you me, Major, this is the only way you can make sense of what's down there. Once you are in the trenches, you keep your head down and the world shrinks. Don't worry, we are too far away for any small-arms fire to cause us any bother and any artilleryman who could hit us would deserve every medal the Germans have. Start nearest to us. See those farmhouses, sir? Not a roof between them? Billets for the men either on their way up the line or down it or just having a few days' respite. Right, move forward, follow one of the new roads. You should be able to see some dark lines? Running north to south? That's left to right, see? Got them? Reserve trenches. You'll find you can't keep men constantly right at the sharp end, they have to be rotated. Now branching off from those – steady, wind's shifting a little, *Florrie*'s just righting herself again – branching off from those are the communication trenches that go towards the forward trenches. They zigzag, right? Most trenches do, you'll find. If not zigzagged, then they are castellated, like battlements. It means there is no clear line of fire for any interloper and that shell blasts won't funnel down them for miles. The traverses, that's the correct term for non-linear trenches, they contain the shockwave, you see. They learned that the hard way. The next row running left to right, that's the support trenches, one back from the front line. That's probably where you'll find your lot. The Regimental Aid Posts. Then, more communication lines run to the main fire trench system. The front line proper. See the parapets and the sandbags? And beyond that, the wire and the anti-cavalry obstacles? And then . . .'

'No man's land,' the major said, the first sight of it drying his mouth.

They were high enough now that the major could see a similar pattern repeated on the German side – obstacles, wire, trenches, lazily zigzagging communications lines, and yet more trenches. It was almost a mirror image. But it was the gap between the two opposing armies that caught and held his attention. It went on as far north and as far south as his powerful glasses could see. In some places it was a black strip of featureless mud, unless you counted shell holes and rusty wire as features, in other sections a few benighted trees and shrubs were clinging on for dear life.

He was surprised to find this death strip was not a consistent size. He supposed that the two sides had not dug their trenches according to any blueprint, but simply where it was expedient to do so as the war ground to a stalemate in late 1914. Therefore, this contested band separating the Allies and the Germans randomly swelled and shrank in width, as the two front lines grew closer together or retreated away from each other.

No man's land was like a wayward river, an apparently permanent fixture of the European landscape, snaking over seven hundred miles, from the Belgian coast to the Swiss border. Except the only thing that flowed in this waterway and burst from its banks to inundate the surrounding countryside was human misery and suffering. He was, he realized, looking straight at the belly of the beast that was sending the Empire's young men home in pieces, or consigning them to an eternity in the soil of France or Belgium. Here be Dragons, indeed.

Now he could see the method in the Deputy Director's kite balloon madness. It was to give the uninitiated a taste of what was to come, to bring home the enormity of the task facing anyone who thought they could make a difference to the course of a war being fought on an unimaginable scale. To dent the resolve of an old doctor, a veteran of a different kind of war, a persistent nuisance who should, perhaps, be contemplating his retirement rather than insisting there were new ways available to save the lives being snuffed out on those plains below.

There came the boom of an artillery piece, and, closer, the manic chatter of a machine gun. A plume of dirty smoke rose from the north and wood pigeons clattered from the trees beneath them. It appeared breakfast was over. And so was this jaunt. He lowered the binoculars.

'Excuse me,' said the major as he reached across, past Slattery, and yanked at the slow-bleed valve. *Florrie* gave a hiss and whistle of protest and the major felt his insides lift as she checked her rise and began to sink.

Slattery looked puzzled. 'I haven't finished, sir. There's a lot more—'

'Apologies, Lieutenant, but I've seen enough for one day,' said Major John Hamish Watson of the Royal Army Medical Corps. 'And I've got work to do.'

TWO

It was daylight by the time they had managed to find a bed or a corner for all the new arrivals and make sure their immediate concerns were dealt with. The medical staff never knew what time the trains would arrive at Bailleul hospital, even though it was less than a dozen miles from the front. An hour's notice, if they were lucky. Ten minutes sometimes. This one came in at close to two in the morning with a half-hour's warning and two hundred wounded. By the time they reached this stage of the medical evacuation chain, a conventional fixed hospital, the soldiers should have received good basic care and surgery where required, but sometimes the mobile medical units close to the front were overwhelmed and the wounded were simply shunted down the line with minimum intervention.

That had clearly been the case here, as there were still boots to be cut off feet that hadn't been out of them for weeks, primitive field dressings to be changed, wounds to be irrigated, limbs to be amputated. And lice to be avoided. Which was nearly impossible. You even ran a risk of infestation if you handled the severed limbs – the grey-backs seemed happy to wait their chance to jump ship from excised to living flesh.

Mrs Georgina Gregson had dumped the stiff calico over-dress they wore on top of their uniforms for dealing with lousy new arrivals — tight at the neck and tied at the sleeves — at the laundry. She was too exhausted to eat, however, and, after picking up a jug of hot water, had gone straight back to the tiny room she shared with Alice Pippery.

Her roommate was already in bed; the ill-fitting curtains meant she could make out her barrow-like shape beneath the blankets. She closed the door as softly as she could and began to undress. Two cot-beds, two lockers, one shared wardrobe, a mirror, a stool and, in the corner, a tiny and temperamental stove. She knew the position of everything in the room by heart, so undoing laces, rolling down stockings and pulling off her uniform and hanging it up in the half-light was easy.

She had just smoothed out her cape on its hanger when she heard a squeak. Mice, was her first thought. They infested the lower floors of the hospital. They weren't as disgusting as the rats that sometimes ventured into the tented quarters, perhaps, but they would chew through anything in search of even a morsel of food. Many a nurse had found her camisole or knickers shredded because of a carelessly stored biscuit or chocolate.

There it was again.

It wasn't a mouse. It was Alice.

Mrs Gregson moved over to the cot and laid a hand on the blankets. They were vibrating with a familiar rhythm. She came across it on a daily basis, but especially on the night shift. The men in her charge were past caring about any shame at showing any such weakness.

Miss Pippery was crying.

'Alice?' She threw back the blankets and squeezed herself in beside her. Alice shifted in the bed, spinning around and sliding her arms around Mrs Gregson. She responded in kind, careful not to squeeze too hard. She always felt it wouldn't be difficult to crush Alice with one strong hug. She could feel her friend's heart beating against her chest through her nightgown, as fast as a frightened rodent's. Alice's cross was digging into her collarbone, so she moved it to one side.

'What is it, Alice?'

No reply. Just a long, ululating sob. They all had days like this. Days where you felt the dark waters of despair close over your head. The only surprise was that there weren't more of them. She stroked Alice's hair. It was straw-like to the touch. She ran a finger through her own red curls. Worse. Before the next shift, she decided she would take them both down to the bathhouse and bully, cajole and demand enough hot water to scrub them both and check they were free of any infestation.

'Alice? What's wrong, dear?'

'Matron said I had to go on the cookery – ' the sentence was punctuated by a catch in the throat – 'roster. I can't cook. You know that, George.'

'I do. People still talk about your porridge pot.'

It was difficult to tell whether her response was another sob or a stifled giggle. It was true that Miss Alice Pippery had once made the worst porridge since Goldilocks picked up a ladle, but stirring a great vat of the stuff on a Soyer stove, without it sticking, was no easy task.

'What did Matron say?'

'That "can't" shouldn't be in a VAD's vocabulary.'

They were both members of the Red Cross's Voluntary Aid Detachment, which put them on the lowest rung of the nursing ladder. In fact, sometimes they weren't even allowed to touch the ladder at all.

'Remember that first hill climb? At Outersley? On your brother's motor cycle?'

She felt Alice nod against her shoulder.

'When you looked up that hill, saw how steep and muddy it was, what did you say?'

A mumble.

'What was that?'

'I can't do it.'

'And where did you come?'

'Third.'

'Third,' Mrs Gregson said triumphantly. 'And where did I come?'

'Fifth.'

'Fifth.'

'But that was only because you put rocks over my rear wheels because I didn't have the weight to get any traction, wasn't it?'

Mrs Gregson laughed at the memory of the subterfuge. 'Tactics.'

'And then they disqualified me.' Alice punched her lightly on the shoulder. 'And my parents said you were a cheat.'

'And a liar,' she added proudly. 'And I think "a malign influence" was mentioned.'

They lay in silence, still intertwined, considering this.

'I never thought that, George, ever, even when we broke down in the Lake District and I almost caught pneumonia. If it wasn't for you I wouldn't be here.'

'What, lying cold and dirty in a bed, scratching at your lice sores, not having slept properly for months, a lowly VAD who is about to start peeling potatoes as her contribution to the war effort? I hope you remember me in your prayers.'

'I do, George,' she said solemnly. 'Of course I do.'

She had been teasing. She had momentarily forgotten that for Alice, levity and religion could never happily co-exist.

'Do you miss him? Mr Gregson?' Alice asked at last, her voice tremulous as she picked her words carefully. 'At times like this?'

Mrs Gregson raised herself up on one elbow. 'What really happened today, Alice? This isn't about cooking, is it? Or how warm Mr Gregson used to make my bed. Come on, something breaks our hearts every day. I lost one I was fond of the other week. Private Hornby. Lancashire lad with an accent thicker than your porridge. He was fine when I went off shift, when I came back . . .' She let it tail off. She didn't want to recall too vividly the state the boy had been in.

'Mine asked me to let him die,' said Alice, then caught herself. Mrs Gregson felt her stiffen. 'No, that's not right. He asked me to kill him. Not in so many words, but that's what he meant.'

She had heard of that before. A frightened lad, maimed beyond recognition, perhaps, or knowing he was going to die no matter what the doctors tried. Even heard tell there were some nurses who had acceded to the request. 'And what did you say, Alice?'

The door opened with a loud squeal from the hinges and a hand reached in to turn on the light switch. The single, unshaded bulb flickered into reluctant light.

As she rolled over to see who was disturbing them, Mrs Gregson unbalanced on the edge of the mattress and crashed to the floor, crying out as the wind was driven from her body. 'Jesus.' She remembered herself. 'Sorry, Alice. I mean, good grief.'

When she had finally lowered her legs and raised her head, she could see Elizabeth Challenger, their formidable matron, standing in the doorway, hands on generous hips.

'Pippery. Gregson. What on earth are you doing?'

'It's my fault, Matron—' Miss Pippery began.

'I thought I felt a mouse in my bed,' said Mrs Gregson. 'I have a phobia of mice.'

The matron smirked at the thought of Mrs Gregson fleeing from any small furry creature. 'Well, I wouldn't worry too much about that, you've been asked to report to the Senior Medical Officer in Charge for reassignment.'

Now the matron had Mrs Gregson's full attention. She sat bolt upright. 'Where?'

Matron shook her head. 'I have no idea. But wherever you are going, you'll be going there with a Major Watson.'

THREE

Sergeant Geoffrey Shipobottom hammered his fist on the doorpost of the officers' dugout. He waited until a muffled voice told him to enter, pulled the gas curtain aside and ducked into the dim interior. The captain was sitting at the rough table, papers in front of him, pencil in hand. Cecil, his Jack Russell, was lying at his feet, eyeing the newcomer with suspicion. Lieutenant Metcalf was lying on one of the bunks, smoking, a small, leather-bound volume of poetry propped on his chest.

Shipobottom kept his head down as he approached the captain, which made for an awkward salute. The bunker was well constructed of timber, steel plate and sandbags, but the ceiling was far too low even for men of average height. Which Shipobottom certainly wasn't. Must have been built by Welshmen, Lieutenant Metcalf had joked when they had taken up residence.

'What is it, Sergeant?' Captain Robinson de Griffon asked.

Shipobottom detected a brittle, impatient edge to his voice. Not like the captain at all. 'There's a balloon gone up, sir.'

The two officers exchanged glances and Metcalf swung his legs off the bunk. A balloon was often a sign that a barrage was imminent. And after a barrage came an assault on enemy lines.

'How many?' de Griffon asked.

'Jus' the wun, sir.'

'And how far away?' asked Metcalf.

'Can't rightly say, sir. Not close. Not too high yet, either.'

'Shipobottom,' said Metcalf impatiently, 'one swallow does not make a spring. And a solitary balloon does not make a barrage.' It was customary for at least four to be launched prior to any artillery action, spaced several miles apart.

'No, sir. But, y'know, the men was wondering. If you'd heard anything, like.' His eyes darted to the field telephone. 'That might change things.'

De Griffon studied the big man before him. Like most of the soldiers in his company, Shipobottom had worked at the Lancashire cotton mills. He was taller and bulkier than most of his compatriots, however, with the exception of Corporal Platt, and with a startlingly bulbous nose that suggested a good proportion of his wages never made it to the family home.

'Sergeant Shipobottom, I intend to hold a faces and rifles inspection shortly. Tomorrow, full kit. Then, as far as I know, we will be marching out of here for a well-deserved rest. And as we march, I want anyone who is watching to ask: who are those smart lads? And the answer will be, those are the Leigh Pals.'

Metcalf jumped in. 'And if we find anyone who is dragging their feet or dishonouring the uniform, it'll be Field Punishment Number One before he can undo his puttees. Is that clear?'

Shipobottom was taken aback. 'Sir.'

De Griffon waved him away with his pencil. 'Dismiss. And,

Shipobottom, tie back that gas curtain, will you? Can't breathe in here.'

Taking the hint, Metcalf rose and stubbed his cigarette out. Once Shipobottom had gone, he asked: 'More tea, sir? There's some condensed milk left.'

De Griffon nodded. He reached down to ruffle the dog's fur. 'What is the matter with Shipobottom? He's prancing like a filly on hot coals.'

Metcalf primed and lit the stove. 'He went to a fortune-teller in Cairo before we left. Apparently, she told him he'd come to a sticky end.'

De Griffon leaned back in his chair and put his hands behind his head. His blond hair bunched beneath his fingers. He must get it cut. Grew like corn on a hot summer's day. 'She probably thought he was bound for Gallipoli. Not much clairvoyance needed to predict what fate would befall any soldier sent there.' They had missed being transferred to those hellish beaches by a whisker. 'Still, that doesn't mean it won't happen to him out here. Or, indeed, any of us.'

The nihilism of that remark was so uncharacteristic of the captain that Metcalf was emboldened to speak up. 'I hope you don't mind me asking, sir, but is everything all right with you? You seem a bit out of sorts.'

De Griffon's blue eyes seemed to grow a shade paler as they turned on him and Metcalf thought he had overstepped the mark. They might both be officers, but Metcalf was a Manchester Grammar School lad, who had once spoken in an accent not much different from Shipobottom's. Metcalf was considered to be – and expected to act like – a gentleman as long as the war lasted, but they all knew his was a temporary promotion to the gentry. The captain, on the other hand, was as blue-blooded as they came.

The chair landed on its front legs with a thump, and de Griffon stood, remembering to crick his neck at the last moment. 'Do I? Was I hard on Shipobottom? I thought your threat of the field punishment was perhaps unnecessary, I must say.'

Metcalf shifted uneasily. 'Sorry, sir. I was simply backing you up. If I spoke out of turn—'

'Don't fret about it,' he interrupted. 'You know my family, don't you, Metcalf?'

'Not personally, sir.'

'No, of course not.' Metcalf's parents owned several large hardware stores in Leigh, Preston and Salford. They had supplied the de Griffons with goods and chattels, but had never socialized. Although, Metcalf reminded himself, here they were having tea, almost as equals. His parents would be thrilled.

'Give me one of those gaspers, will you?' de Griffon asked. He took a cigarette from Metcalf and lit it from an oil lamp. He walked over to the doorway and exhaled from the corner of his mouth, so that the smoke drifted out into the reserve trench. What with the black tar from lamp wicks, the constant cigarettes, not to mention the tang of rat piss and the sour smell of unwashed clothes and bodies, the atmosphere in any dugout was oppressive and rank. He saw no reason to add to it.

Cecil trotted over and slumped to the floor next to him. De Griffon gave him a friendly prod with the toe of his boot and the dog began to worry at the leather with claws and teeth. 'You know, Bertie – the Prince of Wales – once called my mother "a professional beauty". Queen Victoria had thought her "too fast" because, when the fancy took her, she shot with the men at Sandringham. Quite a character, Mother. And she shot until quite recently. Flitcham, where I was brought up, was once a sporting estate to rival Holkham, Malden and Quidenham. You've never been?'

'No, sir.' His family was not the sort to enter a place like Flitcham by the front door.

De Griffon puffed on the cigarette, his face grown slack as he recalled his boyhood, his features for once devoid of the worry lines the war had gifted him. The captain looked just as he must have done in peacetime, Metcalf thought, a well-groomed, handsome young man with the confident afterglow of a good upbringing, secure in the knowledge of an equally privileged life ahead for generations to come.

'A bag of two thousand or more a day throughout November was not uncommon,' de Griffon continued. 'If Sir Ralph Payne Gallwey or Lord Walsingham were visiting, that could be doubled. We had the most beautiful shooting brake, an Albion, to ferry us around. I still remember the wicker baskets of champagne for the guns and the ginger beers for the beaters that would be lugged out to Shillingham Wood. Then, a little more than two years ago, everything changed. The pheasantries are empty now. The partridges strut around as if they own the place.'

Metcalf, never having heard his captain divulge such personal history before, poured the hot water into the metal teapot and kept silent. He wasn't sure of the form at this kind of confessional. Did he comment, make sympathetic noises and gestures or simply keep his mouth shut? The latter was surely the safest option.

'My father took ill. Horrible, terrible disease. Wasted away before our eyes. We were lucky, we had a chauffeur, Harry Legge, who was devoted to him. Turned him every four hours to prevent bedsores. Day and night. That's real, genuine devotion. Drove into town every two days to fetch Dr Kibble, then drove him back. Fed my father three meals a day, which was far from easy. We were terrified Legge would volunteer or be called up. We even put up with his amorous adventures with the housemaids and the cook. Then my father died. Which was a relief. Couldn't even speak at the end. But my mother went into a mourning that would have done Queen Victoria proud. Legge, poor chap, got blind drunk and crashed the motor car and put paid to his chances of ever serving. Terrible limp. My older brother was already in the army. I decided to enlist to make sure I could get a commission here, with the Leigh Pals. At least it was a battalion I had a connection with, no matter how distant.'

At this point Metcalf risked a nod, because he knew some of the background. Although the de Griffons owned several large cotton mills in Leigh, Lancashire, Lord Stanwood was for the most part an absentee landlord, spending his time at Flitcham, his Gloucestershire seat. Ever since the strikes of the 1890s, he had left the day-to-day running of the mills to his hard-nosed managers. By his own admission, Robinson de Griffon was a stranger to the town that had created so much of the family wealth.

'Then this came this morning.' He picked up a single sheet of oft-folded paper and handed it across. 'Please keep it to yourself.'

Metcalf was flattered that he was to be taken into the captain's confidence, but also apprehensive about the contents of the letter. He doubted it was good news.

'It's the original. My mother forwarded it. Go on, read it.'

Dear Lady Stanwood,

I am certain by now you will have had either a telegram or a telephone call to inform of the sad news I have to impart, but I thought you might welcome some further details. I regret very much to inform you that your son 1st Lt. Lord Charles de Griffon, No. 677757 of this Company, was killed in action on the night of the 31st instant. Death was instantaneous and without any suffering.

The Company was taking part in an attack on an enemy position situated high on a ridge. The attack was successful, and all guns reached, and we established new strongholds on the enemy lines. Your son was instrumental in taking one of the positions in fierce fighting. However, the enemy counterattacked that night, with a heavy bombardment. Your son's dugout suffered a direct hit. At this moment, due to a continued enemy presence, it has proved impossible to get his remains away and he lies in a soldier's grave where he fell. It will be some consolation, I am sure, to know he has been recommended for an award for gallantry thanks to his actions leading his platoon onto the ridge that night.

The CO and all the Company deeply sympathize with you in your loss. Your son always did his duty and now has given his life for his country. We all honour him, and I trust you will feel some consolation in remembering this. His effects will reach you via the Base in due course.

In true sympathy,

Yours sincerely,

Captain R. E. March

'Is that tea ready?' asked de Griffon, as he screwed his cigarette into a brass ashtray, fashioned from the flattened fuse of a shell casing.

'Sir.' But Metcalf continued to stare at the letter. It took a few seconds for the lieutenant to comprehend, beyond it involving yet another family tragedy, its true consequences. He held up the piece of paper.

'I'm truly sorry about your brother, sir. But does this mean that you're—'

'It does, Metcalf. It bloody well does. With Charlie dead, I am now Lord Stanwood.'

When Shipobottom left the officers' dugout he went straight back along the duckboards to the funk hole, an alcove excavated from the side of the trench and lined with old waterproof capes and sections of ammunition boxes. Sitting in it were corporals Platt – a man even larger than Shipobottom – and Tugman, plus privates Farrar and, the baby of the group, Moulton. All had grown up within two streets of each other; all had worked at the mills back home in Leigh; all had joined up within a day of each other, and been trained, in Wales, Catterick and Egypt, in the same platoon. Their battalion wasn't called the Leigh Pals for nothing.

All were watching the billycan that sat on the paraffin stove, waiting for it to boil for a brew. Every man was smoking, rifles and gas masks had been laid to one side, helmets taken off. They were in the reserve trenches, and the nerve-jangling tension that accompanied the hours and days at the firing line was slowly dissipating. Which was why the sight of the balloon had spooked them; if there were a barrage, they might be rotated forward to the support or even the fire trenches, rather than back to a recuperation area. They had heard it happened a lot: a spot of rest dangled like a carrot and snatched away at the last moment. Just one more example of Brass Hat torture.

'What'd the cap'n say, Shippy?' Platt asked, offering him a Woodbine.

Shipobottom crouched down, his bulk almost blocking the light from the cubbyhole, and took the cigarette. 'Ta. Nothin',' he said, his relief evident. 'Balloon's nothin'. All goin' ahead. We'll be marchin' away from here aw reet, although we'll have Metcalf on our backs by the sound of it. But we'll be sleepin' on silk soon enough. Well, stinkin' straw, anyways.'

The others laughed. 'I bet that spooner Metcalf will be sleepin' on silk, drinkin' champagne,' said Tugman. 'With some tart pullin' at his old man while we get tea and biscuits at the YMCA, if we're lucky.'

'Leave it out,' said Farrar. 'He's aw reet.'

'Aw reet? With his bloody little stick and his posh-nob accent,' said Tugman. 'He used to sell me penny bags o'nails in the shop at Crawford Street. And his old man refused my old man credit once when he was tryin' to stop us roof leakin' because the landlord wouldn't. An' now he's all airs and graces, like.'

Moulton mimed playing a violin and Tugman cuffed him sharply around the ear. The boy yelped.

'Oy,' said Shipobottom. 'Stop that. Now. Corporal Tugman. Apologize.'

The truculent corporal did as he was told, albeit with ill humour.

'I think Metcalf's the sort of officer who will lead from behind, if you ask me,' he said. 'I bet he's got no guts.'

'He's one of us,' said Shipobottom, unable to fathom the level of animosity Tugman felt to a local boy made good. 'Leave him be. I've seen you nearly shittin' your pants enough times.' Tugman glared at him, violence in his face. Shipobottom gave a malicious grin back. With that enormous nose it made him look like a crazed Mr Punch. 'Yeah, you wanna give me a clout, Corporal, see where that gets you?'

'At least I haven't been jumpin' at my own shadow since some gypo crone read my palm.'

Shipobottom's grin faded and he aimed his index finger at Tugman.

'Here we go,' said Platt loudly. The water in the billycan was now at a rolling boil and he tossed some black, powdery tea leaves in, then a handful of sugar and stirred. 'Just take it easy now, fellas. Yous all a bit on edge, like, 'cause we're nearly out of here. It's the waiting that's the hardest, innit? Like linin' up to get on the ship at Alexandria under that bloody sun. I hated that. Let's just get it over wit' and get us selves torpedo'd, I thought in the end. Got t'be better than sweatin' me bollocks off an' eatin' flies on the quayside. And here we are, waiting to get out of this shitheap before someone decides it's time for another Big Push, or the Germans want to try out new trench mortar on our heads. Just the same as then. So pack it in, we're all in the same boat.'

'Blimey, Bernie, that's more words than I heard you speak in ten year,' said Farrar.

Both Tugman and Shipobottom smirked at the remark and the atmosphere warmed once more.

Platt poured the tea into five tin mugs, using a home-made strainer, fashioned from wire and muslin, to catch the leaves, which would be reused. 'There you go.'

'Let's hurry that along,' said Shipobottom. 'We got rifles and face inspection later,' he added, remembering what de Griffon had said. 'An' full kit tomorrow.'

'Then, Joseph,' said Platt to Tugman, 'We'll be off to see if we can find you a tart of your own.'

Farrar laughed. 'Well, yours and fifty other blokes. He likes it with others watchin', as I heard tell.'

Once again, the temperature dropped a notch in the funk hole and Tugman balled his fists. Moulton, too young to know what they were referring to, looked in puzzlement from one to another.

'You still got that boil on your bum then?' Tugman asked him. 'Like a bloody beacon it were while you were tuppin' that Frenchie. A reet chip off the old block you were. Y're old man had a spotty arse'n'all.'

Farrar tensed, as if about to leap across the alcove at Tugman. 'What you talkin' about?'

'Don't tell me he didn't tell you,' laughed Tugman. ' "Cock of the Woods" Farrah?'

Shipobottom stood up, not quite to his full height. You were safer from snipers at the rear of the trench system, but it was a habit you kept up nevertheless. Otherwise, one day you might forget yourself in the wrong place. 'Next man speaks out of turn gets my boot up his arse. And these are size thirteen. You'll need a pick an' a rope to get it out. Understand? Farrah? Tugman? Aye. You just keep quiet about all that. Faces and rifles,' Shipobottom repeated. 'Faces and rifles. And let's try and get the fuck out of here in one piece.'

MONDAY

FOUR

'I see you have spent some time in the West Indies, Staff Nurse Jennings.'

The young nurse stopped her unloading of the blood transfusion kit and stared at the Royal Army Medical Corps major. 'I beg your pardon?'

'And that your family were in sugar.'

She gave a small laugh of disbelief and put her hands on her hips. Her eyes widened, so they seemed almost too large for the delicate face. 'How on earth can you know that?'

'A parlour trick,' said the major with a smile. 'Forgive me.'

'That hardly explains how you come to be familiar with my family history, Major Watson.' She paused as a low rumble began, like thunder growling on some distant mountains. She put her head to one side and listened carefully. A curl of dark hair looped free from the headdress and she absent-mindedly tucked it away. 'Their guns. Not ours. You soon learn the difference.'

He frowned as the bright nickel instruments he was laying out on the folding table rattled softly in their steel kidney bowls.

'Don't worry,' she said, 'we're out of range here of all but the big ones, and they tend to be used on the towns and marshalling yards. Not the evacuation railheads.' The Casualty Clearing Station was half a mile from such a railhead, accessed by special wheeled stretchers that ran on a narrow-gauge track. From these improvised tramways, the wounded were transferred to regular ambulance trains.

'I'm not concerned,' said Watson. 'But I have demonstrations to give and samples to stockpile, and I was told this was a quiet sector.'

'Quiet,' she explained patiently, 'means less than a hundred casualties a month. There is no such thing as a totally safe place out here. The guns can start anywhere, anytime.'

Although a relative novice to the front – it was little more than a week since his balloon ride – Watson knew what those falling shells meant. There would be wounded coming through. Casualty Clearing Stations always worked in pairs, and this one, the East Anglian, had been stood down for a few days to enable it to clear the backlog of cases, while another CCS in the same sector remained on alert. If that one, however, ran at or beyond its capacity, the East Anglian would come back into play.

'And we hadn't had a "hate session" from the enemy until three or four days ago,' said Jennings, 'when some foolish . . .' She hesitated. Nurses were directed not to comment on anything but clinical matters, and even then, only if invited to.

'Some foolish what?'

'It's nothing, Major.' Jennings swiftly moved on, pursing her lips at her impetuousness. 'They'll be putting electric lights in here within a few days. About time.'

She looked down at the packing case and lifted out The Icehouse, a wooden and zinc box some twenty-four inches on each side. It had cost him sixty shillings of his own money at Army & Navy. 'What do you intend to keep in here?' she asked as she laid it on the floor of the tent.

'Once the cavity is filled with iced water, it will be used to store citrated blood.'

Jennings looked puzzled. Her grey cape, edged with scarlet, told him she was, like most nurses servicing this collection of tented wards in the grounds of a former monastery, a member of the Territorial Force Nursing Service. It was very likely that these staff didn't keep up with the latest developments, such as the ability to store unclotted blood outside the human body for days at a stretch. From what he understood, few this far forward – be they territorial, reservists, Queen Alexandras or doctors – had much time to read current issues of the *British Medical Journal*. His task, gained only after much inveigling of the RAMC – and that damned balloon ride – was to spread the gospel of the new methodology in hospitals and CCSs.

The RAMC's hesitation in allowing him out here had been ridiculous. Apart from one knee that sometimes crackled and creaked and a *tendo Achillis* that ached after long walks, he was almost as fit as the young doctor who had been wounded at the Battle of Maiwand in Afghanistan. Although, he had to admit, he no longer had that man's waistline.

'Careful with the solution bottles, Staff Nurse,' he warned, as she unwrapped a glass cylinder from its cocoon of corrugated cardboard and newspaper. 'That's our secret ingredient. Hand it here, please.'

There came a deeper rumble and for the first time, he felt the impact vibrate through the wooden floor and the soles of his feet. The canvas stirred and tugged against its ropes on one side of the tent and the roof rippled uneasily.

'That was closer,' said Jennings with a frown, just as the flap of the tent snapped back with a crack like a whiplash. Standing in the opening was the sister-in-charge, her face almost as crimson as the red cape that proclaimed her a full member of Queen Alexandra's Royal Imperial Nursing Corps. The two red stripes on her sleeve told of her rank within her service. The sound of the German guns was momentarily lost beneath her impressive bellow. 'Major Watson!'

Watson carefully laid down the precious jar of sodium citrate solution on the tabletop before he turned to face her. 'Sister? How may I be of assistance?'

'What is the meaning of this?' She pulled back the canvas further to reveal his two VADs, each holding an Empire medical kit. Standing behind them, and towering over the pair by almost a foot, was Brindle, his designated driver, batman and orderly. Brindle's long, sorrowful face was even glummer than usual as he secured the entrance flap open with two press studs.

'Experience dictates that travelling with one medical kit in a war situation is somewhat risky, Sister,' Watson explained patiently. 'I always pack a spare.'

Now the colour on her cheeks was a perfect match for the cape. She waved a rolled piece of flimsy pinkish paper at the two women, who were still holding the heavy medicine chests, stabbing at them with it, as if it were a short sword. 'I am not referring to your *travelling* preferences, Major,' she almost snarled. 'You have brought VADs into my Casualty Clearing Station. *VADs!*'

She made it sound as if Voluntary Aid Detachment nurses were some kind of vermin. And besides, it wasn't strictly speaking her CCS; it was Major Torrance's. But he was at Hazebrouck for a meeting with one of the army's specialists in gas warfare. 'When I was at Bailleul hospital,' Watson said calmly, 'I requested some assistance during this tour of the clearing stations and field ambulances. The Senior Medical Officer in Charge suggested Nurses Gregson and—'

'They are not *nurses*, Major Watson, as you well know. Not qualified nurses. They are auxiliaries. Orderlies. And the Matron-in-Chief herself has forbidden VADs to work this far forward—'

There came another explosion, short and sharp, that made everyone's heads turn to the source. It had come from Mrs Gregson, the older of the VADs. Her companion, Miss Pippery, a tiny thing who looked to be barely out of her teens, took a small step backwards, as if retreating from a ticking bomb.

Mrs Gregson bent at the waist, put down the medical chest, and stepped over it, so that she stood eye to eye with the sister.

Mrs Gregson, Watson estimated, was thirty or thereabouts, with striking green eyes and, beneath the white VAD headdress, a crown of fiery red hair. The sister was probably two decades older, pipe-cleaner thin, with a mouth pinched by years of keeping her charges in line. Now the opening was reduced further, to a razor cut in a rather sallow face.

When Mrs Gregson spoke, it was with a quiet but stinging force. 'Sister, I may not have your qualifications, but I have been out here for more than two years. I was running first-aid stations when the worst the men faced was a turned ankle from trying to march in hobnail boots on French and Belgian cobblestones. I drove for McMurdo's Flying Ambulance Brigade at Mons. Perhaps you have heard of it? I have treated trench foot, venereal disease, lice infestations and lanced boils in men's buttocks the size of macaroons. I have stuffed men's entrails back in place and held the hands of boys who cried for their mothers, such was their pain, and of grown men weeping in fear at the thought of going back up the line. I have carried men's mangled arms and legs to the lime pit, told a private he will never see again, watched men drown in their own fluids from gas, spent weeks wondering if I will ever smell anything in my nostrils other than the stench of gas gangrene. I have shown pretty fiancées what German flame-throwers have done to their future husbands' faces. Then had to deliver the letter that tells them that they have lost those sweethearts. I have seen enough pus to last me a lifetime, Sister, and my hands are likely ruined for ever from all the scrubbings with carbolic and Eusol because, of course, only a *sister* can wear rubber gloves, and I do believe, no matter what your dear Matron-in-Chief thinks, that I have earned the right to go where my betters think I am needed in this war, and I also believe that Major Watson's new method of blood transfusion will save the lives of many who have to this point died for want of fluid and warmth.' She finally took a breath. 'Of course, I am not a nurse, nor would I claim to be. I am a VAD and proud of it.'

Mrs Gregson's short speech never increased in volume throughout its course, but somehow, like a great flywheel pressed into motion, gathered power and momentum as it went. Watson was about to object that is wasn't strictly speaking *his* new method of blood transfusion, but decided to stay out of the contest. It would be like trying to separate two Siamese fighting fish.

The guns seemed even louder and much closer in the brittle silence that descended on the tent.

Sister took her time composing her reply. The heightened colour in her cheeks faded, but she twisted the piece of paper she held in her hands as if she were wringing Mrs Gregson's neck. 'I did not intend to impugn the service you have given. But there are few here who haven't performed the same tasks. Isn't that right, Staff Nurse Jennings?'

'Yes, Sister,' she agreed softly, eyes downcast. 'Although I can't drive—'

But Sister had turned her attention back to the VADs. 'You will assist Major Watson, of course, in his important work, and I assume move on with him once the technique for this wonder treatment has been demonstrated. But I do not want you on the re-suss, pre-op or evacuation wards. Or on the officers' wards in the Big House. It will only confuse the men. I don't want them to think they are getting . . .' She paused for a moment and actually smiled before delivering the blow '. . . second-rate care.'

Staff Nurse Jennings gave a little gasp.

Mrs Gregson's answer was thwarted by the popping of a motor cycle as a signals courier appeared in the doorway. He skidded the bike to a halt, raised his goggles off a dirt-encrusted face and shouted something that baffled Watson: 'Pause!'

'What about the Plug Street CCS?' Sister yelled, pointing to the south. 'Half our staff are on leave.'

The driver shrugged. 'They've been bombed. From enemy aircraft. Direct hits. Not big bombs, but lots of them apparently.'

Sister shuddered at the thought of a shell of any description landing in the midst of a tented CCS and how little protection the thin canvas would provide.

'Casualties?'

'I reckon.'

She snapped her fingers at Jennings. 'I'll send a runner up to the Big House for the surgical teams. You gather the other nurses.' She turned to Brindle. 'Perhaps you can lend a hand at the reception area?' Finally she addressed the VADS. 'And you two girls, would you kindly do your best not to get under our feet?'

Once they were alone, Mrs Gregson lifted her long dress clear of the floor and stomped her foot three times, accompanying each percussive blow with a shriek of frustration.

'Nurse Gregson, I apologize for Sister Spence——' Watson began.

'No, no, don't call me that, she's right. I am not a nurse. Nor am I . . .' her lip curled, '. . . a *girl* of any description. "Mrs Gregson" will do just fine. It's not the first time I have met her kind, Major. Although she is an exceptional specimen.'

'There might, I fear, be extenuating circumstances.'

'I knew, Major Watson, when I first set eyes on you and your tubes and syringes, that you were a gentleman. I don't expect you to take sides. The war between VADs and QAs has been going on almost since hostilities began.' She took several deep breaths and recovered her composure. 'We'll carry on unpacking, Major. You'll be needed at the triage tent initially. We'll have you ready for any transfusions by the time you've finished.'

One thing still puzzled him. 'What did he mean by "pause"?' he asked.

'PAWs,' corrected Miss Pippery, spelling it out, her voice sounding slight and reedy after the robust exchange between the two older women. 'The casualties that are given priority transport from the dressing stations. Penetrating Abdominal Wounds. I think you used to call them Double-Is. Intestinal Injuries.'

He nodded. New weapons, such as shrapnel, needed fresh terminology. And, he reminded himself, new medicine.

'Which means, Major Watson,' said Mrs Gregson, 'we'll be needing your magic blood a lot sooner than you anticipated.'

FIVE

The Tommy would never know just how lucky he was. He only appeared for a fleeting second, a grimy, thin face with, as Bloch could see through the scope, protruding, blackened teeth. The soldier had decided to risk a quick glance between the sandbags, to check all was quiet out beyond the coils of wire in no man's land. In that second, a time span no longer than a heartbeat, Scharfschütze Unteroffizier Ernst Bloch had to decide whether this Tommy was worth one of his expensive bullets and risking the detection of his hide. The cross hairs sat squarely on the face, fixed at the bridge of the nose. Beside him, he felt Gefreiter Schaeffer, his young spotter, stiffen, anticipating the shot. Then the all-too-tempting target disappeared down behind the parapet.

Wait for an officer or a specialist. Make it count.

That was the sharpshooter's mantra. The Tommy had been both a private and a newcomer – his cap was still stiff with the wire that kept its shape. Old trench hands removed it so that the crown collapsed, providing less of a target. Bloch was seeing more and more of the new Brodie steel helmets in his sights now, though. Not that they could stop a shot from him.

Bloch moved his head slightly and found the drinking tube, sucking up a mouthful of water, which he held over his tongue before swallowing. His eyes never left the scope on his father's Mauser sporting rifle. They had been out since before dawn, in this shell hole between the lines, one of hundreds that pockmarked the earth. This one was different, though, because it was next to the root ball of a tree that had been ripped out of the ground and reduced to splinters. The remaining tangle of compressed roots gave perfect cover for a sniper.

The pair also lay under a camouflaged sheet, their faces and hair and hands plastered with mud, so they looked as if they were primordial creatures formed from the killing grounds of Flanders. Bloch ignored the cold seeping up from the earth, the oddly sweet, cloying stink of the decaying bodies and the thin, icy drizzle that had begun to fall from the sullen, featureless sky that sat over the whole of northern Europe. It could be worse, he reminded himself, it could be summer, when battalions of bloated flies filled the air and the stink of putrefaction was enough to make a maggot gag.

Although further north no man's land was being churned and harrowed to a hideous strip of ooze and muck by constant bombardment, here, in the quieter part of the line, you could still see evidence of the countryside's pre-war existence. There were a dozen farmhouses and barns — albeit without their tiled roofs, and with the beams plundered for firewood — in the vicinity. Among the rat- and crow-stripped skeletons of soldiers that littered no man's land were those of the horses and cattle that had once roamed the fields in peacetime.

Behind him, a crop of mangels had gone to seed, a promiscuous riot of stems and leaves that had provided Bloch with extra cover as he had moved into position in the strengthening light of the new day. Now and then he spotted a rusting cultivator or roller, hastily abandoned as war overtook the farmer. This had once been rich, productive agricultural land, toiled by peasants whose lives were much like those of their fathers and grandfathers. It was hard to imagine it could ever return to such an innocent time. Surely the scars they had inflicted on Flanders would last for generations.

Despite the long hours of discomfort, he enjoyed being a sharp-shooter. Not for him the weeks of living in dugouts and skulking in trenches, the world reduced to a narrow corridor of sky above his head. A *Sharfschütze* was one of the élite, allowed to roam free across the front, just as long as he continued to add notches to his rifle butt, which was often a weapon he had used in his days as a *Jäger*, a hunter, before the war. As with the peasants in Flanders, it was all about family tradition; Bloch had been an accomplished *Jäger* like his father and grandfather before him.

'Eleven minutes to your left,' came the whispered instruction. It was the first time Schaeffer had spoken for an hour or more.

Bloch moved the rifle in a smooth, steady arc. Behind the rusting coils of barbed wire, a two-metre section of the British trench parapet had collapsed, the badly packed sandbags falling inwards. Bloch could see the urgent hands and arms of those attempting to repair the breach. He imagined them, standing on the firing step, crouched like apes as they endeavoured to make sure they exposed no body part to enemy fire. It wasn't easy. The British trenches were dug piti-fully shallow. Manna to a sniper.

'Officer!'

But Bloch had already seen the man, noted the distinctive long tunic with Sam Browne belts and the stick under the arm and had decided this was a kill worth having. The discharge sounded enormous to him, but he knew how difficult it was for men in trenches to gauge the direction of a single shot. There was no smoke and little muzzle flash; the cartridges were of his own design, perfected while hunting wild boar. He worked the oil-smoothed Mauser action to chamber another round.

As Bloch refocused through the Goertz sight, he heard the hoarse cries for a stretcher-bearer 'at the double' and watched the periscopes appear, popping up like nervous rabbits from their burrows, scanning the wasteland for telltale signs of his position. He even saw some steel-helmeted idiot put his head up, long enough for him to collect him as a second notch that day, should he so desire. But he held his fire. Now was the time for calm, for holding position, to stay as still as he had been before he had removed that man's head. Soon, a lumbering spotter plane might appear, trying to locate them. Or, at dusk, men would slip out from the British lines on a mission to flush them out, for the Tommies had countersnipers now, special units designed to spot, track and kill people like him.

Overhead, there came a sound somewhere between a whistle and a scream, tardily followed by the boom of the 77mm gun that had launched the shell. Several hundred metres ahead of Bloch, beyond the wire, a column of earth leaped skywards as the projectile exploded between the British trenches. It was the early afternoon bombardment, which always began at one p.m. precisely somewhere along the line. General von Kluck was known to the British as 'General von O'clock' because of his punctuality.

A second round followed, vomiting up another cloud of muck that stayed frozen in the air, like a great oak tree made of soil and splinters and parts of men, before it collapsed into smoke and dust.

The next few detonations produced inky black flowers. Shrapnel shells. Then the distinctive short, sharp thump as the trench mortars joined in, followed by the more sibilant whistle of howitzers. Soon the ground was shaking continually as the heavier artillery batteries added their might.

Some of the rounds began to fall onto no man's land, showering the snipers with fine particles. A thick man-made fog now billowed over the trenches, reducing visibility. The earth was rippling beneath the pair, as if they were lying on the back of an enormous animal, stirring from its sleep. Their organs began to jigger, and teeth rattle in their heads. Soon the noise would consume them, eating at their sanity.

Bloch rolled onto his side. 'Let's go home, Schaeffer. Nobody's going to be sticking their head up while this is going on.' He shouted the words, but even so Schaeffer had to lip read. It was something they'd all grown very skilled at.

The young spotter didn't need telling twice. In less than a minute the two men were sprinting at a crouch through the mangel field. One officer. A poor tally for the day. Still, Bloch thought in the moments before the building crescendo of shrieks and explosions drove everything else out of his head, there was always tomorrow.

SIX

From his pre-deployment briefings at Millbank, Watson was aware that the British Army and the Royal Army Medical Corps had, by a system of trial and bloody error, created a brutally efficient way of dealing with the hundreds of thousands of casualties it took in any given campaign. A man wounded on the front line would first either find his own way or be taken by stretcher-bearers to a Regimental Aid Post. This was the most advanced of the outposts, staffed by a medical officer and three or four orderlies. Minor wounds were dressed there and then.

However, those with not-so-minor injuries were stretchered or walked or sometimes trollied down on an overhead railway system a few hundred yards to the Advanced Dressing Station, usually situated in a cellar or farmhouse. Some men would be patched up and returned to their units, some were allowed to rest overnight and received food and water. The more seriously injured would be passed down the line by horse or motor ambulance to the Main Dressing Station, where some emergency surgery was possible.

Eventually, motor ambulances would transfer the worst cases to the tents and ancillary buildings of the more permanent Casualty

Clearing Station, where the doctors and nurses readied them for evacuation, by train or barge, to a base hospital. There, conventional care could take place, before, if they were lucky, the injured were shipped back home.

It was, at least on paper, a well-drilled system. There was little that felt smooth or efficient about the scene that greeted Watson at the reception tent, though.

A steady procession of battered motor ambulances was emerging from the thin, unnatural fog that shrouded the countryside. They halted long enough for orderlies to grab the stretchers or help down the walking wounded before turning round and heading upstream against the tide of new arrivals. The CCS unloading area was quickly overwhelmed as row upon row of stretchers began to fan out. Most occupants were bandaged or had limbs encased in a Thomas splint, evidence of hasty care at the advanced stations.

Groups of 'walking wounded', caked with blood, yellow mud and black earth, had spread out their capes and sat, with whatever rifles and kit they had managed to bring lying next to them. It had always amazed Watson just how much the modern Tommy was expected to carry – a backbreaking ninety pounds of gear; a sodden greatcoat added another sixty in conditions like this. A Lewis gun or the ammunition for one increased the burden even more.

Almost every soldier who could manage it was smoking, and a fug of Woodbine and Gold Flake mixed with the petrol fumes that hung over the whole scene. Some leaned over and put a cigarette between the lips of a prone comrade, letting him suck in smoke until the patient gave a grateful thumbsup. The eerie thing was, no man spoke or cried out. It was as if they had been robbed of the ability to speak or utter any sound. All they could do was smoke their gaspers as if their fragile lives depended on it. As Watson examined the men, some of the soldiers stared back at him, eyes hooded with fatigue or shock or a mixture of the two.

Orderlies moved among them, collecting up rifles and Mills bombs to be transferred to a kit store. Some argued, not wanting to be parted from their lucky rifle or talismanic bayonet. The orderlies explained that they could hardly sleep with them in a medical ward. In a few cases a label was attached, so a man could reclaim his own weapon.

And still the ambulances came, gears grinding, cabs rocking and twisting on the rutted road. Some of them were the new Vauxhall and Humbers – often bearing the name of the organization or individual from back home who had funded its purchase – but mostly they were of the original generation of ambulance: a lorry chassis with a makeshift body bolted on the rear. There were even some horse-drawn carts with stretchers loaded where once hay, turnips or potatoes would have been transported.

And this a quiet section of the front, Watson thought. What must—

'Major Watson!' Staff Nurse Jennings beckoned him from the open sides of the triage/reception tent, where long trestle tables received the stretchers and each case was assessed before being moved on to the appropriate ward or, in some cases, the mortuary.

'Yes, how can I help?' he asked, hurrying over.

'Over here.'

He stepped into the tent and into a miasma of stale sweat, tart chemicals and fresh blood. A series of barked instructions rang out, mostly coming from a man in a white coat who, beneath it, was seemingly dressed for a round of golf. The accent was American or Canadian, Watson wasn't certain.

'Re-suss! This guy needs morphine. Where's his label? What do you mean it's fallen off? Re-suss! Are the surgical teams in place? Pre-op now. Now! Staff Nurse – get this wound cleaned and irrigated. I've seen farms in Idaho with less soil in them.'

American, then.

'Is the X-ray trailer up and running? Good. OK, soldier, let's see. Well, I'm guessing that hurts like hell, but it's a Blighty. Yup, even the British Army doesn't need men with one knee. Orderly! Get this man to X-ray, please.'

He was striding between the tables, assessing soldiers in the blink of an eye before moving on, but Watson noticed there was always purposeful activity left in his wake. He caught Watson's eye and gave a mocking two-fingered salute.

Jennings pulled at Watson's arm and he swung round and followed her pointing finger. Watson swallowed hard and, for one mortifying second, he thought he might swoon. The man's khaki jacket was covered in blood and ochre-coloured mud. But it was the source of the blood that was so horrifying. Most of the soldier's face, from the nostrils down, had simply disappeared. It reminded Watson of the demonstration models of coloured wax used by his professors at the University of London.

But this was not wax – it was flesh and bone, a series of spongy surfaces, glistening tubes, raw muscle, cotton-like nerves and hard bone, the human workings exposed by the removal of the jaw. Most of the palate had gone, too, and he could see up into the dark corridors of the sinuses.

The sight made him appalled, angry. The wounds from the round bullets used in Afghanistan had caused nothing like this damage. His own intact limbs were witness to that.

'Lieutenant Cornelius Lovat. RC. Sniper wound. He's stopped breathing,' said Staff Nurse Jennings, her voice quavering. 'He was breathing just a second ago. Then he gave a spasm. I took away the dressing, thinking it was suffocating him and . . . that. Shall I call the padre?'

Watson leaned in close towards the ghastly wound, the clinical part of his mind noting the teeth and bone that had been forced into the remaining flesh, the dull shards of metal that would need extricating. And there were the patches of the wound that had been cauterized to shiny circles of seared flesh by intense heat. As he came close one of the man's eyes snapped open, causing him to start, but he held his ground. There was no sight in it, no spark of consciousness. Lovat, thank God, had been rendered senseless. He gently brushed away a pair of lice, no respecters of rank, that had emerged from the lieutenant's hairline.

'It says "M" on his label,' Jennings said. 'They gave him morphia. Could that have depressed his breathing?'

'Possibly.' And perhaps, Watson thought, somebody at one of the dressing stations of the field ambulance had decided they might perform a mercy and given him a larger-than-necessary dose. It would have been understandable.

Watson took the Wilsdorf & Davis from his wrist. They might be considered a touch feminine in London circles, but a wristwatch, especially one with a shrapnel guard like the W&D, made more sense that his usual half-hunter, now he was back in uniform. He unbuttoned the top pocket of his tunic and swapped the timepiece for the ivory-handled magnifying glass he always carried about him, the one with the inscription he valued so much. 'Can you fetch that lantern, Nurse? I need more light.'

She did as instructed and soon he was looking at the damage in even greater detail. It was a struggle to keep a growing feeling of revulsion in check, both at the wound and the weapon that had made it. He was used to the sight of injuries, but this was of a far greater magnitude than he had experienced in his previous life. Perhaps Tiger Mac had been right . . .

Watson straightened up, took a deep breath, focused his mind. He was out of practice, that was all, grown soft. Too much fanciful writing, not enough doctoring. He summoned the dispassionate clinician of old and moved in closer once more.

'I need some forceps,' he said, taking off his jacket and rolling up his sleeves. 'You were right, Staff Nurse Jennings. There's gauze or similar from the dressing occluding the trachea.' Or what was left of it.

There's something else.

The voice in his skull was so burnished and clear, he almost looked over his shoulder for the speaker. But that would have been ridiculous. He knew it could not be his old friend. It was just an echo of times past.

You are looking but not observing. Or rather, not observing with all your senses. Think, Watson, think.

Then he had it, the sensation almost overwhelmed by dozens of others. He concentrated on it alone, slowly isolating it, stripping away the competition, pinning down the few stray molecules in his nostrils. He could smell burned garlic.

Well done, Watson, the voice said, rather patronizingly. Nevertheless, as he worked the compacted material free of the windpipe and the poor wretch made a gurgling sound in his throat, he allowed himself a small smile of satisfaction. Which then faded as he remembered what the burned garlic indicated. Yet another perversion of the art of war.

'Pre-op,' he said to the nearest orderlies. 'Adrenaline chloride on the wound to stem bleeding. And ask the anaesthetist to use a rectal infusion of ether. I'll add it all to his label.'

Watson extracted a stubby pencil from his pocket and wrote the instructions in blocked capitals. 'Understand? Rectal. Plus GSE. *Glandulae suprarenalis extractum*. That's the adrenaline chloride. And I want any shrapnel extracted saved and delivered back to me.' He wrote that down, too.

He watched as the stretcher was slid off the table, to be immediately replaced by another. He scanned the label attached to the man's sleeve, next to the 'wounded' stripe, which showed the poor devil had been hit before. 'PAW', it read, and gave his name and rank. He was with the Royal Scots Fusiliers. Not, Watson noted, from the battledress trousers, a kilted regiment; how those that did wear the tartan managed in the cold and filth of the trenches beggared belief. Watson looked at the abdominal dressing and at the red stains creeping around the side of it.

'Major Watson. Hello, sir.'

He looked up to see a face full of anguish that he didn't, for a moment, recognize.

'De Griffon?'

The man nodded and his face relaxed into the broad, open one Watson remembered from his time in Egypt, where he had been investigating the mechanics of the new blood transfusion methods in field hospitals. De Griffon's unit had been one of his first guinea pigs. 'Good Lord, what are you doing here?'

Robinson de Griffon's head was moving back and forth, as if he were watching an accelerated game of tennis. 'Looking for my men.'

'Your men?'

'Yes. The Leigh Pals. "A" Company.'

'In this part of the line?' Watson asked.

'We are, yes.' He gave a nervous laugh. 'Small world, eh, sir?'

In Watson's limited experience of them, wars made for very small worlds. It was astonishing to him how often he ran into old colleagues from the Berkshires. 'What's happened?'

De Griffon took off his cap and ran a hand over his wayward hair, smoothing it down for a few seconds. 'We were on our way back from the front when a stray shell hit one of the columns. Damned bad—' He turned to Jennings and shrugged apologetically. 'Sorry. Bad luck. Two dead. Shipobottom, Carlisle, Morris, all quite seriously injured. Hoped they might be here.'

His lower lip quivered slightly and Watson thought he might cry. He noticed that de Griffon had been promoted since he last saw the young man. He was now a captain. How old was he? No more than mid-twenties, surely. And unlikely to have known anything like war, given his cosseted background. De Griffon was a far cry from one of the 'Temporary Gentlemen' they talked about. Still, his heart was clearly in the right place and rapid promotion was, he supposed, another feature of this conflict.

'I haven't seen Shipobottom here, no.' Watson didn't recall Carlisle or Morris, but the curiously named sergeant was not a man you forgot in a hurry.

'There'll be another reception tent taking the overspill,' said Jennings. 'About a hundred yards up the hill, on the left. I should imagine they are in there.'

De Griffon looked relieved. 'Thank you, miss. I hope to see you soon, Major.'

'I'll look forward to it,' Watson said. After he had gone he glanced at his nurse before turning his attention back to the new patient. 'That is one anxious young captain.'

'The officers become very protective of their charges,' Jennings said. 'Often they are like father figures to men ten or fifteen years older than them. It's strange to see sometimes.'

'Right, who do we have here?'

'McCall, sir. Is it no' a Blighty, Doc?' the soldier on the stretcher asked in a broad accent once he realized he had Watson's full attention. Beneath the mask of filth was a mere boy of eighteen or nineteen.

'Well, let's take a look,' Watson said noncommittally. Being a Blighty or not was the least of the lad's worries. He had read papers on the survival rates from abdominal wounds, of the festering caused by the soil and cloth forced into the lacerating wounds by the shrapnel. Of the resulting gas gangrene, which caused the skin to inflate until it was as tight as a drum before it split and released, as Mrs Gregson had observed, a smell of putrefaction that, once inhaled, was hard to forget. Some of the isolation wards at Bailleul had reeked of it even after repeatedly being scrubbed down.

Watson registered the wound stripe on the lad's soiled tunic. 'Where did they get you last time?'

'Bullet in ma shoulder, sir. No real damage.' Watson's own, now ancient, wound in the same location stirred in sympathy. 'I don't wan' it to be a Blighty, sir.'

'Is that right?' Watson asked, surprised.

'Aye. Don't wan' to leave ma pals. Don't you believe wha' you hear. There's parts o' this war that're reet gut fun.'

Watson winked, as if they were sharing a guilty secret. The man was right; there was a dangerous thrill to conflict, and marvellous comradeship. Some thrived on it, no matter how gruesome the conditions. There was much Watson had missed when he left the army. That, however, had been a different kind of war. Although he supposed some things never changed – the thrill of being tested in battle and coming through head held high, eating, sleeping and fighting alongside men you would lay down your life for, the bitter-sweet elation of a victory, no matter how small. It could be a euphoric mixture. He had rarely experienced anything quite like it since, apart from when Holmes had stirred him out of his comfortable existence.

'Staff Nurse Jennings, can you fetch me some scissors? Best take a look at what's under here.' He rechecked the label. No 'M'. Just 'PAW', name and rank. 'Did they give you anything, Private, at the dressing station?'

'Like wha', sir?'

'Something for the pain?'

'MO had a wee bit of rum. It's naw too bad.' He managed a cheer-ful grin, but it soon faded.

'Lie down now. We'll get you something. Morphia, please.'

'There is none left,' hissed Jennings.

'What?'

'No morphine. We have sent to the Big House for more.'

'Aspirin, then. You have that?' It wasn't a given, as phenol short-ages had curtailed production of the drug on both sides.

'We do.'

'Then we'll try that.' Aspirin might be a German drug, but he was sure the lad wasn't too fussy. 'Hold on, any *tinctura opii camphorata*?'

'Yes, I believe so.'

It was the weakest of all the opium preparations, but had the edge on aspirin.

While an orderly went to fetch the elixir, Watson cut away the top swathe of bandage. More blood began to well from the edges. 'Doesn't look too terrible,' he lied. 'You lay your head back down, Private McCall. Have a little rest.' He wrote 'M REQUIRED' on the docket. Then 'X-RAY'.

The boy did as he was told, and as Watson worked at removing the layers of bandaging, he spoke softly to Jennings as she fed the boy the newly arrived elixir. 'I meant to explain myself earlier. Before Sister interrupted.'

'You have seen the worst of Sister Spence, Major. She's a good, dedicated woman.'

'I'm sure of it.' He pointed at her neck. 'I meant about that tiny blemish, although I fear that is too harsh a word for such a delicate thing, at the base of your throat. Only the St Kitts sandfly, *Culicoides clasterri*, also found on Nevis, leaves such an attractive, star-shaped scar.'

'Ah, yes. We used to call it the Sweet Itch.'

'And the only business that would take a British family out there, other than perhaps the Church, is the sugar business.'

She raised a quizzical eyebrow. 'Tell me, Major Watson, do you always check your nurses' throats for blemishes?'

Her cheeks dimpled fetchingly as she smiled. He felt himself warming under the collar of his now blood-spattered shirt. He resumed cutting.

'And how do you know about the sandflies of the Caribbean, Major?'

'I think we'll need some towels here. The flies? Oh, I read a monogram. Recommended by . . .' He paused. 'I had a very good tutor, Staff Nurse Jennings.'

Good? The very best, Watson. The very best.

He ignored the comment. It was a trace memory, playing tricks on him. He was aware it could have no connection to his former colleague and friend because, should they pass in the street, Watson knew full well that Sherlock Holmes would no longer give him the time of day.

SEVEN

Sitting in just his singlet and longjohns, Ernst Bloch opened the box of cartridges his father had posted to him and removed the upper layer of the compressed cotton wool that swaddled them. He carefully placed ten of the bullets onto the baize covering of the portable card table at the foot of his bed. They lay next to the pipe he intended to enjoy as soon as he had finished this little task. He wouldn't worry about the smoke from his potent black tobacco affecting his fellow soldiers, because there were none.

Bloch occupied his own cubbyhole in one of the deep, airless dugouts. He was curtained off from the regular troops in his own miniature Siegfried shelter. Nobody in the regular army cared much for snipers, not even those on his own side. The conscientious objectors who cleaned the latrines were held in higher esteem.

Bloch didn't care. At least, unlike poison gas or the flame-thrower, there was still a sporting element to his hunt for a target. It was a way of waging warfare that went back to the Crimea and the Edinburgh Rifles, who had first used telescopic sights to kill Russian gunnery officers. Bloch had done his homework; he could justify his trade in any argument, but it had long ago become tiresome. Let the cannon fodder grumble about him and his opposite numbers on the Allied side.

He weighed the first of the rounds on the little scales he had set up. Then the second and a third. All three were within a fraction of a gram of each other. Satisfied, he stood a steel ruler on its side. A half-moon depression had been milled out of it and into that he slotted the cartridge, adjusting it until he found the centre of gravity. He repeated this four times, noting the balance point was identical in each case. His father had followed his instructions to the letter.

Schaeffer came through with a cup of coffee for him and quickly retired, pulling the thick blanket that doubled for a curtain back into place as he went. He knew that Bloch didn't want to be interrupted while he polished his ammunition or stripped down his rifle. A grunted thanks was the only exchange.

Bloch felt a vibration in the earth, an explosion high above, too distant to register as sound. The German trenches were dug deep and snug, excavated on higher ground, in well-drained soil, which meant they could easily reach forty metres or more into the earth. The British and French were in the soggy lowlands and they were living in shallow gashes in the earth, poorly revetted with wood and parapeted with sandbags to give them extra depth. He had been in the French trenches on a night raid in the early days, before he transferred to the sharpshooters. They were shameful.

'Bloch.'

'Sir.' He put down the bullet he had been wiping with a cloth and stood to attention. The blanket was whisked back and an officer joined him in the compact space. It was the sniping section supervisor, Hauptmann Lux, a Saxon by birth, now attached, like Bloch, to the Sixth Army. Lux was not a tall man, but held himself well, and his uniforms always fitted immaculately. Next to him, Bloch always felt like the unfinished country lad he was. It could have been worse. Lux could have been a prick of a Prussian. That would have been unbearable.

Lux looked Bloch up and down, bemused at a man in his underwear standing ramrod straight, as if waiting for a kit inspection. 'At ease, Bloch. Jesus, it's hotter than hell down here.' Lux took off his cap, wiped his brow and looked around Bloch's impressively neat cubicle. His eyes fell on the needle-nosed bullets. He picked up the scales. 'Private ammunition?'

'My father makes them, sir. They reduce flash and smoke. But weight and balance are critical.'

Lux nodded, not really caring. Every sniper had his rituals, his superstitions and some specialist equipment he believed gave him an advantage over his fellows. 'An officer today, I hear?'

Bloch knew Lux received a daily tally from all his snipers and, for corroboration, their spotters. 'Sir.'

'That is twenty-nine kills, I believe. Or at least, twenty-nine confirmed officers.'

'Yes.' The actual tally was close to a hundred, but, since his over-enthusiastic early days when he shot anything that moved, he had become much more selective.

'One more and it's an Iron Cross, Second Class for you.'

Bloch remained impassive. He wasn't doing this for baubles. He didn't even do it because he hated the British individually; there were times when he felt sorry for the young officers he caught in his sights. But he detested the British imperial arrogance that led the country to think it deserved a hand in every nation's affairs. He did

this job because he believed in a strong Germany that wasn't domi-
nated by an insignificant island with inflated ideas about its
importance. And he did it because he was good at it. 'Thank you, sir.'

'And a week's leave.'

Now Bloch allowed himself a ghost of a smile. However, it didn't
do to dwell too much on the carrot of a few days with Mother,
Father, sister and perhaps Hilde. The army had a habit of cruelly
snatching away a furlough at the last moment on the flimsiest of
excuses.

'There are fresh British units moving into this section,' Lux said.
'Untested. Kitchener's New Army. They've been a long time coming,
eh? The theory is they will get used to trench life in a quiet section.
Learn something from the Scottischers who are already here.'

Bloch was not surprised by Lux's knowledge. The army's intelligence about which divisions and regiments they were facing was
always excellent. He assumed they had good spies somewhere over
the wire.

'A section defended by untried troops is an opportunity for us to
try something different.' Lux indicated Bloch should move to one
side, then took out a map and laid it onto the bed, smoothing the
folds with the flat of his well-manicured hand.

It showed two thick black lines, representing the opposing
trenches, snaking across the page, the loops sometimes coming
close, within, Bloch knew, twenty metres at some points, then
diverging again so that no man's land might be a void of a half-kilo-
metre in width. Lux pointed to a red trace that had been drawn from
Ploegsteert village through the nearby woods. 'This road is the one
they call the Strand. Here, Oxford Circus. Have you ever been to
London, Bloch?'

'No, sir.'

'It doesn't match Berlin. It is far dirtier, more squalid, but it has a certain grimy charm. And they know how to throw a decent dance, I will grant them that. Perhaps you'll be there one day soon, eh? When it belongs to us.' He carried on when Bloch did not reply. 'This area,' he pointed to the east of Ploegsteert Wood, 'is The Birdcage and this is Somerset House. Brigade HQ for the British here. This is where the new officers will be briefed about the sector. And here . . .' another stab at the map, '. . . is the church steeple of Le Gheer. Now, Bloch, thanks to shelling of the woods and a subsequent fire, we believe there is a clear sight-line from this steeple to Somerset House. A good sniper could lie low up there and perhaps pick off half a dozen senior officers at one session. Including . . .' he paused while he took out a newspaper cutting, which he unfurled for Bloch, '. . . this man.'

Bloch studied the grainy photograph of a portly Englishman, a major. Like all snipers he knew his Allied uniforms. The man was emerging from the doorway of an official-looking building, a terrible scowl across his face, as if he were about to bawl out some unfortunate subordinate.

'You know who this is?'

'I think so, sir.'

'Really?' Lux sounded impressed, but Bloch's cousin Willi was in the navy, and had often talked about this man, as if he were engaged in a personal war with him.

Bloch read the caption, just to be certain. His English was poor, but a name was a name and he certainly knew this one. 'Yes.'

'And you could recognize him through a rifle scope?'

Bloch looked at the pugnacious face once more and nodded.

'Good man. Put a bullet through him and it'll be an Iron Cross First Class and two weeks' leave, Bloch.'

But it wasn't the target or the double points for shooting him that exercised Bloch. He looked back at the 'X' marking the steeple and the wiggling traces of the opposing trenches on the map. His real concern was, whatever remained of Le Gheer church, it was firmly on the British side of the lines.

EIGHT

Watson stumbled out of the transfusion unit into a glutinous, all-enveloping blackness and paused, waiting for his eyes to adjust. It was as if his head had been wrapped in a thick velvet cloth and it wouldn't do to break his neck stumbling over the taut guy ropes that played out from the tents in all directions.

He had no idea how many hours had passed since he first saw that jawless man — what was the name again? Lovell? Lovat? So many names, ranks and numbers, so many abbreviations that only hinted at God-awful wounds. The victims had come thick and fast, in such numbers he was initially forced to transfuse soldier-to-soldier, using syringes lined with paraffin wax to try to inhibit the clotting. It was preferable to the previous method, where the radial artery of one man was inserted directly into the median vein of another, and the flow controlled by sutures and thumb and forefinger, but very hit and miss compared to his new system.

Eventually, though, he had been able to collect donations of blood for citration from the lightly injured. Soldiers who agreed to be donors were rewarded with a weekend pass to be used before rejoining their battalion. Thus there had been no shortage of volunteers and he had created a small stockpile, which he had citrated, 'typed' and put on ice.

He wondered what that harpy of a sister-in-charge would say if she knew he had allowed the VADs to help draw the blood. And that all the soldiers had called them 'nurse'. He shuddered to think what acid remarks she would draw up from her well of vitriol.

As his pupils dilated, Watson looked up at the sky and checked off a few of the familiar astronomical markers that were emerging: the Plough, Orion, and the iconic 'W' of the stars of Cassiopeia. This was clearly the same world he had always inhabited, under the same heavens. It simply no longer seemed familiar; he felt as if he had been whisked off to some distant planet, where the earth as he knew it had been subverted and distorted into a hideous simulacrum of the real thing.

Some way distant, he saw the flash of a star shell, briefly illuminating all beneath it with its sickly, over-white light, before it faded, leaving only an after-image on his retinae. There was still a war going on out there, even under cover of darkness. Although they were miles away, he could smell the trenches on the wind: a devil's stew of overflowing latrines, unwashed bodies, cigarette smoke, stagnant mud and rotting corpses that clawed at the senses. Those who experienced the revolting aroma up close for the first time, he was told, were often physically sick. Within a week, they no longer noticed; indeed, they had become part of the stench.

Over to his left he could make out the grim rows of stretchers holding bodies stitched into coarse army blankets. A figure moved among them, sometimes bending down and shining a torch onto a label and writing on a clipboard. One of the padres, no doubt, finding out which of the men belonged to his flock and which to some other shepherd. Chaplains of every stripe, and the orderlies who acted as gravediggers, would be busy the next morning. Watson wondered for a moment how the man's faith was holding up, but he was too weary to start a theological discussion.

He began a slow trudge uphill, towards his billet in the Big House, careful to favour his aching knee. He passed the pack store — once the groundkeepers' shed — and skirted the rectangular beds of what must have been part of the old monastery gardens, now sad and neglected. He caught the scent of thyme and . . . yes, liquoricey wild fennel. Who knew when this patch would be growing their medicinal herbs or vegetables again?

The lawned section of grounds just before the stone steps up to the monastery was pitched with the tents that made up the nurses' quarters. The flap of Sister-in-Charge Spence's bell tent was open as he passed and he glanced inside. Clearly illuminated by a hooded candlestick reading lamp, she was seated at a chipped wooden writing desk poring over a pile of post, a thick brush and inkpot to hand. She was censoring. Something made her look up and she waved him over.

Watson hesitated, swaying slightly as a wave of tiredness broke over him. Unnaturally amplified sounds rattled around his cranium: a distant explosion that cracked the night sky, a man coughing his last some yards behind him, the hum of electricity wires feeding the larger tents, the whirring of clockwork from the mechanical oil lamps used elsewhere, the snorting of jittery horses from a nearby livery stable. He felt like closing his eyes there and then. But he shook his head clear, put one foot in front of the other and went across to Sister Spence.

'Major Watson,' she said as she stood, put the lid on the inkpot and snuffed out the twin candles of the reading lamp, 'I thought some hot chocolate might be in order. Rowntree's.'

'That sounds splendid,' he said with as much enthusiasm as he could muster. He just wanted to get out of his ruined clothes.

She placed the kettle on top of the Beatrice oil stove and spooned the powder into two enamel mugs, talking as she did so. 'No milk, I am afraid. I saw your two VADs giving out teas earlier. Very efficient.' She looked over. 'I hope that was all they did.'

'They assisted me with transfusions. Sterilizing syringes and the like.'

The sly smile told Watson that she didn't believe a word of that, but was prepared to let it pass.

She realized that decorum was dictating he kept one foot outside. 'Oh, do come in, nobody is going to think two dry old twigs like us are up to anything improper.'

Watson wanted to object that he liked to think he still had some sap left in him. But not only would it have been inappropriately forward, looking down at his blood-spattered shirt and jacket, he could see he probably looked positively desiccated. She was right, nobody would imagine him capable of mischief.

Sister Spence's uniform, he noted, was immaculate, as was the interior of the bell tent, with its wardrobe trunk for her clothes, an improvised dressing table holding an ebonized mirror-and-brush set, and a wrought-iron washstand with jug and bowl and, on a lower level, two oblong aluminium hot-water bottles. The only incongruous note was struck by a leather *Pickelhaube*, the infamous spiked German helmet, which hung down next to the Coleman lantern in the centre of the tent.

'A battlefield souvenir,' Sister Spence said, noticing his interest. 'I don't agree with them, robbing bodies is a ghastly business, but it was donated by a grateful Tommy. They can be raffled back home and raise a pretty penny for the medical services. Helmets, medals and those nasty saw-edged bayonets, they fetch the most. And these hideous spiked ones are becoming rare now. Sit there.' She pointed to a folding chair next to her camp bed and he lowered himself into it. He longed for Brindle to appear and pull his Latimers off; his feet were throbbing. A Turkish bath would be the thing. Whenever he felt old and rheumatic, he sought out Nevill's on Northumberland Avenue. He could almost conjure the smell of steam in his nostrils.

The sister appeared to be clairvoyant. 'You know, the monks at the monastery left us one very useful item. A brewery. Oh, don't get your hopes up, not for producing beer. The wooden vats make for very handy washtubs these days. A good soak works wonders, even here. The orderlies should have hot water ready when you get up there.'

He nearly groaned with pleasure at the thought of scrubbing his skin almost raw. That and a pipe of Schippers, an indulgence he had denied himself at the request of Emily – she had always loathed the smell on her clothes and in her hair – and which he was now of a mind to resume. However, having no ready supply of his tobacco of choice, he would have to make do with one of his Bradley's before he turned in.

'And there'll be food. As I said, no milk, but we have plenty of eggs. And bread. Here you are, Major.'

She handed over the drink. As he went to take it, he noted his shaking hand with some surprise. It felt as if it belonged to another man. Yet there it was at the end of his arm, agitating the chocolate in the tin mug, as bad as any delirium tremens he had ever seen. There was something else, too, a pressure building in his chest, and the sensation that only by screaming at the top of his lungs could he release it.

'And this,' said Sister Spence firmly.

It was a hefty tot of rum in a blue crystal liqueur glass, which he took from her and threw back, coughing as it caught in his throat. He felt the pressure behind his breastbone ease as the fiery alcohol coursed down to his stomach.

'Better?'

He nodded. 'You know, it wasn't until I saw the hospital tents from the ship, rows of them along the clifftops, that I began to appreciate the scale of what is happening out here.' It had been a continuous line, running, so he was told, all the way from Calais to Boulogne. 'Then, when I saw the trenches from the air—'

Sister Spence interrupted him. 'Personally, I think it helps if you try and block out what our Major Torrance calls "the bigger picture". Oh, it's all very well getting that if you are a general. But I feel we should concentrate on the case before you at any given moment, as if it is just a singular event. If you try and take in what is happening across Europe . . . it could drive a man quite mad. A lack of imagination can sometimes be a blessing.'

Watson thought he didn't lack for imagination, but even so, he had trouble contemplating the vastness of the medical operation, about how one could multiply this one hospital by one hundred or one thousand, and the tally of young men wounded, maimed and killed that would be at the end of the equation. And Europe was just one theatre and one side of the conflict — there was the Eastern Front, the Dardanelles, Egypt and the Middle East, Africa . . . Perhaps it was the terrible mathematics of such slaughter that had been trying to force its way out of his chest earlier.

'Don't worry, Major. I have had word that our sister CCS is up and running after its attack. We're full. And Major Torrance and Captain Symonds will be back presently, so we'll be up to full strength with doctors. Tomorrow will be an easier day for all of us. Physically, I mean. More rum?'

He shook his head and sipped the chocolate. They could hear the sound of a badly tuned piano drifting in from a billet in the reserve line, somewhere close by. It took him a few moments to recognize the sombre first movement of Godin's 'Valse Septembre' before the wind shifted and the tune was gone. 'Bad news?' he asked.

She looked puzzled. 'I'm sorry? Was what bad news?'

'The telegram. That paper has a very distinctive colour and texture. Was it bad news?' He could see it on the table, next to the mail. It was still twisted like an over-sized sweet wrapper. She had waved and throttled it at the transfusion tent when she and Mrs Gregson had exchanged words. 'It's a Keeper of the Privy Purse telegram, isn't it? Their Majesties regret . . . I'm sorry, perhaps I shouldn't intrude.'

It was bad form, but curiosity had the better of him. There had to be some explanation for her earlier behaviour.

Sister Spence turned her gaze on the telegram briefly, and her chin shook momentarily. 'It's about my brother. Suffered a relapse at a hospital outside Boulogne, the day before he was due to be shipped back to England.'

Watson closed his eyes for a second. It was an effort to open them again. The lids felt as if they had been coated with lead. Was he, after all, too old for this? Should he have listened to the nay-sayers? To Holmes?

'I'm so sorry,' he said.

She gave a brief incline of the head and drank some of her beverage. 'They are all somebody's brother or son, Major. Or husband or sweetheart. Or father. Every last one. I'm not unique.'

'But you are, in that you know what "relapse" means.'

A sigh. 'You know about that, too, do you?'

'It's one piece of terminology that has stayed with me. I came across a case at Bailleul. He managed to get into the medical stores one night. He found the digitalis.'

She stared down into her mug and her features softened into a very different Sister Spence. 'Henry had no genitals left. It sounds like some terrible music-hall song, doesn't it?' The voice was thin and fragile, hollowed out by grief. 'They were blown clean off by some freak of ballistics that left the rest of him intact. He was twenty-two. Can you imagine? He would have thought his life over. Heaven knows where he got a pistol from, but I suspect they won't enquire too deeply about that. I think "relapsed" is a little easier on the families at home than "suicide", don't you?'

'At least while the war is on, I believe it to be a kindness, yes.'

She looked up at him, blinked away a film of moisture and fixed him with a hard stare. Her words recovered their brittle glaze. 'Major, I may have been a little firmer than usual this afternoon . . . yesterday afternoon . . . because of the news about Henry. But that has no bearing on my attitude to your VADs. I won't have them. I won't have Canadian nurses either.'

'Why ever not?' He had come across some fine examples from the Dominion at hospitals both in England and Egypt.

Her face pinched up once more. 'Dances, Major, dances. The Canadians are allowed to go cavorting with officers. To walk out with them. To attend tea parties and dances. It unsettles my girls. It's bad for morale.'

'You could always let your nurses have a cavort or two.'

She frowned at such flippancy. 'I quote Matron-in-Charge Challenger: are we here to go dancing or save lives?'

Can't one do both, he wondered, but the fight wasn't in him. He felt woozy. Alcohol on an empty stomach, perhaps.

'And a lot of these VADs hold dangerous political views. I don't want them to poison the minds of my nurses.'

'What sort of political views?'

'Radical suffragettes.' She said it with a sneer.

'You don't believe in suffrage?'

'Your Mrs Gregson—'

Why did she keep using that possessive? 'She isn't mine.'

'Mrs Gregson strikes me very much as the sort who would have all treated equally. Nurses and VADs. Do you really think a servant should have exactly the same vote as her mistress?'

Sister Spence was clearly a great believer in hierarchy and the natural order of things.

'Actually, I do. Just as the valet's opinion counts as much as his master's views.'

She looked surprised. 'How terribly modern of you.'

Watson smiled to himself. That's not what Emily would have called him. Quite the opposite. But he had adopted some of her more progressive ideas. 'I should be going, Sister. Thank you for the chocolate. Most welcome.' He stood, a little unsteadily. 'As was the rum.'

'Good. I'm sorry if I was rude. You see where politics can get us? I meant no offence.'

'None was taken.'

'Can I offer a word of advice, Major? Medical advice. Just an observation.'

'I am a newcomer hereabouts, Sister, advice would be most welcome.'

'You have to concentrate on the viable ones. You can't save them all.'

'We tried to in Afghanistan.'

'There weren't as many,' she said coldly. 'Nor were the injuries anything like as heinous, I'll wager. Staff Nurse Jennings told me about the poor chap with half a face. I went to see him. There was no possibility on God's earth he could have survived. And I think you knew that. It goes against all our training and ethics—'

'He's dead? Lovat?'

'I am afraid so.'

'Where is he now?'

'In the mortuary tent awaiting burial, I would imagine. Why?'

'He's evidence.'

'Of?'

He explained his suspicions about the wound and the smell of garlic. That something abominable was being used to inflict such disfiguring wounds. Wounds that would always prove fatal.

'You'll have to take that up with Brigade. There are channels for such information.'

'I thought as much. I'm now beginning to wonder if I imagined it.'

Nonsense.

He yawned and determined to ignore the bogus inner voice.

'Good night, Sister. Sleep well.'

'I will, once I have read some more of these,' she tapped the stack of letters, 'and suffered yet more very bad poetry indeed. Sometimes I think I should leave the war-sensitive material in and scribble out the doggerel. It would be a blessing for the recipients.'

He managed a tired smile. 'Good night,' he repeated and was half out into the chill night air before he turned and asked: 'Where is Brigade for this section of the line?'

'Plug Street. Or Ploegsteert, to be more correct. At a place called Somerset House. Not its real name, of course.'

'No,' he agreed. The naming of every inch of the country with familiar landmarks was just another example of homesick men trying to make sense of a world gone mad. 'Sleep well.'

As he pulled at the tape to let the tent flap fall closed, Watson saw Sister Spence reaching for the telegram concerning her brother, no doubt hoping that in the past few hours the words had magically rearranged themselves into a less devastating message.

NINE

Staff Nurse Jennings put a brave face on having to share with the new arrivals. She had wondered if Sister Spence had engineered it deliberately, but in fact, being the only nurse with a bell tent all to herself, and a large one at that, it was the logical solution to the problem of the unexpected VADs.

'This is me,' she explained, after she had lit the lamp. 'So if you want to choose one of those two . . . Sheets might be a little damp, I am afraid. If I'd known you were coming . . .'

Miss Pippery hesitated, waiting for Mrs Gregson to make her selection, but she simply placed her valise on the nearest of the cots. 'This will be fine.'

'We aren't staying more than a week,' said Miss Pippery. 'We'll be out of your hair then.'

'So you'll be here for the top brass?'

'What top brass?'

'Field Marshal Haig and entourage. A surprise visit next Friday. Except they told us about it a week ago. They want it to be a nice surprise. With no surprises.'

'Lots of extra scrubbing?'

Jennings sighed. 'And painting. Lord, it's getting cold. Look, there are two hot-water bottles over there. And hot water at the wash station. It might help take the chill off the beds.'

'I'll do it,' said Miss Pippery brightly, picking up the ceramic cylinders. 'And shall I get you one?'

Jennings shook her head. 'I don't think I've got the energy to undress fully.'

Miss Pippery left and Jennings took off her cape and began to unbutton her dress. 'She's nice.'

Mrs Gregson nodded.

'And your Dr Watson.'

'Yes, he's sweet,' Mrs Gregson agreed.

Jennings frowned. 'He's a little more than that. I mean, he's a very good doctor, too. Worked like a man half his age tonight.'

'Hh-mm.' Mrs Gregson was only half listening. She was busy admiring the slight body that had emerged from under the rough dress and petticoats. 'How on earth do you stay so slim?' she asked.

Jennings looked down at her embarrassing layers of grey, over-washed underwear. 'By never stopping moving? Skipping every other meal? Being too exhausted to eat? And thank you for being tactful. Skinny is what you meant.'

'You think so?' Mrs Gregson had pulled down the top of her own dress and she flexed her right arm and squeezed the muscle with her left hand. 'No, this is what I am talking about. Nothing but beds to make and bodies to shift. I've developed arms like Bombardier Billy Wells. The boxer,' she added, when Jennings looked blank. 'Look at yours.'

The nurse pinched the flesh of her own arm, which was as thin as a child's in comparison. 'Under-nourished, my mother would say.'

'Svelte is the word you are looking for.' She yawned. 'Excuse me.'

Jennings did the same and put a hand over her mouth. Her expression took on a serious cast. She glanced at the entrance, to ensure they were quite alone. Even so, she lowered her voice. Canvas was precious little barrier to careless talk. 'I was brought up in Didcot, you know.'

'Really?' Mrs Gregson asked, puzzled at the sudden swerve in subject matter.

'It's near Sutton Courtenay.'

Mrs Gregson's skin grew even paler in the lamplight. 'Oh.'

'You were big news around there.'

'I should imagine I was.'

'Local papers were full of it. Very rare for them to send a reporter up the Old Bailey.'

Mrs Gregson yawned once more, as if the subject was boring her.

'The Red Devil Case we called it—'

Mrs Gregson spun round and grabbed Jennings' upper arm, squeezing so that her fingers met. It felt like a chicken leg to her, a limb that could be snapped just as easily.

Jennings winced. 'Sorry, that was insensitive.'

'It was.'

'I'm tired,' Jennings said, truthfully. What had possessed her to be so crass and forward? 'Not thinking straight.'

'The thing is, Staff Nurse Jennings, Alice knows nothing of all that. Nothing about Red Devils and Sutton Courtenay. Nothing.'

'Oh.'

'I would very much like to keep it that way.'

'Of course. But could you return my arm, please?'

They heard Miss Pippery approaching with the hot-water bottles.

Mrs Gregson let her grip slacken. 'Do you understand what I am saying, Staff Nurse Jennings?'

Jennings wriggled her arm free. There were scarlet marks where fingers had dug into flesh. 'Please don't worry, Mrs Gregson.' She rubbed at her skin. 'Your secret is safe with me.'

Perhaps so, thought Mrs Gregson, *but which one?*

TEN

The star shell had arced over from the British lines and was now intent on defying the laws of gravity. It hung there above no man's land like a low-slung celestial body, burning with a fierce luminosity that failed to diminish as time ticked by. The ruined countryside was washed in its cold silvery light. It was as if someone had turned the moon up to full power. The merciless brilliance threw shadows of deep, impenetrable blackness. From their respective trenches, spotters on both sides scanned the landscape for movement.

Bloch lay immobile, knowing that to any observer he would appear to be just another ridge in the churned earth. Unless he moved a muscle: the slightest stirring in this tableau might register with a skilled watcher. His eyes were squeezed shut; he must not yield to the temptation of staring at the light. Eventually the artificial star began to head earthwards and as it did so, the chemicals fuelling its brief life became exhausted, and slowly the world returned to shades of grey. The shell landed with a soft thud and gave a last, dying splutter.

Bloch stayed frozen for another minute. Then ahead of him he saw three figures rise from the ground and start forward towards the British lines. This was his escort, his very own raiding party, a *Patrouillentrupp*, experts in crossing no man's land at night. They wore leather arm-and-knee patches, and soft-soled ankle-boots and puttees rather than noisy jackboots. Bloch admired and trusted them enough to put himself in their hands for this section of the journey.

As they moved off, he pushed up into a crouch and followed. The star shells were a double-edged sword. They were excellent for spotting motion within the field of their glare; but afterwards the watchers had impaired night vision for anything up to twenty minutes. Having escaped detection under its spotlight, it actually made the infiltrator's job easier.

In Bloch's head were two vital pieces of information. One was a detailed map of the British trenches, from the square-toothed shape of the fire and support trenches, the winding communication trenches, through to the machine-gun strongholds and the wave-like curves of the reserve trenches. The second item he kept at the forefront of his mind, picked up by a forward listening post earlier, was that night's password. 'Unicorn.' Lux had made him practise it, until he had perfected a growl that hid his German accent.

The trio ahead went down again onto the earth and he followed suit. In a sudden burst, they scuttled rapidly like four-legged cockroaches until they were at a British 'sap', a forward observation trench dug out past the wire right into no man's land. These advanced posts were usually temporary, abandoned once the other side knew about them. Using this would get him under the British wire and into their lines proper. He was beckoned forward to join the raiders as they slithered to the edge of the dugout.

'Unicorn,' one of his companions hissed, then added in flawless English. 'We got us an Allyman.'

'Come on then, let's have 'ee.'

It was all over in a few seconds. The two British observers were subdued with blows from trench clubs. Bloch was given a greatcoat and a cap to put over his own uniform. He peered down into the darkness of the excavation. His mental map told him it would take him to a fire trench, then a communication trench, which would in turn deliver him to a relief trench and then almost to the walls of the ruined church. The chances of his being stopped were slight. If he was, however, now he had put on the British khaki, he would be shot as a spy. That was not an unusual risk: captured snipers were often executed out of hand anyway.

Bloch shook each of the three Germans' hands in turn, popped up the greatcoat collar and set off. The two groggy Tommies were revived, gagged and bundled out of the sap at bayonet point, a precious bonus from the incursion. Lux would have great pleasure adding to the sum of his already considerable knowledge about British deployment.

As he set off along the rough-walled trench, Bloch put his hands in his greatcoat pockets and found a crushed packet of ten Black Cat cigarettes, with four left. If he met trouble, that would be his first course of action. Offer a smoke.

But although he passed a few shallow dugouts and heard whispered conversations or smelled tobacco from within a number of them, they were mainly closed off with crude gas curtains and nobody challenged him. In one open dugout he saw two soldiers running candles over the seams of their clothing, killing lice. They were too intent on their bug hunt to look up. He smiled to himself.

He knew how futile it was and that somewhere behind him, two Germans were performing exactly the same parasite hunt. They were the same army, really, separated by a few hundred metres, a language and a Royal family. In truth, not even the latter.

Away from the firing trenches, he came across the latrines, separate for officers and men, a series of lime-washed pits accessed down a short cul-de-sac from the main trench. He held his breath. They smelled no better than the German ones.

Within twenty nervous minutes he was out of the trenches and inspecting the interior of the church, empty save for the unseen rats that scampered and darted through the rubble covering the floor. He looked up in the yawning space above and could just make out the wooden platform of the belfry in the spire. He would be invisible up there. There was one slight problem that Lux hadn't anticipated.

The wooden stairs leading up to it had been blown away by shellfire.

TUESDAY

ELEVEN

Watson awoke with a start, a formless feeling of apprehension gripping him. His heart was running fast, like an ungoverned motor, and there was a film of sweat around his neck. He knew he had been dreaming, but when he tried to focus on it, the images evaporated like smoke, leaving only a residue of unease. He was aware that someone else was in the austere monastic cell that was his billet. He shuffled up on the straw palliasse, just as the shutters were thrown back. He blinked in the thin beam of grey light. He was expecting Brindle, but the figure at the window was shorter. But then, everybody was shorter than Brindle.

'Hello?'

'Sorry to startle you, Major. Your orderly volunteered for the burial party. Asked me if I would mind bringing you your tea. We didn't get a chance to meet yesterday. I'm Caspar Myles.'

It was the American who had been in the reception tent, the one dressed in golfing attire. Today, Watson could see he had on a sleeveless sweater over a shirt, collar and bow tie. He also had on a pair of wide flannel trousers that would have told even a casual observer that he was not British.

He put the tea on a side table. Then he picked up Watson's pistol, which from old habit he kept close to him. 'Jeez, what's this relic?'

'It's my old service revolver,' Watson said testily.

'Really?' Myles weighed it in his hand. Watson noticed that the knuckles on his right hand were abnormally large and swollen, compared to those of the left. 'Tell you what, Major. Why don't we just put some wheels on it, hitch it to a limber and a team of horses and tow it to the front. Make a great howitzer.' He laughed as he put it down. 'Only joshing you. Look, it's almost eight. I wondered if you'd like to join me on the rounds here?'

Watson tried not to be upset by the man's lampooning of his old faithful companion. 'Of course. I'd be delighted to. But tell me, Dr Myles, what is a Harvard man doing in a CCS?'

The American looked taken aback for a second. 'Who told you I was a Harvard man?'

'Nobody. But you are from Harvard?'

'Of course,' he said with pride. 'Part of the All-Harvard Volunteer Medical Unit. But—'

'Your ring. The three open books spelling "Veritas".'

Myles looked down at the signet ring on the little finger of his left hand. 'Of course. Stupid of me.'

'A colleague of mine once made a study of American college symbols for a monograph, with particular reference to secret societies.'

'This war is my secret society,' Myles laughed. 'My parents think I'm studying in Switzerland. We volunteers didn't have to enlist, so there was no official notification for them to discover. That means no rank, hence . . .' He pointed down at his clothes. 'But, you know, you guys need surgeons and I'm a damn fine one.'

Watson smiled at the brash confidence of youth. The man was not yet thirty. He had a long, unlined face, a well-trimmed black moustache and a disarmingly direct stare. His hair was oiled and side-parted. He smelled of Bay Rum. He was probably something of a swell back home.

'I'm sure you are. And I'm certain we Allies are very grateful for your volunteering, when it's not your war.'

'It felt like it was. Bayoneted babies, raped nuns, executed civilians, torpedoed liners, poison gas . . .' He tailed off. 'Yes, I know some of that is exaggerated. But I think it's a just war. A good war.'

Watson was no longer certain that the word 'good' could be applied to any war. But the Von Bork business, back before the outbreak of hostilities, when Holmes had infiltrated a spy ring operating throughout England, had convinced Watson that there was a cabal within Germany that had very real, expansionist plans for subjugating Europe and controlling the Channel. A 'just' war? Perhaps. Necessary? Yes.

'I had personal reasons, too,' said Myles.

They must have been powerful personal reasons indeed, Watson reasoned. By volunteering, doctors and nurses and ambulance drivers sacrificed their American citizenship. It was little wonder he hadn't told his parents the truth.

Myles gave a lopsided grin and clutched his chest. 'Broken heart, in case you're wondering. Shall we say ten minutes downstairs?'

'Best make it fifteen,' Watson said. 'Takes a while to unseize the old joints these days.'

'Fifteen it is. Rounds, then breakfast.' He bounded to the door and stopped with it half open. 'John Watson, right?'

'It is.'

'The writer?'

It was a while since anyone had made the connection. His rank of major seemed to have swallowed whatever little fame he had achieved as a chronicler back at home. 'I have written, yes.'

'Boswell to Holmes's Johnson?'

'That has been said, yes. Although it is quite flattering to my efforts. I merely chronicled what my friend and colleague—'

'Oh, that English false modesty. Take some credit, man. Can you honestly tell me you brought nothing to the table but mere reportage?' The grin returned, wider than ever when Watson failed to answer. 'Tell me, Major, there was one thing that I always wanted to know. What was *The Repulsive Story of The Red Leech*? I remember reading that as a kid and imagining all sorts of things.'

As a kid? Watson thought. Yes, Myles would have been a child when it was mentioned in passing in *The Golden Pince-Nez*. 'It was a misprint.'

'Misprint?'

'It should have said "red beech". A type of tree.'

Myles looked crestfallen. 'Oh.'

'I just let it pass. The thought of a giant annelid seemed to fire readers' imaginations rather more than a gruesome murder under a tree that is native to New Zealand.'

'Right. That's, um, disappointing.' The American stroked his moustache with thumb and forefinger. 'You know I—'

'Wish you hadn't asked. I very rarely say this, but perhaps some mysteries are best left unsolved. A little mystique is no bad thing. *Omne ignotum pro magnifico.*'

That normally batted off any more questions about *The Singular Affair of the Aluminium Crutch*, *The Home Secretary's Purse* or *The Pursuit of*

Wilson, the Notorious Canary-Trainer, or any of the other unpublished accounts from the Baker Street Years he had been foolish enough to dangle before the readers.

Myles nodded. 'True. Of both literature and women, I suspect.' He winked. 'So, fifteen minutes, Major. Oh, and if you don't mind, it's what you fellows call mufti for my rounds.'

All but the powerful aroma of his Bay Rum left the cell and Watson threw back the blankets, swung his legs over the side of the bed and took a sip of the black, lukewarm over-sweetened tea.

Watson didn't like deceiving, but Holmes had agreed with him at the time that *The Repulsive Story of The Red Leech* was one for which the world was not yet prepared. Perhaps Watson had been reluctant because the villain turned out to be a respected member of the Harley Street community, a doctor who had perverted the practice of hirudotherapy into a hideous form of torture. No, let the American think it was a misprint. No harm done then.

The image of the bloated bloodsuckers they had discovered in the basement laboratory unsettled him and he now recalled his dream and shuddered. It was of an aeroplane, engine sputtering, spiralling out of the sky and hitting the earth, its wings, as fragile as a mayfly's, folding into the fuselage under the impact. Then the screams, the figures running towards the twisted wreckage as a whorl of black smoke rose heavenwards . . .

Heavier-than-air machines. Perhaps something else the world was not yet ready for.

TWELVE

Staff Nurse Jennings had already departed when Mrs Gregson awoke, even though it was not yet seven. Her cot was empty, the bed made with admirable precision. She must have moved like a wraith. The air in the tent was freezing and Mrs Gregson's breath rolled over the blankets like ground mist on a meadow. She kicked away the now cold ceramic cylinder of the hot-water bottle and shuffled up onto the two thin pillows. Alice, she noted, was still fast asleep, not quite snoring, but snuffling, as if in the throes of a dream.

Your secret is safe with me.

She regretted her reaction, now. Jennings's arm must be quite bruised. Perhaps it was an attempt at friendship by the nurse, something they could both share and keep from the outside world? It wasn't a secret, she reminded herself. It was public knowledge. If you knew where to look. She had nothing to be ashamed of. It was simply part of her previous life, the life before Alice Pippery and motor cycles, nursing and war, when there was a Mr Gregson and a household to run and she only ever saw blood when she pricked her finger with a needle. Not the gallons she had seen since.

She knew she should get up and make some tea. Alice would have. But she gave herself another few minutes in the warmth. She would make peace with Jennings. Although she still wanted her silence. It was a multi-layered story, one that would not please Alice one little bit. And she didn't want to lose her.

She must have drifted off because Sister Spence's voice made her start.

'Ladies.' She was standing at the foot of Miss Pippery's bed, arms crossed, looking as if she had slept for fourteen hours on a feather mattress.

'Sorry, Sister,' Mrs Gregson said. 'What time is it?'

'Seven thirty. Jennings has been on ward for an hour.'

'We were just getting up,' said Miss Pippery, her sticky eyes giving the lie to that. She rubbed them clear and threw back the covers.

'Dr Watson has some other duties today, and so I was wondering if I might avail myself of your services.'

'Yes, Sister,' they replied in unison.

'Once you have had your cup of tea.'

'Thank you, Sister,' said Miss Pippery. 'Do you have any task in mind?'

'I do,' said Sister Spence. 'I just wondered how handy you two are with a paintbrush.'

THIRTEEN

An intemperate rain squall was battering the old monastery. Rivulets of water ran down windowpanes — many of which displayed the concussion cracks of artillery fire from the days when the lines were more fluid — and gutters rattled and overflowed. The water was pounding sills and parapets so hard it had a milky opaqueness.

As they walked through the corridor to the officers' ward — a walkway that smelled strongly of fresh paint — Myles explained why he had asked Watson to dress in civvies. 'The men like my rounds because when Major Torrance does them, any junior rank who can manage it is obliged to stand next to his bed. A lot of them who shouldn't, make the effort. They bust stitches, shift dressings. Me, I like things informal.'

They entered what had once been a chapel, although it had been stripped of any religious symbolism and was now the officers' surgical ward. The high roof and soaring stone walls made it chill and a brace of large paraffin heaters were working overtime. There were twin rows of closely packed steel bedsteads facing each other, some with screens around them, behind which, Watson had no doubt, wounds were being washed or irrigated. The smell of Bay Rum was overwhelmed by a riot of familiar medicinal odours. Two territorials, one of them Staff Nurse Jennings, and a brace of orderlies were clearing up the last of breakfast. Jennings looked over and permitted herself a fleeting smile that segued into a more formal inclination of the head.

'Good morning, gentlemen,' Myles bellowed. Many of the patients returned the greeting. Others, lost behind dressings or adrift in their own world, made little or no acknowledgement. 'This, gentlemen, is Dr Watson, who will be assisting me today. Treat him as you would me. Only better. Right, I'll take the left. If you would care to inspect the right?' He dropped his voice. 'We keep them here longer now, instead of passing them down the line. Orders. Too many officers getting out of the war with relatively light injuries. Now, we let them rest up, see if they are fit to return. So don't be too keen to move them along. Nurse!' It was Jennings who came over. 'Brief Dr Watson on the patients, will you?'

'Of course, Dr Myles. Did you sleep well, Major?'

'I did. And you, Staff Nurse Jennings?'

'Well, thank you.' The dark crescents under her eyes suggested a few more hours wouldn't go amiss. 'Although your VADs are not the quietest of company. Shall we start with Captain Morley here?' She indicated the nearest patient. 'Came to us ten days ago. PWSB. Penetrating wound by a secondary body.' This usually referred to items driven into the body by a blast, often the contents of the victim's pockets.

'A couple of teeth in my chest,' the captain explained. 'They weren't even mine.'

'We are seeing this a lot, now,' interrupted Staff Nurse Jennings.

'Shells are throwing up fragments of bones, animal or even human, from the earth.'

Watson stepped closer to the captain. His skin had a strange hue. The eyes, too, showed a tinge of pigment. He put a hand on the forehead. It was cool to the touch.

'Lucky man,' said Watson as they moved on. 'Could easily have become a gas gangrene case.'

'He was, Maj— Do I call you Doctor or Major in those clothes?'

'Whichever feels most comfortable. His colour, though? Jaundice? Gallstones?'

'Apparently not.'

Watson halted and pondered for a moment. He half expected to hear that imaginary voice, but it kept its counsel. This was, after all, his field of expertise. 'What do Percy Shelley and George Bernard Shaw have in common, Nurse?'

Jennings looked flustered. 'Writers?'

'Indeed. But some men would see another connection beyond literature.'

Watson swung back and retraced his steps to the captain. He asked the question again.

'Vegetarians,' said Morley enthusiastically.

'Precisely. Two famous vegetarians,' said Watson. 'Show me the soles of your feet.' Watson impatiently tugged the expertly tucked blankets and sheets free. 'There, Staff Nurse Jennings. Orange. Where do you keep the carrots?'

'My batman makes up a drink each morning.'

'Always carrots?'

'And asparagus if we get it. Haven't had much luck sourcing any of late. Hardly the season.'

'And you've been drinking it over here?'

The captain raised an eyebrow. 'Yes, of course. They hardly cater for men of my persuasion in the British Army,' he said. 'Or indeed in its hospitals. Sorry, Nurse. My mother sends over a hamper of vegetables from Harrods every so often. I share them out. Keep the carrots for m'self, mind.'

'Carotenaemia,' said Watson. 'Harmless. But if you aren't to start looking very oriental indeed, you need to cut out the carrots, vary the diet. I'd prescribe a meat and malt wine beverage stock, but . . . do you have Marmite, nurse?'

'Yes.'

'Two cups a day. And cod liver oil. And no carrots.'

The captain squirmed. 'Doctor, I hate Marmite—'

Watson had already moved on. 'Check him again for diabetes, just in case,' he said softly. 'The carotenaemia can have an underlying cause.'

The next bed contained a cheery amputee – one leg below the knee, one arm above the elbow – who was happy at the thought of going home. He was due to enter the final section of the evacuation chain later in the day, so all Watson could do was wish him Godspeed. He had a feeling, though, that the day would come when his euphoria would sour. He had a tough lifetime as an invalid ahead of him.

The third patient was in a screened bed. 'Second Lieutenant Marsden is in there,' said Jennings. 'Perhaps you had better go in. It's an SIW.'

A 'self-inflicted wound'. Men shot themselves through the foot or hand, hoping to get a Blighty. The cleverer ones, so he had heard, did it through a can of bully beef, to mask the powder burns. It often went hideously wrong, however, when the meat was driven into the bullet hole and festered. The wags called them Fray Bentos wounds.

Steeling himself, Watson pulled back the curtain and stepped into the cubicle. The lieutenant, a lethargic-looking boy with large spectacles balanced on his nose, was sitting up, reading a copy of *Lord Jim*. Both hands looked to be intact. Must be the feet, thought Watson.

'What kind of wound have we here?' he asked.

'Genital, doctor,' said the lieutenant gloomily.

'Genital?' That was a new form of self-mutilation to him. Few were driven to that extreme.

'Went over the top in an *estaminet* when I got here.' An *estaminet* was a local bar that sometimes doubled as something more. 'Bayoneted the young girl, you might say. If you get my meaning.' He gave a weak smile.

'All too clearly, Marsden. I am meant to find that amusing?'

The lad flinched at the change of tone. 'No, sir.'

'Did you wash yourself afterwards?'

'Face and hands, yes. Thoroughly.'

Watson rolled his eyes.

The façade of insouciance the young man was affecting cracked and crumbled. 'There's to be a court martial as soon as I'm better, apparently.' He looked close to tears at the thought. 'I didn't do it deliberately. But nobody here believes me.' He lowered his voice to a rasp. 'They spit in my food.'

'I doubt that.' Syphilis, Watson surmised, and a dose of a persecution complex and self-pity with it too. Venereal disease was classed by the army as a self-inflicted wound, an attempt to be repatriated. 'And how are you feeling now?'

'Weak. Sick. Shocking headaches. It was a *maison de tolérance*. A bloody blue lamp.' A brothel for officers; red indicated a place for other ranks. There was a popular rumour – at least among the other ranks – that once a girl had any form of pox, she was instantly demoted down to a red-lamp house.

'Hold on a moment.' Watson stepped outside. The curtains were to shield the lad from the others, he now understood, not because of any hideous wound but his pariah status. SIWs of any kind were not well received by officers nursing genuine wounds. For every soldier who deliberately maimed himself, there were scores of young men who faced up to doing their duty. Understandably, the latter felt aggrieved when the former were shipped home.

Of course, it could be that this young man was unfortunate in contracting the disease; but there were infected women who would nevertheless sell themselves as a ticket home for a windy soldier.

'What treatment have you given the lad?' he asked the nurse.

'Injections and inunctions of mercury, Doctor.'

'Mercury? Don't you have Salvarsan?'

'Not here.'

'I have some in one of my medical kits. Whose patient is he? Dr Myles's?'

'Major Torrance's.'

Mercury injections were crude and the inunctions – the application of mercury ointments – messy and largely ineffective, but the newer drugs had been slow to catch on among the more traditional doctors and he could imagine supplies being difficult to source.

Across the room, Myles was guffawing with a patient who had two stumps in place of legs. The paraplegic soldier was laughing along with the man who had removed his legs. Myles slapped the officer on the shoulder and moved along. Watson felt slightly envious of Myles's unforced and jovial bedside manner. He had been taught to keep a distance from the patient, even in civilian life. To be detached, analytical and professional. Ah well, the man was from a different country. And a different generation, too, he supposed. Which was almost the same thing.

'What's through here?' he asked Jennings when he had seen the last man, pointing to a thick curtain over a large doorway that had once held wooden doors, judging by the twisted hinges still lolling from the stonework. The door itself had probably been looted for firewood.

'NCOs mostly,' she said, changing the dressing on the weeping stump of a young artillery officer.

'May I?'

'Of course, Major. I'll finish up here. We're going to have you shipped along very soon, aren't we, Lieutenant Walsh?'

The artilleryman smiled, showing he had lost several teeth as well as his right arm. Watson watched her admiringly for a second, fussing with the amputee's bed and carrying on a stream of light chatter designed to make him forget, for the moment at least, just how diminished a man he would be when he returned home.

The wall was streaked with a grey-greenish mould that had colonized the brick beneath a leaking gutter. The gutter had been repaired, but the wall itself, part of the Big House's kitchen block, still looked scabrous. Sister Spence had asked for it to be whitewashed and then for the greenhouse to be 'freshened up'.

'I'd like to freshen her up,' Mrs Gregson said, when she had gone. She had asked for overalls, but Sister Spence did not want any women on her CCS in trousers. She had found them some smocks that made them look like a pair of Humpty Dumptys. An orderly had brought two pails of water and a bag of lime and left them to it.

'I think we should scrape that green off first,' said Miss Pippery.

'Why?'

'Well, the wash won't stick properly. It will flake off within a fortnight.'

'And where will we be in a fortnight?' Mrs Gregson asked.

'I don't know.'

'I do. Somewhere else other than here.' She bent down and tore open the top of the bag of lime. She ripped a fingernail and let out a curse.

'Hello, ladies. Need a hand?'

He was a second lieutenant, a touch gangly, but not unattractive either, with a fastidiously neat moustache and clear green eyes. He also had two balls of embarrassment glowing on his upper cheeks.

'How long have you been standing there?' Mrs Gregson demanded.

'Oh, not long. I was just getting some fresh air. Bit stuffy on the wards.'

'Really?'

'Well, yes, you'd know all about that, I suppose. Bit rum getting you girls to paint, isn't it?'

Mrs Gregson rolled her eyes.

He looked at the bag of lime and the two buckets at their feet. 'But you must mix the lime in at the right proportion, you know. Over-thickening is very common. And you must give it a good old stir.'

'Must we?' asked Mrs Gregson.

'Yes.' He examined the wall and pointed to the mould. 'And you'll have to scrape—'

'Can you fetch us a stick?' Mrs Gregson asked, not wanting another lecture. 'To stir the mix.'

'Oh. Right-o.' He began to look around ineffectually.

'Unless you want to loan us that one.' She pointed at his swagger stick.

'I . . . no . . . I'll be right back. My name's Metcalf, by the way. James Metcalf.'

As soon as he had gone, Miss Pippery spoke. 'He's after something.'

Mrs Gregson agreed. 'You can't usually get an officer to fetch sticks quite so easily. Usually takes a few sessions.'

Metcalf returned with a broken broom handle and, as Mrs Gregson poured in the lime, he proceeded to rotate it in the pot with a practised vigour, mixing the contents without spilling or flicking.

'The thing is, ladies, I am here to see some of the men. Wounded men.'

'You've come to the right place,' said Mrs Gregson. 'We've got hundreds.'

'No,' he corrected solemnly, speaking as if the VADs were particularly dim-witted. 'These are men, you see, under my command. They were hurt in some shelling. The thing is, I have been asked by some of the officers in my battalion to set about organizing a dance. We'll be in the area off and on for the foreseeable future, you see. And we thought, while we are out of the line . . . To be honest, I thought I might kill two birds with one stone.'

The women exchanged glances.

'I mean, while I am here visiting the men, I could ask some of the nurses if they would enjoy the company of officers.'

'We have plenty of officers here, Lieutenant. Whole ones for a change, do you mean?' Mrs Gregson asked.

'I suppose I do, after a fashion. Golly, that sounded cruel.'

'We'll think about it,' said Miss Pippery. Mrs Gregson nodded her agreement. 'On one condition.'

'What's that?'

Miss Pippery flashed a coy smile. 'You help us paint this wall.'

Mrs Gregson shot her friend an admiring glance. She couldn't have put it better herself.

'What? When?'

'Now.'

He looked down at his once pristine uniform, now lightly floured with lime dust. He brushed at it ineffectually.

Mrs Gregson tutted. 'Oh, I'm sure we can find you something to cover that. You *can* paint?'

'I've done my share,' Metcalf said cautiously, wondering how much manual work a gentleman should admit to. 'And you'll think about it? The dance? Perhaps ask some of your chums.'

'We said we would. And Miss Pippery here, Alice, is the very best fox-trotter you have ever seen.'

Metcalf's face brightened at the thought. 'Really?'

'She was taught by Harry Fox himself.'

Miss Pippery's eyes dropped to the floor, in what could have been mistaken for bashfulness.

'Good Lord. Really?'

'At the *Jardin de Danse* on the roof of the New York Theatre.'

As Metcalf began to unbutton his tunic, ready to roll up his sleeves, Mrs Gregson and Miss Pippery were careful not to catch each other's eyes, for fear of collapsing into giggles.

It was shortly after they had finished the wall and were about to move on to the greenhouse that they heard the sound of a man sobbing.

*   *   *

Watson passed through the curtain from the officers' ward and into a small passageway that opened up into another high-ceilinged room, but with larger windows and more natural light. A former refectory, perhaps, although a porous one: metal buckets caught drips from the leaking roof, pinging and plopping in an almost musical sequence. The arrangement was much the same as the officers' ward, with twin rows of bedsteads facing each other. There was only one heater, though, along with an as-yet unlit potbelly stove, and there was a bite to the air.

'Major Watson! Is tha' you, sir?'

He turned to his right. It took him a second to recognize the sergeant as the man's left eye was heavily bandaged and it obscured most of his face. The nose was unmistakable, though.

'Sergeant Shipobottom?'

'Aye, sir. It's Shipobottom. 'Ow do?'

'Your captain said you'd been injured. But we didn't have the opportunity to chat further. What on earth are the Leigh Pals doing here?' He spoke up, as always when dealing with the mill workers, whose hearing had been ruined by the constant clatter of machinery. It made them very adept lip readers, a useful skill in the trenches.

Shipobottom pointed at his dressing. 'Ah took one in the stomach. And a shell splinter in m' eye—'

'No, no, man,' said Watson with a laugh. 'I mean here. Belgium. You were in Egypt, last I saw, marked for the Dardanelles.'

'That's right, but we were away about a month after thee, sir.' There was a time when Watson had been unable to understand the thick 'Lanky' accent of the Leigh Pals, or 'the Lobby Gobblers' as they were sometimes known, but a few months as their temporary MO – where, for a shilling a time and a tot of rum, they had acted as willing subjects for his transfusion experiments – had cured him of that. One curious side effect of the war was that it had thrown together men of different regions and classes who would never have had cause to converse before. This breaching of national (and to some extent, class) boundaries, Watson had come to believe, could only be a welcome development. Even if it made for difficult conversations sometimes.

'Are you all right, sir? No more of that ague?'

'I am, thank you.' Watson had come down with a mild case of malaria, debilitating enough to have him repatriated. 'Quite recovered. No recurring fevers yet, fingers crossed. So you shipped here straight from Egypt?'

'Aye. Like you said, we expected Dardanelles, like . . . but they brought us t' this place. Get us green ones used to trench life, so they say.'

Watson caught a whiff of something on the man's breath. 'Have you been drinking, Shipobottom?'

The man gawped at him, his expression as comical as his name, which he claimed was derived from 'man-who-looks-after-sheep-in-meadow-with-a-stream-at-the-bottom'.

He looked ready to deny it, but then relented. 'Aye. Just a drop, like. Don't tell on me, sir.'

'I won't. But it's not a good idea right now. Not in here. No more. Understood?"

'Aye.'

'And how are the men?'

He looked sombre. 'Bearing up. We lost Captain Leverton, though. A right shame it were.'

'I'm sorry to hear that.' It was true. He had been a fine officer, a good few years older than most. Maturity was in short supply in the British Army. 'How did he . . . ?'

'He got some gypo disease. Terrible it was in the end. Reckon you could've saved him.'

Dysentery, enteric fever and, as he knew, malaria, were rife out there. 'I'm sure they did everything they could.'

Shipobottom's unbandaged eye looked doubtful. 'They've given yon de Griffon a field commission to captain. We all thought it must be because his family is bow-legged with brass. Rich, like. And a nestle-cock we reckoned. But no, the lad done well. I reckon he'll keep the promotion, n' all.'

'I'm sure he will. He seemed very concerned about you.' He knew de Griffon was from a well-to-do family, but he had a common touch that the men liked. What was a nestle-cock, though? Someone used to a little mollycoddling was his best guess. 'And here in France? You've seen much action?'

'Nah. The guns, like. Always the bloody guns throwin' shells at us. Worse thing being the trench foot. Some of the boys, they take their boots off and their feet swell like a freshly baked loaf. I told 'em, you have to keep your boots and puttees loose and rub the whale oil on, but it don't half pong. Dunno how whales put up with the stink. And then this happens to me. Just a scratch under the bandage, so Dr Myles says. I'll be back with lads soon enough, I suppose.'

'And the wife? And family?'

He beamed. 'Peg is champion and the boys an' all, thankee. I wrote 'em a lazy card and had got three letters back.'

A 'lazy card' was a sheet with a set of stock phrases to be crossed out as appropriate. 'Have been wounded in the arm/leg/face/body.' 'Am doing well/better than expected/poorly', and space for the location of the CCS or hospital. Shipobottom, he suspected, couldn't manage much more.

As he looked into Shipobottom's face, a glint in the white of the good eye caught his attention. 'Sergeant, can I just look at the area around your pupil?'

'Sir.'

Watson took finger and forefinger and separated the upper and lower lids. Something was odd there. Amid the reticulate pattern of red veins, he could see tiny flecks of blue. Which meant what? Was it some side effect from the metal that had penetrated his body? He made a mental note to check the other eye, once the bandage was off.

'Is it all right?'

'Yes, fine.'

'I was wishin' for some leave home after all this, you know. I'm right jiggered.'

Watson could hear an unfamiliar trembling in the big man's voice. Shipobottom, the robust, foul-mouthed (when no officer was around) force of nature was genuinely scared. He didn't want to go back up the line. The near-miss seemed to have shattered his nerves.

'But soldiers like this one are too valuable to let go. Right, Sergeant?'

It was Caspar Myles, from over Watson's shoulder.

Shipobottom pulled himself together. 'Yes, Dr Myles, thankee. I'm still a bit mazey, though. A terrible yedwarch, an' all.'

'Mazey?' Myles turned to Watson. 'I only get about one word in three as it is.'

'Dizzy,' Watson translated. 'Light-headed. And a yedwarch is a headache. Did he lose much blood?'

'From the stomach wound, yes,' said Myles. 'He's had saline.'

Watson was all too aware that saline often brought about a remarkable recovery initially, but could be followed by a spectacular collapse. 'You could give him some of the citrated blood I collected. It can work wonders.' He turned back to the patient. 'As the sergeant saw first-hand in Egypt.'

'Do I get me shillin' and a tot this time?' Shipobottom asked cheekily.

'I think you know the answer to that, Sergeant.'

Shipobottom nodded with mock contrition. 'Aye, Doctor.'

Watson turned to Myles. 'Won't take me a second to select the right grouping. You simply have to be sure there will be agglutination or haemolysis in the donor blood.' A thought occurred to him. 'Sergeant, you don't recall your group, do you?'

'Aye, I was group one. The tops.'

Watson had tried to tell this group of guinea pigs that group I blood was in no way superior to group IV – it was simply a terminology associated with cross-matching, but they wouldn't have it. 'Well, there you have it. He can accept any blood – a universal recipient. You simply infuse the citrated blood like saline.' Watson had to be careful. It was a disaster to suggest a fellow physician was in any way deficient or not familiar with current practice.

'So I heard,' Myles said evenly.

'If the sergeant feels up to it, you could move him to the transfusion tent. Some privacy, the VADs can do the monitoring rather than take up valuable time here. Also, with the lamps turned down, it would be a perfect environment to remove the eye bandage. No windows.' It would also be a good place away from big ears and prying eyes for Watson to have a quiet word about Shipobottom's mental state.

'Excellent thought.' Myles cleared his throat. 'Dr Watson, can I have a word?'

Myles steered him to the centre of the room and lowered his voice. 'I just want to ask you a question,' he said furtively.

'Is there a problem?' Watson asked, automatically reducing his own speech to a whisper.

'Staff Nurse Jennings.'

'Yes?'

'You were with her yesterday. In the reception tent.' Watson nodded. 'What do you think of her?'

Watson considered, not sure how the question was weighted. Perhaps he was considering recommending her for promotion or a mention in dispatches. 'I think she has the makings of a fine nurse, Doctor. A sister-in-charge at least. Of course, she's young—'

'No, I mean.' A conspiratorial huskiness crept into the voice. 'What do you think of her? Not as a nurse.'

'I don't think of her as anything other than as a nurse.'

Myles winked. 'Is that right? I thought there might be the age factor, but you never know. Famous writers, eh? Might fancy their chances despite . . .' He cleared his throat, thinking better of finishing the sentence. 'So you don't mind if I have crack at her?'

'A what?'

'A crack. A run at the barn door. Been considering it for a while. Then I saw you two being, well, intimate. Hold on a cotton-pickin' minute. What's this? But I was imagining things, you say. Just thought I'd check.'

Watson felt himself blinking, too fast and too often. 'Dr Myles, if

Staff Nurse Jennings has any dealings with you in that sense, Sister
Spence will have your—'

'Whoa, now.' Myles pointed at his own chest. 'Doctor. Yes? Not
army. Not an officer. The rules don't apply to me.'

Watson wasn't certain that was true. Or at least, that Sister Spence
would make any exceptions where her charges were concerned. 'But
they do to Staff Nurse Jennings.'

'I'd argue that in a court of law.'

'And why are you telling me this?'

'As I say, I just thought you were gearing yourself up for a pass of
your own. I wanted to make sure that I'm not . . . what do you say?
Queering the pitch? I did see her first, y'see.'

'Dr Myles—'

'Caspar.'

'Dr Myles. There is no pitch to queer. But I promise you if you
endanger that girl in any way, either morally or professionally—'

'Oh, don't be such a stuffed shirt.'

' — I'll have you run out and returned to your unit. The All-
Harvards or whatever they were called.' Myles didn't look too
concerned at this rather empty threat. 'I have a suggestion to make.'

'What's that?'

'Find yourself a Canadian nurse. They might be more to your
liking. Now if you will excuse me, Doctor, I have to prepare blood
for your patient and locate my driver.'

Watson turned on his heel and left before Myles could reply.

It was only when he got back to his room and tore off his collar
and tie in exasperation, that Watson realized that, in his hot-headed
response, he'd forgotten to ask Myles for a second opinion on those
blue flecks in Sergeant Shipobottom's eye.

FOURTEEN

Brindle was weeping. He sat on the bed in the transfusion tent, head in hands, his body shaking with grief. Water was streaming off his hair and dripping onto the floor, his clothes were mud-stained and rain-soaked, showing he had been out in the squall that was spitting its last.

Watson, now back in uniform, had entered the ward just in time to hear him emit a terrible wail. Miss Pippery was trying to feed the inconsolable man a mug of hot, sweet tea. Both nurses had some kind of over-smock covering their uniform that appeared to be covered in blobs of dried paint.

'What's happening here, Mrs Gregson?' Watson demanded.

'We found him round the back of the greenhouse we were meant to paint.'

'Paint?' Watson tried to keep the incredulity out of his voice. 'But—'

'Ask Sister Spence. It seems poor Brindle here recognized one of the bodies he had to bury. We brought him here to calm down. I suppose we should get rid . . .' she forced the smock over her head-dress, '. . . of these things.' Miss Pippery followed suit.

When Brindle looked up his eyes were crazed by an unsettling intensity. It was the stare of the madhouse. 'He should not be buried in a mass grave. I told them that. Cornelius deserved better than that.' He put his unnaturally long fingers over his face.

Watson moved across and laid a hand on his shoulder. 'You knew Cornelius Lovat?'

He managed to nod between sobs.

'Look, Brindle, he couldn't have lived like that. Not with those injuries.'

Again the head came up. 'You don't understand. I could have made him a mask. A beautiful mask.' He mimed an act of creation with his hands. 'I knew every inch of his face. They make new ones in London, don't they? At Wandsworth. New faces made of the thinnest copper. I would have done my finest work. He could have been handsome again.'

Watson squeezed his shoulder. The man wasn't listening. The tissue damage was simply too extensive for him to have lived. Sister Spence had been absolutely correct about that. 'How did you know him?'

'From St Martins. He was in the year ahead of me.'

'You're a sculptor?' Mrs Gregson surmised.

'And Cornelius was a painter. A fine one.'

Watson, to his shame, realized he knew very little about the orderly who had been assigned to him. Many of the drivers and dogsbodies, the stretcher-bearers and the gravediggers, were pacifists of one stripe or another, willing to help win the war, unwilling to kill. But now he looked at those fingers again, tracing a human visage in thin air, he appreciated this man had an artist's hands. He hadn't been looking at what was right under his nose. A cardinal sin.

He half expected to hear a nagging voice in his ear, telling how he was looking but not observing.

Brindle began to sob once more. Watson released his grip. He kneeled down and whispered a few words in the man's ear before standing. It wasn't much, but he hoped it helped.

'Miss Pippery. Your convictions are showing. If Sister Spence sees that she'll try and nail you to it,' Mrs Gregson pointed at her friend's neck. The gold cross had escaped and was hanging down the front of her VAD shift. Miss Pippery tucked it away. They weren't allowed to display external signs of their own beliefs in front of the men. It might be a clue to their personality. And they weren't meant to have one of those.

'Right,' said Mrs Gregson, 'let's get him out of those wet things and into pyjamas. Then hot-water bottles.'

'And a bromide sedative,' suggested Watson. 'If you will, Miss Pippery?'

But Miss Pippery's gaze had slipped past him, to something over his shoulder. He turned to see two RAMC-uniformed officers had entered the tent behind him.

'Major Watson? George Torrance.' The CO of the Casualty Clearing Station extended a hand. He was shorter than Watson, with a flushed face, a tightly groomed oblong on his upper lip and a generous stomach pushing against his tunic buttons. 'Good to meet you. May I introduce my adjutant, Captain Symonds.' The junior officer and Watson also shook hands. 'Sister tells me you did sterling work last night. It was kind of you to muck in.'

'I think Sister Spence and your CCS would have managed quite well without me. It's a tight ship.'

Torrance smiled under his close-clipped toothbrush moustache. The man might be carrying a few extra pounds, but he was immaculately pressed and turned out. He looked as if he steam-ironed not only his uniform, underwear and his hair but Captain Symonds, too. His voice, though, was abrasive, part honk and part bark. Watson could see why sick men would struggle from their beds for his inspections. 'You've met Caspar Myles, I assume?'

'I have run into Dr Myles.' Watson had tried not to bristle, but he clearly gave himself away somehow.

'I know, I know, somewhat unorthodox. But a fine surgeon. He came to us by accident and, well, we've managed to hold on to him.'

'We are very much looking forward to hearing about the new transfusion methods,' interrupted Captain Symonds.

'And it would be my pleasure to show you.'

'Excellent,' said Torrance. 'And perhaps a demonstration for Field Marshal Haig when he comes? Show him we aren't still in the dark ages at the CCSs. I'm sure we have plenty of subjects—'

'Perhaps we could discuss this later, Major Torrance? I'm going up to Brigade at Somerset House.' Watson looked at his watch. Half the morning had gone. He cast a glance at Brindle, now being tucked into bed by Mrs Gregson, while Miss Pippery prepared the sleeping draught. Brindle had offered no resistance to Mrs Gregson; his limbs looked to be made of India rubber. The man was clearly going to be useless for some time. 'However, I seem to have mislaid my driver.'

Although Watson was quite capable of operating a motor car, it gave him no pleasure, and it certainly wasn't the done thing for an officer to turn up at Brigade behind the wheel of his own vehicle.

'Don't worry, Major Watson. I've had enough of whitewash for one day. If it's only a ride to Brigade you need,' Mrs Gregson pulled off her VAD headdress and a riot of auburn hair sprang free. 'I'll drive you there.'

FIFTEEN

Bloch looked at the photograph of the man he had travelled across no man's land and through enemy lines to kill. He did it dispassionately. To Bloch, he was already dead, an inanimate object. A 'target', pure and simple. It was one of the first things he had taught himself. Don't think of them as people. They are walking bull's-eyes. Don't wonder if they had families, friends, lovers. Just do the job and get out.

He shifted position slightly, as quietly as he could manage. He had come alarmingly close to being discovered several times. As the hours of darkness drew to a close, men, machines and animals were on the move, making one final hasty journey before the creeping light from the east betrayed them to the enemy. The munitions drays, the food and fresh water convoys, the tumbrils, the medical supply ambulances and the columns of reinforcements, and those being relieved, all took up their daylight positions, for, thanks to men like Bloch and his close contemporary, the artillery spotter, this was a war of armies and services that moved primarily at night.

He had lain in the nave while British soldiers stepped in for a quick cigarette, coming inside in the hope that the glowing tip would not attract the attention of a sniper. If only they knew. Others had relieved themselves against the walls, grunting with pleasure as they splashed noisily, whistling softly as they buttoned themselves up. Once, he heard someone enter and cry to himself, the sobs stifled and then quickly squashed altogether when the weeping man heard a voice.

'Sir? You in there, sir?'

A sniff. 'Just coming.'

He picked up other conversations from nearby trenches, meaningless apart from a few clearly enunciated words, often 'fuck' or 'shit' or 'bugger'. The smell of tobacco that came from these soldiers made his nose twitch and his lungs ache for some. That was for later, he promised himself, when he was back behind his own lines, writing home to tell them to restock the larder and to alert lovely Hilde that he was on his way back to her.

In between all the dawn activity in and around the tower, he had worked as quickly and as quietly as he could at solving his problem. He had found four fragments of bell rope that, when securely knotted together, he had managed to toss up and loop over one of the exposed beams just below the belfry. That was when the sobbing officer had entered the space, and Bloch had been forced to crouch in the corner, hoping the man was emotionally distracted enough not to notice the twin filaments freshly sprouted from above, swaying like jungle creepers. His hand was on his bayonet, and he was ready to spring forward and open the man's neck should he show any curiosity. But he hadn't; nor did any of the other transient visitors.

Eventually, with his rifle strapped across his back, he had grasped the bell ropes and hauled himself up, using the wall for leverage as sparingly as possible in case he dislodged a stonefall, until he was able to drag himself up onto the platform. Then, once the burning in his hands had subsided and his shoulders stopped complaining, he had pulled up the bell ropes and coiled them on the floor of the belfry. He had taken off and smoothed out the greatcoat next to the coils, unpacked his rifle, water bottle and rations and lain down on the coat in front of the westerly opening in the belfry's stonework – once delicately louvered but now a gaping hole – gradually making himself comfortable.

He was still lying there when dawn aimed its first gun-grey rays of light at Somerset House, and, through the telescopic sights, he could clearly make out all the features of the sentry standing at the front entrance.

He smiled to himself. Half a chance, that was all he needed, and Lux's special target was a dead man.

SIXTEEN

The showers had abated and the clouds slid away in a single smooth action, like a dark curtain being pulled aside to reveal the blue underneath. For once the air smelled of nothing more than the oils and spores released by wet earth and turned soil, and it reminded Watson of travelling briskly down the Surrey lanes in the aftermath of a rainstorm on a spring day, the hedgerows dotted with green shoots, ploughed fields steaming in fresh sunshine after the squall had moved on. He could almost hear the clop of hoofs, the encouragements of the trap driver, feel the old excitement as they faced solving another enticing puzzle together. Such a simpler world back then. The world, he reminded himself, that most of these young men imagined they were fighting to save.

He leaned against the wing of his Crossley 20/25 staff car while he waited for Mrs Gregson and lit one of his Bradley's, breathing deeply of the slightly sweet smoke. Women's tobacco, Holmes had called the blend, but Watson liked the contrast – his choice of cigarette was light and refreshing, his pipe of Schippers muscular and invigorating.

The only activity around him was the grim scurrying back and forth of the blank-eyed burial parties and the attendant chaplains, so instead he watched three slow pusher observation biplanes crawl overhead, almost stationary against the pale sky, making their stately way towards the German lines. He thought of ducks, flying towards the waiting guns of hunters. Beyond them, though, at a far greater height, he could just make out three other cruciform shapes, hovering like kites. Perhaps the lumbering spotters had some guardian angels. He hoped so.

And what of Staff Nurse Jennings? Did she need an unseen protector? Watson knew that he was out of step with modern times and that war created a new, shifting morality, as tricky as the Grimpen Mire to negotiate. Even so, there was something distinctly unpleasant, venal even, about the cold way that Myles had told him that the young nurse was a target. Perhaps the language was misleading; it was possible his ardour was making him tongue-tied and verbally clumsy. He recalled how he had fallen in love with Mary Morstan so readily and how hard he had found it to express his feelings with anything approaching eloquence. It could be that Myles was merely making sure, in his own stumbling fashion, he had no rival for the nurse's affections.

And his terrible spur-of-the-moment, second-hand slander of the Canadian nurses' morals. Sister Spence's disapproval of their dancing was hardly reason enough for him to make his own sweeping assumptions about their behaviour. The thought made him blush. He felt like a traitor to the Dominion, which was sending thousands of men and women across to the war every month. Conscious that he might have made a fool of himself, Watson had left the blood for Shipobottom with Miss Pippery, along with a hastily written note asking if he and Myles could meet to 'clear the air' that evening upon his return. Snap judgements were all very well, but he would have to work with this Myles for a few days at least. He really should give him the benefit of the doubt.

'Right, Major, I'm ready.'

He turned and was greeted by an extraordinary sight. Mrs Gregson had donned a most bizarre outfit, a heavy leather belted coat over a long leather skirt, which was split to reveal a pair of britches. She caught his expression. 'My motor-cycling clothes. Messrs Dunhill of Conduit Street.' She gave a little curtsy, pulling out the lower part of the garb. 'Modest yet practical.' She produced a bright green headscarf from her pocket and began to tie it around her head.

'Isn't that rather . . . conspicuous?' Watson asked.

'Ah, Major, I can tell you don't know about the Green Women of Pervyse. I think you should sit in the front,' she said as he made to climb into the rear. 'I'll explain why in a moment. You there! Orderly! Know how to crank a car?'

A stretcher-bearer, smeared and caked in mud, his eyes dull with exhaustion, nevertheless nodded gamely.

'Do the honours then, will you?' she asked, passing him the starting handle.

'Yes, ma'am. Pleasure.' Watson had nothing but admiration for the bearers. It was debilitating, backbreaking work, hauling the dead, dying and wounded through trenches and over shell-pocked land. Yet still the majority would go the extra yard for you. Even risking a dislocated shoulder by cranking a car.

Mrs Gregson slid behind the wheel and began to fiddle with the controls, easing out the choke. 'Back in the early days, when the war was still much like a game between gentlemen, we volunteers asked permission to collect the dead from the battlefield. The local German commander, rather a nice chap, said that if we wore bright headscarves, then we would not be mistaken for soldiers and the snipers would spare us. And so it proved. There was a set of curtains lined with green silk in the house that formed our casualty station, so we used that to make scarves for ourselves. The Germans were as good as their commander's word. Anyone who even nicked one of us had hell to pay from their own side. We became invisible. And now— Thank you!' she said as the Crossley rocked into life and she retrieved the handle from the orderly. 'And now it is a widespread notion, so I understand, among the enemy that anyone wearing such headwear should be immune. However, a man sitting in the rear of a staff car, that man is assumed to be a high-ranking officer and, therefore, a prime target. And this —' Mrs Gregson banged the driver's door, which, like the bonnet and the passenger side, bore a large Red Cross — 'is no protection at all.' She slapped his leg, making him jump. 'You're safer up here with me, Major.'

With that, she engaged the gears and they leaped forward and left the CCS to splash down the rutted, potholed track that would lead them to the main road.

'I am heading west first,' she said, pointing at the map in its dashboard holder. 'There'll be too many diversions and the Military Police have roadblocks closer to the front. Deserters and spies. Especially spies. You have papers with you?'

Watson nodded. 'You don't mind being driven by a woman. Major Watson?' she asked as she deliberately fishtailed on a patch of mud, oil and grease by the entrance gates.

'Not at all, Mrs Gregson,' he said calmly. 'It's one of the many prices one must pay in wartime.'

Her eyes flicked to him, unsure whether he was joking. 'You could call me Georgina away from the workplace, Major.'

There was plenty of traffic on the still rain-slicked road, a mix of horse-drawn, motor lorries, ambulances and even the occasional omnibus that had been pressed into service. She operated the jerky wipers every thirty seconds, which squeaked and smeared the screen with mud. He wondered that she could see where she was going, but she drove with confidence. Or recklessness – he couldn't quite tell.

As they put some distance between themselves and the fighting, the flat countryside quickly took on a relatively normal aspect, as roof tiles ceased to be a rarity, and Watson could see farmers at work and livestock that didn't have to be in fear of their life. Birds of prey hovered over the fallow fields, ready to swoop and chaffinches flitted alongside the car in relays. There were regimented rows of poplars, all intact, striding into the distance. Normally, this would be a rather uninspiring, uniform landscape, but now it looked magical, like a fairground diorama. Even after just a few days at the sharp end of the war, to him the everyday had become extraordinary.

'We'll turn south at Nieuwkerke. Are you listening, Major?' she prompted.

'Sorry, yes, Mrs Gregson. South at Nieuwkerke.'

'Are you feeling quite yourself? You seem rather distracted.'

He told her, briefly, about the boorish Caspar Myles and his concerns about the man's intentions. He was taken aback when she laughed.

'If we are to protect the honour of every young nurse on the Western Front, Major Watson, then we do have our work cut out.

She is an attractive young lady.' And possibly a slippery one, too, she thought. 'As they say where I come from: "Young gals, yer should kip yer 'and on yer haupney."'

Watson shifted uncomfortably as he interpreted that. 'But—'

'But your concern speaks well of you. If it is a paternal concern?' There was mischievousness in her voice.

'Of course. What else?' he objected.

'Strange,' said Mrs Gregson with a self-pitying sigh, 'in my experience nobody seems too concerned about the honour of an ageing widow.'

'Mrs Gregson, you aren't . . .' The words seemed to run out of momentum, as if they had wheels and had ploughed into sand. A trap, he realized too late.

She giggled. 'I'm teasing you, Major.' She glanced at the map once more and back at a distant church spire. 'Why, Miss Pippery and I had an offer too. To attend a dance.'

'Sister Spence will—'

'Please.' She pursed her lips as if she had just tasted something sour. 'It's such a lovely day. Don't spoil it.'

'She might not be able to stop you, but she certainly wouldn't allow any of her girls to go.'

'Well, there'll be plenty of officers to go round for Alice and me then.'

'And who delivered this invitation?'

'A Lieutenant Metcalf.'

'Can't say I've had the pleasure.'

'One of the Leigh Pals' officers. Quite pleasant in a sort of hopeless way. And, well, Alice, Miss Pippery, and I would like to discuss it with you.'

'Me? I'm not a great dancer.'

'Not to dance, silly. About the best way to approach Sister Spence.'

'Oh.' For a second he felt slighted. He had been known to turn heads at regimental balls once upon a time. 'I'm not sure there is a way to approach her.'

'Not for us. But you. You have a way with words, Major Watson.'

'Nonsense.'

'Then what did you say to Brindle in the tent? If it isn't too personal.'

'I said I knew what it was like to lose a close friend. A male friend.' And to have them miraculously restored and, through impetuous and impecunious language, lose them again. Although he hadn't added this latter. 'And how life does, as it will, go on. But you must treasure the memories that you have, not destroy them with bitterness at the way things turned out. Platitudes, really.'

'I doubt he thinks that.' They passed a picturesque red and white windmill with one of its sails missing, but still turning, yet another amputee doing the best it could. 'Are you married, Major?'

'I was. Mary, my first wife died, along with our child. Goodness, more than twenty years ago now. Emily, my second . . .' The pain was fresher, he realized. The sadness over Mary had grown faint with time, the ache a dull one, the regret at the stillborn boy muted, the rage of helplessness passed now, like a storm moving on to torment others. The shame, too, had diminished, the impotence of a doctor who couldn't save his own wife or child. The thought of Emily, though, brought a fresh stabbing in his chest, a feeling of breathlessness and the pin-sharp image of her face to mind. The scrim of time had not yet done its work.

Mrs Gregson threw him a concerned look. The note of his

breathing had changed. 'I'm sorry, Major. If it's difficult . . . it's really none of my concern.'

Watson hesitated. He knew that it didn't do to fraternize with one's staff, to share too many personal insights; on the other hand, he was ashamed of himself for not knowing more about Brindle. Other men, a special kind of man, might be able to surmise a fellow's profession, marital status, place of work and habits and hobbies from a cursory glance, but he was not that person, as had been demonstrated to him time and time again.

'Emily was fascinated by modernity. By the way the twentieth century was to be a time of electricity, the motor car and the aeroplane, of grand scientific breakthrough, and how it would bring an end to disease and to . . .' he gave a snort, '. . . to human conflict. Myself, I am a creature of Victoria. Emily was younger than me, a child of Jules Verne, H. G. Wells, Blériot, Marconi. She wanted to try the new flying machines and, much against my better instincts, she persuaded me to allow her to go up with Gustav Hamel, looping the loop over Brighton racecourse.'

'And . . . ?'

'Oh, and she became besotted, with flying and flyers. Not in the romantic sense . . . well, perhaps that too, a little. Emily saw the pilots as the new knights, off on quests to conquer the dragon of the air. She was killed on her fourth flight, at Meyrick Park, as was the pilot. I think you want to turn left here.'

'I'm sorry,' she said, hesitating at the crossroads, before swinging them south. 'About your wife.'

'It was my own fault. I should have forbidden it.'

She glanced at him. 'I suspect you are not a man who would suffocate his wife's ambitions just to keep the status quo. Your own ambitions, perhaps.'

'What do you mean?'

'Major Watson, I have read your works, like almost every other literate person in England. I can also read between the lines, the way you bit your lip, how you had to pretend that you were as in the dark as the reader, how you allowed that man to hog the stage like some cheap music-hall act.'

'Mrs Gregson!'

She slowed the car as they came up towards a pair of straight-backed mounted military policemen, who fixed them from under their red caps with piercing glares that never wavered. Watson could feel the suspicious gaze drilling into the back of his neck after they had passed the pair.

'My goodness, those cherry-knobs would make Our Lord feel like a sinner,' Mrs Gregson said and muttered something under her breath, which Watson realized was a remarkably crude profanity. 'Sorry, but they give me the willies.'

Before he could press her further on her obvious discomfort, she accelerated, swerving to overtake an ammunition truck, causing consternation to the driver of a lorry coming the other way. The bleat of a horn sounded as she tucked back in, throwing Watson about in his seat.

'All I was trying to say, Major Watson, and I appreciate it's not a popular opinion, is that your Mr Sherlock Holmes always struck me as a vainglorious, smug, drug-addled, insufferable prig of a woman-hating clever-clogs.'

They drove the rest of the way to Somerset House in silence.

SEVENTEEN

Caspar Myles pushed home the last of the eight syringes of the citrated blood through the rubber tube and the glass cannula and into Sergeant Shipobottom's median basilic vein. Behind him, Miss Pippery hovered, ready to take the transfusion kit, strip it down, and sterilize it.

'Almost there,' he said to the one-eyed man. 'Feel all right so far?'

'Aye,' said Shipobottom, although there was a small film of sweat on his top lip. Myles was well aware that introduction of blood might well cause a temporary reaction. Watson had acted as if he were the only man to have ever heard of the blood transfusion technique.

'Now, we've had news that your unit has been told they'll stay at the rest area for a few days of *petit repos*. I suspect some of your chums will be in to see you.'

'Lieutenant Metcalf already came. Bit early for my liking, but he's a good lad.'

'Excellent. Well, with a bit of luck, next time you'll be looking back at him with two good eyes. OK?'

'Aw reet, Doctor.'

'Aw reet, Sergeant,' Myles mimicked in reply. 'Now, Miss Pippery here — is that right? Miss Pippery?'

'Yes, Doctor.'

He knew her name perfectly well, but enjoyed the way her eyes flicked down to avoid his gaze when he asked it. 'Miss Pippery will be looking after you until Dr Watson returns from his hush-hush trip to Brigade. You might feel somewhat warm, perhaps a tad breathless. Tell Miss Pippery if that is the case. We've put extra blood in, so your heart might need to pump a little harder. It's like any machine given an extra load to carry. And we've put in someone else's blood, so there might be a tiny reaction to that.'

Shipobottom said something in his mangled version of English that Myles couldn't understand. Judging by Miss Pippery's look of bafflement, it was a mystery to her, too.

'Good man,' he said and tapped the sergeant's leg under the bedcovers. He removed the cannula, swabbed at the welling of blood, then put on a wad of cotton wool and a gauze covering, held in place by sticking plaster.

'Right, Miss Pippery. I have my rounds in the men's post-op tent. Can I leave you to . . . ?'

'Of course, Dr Myles.'

'You're in charge.'

She wished Mrs Gregson were there, but she was determined not to show that. It would do her good to have a little independence. Everything she had come to — motor-cycling, the suffragettes' fund-raising, nursing — she had come to through Mrs Gregson. 'That widow woman is a bad influence,' her bank manager father had said. 'No good will come of it.' Although he later grudgingly admitted to being proud of his daughter's war work.

'I'll be back later, Miss Pippery.'

They watched Myles leave and, as soon as the tent flap had dropped back into place, Shipobottom repeated himself, speaking slowly to be certain he was understood. 'Whose blood were it then?'

Miss Pippery began to collect up the detritus of the transfusion. 'Oh, we don't keep a record of names. Only of the blood type and date.'

'So could be any bugger's?'

Miss Pippery had come across this before. There would be a prejudice against having a transfusion of fluid taken from Jews or Catholics – her own persuasion – or even anyone with a vaguely German- (or indeed foreign-) sounding name. She had even seen one soldier in the base hospital, on discovering that the donor had been a 'kike', insist they take out the half-litre of blood they had put in, as if it could be isolated once it had been swept through arteries and capillaries.

'What are you worried about, Sergeant? It's all good British blood, collected from our own soldiers.'

'Aye, that's as mebe. But when we did t'in Egypt, we was all pals. From same town. We all knew where each other had been, like. I jus' wan' yous t'promise me one thing.'

'What's that, Sergeant?'

''Tain't from no Yorkshireman.'

EIGHTEEN

Caspar Myles had an hour to himself following luncheon and, after picking at an indifferent stew, he returned to his cell. There he stripped off to his undergarments and washed himself in cold water, before selecting a fresh outfit and bundling up his morning clothes for the laundry. He always tipped the local women who did the washing very well, and he could be sure his dirty linen always received special treatment and would be returned, starched and pressed.

Before he placed the discarded items outside his door, he checked the pockets and came out with the note from Watson. The one about clearing the air. Well, perhaps the old man wasn't so bad after all. And equally, maybe he shouldn't have been quite so forthright with an Englishman. They liked everything codified, it seemed. Beating about the bush was their national pastime.

He sat on the bed, suddenly weary. He missed his fellow country-men, the lightness of the conversation, the shared references, the sports and the gossip. Even a man like Watson, someone with a little celebrity to illuminate his life, seemed unable to enjoy it, to revel in his status as an author of some fame. Where was the spirit of Empire? This war must have crushed it out of the entire race.

Perhaps that was why he was finding the women even less open and less carefree than he had grown accustomed to in Boston and, especially, on the voyage over, when excitement and fear had loosened some stays. There had been scandalously close dancing, walks around the decks under the stars, hasty kisses in shadowy corners between the lifeboats, even hushed, giggly cabin visits. He thought the febrile atmosphere had boded well for his time in Europe.

Everyone had told him – and even the newspapers complained – that British women had become 'loose' thanks to the war. God only knew how tightly buttoned they must have been before the conflict. He was surprised they could draw breath. Yet here he was, months in the field, and only the local girls on offer. And he didn't want to end up being rubbed down with ointment of mercury like that snivelling Lieutenant Marsden.

And what about little Staff Nurse Jennings? How could he explain her sudden blossoming? She had been immune to Myles's charms, both physical and verbal, for weeks and he had assumed she was simply one of those girls who had no interest in any man unless he was a suitor approved by daddy. And then along comes this relic of the penny dreadfuls and there are the signs he had been hoping to elicit – the pink bloom high on the cheeks, the fluttering of eyes, the shy smile. Perhaps it was to do with celebrity, but it was entirely likely Jennings had not connected the ageing, unassuming major – who had clearly been handsome in his youth, although that was sometime past – with the biographer of the great Sherlock Holmes. Yet something had got her all aflutter.

Myles knew he had to be very, very careful. He remembered the last time he had been sweet on a girl and failed to act until the last moment. The delay had been disastrous. He still recalled the screams from the nurse as they filled his ears. 'No, Doctor, no! Stop! Now! Please!' And the pounding of blood in his head that drove him on and on and on until . . . until the squeals had turned to sobs and Jackson and Everett had burst in and stood there, horrified at what he had done.

Quite how Cotterall had managed to keep a lid on what could have been an almighty stink was beyond him, but the man was the issue of a long line of politicians and diplomats and he used all his hereditary guile – and no doubt connections back home – to make sure the All-Harvard Volunteers was not disgraced before its work had begun. Banishment was the price Myles paid. Exile among the slovenly, melancholic, primitive British. Now he had no country and no friends of his own kind to call upon.

Myles looked down at his hands. His fingernails had dug deep into his palms. The misshapen knuckles of his right hand were white. There were flecks of blood at the fleshy base of his thumb. He slowly uncurled them, and they straightened more like talons than fingers.

He mustn't wait so long to strike this time.

The thought of action gave him a fresh burst of energy. Myles pulled on a clean pair of trousers, hoisted up the suspenders and went down onto his knees. From beneath the rough bed he pulled out a mahogany box, placed it on the mattress and unclipped it. He pushed back the lid and enjoyed the metallic tang of gun oil as it filled his nostrils.

NINETEEN

Bloch was disappointed to discover that there were several entrances to Somerset House. Throughout the morning he watched vehicles arrive and depart, but always from the far side of the building. The main doorway, with its ornate archway, topped by a rampant stone lion, was at the outer limit of his preferred range for a guaranteed kill. Anything else, such as the rear of the house, would be a wasted shot and risked giving his position away to boot. And the single sentry on the door, picking his nose when he thought nobody was looking, he was not worth a bullet of any description.

Despite its nickname, Somerset House was no English building, but a collision of Flemish and French influences. Extravagantly gabled, it also featured two needle-sharp turrets, one of which had been neatly sliced off at the top, like a boiled egg at breakfast. The external rococo plasterwork was pitted and, in places, had been dislodged altogether. Many of the heavily mullioned windows still had their glass intact and most were hung with either blast or gas curtains on the inside, which made the chances of an interior shot impossible in most cases. Even where he could see silhouettes, he was unable to ascertain identity or rank.

So, Bloch lay there, waiting for his luck to change. One shot he would have and then . . . ? His choices were stark. He could slither down the ropes and, in the Tommy greatcoat, make a run for his own lines. The image of his body spread-eagled on the wire flashed into his mind. He had seen too many out there, crow fodder for days on end, to want to finish up like that.

Or he could lie low, hope they would not compute the angle of the shot, that they would not even countenance that their lines had been breached and assume it was either one of their own bullets or some terrible accident. Then, after dark, he could try to retrace his steps.

Would Lux have considered this dilemma? Of the problems of reversing his penetration? No, he decided. To exchange one sniper, no matter how good, for a high-ranking, even iconic, British commander was a worthwhile trade to him. Bloch was surprised to find he felt no bitterness; he might have made the same calculation in Lux's position. But he did feel a welling determination: to surprise Lux by returning alive from this foray. The look on the man's face would be as gratifying as any Iron Cross.

There was more movement and he turned his attention back to the scope. In the lane on the far side of the house he could see a vehicle arriving, a staff car, and this one followed the wide gravel drive around to the front of the building. He squinted through the scope. A girl with a green headscarf. He remembered that from the early days. Next to her a . . . what? An officer. But one who sat in the front?

He ran through the possibilities. If she had a green headscarf, she was in all likelihood a nurse of some description. It had been the Red

Cross who had negotiated their immunity back in late 1914. And, yes, there was its familiar symbol on the door. Which meant the man in the passenger seat was probably a doctor. Bloch focused on the face. Not a young one, either. A senior medical man. Worth, what?

If he killed this doctor, who would miss him?

There he was, breaking a golden rule. Thinking of him as a man. Think of him in terms of damage done by killing him. A senior doctor was a man who saved British lives. Who made broken Tommies fit for duty once more.

Put a bullet through him now and how many soldiers who would otherwise have returned to the trenches would die? It could be that he had arrived with news of a great new medical breakthrough. That could perish with him. Taking him out of the picture might mean dozens, scores, even hundreds of collateral deaths. A triumphant blow for Germany. The thought had tensed his right index finger.

On the other hand, he might be here to treat some general with the pox, patch up a wounded colonel or visit a friend.

Bloch relaxed the pressure on the trigger.

He watched nurse and doctor exchange a few terse words and the doctor went inside, carrying a bag of some description. The woman stood by the car and lit a cigarette, smoking with an intensity that bordered on fury. There was something fascinating, even slightly erotic about the action, and he let the cross hairs linger on her features, a mere voyeur for a few seconds, rather than a killer.

Bloch heard the half-hour chime from a distant clock. He had been in place for almost six hours; still, he had stalked for longer, both with his father and in no man's land. He let his mind empty. This was the luxury of his chosen profession. The average soldier would be wondering why he was fighting and perhaps dying, what his role was in the schemes that the generals back in Berlin were hatching. For a sniper, the war was reduced to simple, straightforward basics. Bloch had no need to dwell on the unknowable strategies, tactics and campaigns devised by his betters. His task was simple. Kill and move on. Then do it again.

Another thirty minutes passed before the double doors swung back and the doctor stepped out. But he was not alone. The companion stayed in the shadow for a moment, but as the two shook hands the man moved into the light. Bloch's heart flung itself against his ribcage like an animal trapped behind bars of bone, and he made an effort to slow it, and control his breathing.

He recognized the face from the clipping Lux had given him. The men were stationary now. He could take both if he wanted. Why not? With minimal movement he chambered a round and moved the sights so they rested in the centre of the target's chest. He counted to five, making sure that everything was calm and stabilized, and squeezed the trigger.

TWENTY

Mrs Gregson swung the front of the Crossley round so it was parallel to the front of Somerset House. Watson looked up at the sad, scarred edifice, and then to his left, down through a swathe of fallen trees to a lonely church tower and beyond that, a smudge of smoke that hovered over the lines. Gas? No, too high, too thin. He looked at his watch. It was just gone 12.30 p.m. Where had the morning gone?

Once the staff car had juddered to a halt and given itself a shake like a wet dog, Watson grabbed his Gladstone bag from the back seat. 'I expect I shall be thirty minutes or so.'

'Shall I come in with you?'

'I'd prefer it if you waited with the car, Mrs Gregson,' he replied coldly. It was their first exchange since her intemperate outburst about his former colleague. She had only been playing devil's advocate, but Watson had reacted as if she had goosed the King in public.

'As you wish.'

After saluting the sentry, then jumping through the inevitable hoops held at a variety of angles by a team of impossibly young subalterns, Watson was eventually shown towards the rear of the building, to what had once been the ballroom of the grand house. In the reception area and cloakroom sat an immaculately dressed but sour-faced captain, who agreed that, yes, he had been informed of his request to see Lieutenant-General Phipps as a matter of urgency, but, as perhaps the major could hear, the general was busy.

What the general was busy with beyond the white, gilded doors to the ballroom was trying to interrupt a tirade from an angry fellow officer. There were thumps of punctuation during the speech, as one or other of them banged a desk, and low growls of displeasure that made it seem as if there was a large cat, a lion or a panther, in there with them.

'I don't mind waiting,' Watson said to the captain.

The adjutant indicated a ridiculously ornate padded chair that might look more at home in a boudoir. 'I'll stand,' said Watson.

The door of the ballroom was flung back, making them both start, and for a moment Watson thought he must have been correct in assuming a wild animal was in there, for the man who emerged was snorting and snuffling like a bull about to charge. It was a second before Watson recognized the belligerent officer and took a step forward.

'Sir.'

A pair of narrow eyes turned towards him, failed to register who he was, and turned to the captain. 'Where the blazes is Hakewill-Smith?' he demanded.

'In the mess, I believe,' replied the captain evenly.

'Sir . . .' Watson repeated, but the lieutenant-colonel strode off and out down the corridor in search of the doubtless unfortunate Hakewill-Smith.

The adjutant picked up his telephone, spoke a few quiet words, and then looked at Watson. 'You can go through now, sir.'

Phipps, a precise, straight-backed man in his early fifties, was gazing out of windows that were not masked by curtains, and the room was bright and airy compared to the rest of the house. His view was of the main drive, down to the stone gates that opened onto the road to Ploegsteert, and the surrounding woods. It all looked deceptively normal.

The ballroom in which he stood had been converted to an office with the addition of filing cabinets, a blackboard and a great slab of a desk, on which various maps and papers were laid out. At one end of the room was a cocktail cabinet, its flap down, on which stood a series of balloon brandy glasses and cut-glass decanters. A Louis XIV-style side table held an ornate ormolu clock, the face held aloft by golden cherubs, and a vase of fresh flowers.

'Major Watson?' Phipps asked as he turned. 'Do come in. Close the door, just in case he comes back.'

'Was that . . . ?' Watson began, not sure he could believe his eyes.

'Of course. Who else would come in and treat his commanding officer with such contempt? I don't know why French gave him the command. I should imagine over Haig's objections.' He was as much thinking aloud as addressing Watson. 'Man has too much to prove now, he's become reckless.' Phipps stopped himself. 'Can I get you some tea, Major?'

'No, thank you, sir.'

'Something stronger?' He indicated the cocktail cabinet.

'No, thank you. I don't want to take up too much of your time.'

'Oh, take all you wish. I have to say, Major, I am a great admirer of your work. Such a tonic when I was in South Africa. The copies of the magazine were in shreds by the time the Officers' Mess had finished with them.'

'Thank you.' Watson had the sudden impression that it was whatever small fame he enjoyed that had gained him entry to see the General Officer Commanding, a veteran of the Boer War apparently, rather than any medical or military concerns. He so hoped he wasn't going to start asking about the unpublished adventures.

Phipps, though, sat down behind his desk and invited Watson to take the chair opposite. Instead, Watson placed the Gladstone bag on the desk, opened it and took out a carefully folded piece of linen. 'These are fragments recovered from a wounded man at the East Anglian Casualty Clearing Station. He had most of his lower face blown clean off.'

He unfolded the material to show the small pile of metal shards he had insisted be saved after their extraction from Cornelius Lovat's jaw.

'Shrapnel?' Phipps asked, running a fingertip down one side of his moustache. 'Well, that's hardly new.'

'Sniff it.'

'I beg your pardon?'

The ormolu struck the quarter-hour.

'Sniff it, sir. It's faded over the last day or so, but a good nose can still detect the aroma. I suspect you have good olfactory abilities.'

Phipps frowned. 'Why would you say that?'

'The selection of glasses on your cocktail cabinet suggests you are a man who likes to savour the aroma of a good brandy or port. Similarly, the flowers, which I suspect are not easy to obtain at this time of year, indicate a man with heightened sensitivities.'

Phipps's face crinkled into a grin and he wagged a finger at Watson. 'Ah, I see now. A touch of the old deduction.'

A silly piece of vaudeville, thought Watson, but he nodded sagely. No man would deny such flattery, even if it was completely untrue and he had the senses of an earthworm. Phipps picked up the fabric and held it to his nostrils, breathing deeply. Watson watched a range of emotions cross over his features, until, after a long minute, he put the cloth back down.

'Is it . . . onions?'

Slightly better than an earthworm, then, but no bloodhound. 'Very good, although you may also have perceived undertones of burned garlic.'

'Of course, of course.' Phipps touched his forehead, as if admonishing himself. He waited for a few seconds before asking. 'And that means . . . ?'

'Cadet's liquid. I think the bullet contained a quantity of Cadet's liquid, perhaps at the core of a charge of fulminated mercury.'

'A rifle bullet?'

'Yes. A particularly wicked one.' He described the facial wound in detail.

'An ordinary high-velocity bullet can cause extensive damage too. But this does sound like it is of a different order. And this unfortunate Lovat?'

'Dead. I should have realized at the time he could not be saved. Cadet's fuming liquid, to give it its full title, means that, should the victim survive the gunshot, the arsenic in the compound will still kill him. All of which contravenes the Hague Convention.'

'You have come across this before?'

'Twice. Never as propellants, but in static explosive devices designed to cause mayhem. Once with Latvian anarchists and once, it pains me to say, with planned suffragette outrages.'

'You know there have been claims and counterclaims about such bullets. At the beginning of the war, any British officer captured with flat-nosed rounds in his revolver – standard issue for some years – was liable to be shot on the spot. And we found German dum-dum bullets, of course. Hideous things.'

Watson was about to mention that such expanding rounds got their name from the British arsenal at Calcutta, but held his tongue. Phipps would be well aware that there was a degree of hypocrisy at work whenever anyone condemned the other side's atrocities.

'Such things have paled beside the use of flame-throwers and poison gas,' Phipps continued. 'But your bullet seems to be in a different league from even a dum-dum.' He put his fingertips together. 'I can issue a field notice, asking for front-line officers to be on alert for such wounds and report them, and I can write to the International Committee of the Red Cross, alerting them to a possible breach of the Hague and Geneva Conventions. And of course, mention the threat to Field Marshal Haig when he arrives, so he knows to keep his head well down when we tell him. Don't want the Field Marshal having his skull split open in my sector.'

No, Watson thought, I bet you don't. Not a career-enhancing scenario. 'I was told he was visiting medical facilities.'

'It's a bit of a Cook's Tour to be frank. He's mainly to inspect the Ypres salient proper. Pretty beastly up there.' Watson knew 'up there' was only a few miles distant. 'No doubt hatching some scheme to break the stalemate. But he also intends to visit us here at Somerset. You know this was a quiet sector until someone decided it might be a grand idea to start shooting the new rifle grenades over at Fritz.'

'Yes, I'd heard. One of my nurses mentioned much the same thing.'

'Ah, well. Keeps us all on our toes, I suppose.'

Watson, his objectives achieved, made some small talk before he repacked his Gladstone and took his leave. As he stepped back into the anteroom, he was surprised to see the lieutenant-colonel who had stormed out of the office thirty minutes earlier, sitting, brooding in the over-elaborate chair. The adjutant was nowhere to be seen. He stood as soon as he saw Watson.

'There you are, Major. My apologies for not recognizing you earlier. Uniform threw me.'

Watson held the door open for him to re-enter the ballroom.

Colonel Winston Churchill shook his head, making his jowls wobble. 'No, no. Shut that. It's you I want to see, not that shrinking violet in there. Dr Watson, I do believe I have the perfect case for you.'

TWENTY-ONE

Lieutenant Metcalf found a large scrubbing brush under the sink in the kitchen at Suffolk Farm, A Company's billet. He used it to get the last of the whitewash from under his nails. He had quite enjoyed the physical work of painting and had enjoyed the company of the two nurses even more.

He was not sure that his mother would have approved of them, mind. The red-haired one in particular, Mrs Gregson, was positively intimidating. He imagined her coming to tea and the look on his mother's face when she let forth with some of the rather fruity opinions she had about the war and women.

'It'll never be the same again,' she had said. 'Women won't have to break windows to get the vote. Because men will have seen them at their best – away from the washing tub and the hearth.'

Mrs Metcalf thought suffragettes were some kind of inverts, who needed only a strong man to make them see the error of their ways. She was very baffled when a significant number of men – some of whom she admired – turned out to support the idea of universal suffrage. But he was getting ahead himself. He had never brought any girl home for tea yet, let alone one as sparky as Mrs Gregson.

'How are the men at the hospital?' asked de Griffon as he entered the kitchen, ducking to clear the low door beam.

'Bearing up for the most part,' Metcalf replied. 'Shipobottom was a little windy. How was the ride?'

De Griffon had been up early to exercise Lord Lockie, his horse. 'Excellent. You don't, do you? Ride?'

'No, sir.'

'Pity. He's a fine horse and a few miles east of here you could almost forget there is a war on. Have you seen Sunderland?' This was their batman. 'Need to get these boots off.'

'He's gone scavenging for food. Promised us eggs. And milk.'

'Have to make my own tea then, I suppose.' De Griffon set about filling the enormous black kettle. 'How are you getting on with the dance?'

'Oh, I've found some likely candidates.'

'I passed a barn down the road. Peeked in. Clean and dry. Make a good spot for it. Just have to track down the farmer and see how much he'd want.'

He placed the kettle on the hotplate of the range. He touched the metal. It was barely tepid. 'We'll be lucky if that boils in time for breakfast.' He used a cloth to open the stove's door. 'Send one of the men to gather some more wood, will you?'

'Sir.'

There was a knock on the door and de Griffon walked through to answer it. When he returned his face looked glum.

'What is it?' Metcalf asked.

De Griffon held up the written orders. 'I think you'd best postpone the dance. We haven't got a week here. Apparently one of the replacement units didn't make it. We've got three days at the most and we're back on the front line.'

Metcalf stopped drying his hands as this sank in. 'You want me to tell the men?'

De Griffon blew out his cheeks and sighed. 'No. Leave it to me. Just as long as they get a hot bath before we turn them back around, they'll count that as a decent result.'

'And the wounded at the CCS?'

'Will just have to join us when they can. If they think they can sit this one out, they've got another think coming. We're all in this together, Metcalf. The Leigh Pals will live and die together.'

That, thought Metcalf, is what worries me.

TWENTY-TWO

As they walked down the corridor towards the front entrance of Somerset House, Churchill worked at lighting a cigar the size of a cavalryman's lance. 'I had no idea you were out here, sir,' Watson said,

'It took some string-pulling, I can tell you.'

Watson was well aware the former Home Secretary had been driven from his position as First Lord of the Admiralty after the fiasco of the Dardanelles and cast into the wilderness. 'But eventually they gave me the Royal Scots Fusiliers, just to shut me up. A fine bunch, though. Distrusted me, a Sassenach, at first, of course, especially when I turned up with my own bath and boiler, but it's a wonder what a round of clean, dry socks for every man can achieve.' He chortled, his face wreathed in smoke from the newly caught cigar.

'I'm sorry you witnessed the scene earlier. Phipps is one of those who want us to sit on our hands and wait for the Germans to make the first move. My God, I have experience of fighting the Boers too and yet it appears we learned nothing. Small, light skirmishing units, highly mobile, stirring things up a bit. That's what we need. Not sitting in slits in the ground, year after year. We need to remind them we still have a fight in us.'

Watson knew instinctively that it had been Churchill goading the Germans with rifle grenades to elicit a response in his sector. It was he who had brought the 'hate' – the bombardments – down on the heads of a quiet stretch of the line.

'Watson, I don't think I ever told you how grateful I was that you never wrote up what you would doubtless have called *The Adventure of the King's Wife*, or some such.'

Watson was offended. 'I felt it was my patriotic duty not to do so.'

'Quite. One thing that always puzzled me,' said Churchill, halting in the gloomy hallway beneath the skeletal remains of a glass chandelier, stripped down to a few lonely pendants by percussion and concussion. With the windows heavily curtained, light was provided by a string of guttering electric bulbs that weren't up to the job, 'was how he knew I had come straight from the Reform Club when I pitched up at Baker Street?'

Churchill had been smoking a Home Spun Broad Leaf No. 2, a Cuban cigar imported exclusively by the Wine and Cigar Committee of the Reform Club. But as a distant voice reminded him: *A conjurer gets no credit once he has explained his trick.* 'I am afraid I am not at liberty to tell you, sir.'

Churchill narrowed his eyes as if he were going to bark an order to reveal all, but eventually smiled. 'Well, I have a most mysterious occurrence that I would welcome your help on. Let's call it *The Case of the Man Who Died Twice*. The events—'

Watson could feel his curiosity being aroused. He could not allow that to happen. 'Sir, I am afraid I am acting merely as a medical doctor here. Not a companion or a foil or a biographer. Certainly not any shade of detective.'

'That may be so. But you have contacts. I didn't expect him to be here in person, but I thought if anyone can engage the great consulting detective—'

'It pains me to say this, sir, but the partnership is dissolved.'

Churchill's jaw sagged, and only his moist and fleshy lower lip kept the cigar in place. 'Dissolved?'

'He is happy keeping his bees and walking the Downs, his conscience disturbed only occasionally by the rumble of the distant guns, or so I would imagine. I am here to do what little I can to alleviate pain and suffering. We – he and I – are no longer in the business of deduction.'

'Really? I'm sorry to hear that.' Churchill opened the door to allow Watson to step through. 'But perhaps you would consider taking a look at the facts in the case?'

'Until the war is over, I am simply a medical man.'

Winston stepped out into the fresh air. Mrs Gregson, seeing Watson was readying to depart, fetched the starting handle to fire up the Crossley.

'Ah, well. So be it.' Churchill held out his hand. 'Thank you again for your work on the Mylius case. I'm sorry it can never be officially recognized.'

'It was a pleasure.' Watson wasn't lying. He longed for the days when an average week might involve helping Holmes save the royal family from disgrace, a game played out in the library at the Athenaeum, the drawing rooms of the great stately homes of Hampshire, the Old Bailey and even Buckingham Palace. He would never have countenanced such a statement at the time, but life was so much simpler then.

He came back to the present when the clocks in the house began a staggered chiming of one o'clock, a sound that merged perfectly with the whistle of an approaching German shell.

The first 105mm round of the afternoon bombardment detonated close to the lonely tower of the church, the great thud in the earth causing the structure to sway alarmingly. As Churchill and Watson watched the dirty fan of earth spread, both were aware of a smaller explosion behind them, as part of the plaster disintegrated into fine powder. Watson felt the heat cross his face and his skin prickle with the impact of dust and stone and caught a noxious garlicky smell.

The sentry stepped across, blocking the doorway and putting himself in harm's way to cover the colonel. He was rewarded with a round in his chest, which imploded into a grisly crater. As the sentry went down, Watson grabbed Churchill by the arm and hurled him back inside the hallway, yelling over his shoulder for Mrs Gregson to follow them in.

As she dropped the handle and sprinted, a salvo from a battery of Minenwerfer landed in the trees and backtracked towards the steeple, the noise building with each fall, until it was like a continuous series of hammer blows.

The concussion from a Minnie shell the size of a railway carriage snatched at Mrs Gregson and hurled her across the threshold into Watson's arms. They collapsed into a heap in the hallway.

Watson was back on his feet when two things happened: firstly the Crossley was picked up and flung against the front of Somerset House, the bodywork twisting and crumpling as it shattered windows and stonework, and one of the rounds took out the brickwork at the base of the steeple of Le Gheer. Despite the flying shrapnel and splinters, Watson stood at the side of the doorway, transfixed, and watched the tower totter like a drunkard before it fell, poleaxed, into the surrounding wood, with a ground-shaking boom that, just momentarily, blotted out the kettle-drum roll of enemy shellfire.

TWENTY-THREE

Sergeant Shipobottom's skin was contracting. He could feel it tightening all over his body. It was as if his entire epidermis was shrinking, like over-boiled cotton.

He managed to roll over onto his side and look around the transfusion ward. There was one other patient, a driver, they had said, but he was busy talking gobbledegook in his sleep. There was no nurse.

His skin was itching now, little islands of intense irritation, popping up over his neck and torso. He began to scratch and as he did so his fingers started to burn. He could feel something within them constricting, causing the fingers to bend. He held them up in front of his one good eye. His hands were becoming claws, like that old woman in Cairo who had told him . . .

A scream tried to escape his throat, a cry for help, but it wouldn't form. His throat was tightening too. It sounded more like a gargle than a shout. It was coming true, her prophecy was coming true.

A wave of sweaty panic broke over him and he tried to swing out of the bed. But the itching started again, so intense it was as if he were being branded with a thousand tiny irons.

He slumped back on the bed and the pain subsided for a moment. He breathed as deeply as he could. *You might feel warm*, they had said after his infusion. *Warm?* Friggin' agony this were.

Then he heard it. A low whistle, picking out an old folk tune, the sort they played on fair days. He managed to pull himself up in the bed, but he couldn't see clearly thanks to the moisture filling his eye. He could just make out that there was a third person on the ward, cloaked in shadow, standing by the central tent pole.

Then, some words to match the tune came.

This the story of two sisters, sisters
good and true,
They worked the reels in Lancashire,
and only wanted their due.

More whistling.

'Who's tha?' Shipobottom managed to croak. 'Who's tha'?'

There came a low, soft laugh. The only answer was another verse.

They asked for men and women to be treated the same,
to be treated all alike,
And if that was not to be, they promised a bitter strike.

Well, you won't strike, you cannot strike, you will not strike, said the boss,
For the Lord will hear of it, it'll surely be your loss.

Oh, we can strike, we will strike,

we are ready to fight.

And you can tell the Lord,

his mill will close tonight.

'Think on that,' the shadowy figure said.

'On wha'?' Shipobottom pleaded in a voice that wasn't his own. 'Wha' y'on about?'

'Think on Trolley Wood.'

Shipobottom slumped back. He sensed the singer of the song was leaving. Trolley Wood?

A small copse, close to Blackstone Mill, a ring of oak, hornbeam and birch encircling a lovely glade, rich with bluebells in spring, a prime picnic spot and . . .

The implication of that place name had just hit home when his agony moved to a new phase. Like steel cables being wound by a winch, the tendons and ligaments in his face and neck began to shorten. He felt muscles bulging and his features being distorted. Trolley Wood? Is that what this is all about?

Again Shipobottom tried to cry out, but to no avail. The mechanics of his face had been hijacked. The lips were being pulled back and up, the jaw down and, slowly but surely, his dying body was producing a terrible, unnaturally hideous grin.

TWENTY-FOUR

The blitz from the German guns lasted for fifty minutes in all, although to those beneath the falling shells it felt far longer. Incredibly, the main building of Somerset House suffered no more than a glancing blow and a motor car being flung into its edifice. But ancillary buildings and tents had been hit, and the nearest communication and relief trenches badly damaged. Many vehicles and a number of horses were out of the war for good.

It was fortunate indeed, as he would later remark, that Watson had brought his Gladstone, which contained one of the John Bell & Croyden 'Colonial & Overseas' emergency medical kits. It gave him the bare essentials to treat the injured; anything else would have to be improvised.

They used one of Somerset House's subterranean kitchens as a makeshift field-dressing station. A sturdy cherrywood table, assiduously scrubbed with blocks of lye and lard soap by an admirably unshaken Mrs Gregson, acted as an operating surface, while less serious cases were sat in wicker chairs to have their facial wounds tended. Mrs Gregson had found a laundered smock, skirt, petticoats and apron in the laundry press of the great house. She had shed her motor-cycling clothes – Watson had left the room, even though she had assured him that the combination chemise and drawers with long wide legs that she wore under the Dunhill left everything to the imagination – and donned the servant's clothing, even though, as she was at pains to point out, they had once belonged to a very large servant indeed.

With the electricity supply gone, and no windows to let in daylight, they worked by oil lamp and candles. Most of the injuries they saw were from shrapnel or flying glass. A few men, caught in the open, had been killed. Several had been reduced to 'wet dust' – a smog-like mist of blood and brains and muscle, the remnants of a pulverized body, that filled the air for a short time before falling to earth. There would be nothing of those unfortunates left to bury.

Of the survivors, the more heavily wounded were shipped off to the nearby CCS, having been assessed by Watson and tagged using the cache of gummed labels Mrs Gregson had found in the pickling room.

Phipps had been one of the last patients, who came to have a gashed hand – inflicted during the clear-up – treated and he explained that during the night German sappers, under a cloak of absolute secrecy, had laid a branch rail line to enable them to bring up several large guns and some large-calibre Minenwerfen on flat-bed trucks. The British had been able to return fire eventually and had caused them to withdraw. The British guns were expected to saturate the area around the new rail lines soon, ensuring there would be no repeat for the time being. Phipps then invited both Watson and Mrs Gregson to join him for dinner in the mess, as there would be no transport available to their CCS until either late that night or early the following morning.

When the final casualty had been dealt with – a young man with a smashed face, burst eardrums and the clothes blown off his back – Mrs Gregson put the copper kettle on the range to boil once more and indicated Watson should sit down.

'I need to look at that eye of yours,' she said.

He was aware that it had been stinging, but when he took a look in the medical kit's pocket mirror, he could see it was red and angry. 'Dust from the sniper round,' he said matter-of-factly.

'What sniper round?'

He explained his suspicion that an attempt had been made on the life of Churchill or himself or both moments before the first shells had fallen. Or possibly at exactly the same time. One bullet had hit the wall; the other had exploded in the chest of the poor sentry.

She poured out some of the boiling water and let it stand. Her brow furrowed. 'I don't know much about guns. Although I know what they do to the human body. But to fire to here from the enemy lines, is that quite some feat?'

Watson recalled what he knew about sniping from studying the career of Sebastian Moran, the big game hunter and would-be assassin of Sherlock Holmes. 'A good rifle is accurate to six hundred yards. Perhaps eight in the hands of an expert with telescopic sights. That is far exceeded by the distance to even the first of the German trenches. In solving a problem of this sort, one needs to be able to reason backward. I can only conclude the weapon was fired from our side of the lines.'

'A traitor?'

'An infiltrator. And if I am not mistaken, one who was secreted atop of the church steeple we saw fall. I watched it go down, in the hope I would see such a figure, but no.'

'How . . . that's impossible. For a German to walk through our trenches undetected.'

'Unlikely,' he conceded. 'But not impossible.'

'Head back, please.'

Using a syringe and the cooled, sterilized water she began to irrigate the eye. She held her fingers lightly under his chin, gently guiding his head this way and that. He found himself enjoying the sensation.

'Major, I would like to apologize for being so rude about your friend.'

'You are not the first to take him wrong.'

'I am not apologizing for the sentiments. Keep still. I swear, doctors are the worst patients of all. I stand by those.'

'You are being unfair. Let me see, what are the charges? Vainglorious? Yes, he has a healthy regard for his talents. I myself wrote on several occasions that I sometimes found his egotism repellent. But he rarely pursued cases for financial reward or glory. Drug-addled? Only if there is nothing to engage his intellect and his attempts to unravel the mysteries of the hive have kept his mind busy of late, I believe. Smug, I think you said? He is pleased when he is right, and he is right more often than not. And . . .'

'Woman hating.'

Watson hesitated at that one. In fact, all the charges had a tiny element of truth. But 'hate' was far too active an emotion to be accurate. 'Indifferent' might suffice. 'Well, it is true he does not dwell on the fairer sex overmuch. And never will. But there was one woman . . . perhaps two.' Watson had harboured high hopes for

Miss Violet Hunter, the governess of Copper Beeches, whom Holmes had once seemed rather taken with, but that had come to naught. Once the case was over she was dismissed from his mind.

'I am talking about the idea of suffrage. Of women's rights. Was he not responsible for gaoling several dozen suffragettes?'

This was not a case Watson had been involved in. He recalled some of the details, however. 'My dear Mrs Gregson, were those same women not involved in a scheme to burn down the Houses of Parliament?'

'While they were empty,' she objected.

'They are never empty. There was a risk to human life. A crime was planned and was thwarted in the nick of time. The suffragette movement had moved from being a valid − yes, I'll admit valid − movement of protest to one of terror and intimidation.'

'Some of those women were friends of mine.'

'Really?' He pulled his head round to look at her. Sister Spence had been right about political VADs. 'So it's a dislike for personal reasons we are about talking here?'

'Keep still, Lord above. Why do you defend him so? I mean, you will admit to no flaws.'

'Of course I will. The flawless man does not exist. I would rather judge him by his virtues. I defend him because he is my . . .' Say it. Friend. Except no longer could he call him that with any degree of certainty. Watson knew how ruthless he could be with those he deemed to have been disloyal. Even so, that was no reason to disown him or what they had been through together. 'Because the world is a better place for him.'

'All done. Blink.'

She gently mopped at his watering eye. 'I should keep my

opinions to myself, Major. I'm sorry. It's one of my own many, many flaws.'

'And the *Strand* is hardly a penny dreadful.'

'Yes, yes, granted.' She was keen to move along now. 'Why didn't you tell the general your suspicions about the sniper?'

'Two reasons. I think we should wait until we are certain it is all clear out there before sending anyone to inspect the ruins. Plus, one has to hold back some subjects for conversation over dinner. It could be a very long and very dull evening otherwise.'

Mrs Gregson laughed and began clearing the instruments from the tabletop, preparing for another scrubbing down.

'Of course we won't get a word in edgeways if Churchill is there,' he added. The colonel would no doubt insist on telling him the tale of *The Man Who Died Twice*. Under normal circumstances Watson's curiosity might be aroused, but he was wary of being drawn into any scheme involving Churchill. He might be a wounded animal after Gallipoli, but he was still a politician first and foremost and a bruising bare-knuckle fighter when he needed to be. Watson's instinct was to keep away.

Mrs Gregson splashed soapy suds onto the cherrywood surface. 'How the dickens do you know Winston Churchill?'

Watson wondered how much to say. In 1910, the editor and pamphleteer Edward Mylius had accused the new King, in print, of being a bigamist, of having hastily married an admiral's daughter in Malta while he was a junior naval officer. Mylius had even threatened to produce the woman.

It was Churchill who had pressed George V into the highly unusual step of suing for libel, arguing that the magazine the *Liberator* had been available to buy along the Strand and the

Charing Cross Road. Churchill, remembering the rumours in court circles that Sherlock Holmes had performed services for the Kings of Bohemia and Scandinavia, the Dutch royal family and – as was by then well known – the unfortunate Lord St Simon, who managed to lose both his wife and her fortune on his wedding day, had hit upon the idea of using Holmes to disprove the allegation. Which he had done with ease, briefing the Attorney-General, who in turn had given Sir Richard David Muir, acting for the Crown, the ammunition to procure a year in prison for Mylius. 'A small matter of no consequence,' said Watson airily as he repacked his Gladstone.

'As you wish,' she said tartly, recognizing the evasion.

He relented a little. 'A matter of some consequence I have given my word not to discuss.'

She nodded to indicate that this was a more acceptable response.

He paused to watch her scrub, which she did with some force, admiring the precise sweeping movements that made sure no inch was left untouched by the brush, the way she lifted one leg as she bent over to reach the far corner. There was something quite mesmerizing about—

'Major Watson?'

It was Captain Hatherley, Phipps's adjutant. Watson was jerked from his reverie. 'Yes? What is it?' he asked too sharply.

'I am sorry to disturb you, sir, but a request has been telephoned through, asking for you to return to the East Anglian Clearing Station immediately.'

Watson and Mrs Gregson exchanged puzzled glances. For his part, he was not entirely disappointed to forfeit a tedious dinner, but he wondered about the change of plan. Was someone trying to get rid of him? Churchill perhaps? 'We seem to have lost our transport, Hatherley.'

'I explained this to . . .' he studied the piece of paper in his hand, '. . . Major Torrance. He has sent a vehicle over to pick you up. It appears there has been a death, sir.'

'It's a Casualty Clearing Station,' objected Mrs Gregson as she removed her apron. 'There are always deaths.'

'That may well be the case, miss.' Hatherley consulted his document again. 'But apparently this is a very singular death that demands Major Watson's immediate attention.'

TWENTY-FIVE

The pain was so intense that Bloch wanted to cry out, but he knew he couldn't. Drawing attention to himself would be fatal. He felt as if a wild animal were gnawing at him where he lay, and he had to play dead, while it nipped and ripped and chomped. The world had faded; his eyes could no longer see anything but shades of grey, sounds were muffled and distant, as if he was already in his coffin in the ground. This was, he felt, the last station on the line before oblivion.

No, he told himself. He wasn't ready to board that particular service yet. He needed to live.

Bloch became aware that the shellfire had ceased when the ground stopped shaking. He strained his damaged ears. The low hum that was left in place of silence was unwavering. It was time to move.

If he could.

He tried to get a sense of where his limbs were in space. His left arm was under his body, filled with pins and needles. His right was ahead of him, held down by some great weight. One leg was free but the other, again, was fixed and immovable. He arched his back, enough so he could release the trapped left. The action disturbed a layer of stones, which skittered away. He tried to raise his head, which caused more disturbances, but daylight bled through his eyelids. Not completely buried then. With the newly freed arm, he groped forward and found the wooden beam trapping its companion. Three heaves and he had both arms free. Now time was of the essence.

Bloch pushed himself up on his hands, releasing the upper body completely. He was in the woods, where the tower had fallen and taken some saplings with it, and for the moment he appeared to be alone. He crawled clear of the mess of stone and timber to a patch of damp ferns and lay on them, panting, his face throbbing and burning. His eyes were full of grit and when he touched his ear, there was blood on his fingertips. A brush of the nose and his eye almost burst from his face. Broken. A roughness on his tongue told him that his front teeth were chipped. He desperately needed a drink of water, for his throat was coated in fine powder, and swallowing felt like he was trying to force an ostrich egg down his gullet.

He stood, shakily, releasing a shower of grit around him and pulled at his clothes with numb fingers. The leatherwork came off easily enough and, after removing the pistol and the bayonet, he threw them into the bushes. He had already lost one boot and the other he kicked off. His tunic was stiff with dust and debris, and undoing the buttons took an age, but eventually he was down to his underwear. A sudden shiver took him. How incriminating were the singlet and longjohns, he wondered. He couldn't take the chance. He pulled those off too and walked deeper into the forest, hoping he could circle back round towards his own lines.

Luck was with him. He found two Tommies, buried by the collapse of earthworks. One had lost his face; the features had been neatly excised and cauterized by a piece of hot shrapnel, leaving a grisly, shiny oval where his face should be. Nearby was a folded pile of something grey and pink. The other soldier was intact and still alive, albeit barely. His eyelids were flickering as he dropped in and out of this world. He plunged the man's own bayonet into the body, twice. A simple reflex, he told himself. From the other he took the identity disc and slipped it over his head. The boy was younger than he, or appeared so in death. No matter. Soldiers often aged decades at the front, only to see the years fall away as they were freed from the worry and cares of this life.

The lad was wearing an unofficial ID bracelet, which Bloch also took. Stripping the body proved as arduous as removing his own clothes. The trousers and socks were all he could manage, before exhaustion overwhelmed him once again. He rifled the pockets and found a water bottle and a pouch of iron rations. He gulped down the water and ate the hardtack biscuits, cheese and the beef cubes from the ration, then scooped out handfuls of the bully beef from the tin. He also found the man's paybook, which he pocketed.

Fatigue hit him again and the mixture of foodstuffs in his stomach made him feel queasy. He knew he couldn't be found next to the two bodies and further undressing of them was beyond him. He pulled on the trousers and kicked at the soil to bury the lower half of the Tommy he had become. Then he headed towards what he thought was east again, losing the incriminating blade in a shell crater.

It was no more than five minutes before he staggered into a clearing where three genuine Tommies were manning a machine-gun post in a shallow depression, protected by a half-moon of sandbags. Its field of fire was a narrow forest track through the trees. It was an ambush for any German incursion that might follow the bombardment. The NCO in charge stood and levelled a Lee Enfield at Bloch and yelled something. No words appeared to come from the mouth. The sergeant signalled the Vickers crew to remain at their stations and took a step forward.

Bloch went to raise his hands, but his balance deserted him and he fell to his knees. The sergeant, still pointing the rifle at him, crossed the clearing in long exaggerated steps. He bent and lifted the ID disc with his free hand. He shouted something else, back to his comrades. Slinging the Lee Enfield over his shoulder, the NCO put his hands under Bloch's armpits, lifting him back on his feet. He flopped Bloch's right arm around his neck and began to half-march and half-drag him towards Somerset House.

Once there, a blanket and some boots were found, tea provided, cigarettes, and, after a lengthy wait at the back of a queue, during which he pointed to his ears whenever anyone addressed him, a kindly British doctor and his firm yet attractive nurse – the same ones, he eventually realized, he had sighted in his cross hairs – cleaned him up as best they could. This involved extracting two teeth, multiple splinters and stones, straightening his nose and placing a fat dressing over the centre of his face. After they had finished, they found him a cot to lie on until he could be transported to the rear. If he could have managed it without agony, Bloch might have smiled at the irony of how things had turned out.

TWENTY-SIX

It was dark by the time the ambulance dropped them off and a reception committee had formed in the doorway of the transfusion tent. It wasn't a happy band; the frown lines on their faces were cast as deep crevices by the glow of two hurricane lamps. There was Major Torrance, Caspar Myles, Sister Spence comforting a red-eyed Miss Pippery and Robinson de Griffon.

The moment Mrs Gregson stepped down from the ambulance, Miss Pippery rushed over and hugged her before bursting into sobs.

A Jack Russell tied to one of the tent posts gave two yaps, before de Griffon gave it a sharp rebuke. He then turned and saluted Watson. 'Good to see you again so soon, sir,' he said.

Before Watson could answer, Myles crashed in. His words were heavy with aggression and rancour. 'What did you put in that damned blood of yours, Watson?'

Watson turned towards Myles, not certain he had heard correctly. 'I beg your pardon, Doctor?'

'The blood was bad, Watson. Damned bad.'

Torrance tutted at the impertinence then barked: 'Gentlemen, if you would give Major Watson time to draw breath—'

'Which is more than poor Shipobottom will ever do,' Myles muttered.

'Shipobottom?' Watson asked. 'Shipobottom's dead?'

'I am afraid so,' said de Griffon glumly. 'I rode over to tell the men the news, that we were being taken back up the line and . . . well, yes he died.'

'And in the most awful way imaginable,' added Myles.

Part of him wanted to rush inside at once, but Watson tried to remain calm and professional. 'May I see the body?'

'I think you should,' said Torrance, for once lowering his voice.

The group shuffled aside and allowed Watson to enter. Brindle had been moved. There was but one bed occupied but the figure in there was unrecognizable. It was all Watson could do to stop from crying out at the sight of poor Shipobottom. There were deep scratches on his cheeks, where the poor chap's nails had raked the skin and torn at the bandages that had covered his eye. The upper chest also showed breaks in the skin. The hands were folded and locked like claws on his chest, and had been tied together with crepe bandages, presumably to try and stop him attacking his face and throat further.

All that was bad enough, but it was his facial expression that was most remarkable and disturbing. The eyes bulged, the skin around the face was tinged with blue and the tongue lolled from a mouth that had been drawn back into a demented grin. Poor Shipobottom looked like some grotesque poster advertising a circus freak show. It made Watson's stomach turn just to look at him.

'How long has he been dead?' Watson asked, his mouth suddenly dry.

'Several hours,' honked Torrance.

'And the facial muscles haven't relaxed at all?'

'Does it look like it?' demanded Myles. 'He's a damned gargoyle in flesh. Look at him, man.'

'I am looking,' snapped Watson, his weariness making him irritable. 'In fact, I'd like some time to examine the body in private.'

'So you can come to some other conclusion other than you fed this man poisoned blood,' Myles suggested.

'We don't know that,' objected Torrance, albeit without much conviction.

'Will somebody please tell me the sequence of events? Miss Pippery, can you help?' asked Watson.

The VAD gave an enormous sniff and nodded. Mrs Gregson squeezed her hand to steady her nerves. 'I was monitoring the patient, the way we agreed, when Captain de Griffon—'

'Hold on. Is that de Griffon as in the Norfolk de Griffons?' Mrs Gregson asked.

Watson felt another flash of irritation at the unnecessary interruption. Mrs Gregson had no sense of decorum or timing.

The young captain gave an ingratiating smile. 'It is. Do you know—'

'I know all about the de Griffons,' Mrs Gregson muttered, 'enough to not want to share a room with one.' With a final pat on Miss Pippery's shoulder, she left the tent. De Griffon looked perplexed.

'Excuse me, gentlemen.' Sister Spence, mouth pinched in fury, went after the VAD.

Watson, although puzzled by Mrs Gregson's behaviour, did not want to be distracted. 'Please continue, Miss Pippery.'

'Well, Captain de Griffon arrived to look in on the sergeant.'

'And what time was this?'

'Two o'clock,' said Miss Pippery. 'Perhaps a little later.'

'And when did the patient first display symptoms?' Watson asked.

'He already had a fever by that point. I was quite concerned about it,' she said.

'And then . . . ?' Watson prompted.

'He began fitting,' said de Griffon. 'Quite badly.'

Miss Pippery nodded. 'Tonic-clonic seizures, about ten minutes apart. I sent for Dr Myles at once, of course.'

The American jumped in. 'When I arrived his pulse rate was 145 and wild. He was beginning to show signs of the cyanosis. I gave him oxygen. But nothing worked. It took him four hours to die.'

Watson examined their faces. De Griffon looked numb and Miss Pippery terrified that everything was somehow her fault.

They could hear raised voices from outside. Sister Spence and Mrs Gregson were going at it hammer and tongs. It was difficult to establish which of them had the upper hand. It sounded positively gladiatorial.

'Do you think,' asked Torrance evenly, 'that it could be contamination of your stored blood? Or perhaps the method of anticoagulation? Sodium citrate is toxic.'

'Not like this,' said Watson, pointing at Shipobottom's twisted visage. 'And not at the dilutions we use. Nought point two of one per cent in this case.'

'Could the dilutions have been wrong?' It was Sister Spence, returned to the tent, her face flushed. 'It has been known in inexperienced hands for a point two per cent to become two per cent or even twenty per cent solution.'

Sister was clearly suggesting that the VADs had somehow compromised the transfusion process. Watson was having none of that. 'I prepared the anticoagulant. I have absolute confidence the dosage was correct. Besides, all an excess dose does is inhibit clotting. If he had haemorrhaged to death . . .'

'Well, something caused this . . . this horror,' said Myles.

De Griffon kept a steadier tone. 'I'm no medical man, but could it be something contagious? I am concerned for my other men. They'll be in very close proximity once we move back to the front.'

It was a good point and the three doctors looked at each other for an opinion. There was a contagious division, a series of three isolation tents in the old orchard, accessed by an avenue of trees that ran through the monastery gardens, where TB and typhoid cases were sent.

'I think that's unlikely,' said Watson.

'But you can't be sure?' de Griffon asked.

'Not until I have examined him, no.'

'I think we had better isolate this tent, just in case,' said Torrance gloomily. 'And keep an eye on anyone who has come into contact with the deceased. We should seal the body in a canvas bag.'

'I'd still like to examine him thoroughly before any of that,' said Watson. 'Alone, if you don't mind. I shall, of course, report my findings back to you.'

'If you have any findings,' muttered Myles.

'Very well,' said Torrance. 'But for the moment, Major Watson, I shall have to suspend any further blood transfusions using your method. We shall return to patient-to-patient direct infusion where necessary.'

'Of course.' Watson began to unbutton his jacket. 'Did anyone think to take a blood sample for analysis?' He waited for an answer from Myles or Torrance. None came. 'No? Very well.'

The others left for other duties, leaving only de Griffon and Watson alongside the deceased.

'I'm sure it's not your fault, Major,' the captain said.

Watson shrugged. 'At this stage, it is best not to rule out any possibility.'

'And the American doctor—'

'Dr Myles.'

'Yes. I simply think he feels wretched because he couldn't save him. It was a pretty ghastly sight to be honest. You come expecting to see some terrible things at the front, but not at a hospital, surely?'

They peered at the cyanotic face and the hideous grin. Myles had been right about one thing: it was an expression one only normally saw high up on church walls. Watson gave an involuntary shudder. 'No. Not at a hospital,' he said. 'If you will excuse me, I have to get along. Unless you want to stay and . . . ?'

De Griffon gave a little smile. 'I think I shall leave this to a professional. The 25th are scattered across the reserve lines at the moment. If I'm not at regimental HQ, I'll be with the 9th Platoon of A Company, billeted at Suffolk Farm. That's Shipobottom's company. We're there for the next few days. Perhaps you could send word of any results to myself or my lieutenant? Metcalf. The men, they'll want to know. Shipobottom was well liked by them.'

'And by me,' Watson said glumly.

'Yes. And, of course, I shall have to write to his next of kin. It will be useful to know the cause of his death. Well, good night, Major. And good luck getting to the bottom of this dreadful business.'

'Good night, Captain.'

Watson stood for a few minutes, looking at the corpse, waiting for the phantom voice in his head to proffer an opinion, a strategy, even a little comfort, but none came. *You are on your own*, he told himself, *as it should be. This is your field of expertise now. No more ghosts.*

It felt like freedom.

'Major Watson.'

He turned to see Mrs Gregson, looking contrite. 'I'm sorry for my behaviour. I have apologized to Captain de Griffon. Sister Spence was right. I brought my personal feelings into a medical area. No nurse should ever do that. No self-respecting VAD either, as she reminded me. I have agreed with Sister Spence that I shall go back to Bailleul tomorrow.'

'What on earth was the matter? Do you know the captain?'

'The captain? No. His family. And only by reputation. The de Griffons were . . . are mill owners in and around Leigh, although they are not from those parts. They live down south in some big pile. Absentee landlords, you might say. My father, when he was a young solicitor, acted for the first unions in the mills. I can't say the de Griffons were model employers or enlightened in their attitude to organized labour. They broke several strikes at the mill most brutally. Bullied the organizers and worse. Of course, that was before the captain's time. But in my household the de Griffons were a byword for unnecessary cruelty.'

'I don't see much evidence of that in Robinson de Griffon. He seems genuinely concerned for his men.'

'No, I agree, he seems decent enough. I might have been hasty in my judgement. And not for the first time.' She pinched the bridge of her nose. 'Can I assist you here, Major?' she asked, unhooking a lamp from the doorway and bringing it across to increase the illumination over the corpse.

'Aren't you tired after today's exertions, Mrs Gregson?' The strain of the last twelve hours had drawn her features; the harsh lamplight made her look older than her years. Although, he admitted, she had a very attractive middle age in prospect.

'Aren't you?'

He nodded. By the same token, he must look like Methuselah. 'I am weary, yes. And I have an unexpected craving for a glass of Beaune. But there is work to be done here.'

'Then we shall do it together.'

'Thank you.' He retrieved the magnifying glass from his jacket. 'Perhaps you will hold the lantern close to the body while I go over every inch of this poor chap and see what he can reveal to us.'

'Of course.'

He stood back and contemplated the twisted body once more. The agonies of his demise were etched in his features. That in itself was passing strange: muscles usually relaxed after death. No, *always* relaxed. Even the most tortured final hours normally give way to an impression of being at rest or peace that brought some comfort to the bereaved. Not here. The savage contractions had denied poor Shipobottom that kind of dignity. Nobody looking upon him could have any doubt about the grim manner of his passage from this life.

'You know, Mrs Gregson, I didn't want to say in front of the others, for it might have sounded too defensive, but I do believe I have seen these symptoms before.'

Her answer, low and fearful, made him shiver once more. 'Dear Lord. I'm relieved to hear it. Because so have I, Major Watson. So have I.'

TWENTY-SEVEN

The blade slid smoothly into the skin, parting the fat, cartilage and the walls of blood vessels. He twisted it, moving it in a circular motion back and forth to make sure that maximum damage was done to the tissues. The man's eyes looked up at him, imploring, and Bloch found himself shaking his head, in sorrow and regret. *If only you hadn't woken up*, it was meant to convey. *If only you hadn't seen me going through your pockets, prior to me slipping into your uniform. If only you had not made to cry out in alarm. I wouldn't be here now, digging into your neck with your own clasp knife, my hand clamped firmly over your mouth. You probably thought I was some kind of common thief. I am a very uncommon thief.*

The sergeant stopped struggling after a while, although blood continued to squirt out over Bloch's hand and onto the blankets and sheets. Eventually he felt the geyser slow and he risked letting go of the man's mouth. Fate had put this man in the same room as he, the same capricious fate that had decided there were no more transports available that night and the opinion, voiced by a medic, that a decent sleep might see a change of fortune for the pair. Well, this night had certainly seen that for the sergeant.

Bloch rinsed the knife and his hands in the enamel bowl that stood on the makeshift nightstand. He dried them on the sheets of his cot and then set about completing his dressing in the sergeant's uniform, which fitted him reasonably well. A little short in the sleeves perhaps, but an ill-fitting uniform was no novelty in any army, and would not arouse suspicion.

It was raining outside again, and he knew this would suit his purpose admirably. He would stride out of the headquarters and make his way to where he had stolen the identity of the Tommy. He would grab one of the rolls of barbed wire and, exuding as much confidence as possible, head towards the trenches. Everyone would be alert for a German coming towards them. Few would expect one from behind. Especially one who looked intent on repairing the coils of wire that had been blasted apart by the German guns. If he could make the Warnave Brook, to the south of where he was now, a watercourse that pierced no man's land, he could follow that to safety.

Of course, he would need a hefty dose of luck to get into no man's land in the first place, and an even bigger issue of it if he were to avoid being shot by his own side as he approached the German lines. The drumming rain he could hear would help; the men on both sides would be dreaming of the warm and the dry, and taking advantage of any opportunity to avail themselves of it.

He finished buttoning up the tunic, put on the sergeant's steel helmet and shouldered the man's Lee Enfield. He practised a salute. Something told him, looking down at the man's throat, the wound raw in the guttering candlelight, that luck was on Ernst Bloch's side that night.

TWENTY-EIGHT

The weather had resorted to bullying once more. Low, ominous clouds rolled across the entire region, blotting out the moon and the stars, and a cutting east wind sprang up. It drove before it a slanting, icy rain that suddenly gave way to hailstones the size of boiled sweets, which battered Watson as he staggered up the hill to his billet in the Big House. He was drained of all energy. His breathing was shallow and his old wounds throbbed mercilessly. The lumps of ice were like blows of recrimination, and he cried out as they drummed on his exposed knuckles as he raised his hands to protect his face.

By the time he reached the monastery, the marbles of ice had reverted to sleet. Breathless, sodden and miserable, he trudged up to his room, lit the lantern and then the circular radiator lamp on the floor, and collapsed onto the bed fully dressed, tempted to sleep where he lay. Some nagging feeling, though, made him uneasy. Despite his hasty entrance, he was aware that the room was not entirely as he had left it. Colder, yes, but there was something else. The picture had changed. He levered himself up onto his elbows. The first of the alterations was easily located, as his head had flopped down on it. The post corporal had been, leaving a foolscap package on his pillow. It took him a moment to spot the second: there was a mahogany box on the chair that sat beneath the tiny window.

He pushed off the bed and went over to this. He undid the two brass catches and lifted the lid. Inside was a gleaming, seemingly unused pistol. A Colt .45 1911, an automatic pistol, of the sort much coveted by young officers, being deemed more modern than a mere revolver. Watson had heard that complexity was its Achilles heel; that, in the gritty mud currently filling the trenches outside, such a lovely weapon might malfunction. But, as an old soldier who appreciated such things, he had to agree it was a sleek, handsome weapon.

There was a folded note with it, which he read.

You won't need wheels for this. And I cannot foresee me having much use for it. But just in case you ever run into any more gigantic hounds.

Apologies for my crassness earlier.

Caspar Myles

He couldn't accept it, of course. Not now, not after the way the American had spoken to him and his own petulant responses. Not that he bore Myles a grudge. Who could blame him for being suspicious of the blood? He wasn't certain that, had positions been reversed, he might have made similar accusations. Although he would have behaved with more temperance. Still, the pistol was a nice gesture.

Then it struck him. This over-generous gift pre-dated the confrontation about Shipobottom. The American had left this after the exchange over Staff Nurse Jennings. Well, he was certain Myles would accept it back now; he clearly thought Watson a bungler at best, a murderer at worst. But then Myles didn't know the two crucial pieces of information the night had given him. One was the markings revealed by his magnifying glass, scores that had been inflicted post mortem. And Myles did not know that Shipobottom was not the first to die like this. Mrs Gregson was adamant she had seen that grin and the blue skin before.

So the question to be answered was, superficially, simple: were there any similarities in the two deaths, Shipobottom's and the one seen by Mrs Gregson? Had the first victim had a blood transfusion? Was it possible that something in the environment of the trenches somehow reacted with elements in the blood to create a toxic condition that could not be duplicated in a laboratory or in the heat and dust of Egypt? After all, gas gangrene was a disease seemingly unique to Flanders and France, a product of fighting on and, perhaps more to the point, in heavily cultivated soils, rich in manure.

But the marks on the body? How to explain away those? The scoring he had found was definitely man-made.

Or woman-inflicted. Yes, or woman. Don't make the mistake of leaving out fifty per cent of suspects due to their sex.

Plus there was a third factor he had kept to himself. Shipobottom's eye had shown signs of blue flecking when he examined him at the Big House. *Before* the transfusion. Whatever had killed him had begun its work before he had received his fresh blood. If only he had mentioned the blue spots at the time; now it would seem like a retrospective revision, an attempt to shift the blame away from the blood.

Just for a second Watson felt his head spin.

This had been a pivotal skill for Holmes. The ability to hold a half-dozen scenarios in his mind at once, examining each one in detail, while maintaining a questioning overview of the whole case. It was akin to the ability that great chess players were believed to possess, the mental flexibility and acuity to analyse the strategic and tactical outcome of a great many potential moves. And Watson had always been a middling chess player. Cards were more his forte – nap, loo, piquet, poker. Games that relied on a hefty dose of chance, he reminded himself.

He closed the gun box and flipped down the catches. He would return it to Myles in the morning.

Next, he crossed over and, using his penknife, carefully slit open the packet, pulled out the magazine within and dropped it on the bed. What he saw looking back at him from the rough blankets made him reach for his cigarettes.

He smoked for some minutes before he finally flipped open the pages. The table of contents of the *British Bee Keepers' Journal* told him that on page 43, he should find the article trailed on the front: 'Towards an Understanding of the Worker Bee's Dance'. The article in question was credited – as had been proclaimed on the cover – to Mr Sherlock Holmes. However, in the more comprehensive listings within, it was noted that there was a co-author (the name in smaller type), a Thomas Patrick.

A co-author?

For a second Watson thought this might have been sent by some old adversary, taunting him, exulting in the broken partnership. He looked at the postmark. A Lewes stamp. And the envelope was San Remo, linen lined, which he knew was a favourite. And the gum? A scent of strong tobacco. No, it was no tease. It was from the retired detective himself.

He gaped the end of the envelope and peered in, then took the journal by the spine and shook it. No note or card fluttered out. He flicked the pages, searching for an inscription or notation. Nothing.

Thomas Patrick? Obviously some fellow apiarist. Reluctantly he turned to page 43, which was adorned with a large photograph of a crowded comb, over which white directional arrows had been super-imposed to represent the movements of one of the inhabitants of the hive. To the layman this was gobbledegook, like those beginners' guides to dancing that purported to show the foot movements. He read the first line of the article.

'My years of investigation as the world's only consulting detective . . .'

His years of investigating?

'. . . revealed nothing in the criminal annals that has been quite so baffling or exciting as trying to decipher the code of the humble honeybee.'

Hah. He could name a dozen cases that were intellectually the equal of . . .

'Yet during the past three years, my colleague and companion, Thomas Patrick . . .'

Well, really. That was just too much. Unforgivable. *Colleague and companion?* The man had set out to wound. And had done so.

'Despite the best efforts in the last century of august apiarists such as Leon Alberti and Auguste Kerckhoffs, the mechanism by which . . .'

Watson scanned the following pages, picking out words and phrases and sighing. Holmes had always been admirably succinct in speech; he could analyse and solve a conundrum and present the solution not only quickly but eloquently. But here, he was rambling and imprecise. Did this bee-lovers' rag not have an editor?

Watson took a deep breath. He was tired, emotional and, he had to accept, not a little jealous of the new collaborator. Who on earth was he? He could think of no intimate of that name and Holmes had never mentioned any enthusiasts he admired. Patrick? he said to himself, rolling the name around, like a kitten batting at a ball of yarn. Thomas Patrick? Holmes and Watson had always had a good, solid ring about it. But Holmes and Patrick? They sounded like bankers or a small-town firm solicitors of oaths. Perhaps even pawn-brokers. Anarchists.

He picked up the magazine, stuffed it carelessly back in the envelope and tossed it towards the chair, hardly caring when it missed and slid to the stone floor. He began to unbutton his tunic, eager for a wash and for sleep to come quickly without, he hoped, too many dreams of poor Shipobottom's distorted death mask. Or, for that matter, *Apis* bloody *mellifera*.

TWENTY-NINE

Watson did not dream of human gargoyles or of foraging honeybees. Instead, his exhausted and over-worked imagination took him back to their final meeting on the Downs. It was more like one of the popular newsreels than a dream, almost a verbatim account of what took place, apart from the colours. The green of the Sussex grass was of a far more intense hue than usual and the sky looked like a storm straight from Turner's brush, dashed with livid purples and scarlets. The order of the conversation was jumbled, too, but the sentiments intact.

On the day in question, Watson had called at the cottage. There had been a cold lunch accompanied by a glass each of Montrachet. Watson had given Holmes a present, a leather-bound, heavily illustrated treatise on the morphology of bees by René Antoine Ferchault de Réamur. Holmes had presented him with a handsome magnifying glass with a touching inscription. Then, a walk was proposed.

In the dream, as in reality, Holmes had stopped within sight of Firle Beacon and turned to face Watson. It was the first time the detective had spoken since they had left the cottage.

'I must say, you look quite dashing, Watson.'

'Thank you. Aquascutum does wonders for a man's figure. And you look well. A little thinner, perhaps.' Gaunt might be closer to the truth, he supposed. Holmes's skin had a chalky quality, as if minerals had leached out of the soil. He was dressed in a rough tweed jacket, with a matching hat that sported thick earflaps, and breeches with buttoned gaiters atop a pair of stout shoes. In his hand was the dark walking stick with a bulbous head known as a Penang lawyer.

'I am lacking Mrs Hudson's breakfasts, Watson. I have a girl but, alas . . .'

'And you are sufficiently busy? In the mind?'

He laughed, for he knew what the doctor was getting at. 'Fear not, Watson, the puzzle of the bees, and the extraction of the honey – remind me to give you a pot – are more than enough distraction from the seven per cent solution. You may search my cottage—'

Watson hooted. 'I have just seen your cottage. It would take a week to tidy the newspapers and the old files.'

'Ah, we have a routine. Once I can no longer make the front door unimpeded, my girl throws out whatever is on the floor. Now, Watson, I have a little proposal for you.'

He felt a *frisson* of the old excitement, those moments when the detective would look out of the bow window and announce a very curious visitor, or gather his flap-eared travelling cap and ask him to bring along his service revolver. But he sensed this would be something more prosaic. 'And that is?'

From now on the dream encounter followed exactly the real thing, the only addition by his unconscious being the broiling, rapidly darkening sky.

'If you tell me where your offices will be in Wiltshire, I shall endeavour to come across to that county once a week. Breakfast, lunch or dinner. A venue of your choosing.'

A gloom fell on Watson. It was an attractive offer. 'But I won't be based in Wiltshire.'

'No?' Holmes looked surprised. 'Aldershot, perhaps? That's not too far. Or London?' He sounded excited at the prospect.

'I have asked to go overseas. As part of a front line Medical Investigation Unit.'

The reaction was unexpected. His friend threw back his head and roared with laughter, his bony shoulders shaking. 'Don't be ridiculous, Watson,' he said at last.

'I am, as you have said before, an old campaigner.'

'With an emphasis on the old. Why, you were limping and wheezing before we were half-way here.'

Watson pointed at Holmes's Penang lawyer. 'I did not have a benefit of a stick.'

'This? An affectation. I have all my old energies and appetites intact. Come, Watson, you cannot be serious. Do you really want to go over there?' He pointed south with the stick and repeated a popular phrase from the current headlines. 'To rescue plucky little Belgium?'

Watson became aware of a crackling sound. There was a restless kite above their heads and, at the other end of it, a young lad looking disturbed at their cross words. Watson raised a hand in greeting, to show there was nothing to be concerned about, but the boy ignored the gesture and returned to wrestling with his aerial charge. Watson turned back to Holmes. 'You once said that this war would bring us a cleaner, better, stronger land.'

'And I believe that to be so. But war is a young man's business, Watson. And when you were young, you took two bullets for your country. Debt paid. In fact, you are very much in the black. You belong behind a desk.'

'If I were to spend the war in some stuffy Whitehall office, it would be me reaching for a seven per cent solution.'

'You never had that much imagination, Watson,' he said, somewhat cruelly. 'Let me tell you, as a dear friend, that you have never been the same since the death of Emily—'

'Of course. I loved her. It was a terrible waste. I grieved—'

'And grieve still. Oh, I know time is the great healer, and I bided that time. And bided. You became rash. Distracted. Sentimental. You wrote poetry, Watson. *Poetry.* And I tell you, this army nonsense is all too soon. I was worried about you at the time of that Von Bork business. How you moped those two years I was away. Oh, when you come to write it up, what will it be? His Last Case? I am sure you'll gloss over your own condition at that time. Let me tell you, it was cause for concern. And I am not sure the balance of your mind has yet recovered.'

'Because I wrote poetry?'

He pursed his lips. 'Not entirely. Although it isn't your forte.'

'Because I want to serve my country?'

He hissed his answer and banged his stick on the ground to back up the words. 'Because you want to put yourself in harm's way. Deliberately.'

'Now who is being ridiculous? For once your analytical powers fail you,' Watson declared. 'I am not hoping for release from this life. I am a doctor. I want to save lives. The lives of our soldiers.'

His face drained of blood, as if he was shocked at his skills being slighted. 'For goodness' sake, Watson, you were always the practical one in the partnership. You told me your surgical skills had slipped. You even put it in writing when reporting the Godfrey Staunton case.'

His memory was slightly faulty; Watson had admitted his once assiduous habit of keeping abreast with the very latest medical developments had fallen by the wayside somewhat. He had since remedied that. 'That's as may be, but there is more to being a medical man than the knife.'

'You told me there was a position at the War Department Experimental Grounds. Wiltshire, you said.'

'I did not like the type of work.'

'Well, I forbid it. I forbid you to go to war.'

This re-emergence of the old, infuriating high-handedness stunned Watson. 'You cannot.'

'Can't I?' The arrogant matter-of-factness of his next statement was even more exasperating. 'I shall write to the Director-General of Medical Services. I shall explain my misgivings about your mental health.'

Watson felt his vision cloud, and he was suddenly viewing the world down a long, dark tunnel. A hammering began in his temple. 'Should you do that, it would be the end of our friendship.'

A brittle silence thickened around them, save for the whistle of the wind off the sea and the snap of the kite.

'Very well,' Holmes said at last. With that, he turned and walked off the way they had come, stabbing at the ground with the Penang lawyer with each stride.

Watson was struck by the enormity of what had just happened, how a few cross words had escalated to the kind of impasse that could strain a relationship for years. For ever.

'Holmes!' he shouted at the retreating figure. 'Holmes! Come back, man.'

The kite-flyer was standing watching him, something like sympathy in his young eyes. Watson took three steps along the path and tried one last time, filling his lungs for a final bellow. 'Sherlock Holmes!'

But the long legs had done their work, the wind gusting across the Channel from France snatched at his words and the now distant detective showed no acknowledgement that he had heard.

WEDNESDAY

THIRTY

Despite such a vivid reminder of the parting of the ways, Watson awoke with a fresh energy. His mind, so clouded and woolly the night before, had sharpened overnight. The knots that had clustered behind his brow had dissolved. Brindle, who appeared to have suppressed his grief at his friend Lovat's death, arrived with hot tea, warm water, a fresh uniform and two white medical coats.

Watson thanked him and requested breakfast in his room, not being ready to confront what was sure to be a Mess that had already set its face against him and his transfusions. Nor did he want to spar with Caspar Myles just yet. Not until he had more ammunition.

While he waited for his eggs and toasted bread to arrive – plus, he hoped, bacon and perhaps some tomatoes – Watson wrote in his notebook. He had been very remiss in his questioning of the various individuals who had encountered poor Shipobottom at one stage or other of his illness. He needed a timetable of events. Plus a note of all who had been alone with the deceased for any length of time. He then wrote down a full account of all that had happened to him since his arrival in the CCS. Not, as he once did, for posterity, but because he felt certain he would be called to account for his actions at some stage, and as Ho—

— and as he knew, even the most trivial details might turn out to be important.

Especially the trivial details, came the soothing voice. But he wasn't listening to ghosts. Not today.

Once breakfast had been dispatched, along with more tea, Watson found himself pom-pomming Tchaikovsky's Third as he hurried down towards the transfusion tent. The weather looked to have settled in as uniformly dreary. A slate-grey cap sat over Northern France and Benelux, and the rain, while not quite as punishing as the previous night, was steady and chill.

Wrapped in his Aquascutum, he slithered along paths that were now filmed with treacherous mud. Here, the stuff was brown, with the consistency of caramel, stretchy and sticky. Down the road, it was yellow and slimy. Elsewhere it was a grey-greenish fluid, viscous like rice pudding, and in yet other places it was black and putrid and dried into a coating as hard and brittle as toffee. 'Mud' hardly did the malleable substance justice. He had read Captain Scott's account of his last journey and how he catalogued the various states that ice and snow could adopt. Watson thought they needed a similar vocabulary for the liquid soil of Flanders.

Once inside the tent, he divested himself of his coat and tunic and began to look around. The body, its torment now hidden within a stitched blanket, was where he had left it. But it wasn't the deceased that interested him for the moment.

Instead, he began to test the walls of the tent, looking for rents or ventilation openings. He knew only too well that death could enter a room in many ways, through a false ceiling, a ventilation shaft, a trap door. But there was little to suggest anything of the sort here. True, someone could lift up the skirts of the tent and come in, but the rain had done its best to remove anything that might be helpful in that regard. Still, he went over the ground, looking for incriminating imprints, just in case. No stone unturned, as he told himself.

Afterwards, his back aching from all the bending, he sat on one of the empty cot-beds. It had been foolish to think a solution would spring out at him fully formed. But there was one aspect he could eliminate very easily indeed.

He stood and crossed to where the Icehouse box stood on a trestle table. He twisted the two barrel-locks and opened it. To his relief a wash of cold air hit him in the face. Most of the ice had melted, but only just: the temperature had not risen above . . . he looked at the dial thermometer . . . thirty-nine degrees. One short of the maximum. He would have to refill it shortly.

From the cold cavity he extracted one of the glass bottles and then resealed the lid of the box. Watson was a group IV, a universal donor – his blood could be given to anyone with relative safety – but he could only receive a transfusion from his own kind. Fortunately, IV was well represented in the population, and he actually had two 500cc samples of it. He quickly located a sterilized cannula and was rolling up his sleeve when he became aware that someone was watching him.

'What do you think you are doing?'

Staff Nurse Jennings stood close to the entrance, the bottom of her long grey woollen coat weighted with fresh mud. She was wearing gumboots several sizes too large, with her regular shoes in her hand.

When he didn't reply, she said: 'I heard all about the incident with the sergeant. What use is it testing the blood on yourself, Major?'

'Every use.'

'But it might have been one contaminated batch.'

He finished rolling up his sleeve. 'All samples were treated equally, Staff Nurse Jennings.'

She took off her coat and slid out of the gumboots. 'But what if . . . ?' Her eyes darted towards the canvas-shrouded corpse. 'What if it does that to you? If you start to fit?'

A fatalistic shrug. 'Then I have my service revolver in my coat pocket.'

'Major!'

He gave a smile he hoped was reassuring. 'I am not serious. I am absolutely confident that I am in no danger. Check my pockets. There is no revolver.'

She looked relieved.

'Why are you here, Staff Nurse?'

'I was asked by Mrs Gregson to find you. With this.'

She handed him a grey papyrus Regia envelope. His name was written, in a lovely copperplate, on the front. 'Where is she?'

'Gone back to Bailleul.'

'The foolish woman,' he snapped. 'I needed her here. And Miss Pippery? Has she fled the coop also?'

'No. She is with Sister Spence. I fear her nerves are shot.'

'Good, good. I mean that she is here, not about her nerves. I shall need to question her later.' He stuffed the letter into his trouser pocket, still wondering how Mrs Gregson could be so selfish. 'Well, Staff Nurse, I was going to carry out this procedure for my own personal satisfaction, but, fortuitously, it appears you can be my witness.'

He began to lay out the necessary paraphernalia for his transfusion of blood.

'I'm not entirely certain—'

He spun around. 'Staff Nurse, I will do this either with or without you. You can always leave. I only ask that you tell none of the others what is occurring just yet. But if you are staying for my venesection, I need you to make a two-inch incision above my median basilic vein to expose it.'

He was slightly perplexed by the forcefulness of his tone. It had echoes of a decisiveness that was usually quite alien to him. He supposed because he had to accept that there was no leader to follow now. He was no longer the shadow, the sidekick, the note-taker, the foil. No more rhetorical 'What would Sherlock do?' questions for Watson. It was a time for standing on his own two feet. And enjoying it, he added.

'You would trust a nurse with surgery?' She was genuinely perplexed. A doctor allowing a subordinate to wield the knife was unheard of.

'I would trust you.'

She gave a solemn nod and straightened her headdress. 'If you are to be my patient, please sit on the bed here. Do we need to warm the blood, as it has been on ice?'

The question seemed naïve, but he remembered this was all new to her. 'No. It makes negligible impact on core temperature. '

'And how much will you require?'

'Five hundred cc should be enough.'

'A local analgesic might be in order.'

'There's eugenol. In the cupboard there. And, more pertinently, a bottle of brandy at the rear.'

After she had painted his arm with the solution and poured him a tumbler of the alcohol, she prepared a tray with sutures, scalpels, syringes, iodoform and tubing. He admired the precision and neatness of her display.

'How long have you been with the service, Staff Nurse Jennings?'

'Almost six years. Well before war was declared. My elder brother died in St Kitts and we came back to England. There was money from the sale and my father set up in business. It was all a terrible shock after the Caribbean. There, at least, there was some freedom from convention. You have no idea how proscribed the life of a young woman from a well-to-do family in Didcot is, Major. All laid out, from cradle to grave. To be frank, being a Territorial meant at least a few weeks' a year escape from Mother and Father and their endless introductions to suitable young men. It was a very mild rebellion. I never had it in me to become a suffragette like your Mrs Gregson. I was too cowardly, I think. '

'Mrs Gregson told you she was a suffragette?'

She smiled a smile that suggested shared secrets. 'She didn't have to.'

'No. I think it's written through her like a stick of rock,' he laughed.

'I think she and I got off to a bad start.'

'We've had our rocky moments. She doesn't always choose the smooth path.'

Jennings seemed to want to say something else, but apparently thought better of it and turned her attention to the job in hand.

'And was there a suitable young man?' he asked.

She stopped unscrewing the top of the Lysol bottle, as if considering how to answer.

'Since you ask, yes. There was. Is. But he released me from any understanding until after the war.'

'That's very considerate of him. Many young men have insisted on a formal engagement before leaving. Or a wedding.'

She arched an eyebrow. 'If there is one thing Mother won't stand for, it's a quick wedding. She's been planning it for more than two decades now. I think we're ready for you, Major.'

'And what about Dr Myles?'

'What about him?'

'He seems rather struck on you.'

'Really? I hadn't noticed.' She began to move the items on her tray around at random.

'Forgive me for asking, but it has been preying on my mind. Has he made any suggestions that might compromise you profession-ally?' Watson asked.

She fluttered her eyelids at him in a deliberately exaggerated way. 'What kind of suggestions, Major Watson?'

'You know exactly what I mean. Improper suggestions.'

His nostrils filled with the smell of cloves from the eugenol. He took a mouthful of the brandy and gave a small cough as it attacked his throat. Not the finest.

'Keep still now. Arm over this bowl. There'll be blood.'

'I'm counting on it.'

She hovered over the skin. He could see the tip of the scalpel shaking. 'Don't be tentative.' He flinched as the blade entered the skin and the first deep red globules formed.

'Improper by my standards or Sister Spence's, Major?' she asked, more to distract him than anything else.

'Either. Ouch. I think that incision is long enough. You need to go deeper now.'

She worked for a few moments in silence, her forehead lined in concentration, the tip of her tongue showing between her teeth. 'All right, Major, that's exposed. I don't mean to be rude, but I'm not sure Dr Myles is any of your concern. Not away from medical matters. Remember, I joined the Territorials to get away from suffocating parents. The world has moved on, you know.'

He suddenly felt like an over-protective grandfather. 'You're right. My apologies. But my background has made me insufferably inquisitive. And I wouldn't want anything . . .' He cleared his throat again. 'Right, back to the business at hand. You need to insert a traction ligature, to close the vein when we are done.'

Her hands were steady now and she did as she was told. 'I'm ready to put in the first syringe. Are you entirely certain you wish to proceed?'

'It is the only way to convince some people that my blood didn't kill Shipobottom.'

'Nobody could really think that, surely.'

'Possibly in preference to the alternative.'

'Which is?' she asked.

Watson hesitated to answer. It didn't do to spread suspicions as if scattering seeds on a ploughed field. But he was trusting her with this procedure, which meant, subconsciously, he believed her to be untainted by these incidents. 'That there is a murderer in our midst. Someone who is not only making sure that the victim suffers, but takes care to mark the victim, as if keeping a tally. A person who thinks the war is simply not killing our young men fast enough.'

'My goodness. A German spy?' she asked.

'My first thought. But, no. Where is the advantage for a spy? Unless Shipobottom was a source of important intelligence? I suspect he could tell the enemy where the regimental rum ration was stored and how much each barrel contained to the nearest tot. But anything more than that . . . no, whoever did this is someone from our own side. And murdering for reasons we can't, as yet, even guess at.'

'Golly,' was all she could manage this time.

'So let us eliminate the citrated blood as a contributory factor, eh?'

The eugenol was a poor analgesic, as he had expected, and his arm was rippling with pain, but he clenched his jaw. She inserted the cannula into the glistening cylinder of the vein and slowly pressed the plunger. The walls bulged alarmingly as the blood flowed in.

'That's nothing to worry about.'

'Dr Myles did invite me out to accompany him. To a dance. But I am afraid I had to disappoint him. Sister Spence has an attack of the vapours at the very mention of the word. So he has asked me to dinner in town. In Armentières, no less. He claims the normal rules of fraternization do not apply, as he is not an officer in any army.'

'And what did you say?'

'Second syringe now. Are you comfortable, Major?'

Comfortable wasn't the word he would have chosen. He looked up into her young face, as yet unlined, her blue eyes clear and shining. Mary had not been much older when he first laid eyes on her. It was easy to see why the soldiers fell in love with these young girls. After the rough horrors of the trenches, the debasements and the deaths, the bellowing and cursing and petty squabbles, the gas and the constant, debilitating shelling, these pristine visions of womanhood really must seem like angels, come down to walk among men and minister to their every earthly need. He shook his head. It was possible those clove fumes were addling his brain. 'A little more brandy when you are between infusions.'

'Certainly. And I told Dr Myles I would not even contemplate a dinner this evening without a chaperone.'

'Well said, Staff Nurse. And whom did you nominate as your protector?'

'You, Major Watson.'

Twenty minutes later, as they were resterilizing the equipment, Watson felt the first prickles of fever on his forehead.

THIRTY-ONE

Bloch remembered little about how he had reached his own lines and been evacuated away from the front. He had avoided being shot by his own side, he recalled that much. A collapse into an officer's arms. Alcohol forced between his lips. Then a café in a shattered street, hardly a wall standing, the floor tiles covered with straw to soak up the blood. Then an ambulance transfer to the building where he was now, something approaching a normal hospital. It was close to a railway; he had heard the clank and huffing of the trains through the night. It was said the wounded were always moved back to Germany after dark. That the sight of the maimed might be bad for civilian morale at home.

The men in Bloch's immediate vicinity seemed lightly wounded, although the infantryman next to him was a *Pfeifer* – a whistler – who had received a throat wound. It was most likely the type of wound that would take him home. He hoped so. He wouldn't last five minutes in a trench dugout making an irritating noise like that. Someone would finish the job the Tommies had started.

Bloch shuffled up in bed and took in more of his surroundings.

The rectangular room was subdivided by wooden screens, either to shield the badly wounded from the lightly injured, or officers from other ranks. The enormous floor-to-ceiling windows were criss-crossed with blast tape. There were dark coloured squares and oblong panels on the heavy wallpaper, the phantom remains of portraits and landscapes that had once graced the spaces. Two enormous chandeliers, mostly intact, were still in place. He supposed they were too difficult to remove for safe storage. It was, he would imagine, a former dining room. From hosting sumptuous dinners to collecting the deformed and the damaged, it was quite a fall from grace for such an elegant space.

He ran his hands over his face, wincing as he touched unfamiliar protuberances beneath the bandages that masked the centre of his face. His tongue found the gaps in his previously perfect teeth. They were enormous, like canyons. His left hand had the little finger splinted and strapped to its neighbour. At least he could hear now, although occasionally there were high-pitched whistles, of the kind that *Pfeifer* was making, but seemingly generated from within his cranium.

A *Frontschwester*, one of the front-line nurses, strode past and he shouted for her. She looked down at the porcelain container in her hand and indicated, with a wrinkle of her pretty nose, she needed to dispose of something within it first.

He watched her go, a tall, broad-shouldered girl with, beneath her cap, corn-coloured curls. The *Feldpuffordnung* – the widely circulated, semi-official guide to setting up a field brothel – suggested that there was no need for any such facility if there was a hospital staffed with Red Cross nurses nearby. This, part of him thought, was a terrible slander. On the other hand, he had heard all the dugout tales of comely *Frontschwestern* using unconventional means to nurse a man back to health or raise morale.

The thought caused an unfamiliar movement against his leg and he shifted uneasily when the nurse returned, as if she could see through the blankets that covered him. She examined the piece of card pinned above his bed and asked: 'How can I help, Unteroffizier Bloch?'

A thick Swabian accent, also strangely erotic. He was beginning to see how such stories about nurses' behaviour could arise.

'Is something funny?'

'No, forgive me. I was just thinking . . . you remind me of my girlfriend back home. Hilde.'

'That's odd,' she said solemnly.

'What is?'

'You must be, oh, the hundredth man today to tell me that.' She smiled and the tops of her cheeks bulged, like tiny, rosy apples. 'I apparently look like every Olga and Heidi and Karin and Erna—'

'I'm sorry. I bet you do remind us soldiers of all those girls.'

'Only because I am a woman. Any German woman would remind you boys of home. I can't blame you. This war . . .' the sentence tailed off. 'And you soldiers aren't too fussy.'

'What's your name?'

'My name is Nurse,' she said, although not in an entirely unfriendly way. 'Now what was it you wanted?'

'Where am I now, exactly?'

'A château to the north of Menin. Now Field Hospital Number 19. Is that all?'

'A mirror.'

She shook her head, as if he had asked for the moon. 'Why on earth would you want that?'

He touched his face. 'To see what they've done to me.'

'You can't see anything because of the dressings. And there is bruising. Swelling, too. Wait a few days. You don't look too bad.'

'I'd say it was an improvement.' Hauptmann Lux, turned out as if for the Kaiser's birthday parade in dress uniform with medals, stepped from behind her. He had a canvas bag slung over his shoulder that he placed at the foot of the bed. 'Staff Nurse? Do you mind?'

She gave a small curtsy and left. Lux stared at him for a few moments before speaking.

'Well, Bloch, I've seen worse.' He took off his gloves, leaned in and parted the sharpshooter's lips, as if inspecting a horse. 'I'll have the section dentist sent over. That is one area in which we have the advantage of the enemy. They don't bring dentists to the front. Mind you, have you seen their teeth? Probably a waste of time.'

Bloch found it hard to share in the joke. A few less dentists, a few more snipers wouldn't go amiss, he thought.

'Now, do you feel strong enough to report?'

Bloch thought he meant for duty, but he then realized that Lux wanted a verbal account of his action. 'Of course, sir.' He took a sip of water and gave a concise but detailed recap of his adventures from the moment he went out into no man's land with the *Patrouillentrupp* until his return almost twenty-four hours later. Lux listened in silence for the most part, interrupting only when Churchill appeared and cursing when Bloch described the bombardment that firstly ruined his aim and then brought down the church tower.

'Remarkable. I owe you an apology, Bloch.'

'Sir?'

'I did not know about the artillery barrage in that sector. Nobody did. Or I would not have sent you out. That is the trouble with this army. The right hand does not know what the left is doing and neither of them have a clue what the air force is up to. You know those idiots bombed one of the British casualty stations the other day? I think they thought the red crosses on the roof were target markers.' He shook his head in despair. Such folly led to tit-for-tat raids; before they knew where they were, the Red Cross symbol would be meaningless. 'But you did well. And the sergeant you eradicated for his uniform? That counts as half a kill. Twenty-nine and a half points. No Iron Cross, I am afraid, but perhaps some leave once you feel well enough? How does forty-eight hours sound?'

Not long enough, Bloch thought. With military rail traffic given priority it could take that to get back to Düsseldorf. 'That's very generous, sir.'

Perhaps he could arrange for Hilde to meet him half-way? That might be possible. He would write as soon as this stuffed shirt had gone.

'Don't mention it. And I have something else for you.' He reached down into the canvas bag and brought out an object swaddled in soft cloth. He handed it over. Bloch unwrapped it. It was a telescopic sight, although the distal end was enormous, almost the size of a saucer.

'What is it?'

'The new Voigtländer illuminated night sight,' Lux said with pride, as if he himself had crafted it. 'We have permission to undertake field trials. With and without atropine as a mydriatic.'

Atropine eye drops – extracted from deadly nightshade – were used to dilate a sniper's pupils, increasing the amount of light to reach the retinae. The disadvantage was that the user became very susceptible to glare and losing his night vision altogether. It also caused blurred vision and heart palpitations if you weren't careful. Bloch was not an admirer.

He peered through the eyepiece and moved the sights so that the cross hairs rested squarely in the middle of his superior's face. 'Heavy,' he said.

'It's worth it, believe you me.'

'I'll need a new rifle, sir.'

'Of course. And ammunition. No more home-made efforts, Bloch. The new *Spitzgeschoss mit Stahlkern* round is armour piercing. A fresh Mauser Gewehr rifle, those bullets and the scope and I'm sure that Iron Cross will be yours any day now.'

'I'm sorry about Churchill, sir.'

'Ach, do not worry about that. You've proved a special kind of man can get behind enemy lines and back again, with the right planning. You missed him this time. There'll be another. Eh, Bloch? We'll get him next time.'

But Bloch didn't answer. He was too busy looking at the damaged stranger reflected in the unforgiving glass of the telescopic sight.

THIRTY-TWO

'Murder?' Torrance rolled the word around his tongue, as if it assessing a fine claret. 'Murder? Have you taken leave of your senses?'

Watson shifted in his chair. They were in Torrance's office, a room that had once been the abbot's sanctum. It was lined on three sides with bookshelves, all empty apart from a few military manuals, with the fourth wall taken up almost entirely by mullioned windows that overlooked the nearest tents of the CCS. Dense sheets of rain obscured the rest.

'Yes, that's correct.'

'Are you all right, Watson? You don't look too good.'

'Just a small post-transfusion reaction. I'm feeling better by the minute.' He mopped his brow. 'It isn't unusual. I suspect our method of cross-matching blood is a touch crude and sometimes our bodies remind us of this fact.'

'A transfusion? Why have you had a blood transfusion?'

'To demonstrate that whatever caused the death of Shipobottom was not related to the blood I gave him. I considered every aspect, and can think of no other explanation than that the man was murdered.'

Torrance began to quake. A ripple ran through his body, his shoulders heaved and he let out a great blast of laughter. 'Why on earth would anyone want to murder the already dead? Every man sent back up the line is likely to die within weeks or months. We lost 1,500 men at the battle of Mons, then 80,000 at Marne a month later. Total Allied casualties at Ypres? About 150,000. The British alone lost 50,000 at Loos. How many do you think will perish in the next big push? Five thousand a day? Ten? Twenty? There is murder, Watson, on an unprecedented scale, but it isn't happening in forgotten little aid stations behind the lines.'

His face had gone quite red and he began to excavate his briar with a pocketknife.

Watson was having none of it. 'Don't you see, that this is the perfect place for a murder? Bodies, dead bodies, have lost all currency. They matter not one jot. Stabbed, shot, gassed, blown to smithereens, rotted away from gangrene – there are so many ways to take a life, they have lost any value. I have only been here a few days and I feel it happening to myself. The care and compassion we would have over one lost soul has been swept away. We doctors always run the risk of becoming inured to suffering. But here, that impunity is the only way to survive and keep your sanity. And against that backdrop, in the midst of this indifference, it would be so easy to commit a murder.'

Torrance looked unimpressed. 'I ask again, why? Why go to such lengths when, as we agree, the odds are that this conflict will take the victim at some point anyway.'

This was the important question. Who profits from the act? No real answer had yet presented itself. 'Perhaps the murderer wanted to be certain of the man's death. Dear God, some of our youth must survive this war; nobody can be one hundred per cent sure of any one man's demise. Perhaps he wants to, needs to, witness the event for himself. Or, indeed herself. It is also possible that it is important to the perpetrator that the victim knows who is killing him and why.'

Torrance tapped the bowl into a saucer, making a cone of ash. 'That smacks of melodrama, Watson, not fact. A field in which you are something of an expert, or so I hear. Never read any of your stuff myself. But I am of the opinion this was a form of tetanus. An involuntary muscle spasm, a lockjaw. I admit the symptoms were peculiar in their strength, but I have seen many strange things since I came out here. Things beyond reason. Who knows if it wasn't a delayed reaction to gas? Or a rat bite? They have become monsters, feeding on the dead. Or perhaps something from the damned lice they all carry. Now, if you tell me that I should keep an eye out for similar occurrences, I would agree. But murder? You want me to call in the Military Police, do you?'

Watson spoke more calmly this time, but still with conviction. 'It is not tetanus. The cyanosis tells us that. There are no breaks in the skin consistent with a rat bite. I have seen rat bites, by an animal as unfeasibly large as they grow in the trenches, albeit a type native to Sumatra. Unmistakable. There were no such marks. The symptoms we witnessed, Major, are called *Risus sardonicus*, the sardonic grin. Although this seems to be a peculiarly powerful version of it. It is the result of an alkaloid poison. I have come across these toxins before. I had hoped never to do so again.' Watson didn't want to go into details of the case known at The Sign of Four. That would involve thinking about Mary again, and he needed to stay focused on this case, not dwell on his past.

'If — and I mean *if* — there has been a murder, whom do you suspect?' asked Torrance.

'I need to question Miss Pippery further, to establish a time sequence and who had the opportunity to enter the tent. But, of course, the poison might have been administered prior to him entering the transfusion tent. It could be a slow-acting toxin. I saw blue flecks in the white of Shipobottom's eye earlier that morning. It might have been the first expression of the symptoms.'

'In other words, you have not the faintest idea.'

Watson wiped his brow once more. How he wished at this moment he could have said, with the confidence of a Holmes, that he had all the pieces of the puzzle in hand and merely needed a few hours to complete the picture. But it would have been a downright lie. 'No, but I am confident—'

'And you have a motive?'

'Not yet.'

'Did this Shipobottom have any obvious enemies?'

'He seemed to be well liked. I need to question his platoon.'

'*You* need to question?' Torrance demanded. 'By whose authority?'

That was a good point. He and Holmes had always assumed every right to investigate on behalf of clients. In the army, though, it was different. Who was the client? Shipobottom was hardly in a position to give his permission to investigate. 'Well, perhaps we should call in the Military Police then.'

Torrance began to stuff tobacco into his pipe with some force. 'My dear Watson, I am sure life as a blood doctor is dull compared with your old adventures. I am afraid you have a case of over-active imagination. Not everything we can't explain is a crime. And you are not a policeman or even a detective. You are a member of the Royal Army Medical Corps.'

'And as an RAMC doctor, I need to clear the reputation of the citrated blood process. I am not looking for extra adventure, Major Torrance. How many volunteers as either donors or recipients do you think we'll get when the rumours start to fly about the manner of Shipobottom's end?'

'All the more reason not to make a song and dance about one, single unexplained death amongst so many.' He pointed the stem of his pipe at Watson. 'I want that body disposed of as soon as possible.'

'You aren't inclined to contact the Military Police?'

'On such flimsy evidence?'

'Are you worried about Field Marshal Haig's visit?'

Torrance twitched as if he had stepped on a live wire and Watson knew he had hit a nerve. The thought of the CCS being overrun by MPs and the shadow of an unsolved murder – with a grisly corpse to boot – hanging over it was not one he relished.

'I am more worried about you making a fool of yourself.'

Watson, though, was not yet out of ammunition. 'There was another curious aspect of this case. There were small incisions on the chest. Quite tiny, and not difficult to overlook with the naked eye. But they were easily spotted under a magnifying glass. I suspect the scores were made post mortem, as there was little or no blood.' Watson reached over and grabbed a pencil, sketching the marks in the column of a report. He held it up. 'Like this. Does this suggest anything to you?'

IV

'Is it a symbol?'

'Yes. A Roman symbol. It is the number four. Do you see? The Roman numeral for four. It just so happens the downstroke is longer than the V.'

'Which suggests what exactly?' Torrance asked, lighting his pipe and sucking loudly, generating a sudden billow of blue-grey smoke.

'I think, Major Torrance, we have been witness to victim number four.'

Torrance looked cross. 'Meaning?'

'Meaning, it rather raises the question, who were victims number one, two and three?'

THIRTY-THREE

Mrs Gregson was only too aware that if she reported to her sister-in-charge or matron, she would be assigned duties immediately. So she avoided her old wards, which wasn't difficult. Bailleul Hospital had once been a sprawling sanatorium housing TB sufferers from across Belgium. As well as the formidably gothic bulk of the main house, the grounds held a dozen isolation cottages and exercise and rehabilitation centres. It was to one of these latter single-storey buildings, now called the Notifications and Effects Department, that she headed.

The main N&ED operation took place in a single large room, containing rows and rows of open metal shelving, stacked high with boxes of belongings of the deceased. A team of orderlies worked at low wooden benches, packaging and sending on the deceased's effects, either back to the regiment or the next of kin. The process generated a prodigious amount of paperwork, which was stored in the old gymnasium next door. Somewhere within the bureaucracy of those adjacent rooms was the confirmation she was looking for. That Shipobottom was not the only soldier to have died with a dreadful grin on his face.

Overseeing the N&ED was a mono-headed Cerberus of a warrant officer, Arthur Lang, who occupied a desk that all but blocked the opening where double doors once stood, barring entry to the main room.

Lang was the kind of man, Mrs Gregson knew, who thought women should be kept on a leash just long enough to enable them to shuffle from hearth to bed and back again. He had a moustache that dipped and rose again on each side, so it looked like the letter 'w', and beady, suspicious eyes the colour of coal tar. They had sparred in the past when he had discovered her background. He clearly read the popular press, for he remembered her nickname, the Red She-Devil. She thought all that had been forgotten with the war. Apparently not.

'Well, Mrs Gregson,' he said, raising an eyebrow. 'It's been a while since we saw you down here. And empty-handed. Have people stopped dying on your rounds?'

VADs usually brought down the cardboard boxes of meagre belongings for cataloguing.

'I am afraid not. Death hasn't taken a holiday. I was simply reassigned for a few days.'

'And you missed me, did you?'

'Only your wit and good looks.'

He beamed. 'Oh, there's more to me than that.'

'That's not what Mrs Lang tells me.'

He sniggered at this. 'Well, I have missed you, Mrs Gregson. For all the wrong reasons. What can I do for you?'

'I need to check up on a case history. See the copy of the death certificate. You'll have it on file.'

He snapped his fingers at her.

'What is it?'

'You'll have a doctor's enquiry docket?'

'No, it's a very simple matter—'

'And so is a docket. Signed by a doctor. It's a question of confidentiality.'

'I don't need anything confidential,' Mrs Gregson said. 'Surely it's a matter of public record.'

He leaned forward and lowered his voice. 'Everything here is confidential, Mrs Gregson. We have to allow them some dignity in death. We can't allow any Tom, Dick or She-Devil to come rifling. Can we? How do we know you aren't working for some gutter newspaper, looking to see what became of Lord So-and-so?'

She looked over his head. She daydreamed about breaking in at night, accessing the gymnasium, and stealing away without leaving a trace. Like something out of Angela Brazil, she concluded, and about as likely.

She made eye contact with Lang, wondering if she had the nerve to lift up the ashtray and crown him with it, then bully the others into handing over the document. But threatening them with a loaded ashtray was hardly an effective strategy.

'Please?' Mrs Gregson asked.

'No.'

'Just this once.'

'You aren't entitled.'

'What about a dirty postcard then?'

His eyes narrowed with suspicion. 'A what?'

'A mucky picture. About a tanner. Isn't that the going rate? Two bob for the really filthy stuff.'

His moustache twitched and two fiery red spots appeared high on his cheeks. 'I don't know what you are talking about.'

'There's an orderly on Spyon ward. Gordon is the name. Got a pocket full of them. Shall we go and ask him where he gets them from?'

He looked over his shoulder, to see if any his subordinates had heard, but they carried on with their morbid tasks, oblivious to her accusation. 'Mrs Gregson, I assure you—'

'Oh, come on, Mr Lang. I have done the night rounds. It's all you men can talk about. What Fifi or Trixie does or doesn't do with your little gentleman. The special tricks that the French girls have. And the Belgians . . . well, they could show the English rose a thing or two about pricks. I've heard it all. Including how you can buy saucy French postcards. No questions asked about where they came from. But we know, don't we?'

He swallowed hard.

She smiled, enjoying his discomfort. 'I bet Mrs Lang isn't familiar with that sort of thing.'

'You leave Mrs Lang out of this,' he hissed. 'Now look,' another glance over his shoulder, 'it's true that many of the deceased have, what shall we say, inappropriate material in their belongings. What would you have me do? Send pictures of your Trixie with her underwear and worse showing to his mother, sister, wife or sweetheart? With a little note saying, "Look what we found in Albert's backpack", eh?'

'No, and it is very considerate of you to remove it from the effects. But you are supposed to incinerate them. Not resell them around the wards.'

'You're bluffing. You can't prove a thing,' he said with a leer. 'And you can suck my big fat cock.'

If it was an attempt to intimidate or shock it was a very poor one,

Mrs Gregson thought. She had, after all, been both a married woman and a front-line nurse. 'No, but I can make sure the racket is squashed once and for all, can't I? And although that's a very generous offer, I am in a hurry.'

He had to laugh at her insouciance in the face of his deliberate crudity. He had reduced other nurses to trembling tears with less.

'Or I'll go straight to Matron with a complaint about the magic postcards that keep reappearing. Like most matrons sent to the continent, Elizabeth Challenger was a force to be reckoned with.

Lang took a deep, nervous breath and came to a decision. 'Very well. But if I do this and you drop me in it—'

'Why would I? Even She-Devils have their standards. A promise is a promise. Now, it was a soldier who died about ten days ago. He turned blue. He had this look on his face. Of horror.'

'That doesn't narrow it down. Almost every man can summon up one horror or another. Anything else?' There was a hint of impatience in his voice.

She racked her brains for more details. On an overworked ward, with men in need of constant attention, the dead were quickly dismissed. Only the strange colour and the twisted features had caused her to pause, and then just for a moment. Because she'd had to . . . yes, see the show.

'It was the night of the Gasmaskers. You know, the entertainment.'

The Gasmaskers were an all-male troupe of singers, dancers and mime artists, many of whom specialized in dressing as fetching women. They toured hospitals and reserve lines with their sub-music-hall routines. 'He died just before their show.'

'Lucky man. I had to sit through it. I can look at the deaths on that date in the ward logbooks. You did log it?'

'Sister did.'

'As?'

She frowned again. They had wondered how to classify the death. 'Kidney failure, I think.'

'And which ward?'

'I was on Nelson then.'

'Wait here.' He pushed back from the desk, stood and marched towards the entrance of the gymnasium.

She gave a shudder as he left. Somehow the image of what he had suggested she do to him wouldn't be shifted. The last eighteen months had given her a thick carapace and a robust vocabulary that enabled her to spar with the worst of them. That didn't mean she enjoyed it. Descending to their level always made her feel she needed a shower and a scrub with Lysol.

Lang returned, his face having regained its usual pallor. He placed a buff folder on the desk. 'You have one minute.'

Mrs Gregson fixed him with a defiant stare. This, she knew, was dangerous. Lang was not a man who liked to be bettered. She suspected that somewhere down the line, he would find a way to make her pay for this small victory. But, for the moment, she had the upper hand.

Lang gave a harrumphing sound and went off to check on his clerks and sorters, while she leafed through the documents. It was him all right. Edward Hornby by name. Nineteen. Kidney failure.

My left foot, she thought, as she read the description of the symptoms. The blue colour, though, was not mentioned. Nor the claw-like hands. She *had* seen both of those things. Hadn't she? Then she saw something that really did link Shipobottom and Hornby.

She closed the folder. Then she opened it again, glanced up to make sure Lang was still occupied, and ripped the top off the second sheet of paper and then the bottom of the third page. She folded the fragments and slipped them into her pocket.

'Oy!' Lang shouted as she picked up her coat and put it over her head, ready to face the rain.

She tried hard to stop her face burning with guilt.

'Quite finished with that, have you?' he asked.

'I have, yes.'

'And you goin' to sneak off without a by-your-leave?'

'Not at all. Thank you,' she said pushing the folder back across towards him. He picked it up.

Don't open it. Please don't open it.

Lang glanced down at it, ran a thumb across the cover.

'I'm sorry,' she blurted. 'If I was a bit of a bully. Terribly rude of me.'

He savoured the apology for a moment before replying. 'I hope it was worth it.'

She could feel the purloined strips of paper in her pocket. They felt as heavy as a bag of steel washers. *So do I.*

'You might have helped solve a crime. I'll tell you when I have all the facts. But if we do, it will be in no small thanks to you, Arthur.' The flattery sounded as false as a ninepence piece, but he didn't seem to notice.

'A crime? Well, well.' He held up Hornby's records. 'I better put this back safe and sound, then, eh?'

You stupid woman. That's guaranteed he will look now. And notice the damage.
She had to get away and quickly.

'Please. And, Arthur . . . ?'

'Yes?'

'You don't know anyone with a spare motor bike, do you?'

THIRTY-FOUR

The sky apparently had no more moisture left to give and by early afternoon the clouds had thinned, leaving the landscape glistening and dripping. Watson and Brindle had moved the body of Shipobottom to one of the cellars in the monastery, using a wheeled stretcher, and Watson sent a disingenuous message to Torrance to say that the corpse had, indeed, been disposed of. The vaulted subterranean room was chill enough that decomposition should be delayed for a while.

Watson then spent twenty frustrating minutes talking to Miss Pippery, who appeared to have lost her conception of time thanks to her witnessing the traumatizing manner of Shipobottom's death. However, it gave him a rough idea of how the sergeant's last day had progressed. There was one thing to eliminate, however: the possibility that someone had poisoned him before he received the transfusion, as the blue flecks in his eye suggested. And something else to consider: a motive for murdering Sergeant Shipobottom.

He borrowed a bicycle from one of the orderlies and set off for

Suffolk Farm. It was hard pedalling. The access lane from the CCS was a quagmire and had been laid with boards for the ambulances, but these had become slick and slippery, so it was a very unsteady Watson who reached the main road and turned left.

A low sun was worrying the clouds and he soon began to feel warm beneath his tunic and Aquascutum. There was plenty of traffic and he passed three lorry parks, which acted as marshalling areas, sending the trucks out over the whole of the Ypres area, transporting men and materials to near the front, where they would take the final journey under cover of darkness. But horses were still the backbone of any local transport, as testified by the frequent mounds of dung he did his best to skirt.

He passed a field of pack mules, no doubt turned out for some well-earned rest, and beyond them the ruin of what had once been a fortified manor house. Freed from their burdens, the animals stood around as if dazed, and unsure what to do without hundredweights of supplies ruining their backs. Each had a number shaved in its side. Mules were rarely even given names, having a less noble reputation than their equine cousins.

Watson was aware of eyes upon him, and he could see that, atop an intact tower of the wrecked manor house, two soldiers stood, surveying the countryside. Each held a Lee Enfield at the ready.

He heard Suffolk Farm before he saw it. There was the sound of singing and whistling coming across the hedgerows of the lane that led down to it. He recognized the chorus:

> Poverty, poverty knock, my loom it is saying all day.
> Poverty, poverty knock, gaffer's too skinny to pay.

Poverty, poverty knock, always one eye on the clock.

I know I can guttle when I hear me shuttle

Go poverty, poverty knock.

It was one of the mill songs, carried on air that was full of the smells of the countryside after the rain: wet soil, manure and straw, coupled with the odour of livestock and the distinctive aroma of unwashed soldiers. Watson was definitely in the right place. He followed the scent into the farm.

The redbrick farmhouse itself had been sideswiped by the war, with part of its roof gone, replaced by a tarpaulin. As it gusted in the wind it showed a ribcage of roof beams. There were two substantial stone barns, roof tiles remarkably still in place, which, together with the main house, took up three sides of the cobbled courtyard, with a circular stone well occupying the centre of the square.

The forty or so men of the No. 9 Platoon of Company A of the Leigh Pals, a volunteer group of Kitchener's New Army, now part of the 25th (Service) Battalion of the Lancashire Fusiliers, were gathered around this water point, most of them at least partially naked, clumped together to draw what heat they could from the feeble sunshine. Those who were standing had the habitual stoop that told the astute observer that they had just come from the trench system; it took at least a day for some to appreciate that they could stand at full height without risking a bullet to the head.

As they sang, they were picking at their uniforms, squeezing and cracking and generally taking delight in getting some degree of revenge on their tormenters. Somehow they found time for a game of nap or a singsong on the side as they bent to the task of delousing.

'Look at the size of this fucker!' someone shouted before they noticed they had an officer in their midst. One by one, the men began to shuffle to their feet, a mass of pale flesh on the move that reminded Watson of a huge, multifaceted slug stirring.

'At ease!' he yelled. 'For God's sake, as you were, men.'

'Major Watson,' someone shouted in greeting. 'What you doin' in this godforsaken hole, sir?'

'I'm with the CCS just down the road. Where they sent Sergeant Shipobottom. Now, I'm sure you know he fell ill from an infection and, sadly, died. I'd like to have a word with those he was closest to.'

Watson laid down the bike against the wall and turned back to them. Most of them went on with their flecking for lice. 'Don't leave 'im standing there like cheese at fourpence,' said one big lad, pulling on his trousers. 'It's Platt, sir. Corporal Platt as was. I got me three stripes now. Platoon Sergeant.'

Watson remembered Platt. It would be difficult to forget someone of that bulk, in the same way Shipobottom's nose had made an indelible impression on him.

'Congratulations, Sergeant,' he said, trying to sound enthusiastic rather than perplexed. Platt was a big, happy lummox of a lad, strong and, he would imagine, fiercely loyal, but Watson wasn't sure he was NCO material.

'You want a brew, Major?'

'No, I'm quite all right for the moment.'

Platt walked across, putting his ham-sized arms in his tunic as he came. 'Sorry about the state we in. We's expectin' a wheeliewasher.'

These were the mobile bathhouses the Red Cross and FANY nurses operated for men in reserve. The soldiers were delousing in anticipation of a hot shower or bath and perhaps some new underwear if they were lucky.

Watson looked at the grey, goose-fleshed skin before him and said: 'You must all be freezing.'

The young man laughed. 'Nah, thy just a soft southerner, Major.'

Watson stepped forward and peered closely at two of the men's torsos. 'You two. Report to the Regimental MO once you've had your bath. Show him those rashes.'

'Yessir,' they both muttered, and lifted their arms to allow him to inspect the angry, inflamed skin.

'It's scabies,' Watson said. It would mean a week of sulphur-and-lard poultices. He turned back to the sergeant. 'As I said, I'm here about Shipobottom.'

Platt nodded, his moon-face set to grim. 'Aye, bad news, bad news. He was well liked, was Shippy.'

'I would imagine. No enemies?'

'Enemies?' Platt laughed. 'Sergeants always have enemies. The grumblers, like. Why d'you ask?'

Watson ignored the question, along with the growing suspicion on Platt's face. 'And friends? As much as a sergeant can have friends?'

'Private Farrar over there from back 'ome. Same mill. Oy, Albert, get yer keks on and come here. Mason, you too. And there's a lad called Hornby, who was in C Company. He died too. Gassed.'

'And what about Captain de Griffon? How did they get on?'

'Well, at first we all thought he was a bit of a barra-offchilt.' A Baron Rothschild. 'But he's awright, he is.'

'And Lieutenant Metcalf?'

'Well, now that one . . .' He stopped himself.

'Come on Platt, it could be important.' Metcalf, the man who had been hanging around the CCS to badger nurses to come to a dance. Or was that the only motive?

'Well, it's just he's really one of us. Howard over there went t'school with him. Before Metcalf went off to Manchester, like, to get all poshed up. Now he sometimes treats us like summit he stepped in. He's forgotten where he came from, that one.'

'And where is he now?'

Platt pointed to the farmhouse. 'Officers' billet. Along with the captain. They'se got their own baths, lucky buggers.' He lowered his voice and stepped in towards Watson. 'Some was sayin' that Shippy was killed in the hospital, Major. In your care, they say. I said, that's all my eye and Peggy Martin.'

Nonsense, in other words. 'Thank you for your faith, Sergeant.'

'But I'm not liking your questions here, sir. About Shippy.'

'It's just routine, Sergeant. Just routine,' Watson said, using the anodyne phrase he had heard the Scotland Yarders mutter countless times. 'We need to establish the exact cause of the affliction that killed him. What we doctors call Epidemiology.' It felt underhand throwing out high-handed scientific terms designed to bamboozle, but he didn't want the sergeant pursuing the matter. As he expected, the man furrowed his brow.

'Is that right?'

'It's so we can prevent a reoccurrence. We need to establish the syndemic.'

'In case it's like typhoid or some such?'

'Precisely. Now, if I can have a quiet word with these two—'

He was interrupted by the put-put of a motor bike coming down the lane and turning into the farmyard. It was Mrs Gregson, her

Dunhill outfit splattered with mud from her ride. She skidded to a halt and took off her goggles.

'Major Watson,' she said breathlessly. 'The other victim.'

A ripple had gone through the men when they realized it was a woman. Some covered themselves up. Others stood, thinking this signalled the arrival of the portable bathhouse.

'Hornby. From the Leigh Pals. It's the same regiment. This regiment.'

'Victim?' asked Platt. 'What does she mean? Victim? Is it catchin' then?'

'No. It's simply a figure of speech,' said Watson, not wanting to alarm the men. Some, though, had moved closer, sensing a change in the atmosphere.

'The deceased,' Mrs Gregson corrected, 'was from the Leigh Pals.'

'You're certain?' Watson asked her.

Mrs Gregson took out one of the torn fragments of Hornby's medical records and passed it to Watson.

Two Leigh Pals gone. Were there other, unknown victims from the same unit? 'I think, then, we need a word with Captain de Griffon and Lieutenant Metcalf.'

Just then, the door to the farmhouse flew open. Cecil, the dog, exited into the courtyard, yapping in alarm. Metcalf stood there, his eyes wide with shock. His jaw worked but the words jammed in his throat. 'Come quick,' he managed to yell at last. 'It's—'

But before he could say any more, Captain de Griffon pushed him aside and staggered onto the cobbles. His face bore the most terrible of expressions and, as he fell to the floor, his body began to convulse with a violent fit that took hold and refused to let go.

THIRTY-FIVE

The fire had been visible for a hundred miles and across eight counties of England. Soldiers, doctors, nurses and civilians had stood in long, snaking lines on the cliffs of France and watched the flames, blazing like a Saxon beacon from the Viking days. They were unsure what it represented, having no way to know they were witnessing the death throes of a Zeppelin of the German Imperial Navy, fresh from having bombed London. By dawn, the giant leviathan of the air that had beached itself on a Sussex hillside was reduced to a smouldering Duralumin skeleton. By dawn, the first curious visitors began arriving.

Among them was Herbert Cartwright, Boy Scout, whose self-selected task was to monitor the south coast for invasion. Nobody was certain how or why the Zeppelin came down. If it had been intercepted by the planes of the RNAS, it would have exploded in the air over the capital. But then again, the British biplanes could not reach the heights that the dirigibles operated at over London.

It was possible there was a mechanical malfunction or a failure in navigation. Perhaps the skin had been punctured by anti-Zeppelin ground fire, but the beast limped on, its fifteen internal gas cells bleeding out the precious hydrogen, losing height as it desperately tried to cross the Channel to safety.

By the time Bert Cartwright arrived soldiers had been posted to protect the still-glowing wreckage, now stripped to the internal metalwork, from souvenir hunters. Bert was concerned because the machine had come down close to the hollow where he liked to fly his kite.

As he pushed between the onlookers, Bert picked up snippets of information, or at least rumour. The Zeppelin had crash-landed intact. There were no bodies to be found. The crew had torched its own ship – the hydrogen and Blau gas fuel would make this a relatively simple task – to prevent its capture. They had scattered into the countryside but, with no clothes other than their uniforms and no language but their own, they had all been apprehended.

Bert took a notebook from his satchel and began to sketch the enormous cigar-shaped wreckage. He would write a report for his Scout troop. It reminded him of the photographs he had seen of the distorted remains of the Great Yarmouth pavilion, the end-of-the-pier hall burned down in 1914 when the suffragettes were refused leave to hold a meeting there. 'Mad Witches' his dad had called them.

As he was sketching, he glanced over and saw a familiar figure among the crowd. It was the Tweedy Man. Bert had first seen him that day, more than a year ago, when he had been flying his kite. Then, he had been arguing with another, shorter man, a soldier, judging by his cap and the epaulets on his coat. He had often glimpsed the taller one since, striding over the Downs whatever the weather, usually dressed in something eccentric, sometimes the scuffed tweed suit he had on now. The man had aged in the interval since that row with the army officer. He appeared more stooped, his movements stiffer, the once impressive stride shorter. Like everyone else, the Tweedy Man was examining the wreckage but, as he stepped around the perimeter, he was also peering intently at the ground.

As Bert watched him, the man saw something at his feet that took his interest. It was as if an electric shock had gone through him. Dropping his stick – a rough-hewn kebbie – the Tweedy Man pulled something from his pocket and fell to his hands and knees, careless to the muddy, trampled grass and its effect on his clothing. He stopped periodically and peered through his magnifying glass until, satisfied, he moved on, scrabbling this way and that.

When he stood, the man had regained his old, erect posture. He looked around, as if for an ally or witness, and his eyes alighted on the boy. Bert quickly went back to his sketching. He was aware, though, that the Tweedy Man was coming across.

He apologized for interrupting in a surprisingly soft, soothing voice. But he required some help. He could tell, he said, that Bert was a Boy Scout and that his mother worked in a munitions factory (the woven bracelet told him about the scouting and a faint yellow lyddite thumb mark on his shirt collar pinpointed the factory, he later confessed) and was certain his father was doing his bit. Indeed, Bert replied, his dad was a quartermaster in France. So would Bert like to assist His Majesty's Government? He would, he replied, albeit with some nerves. Excellent, said the Tweedy Man, asking his name and then if he could borrow the notebook. On a blank page he sketched a series of what looked like zigzags, with a strange letter P in the centre. It had been written the wrong way around.

Now, said the Tweedy Man, being a Boy Scout, Bert would

obviously have superior powers of observation and, besides, he was closer to the ground than most. He wanted Bert to walk around and find other evidence of this pattern in the soil, where the grass had been scorched or worn away. Could he do that? And he produced a shilling.

Bert, conscious he was late for school, but even more alert to what a shilling could buy him, set out in an anticlockwise direction, while the Tweedy Man walked the other circumference, bent at the waist, sometimes using his kebbie to squat down, then haul himself back up.

To Bert the ground was little more than a trampled mess. The stream of sightseers didn't help, jostling to get as close to the downed dirigible as possible and take photographs with their Vest Pocket Kodaks. He had to detour around clumps of these every few yards, and in doing so he almost missed the first of the telltale patterns in the soil.

He gave a shrill whistle, and the Tweedy Man, upon hearing it, hurried around to where Bert stood, doing his best to stop anyone obliterating the marks. He was breathless when he got there, and Bert pointed to the imprint. Tweedy Man was delighted. He then began to look around, examined the terrain, then pointed with his stick and hurried away from the crash site. Bert, now apparently no longer needed, nevertheless tailed him.

They had gone around thirty yards when Tweedy Man stopped dead. For a second the old boy looked dismayed, twisting this way and that, like a bloodhound that had lost the scent, but, having crouched and used his magnifying glass once more, he saw something that spurred him on again.

They crossed over a bluff, and now there was a steep slope,

leading down to a beech wood. Again he squatted, with no little huffing and puffing, and rubbed something between finger and thumbs. His eyes were taken by a clump of wind-bent bushes just below the ridge to the left. He motioned for the boy to stay back and began to creep towards the shrubs on his toes, the kebbie now held like a staff. Bert couldn't help but notice a rather worrying gleam in his eyes when he turned and made a shushing gesture with his finger across his lips.

With a small cry he leaped forward and parted the branches of the small trees, which revealed a small hollow within their embrace. For a second he disappeared as the twigs closed back over him, but a second later he was out again. Sensing the excitement, such as it had been, was over, Bert advanced on the guilty bushes. The Tweedy Man used his staff to move some of the branches, so Bert could see inside.

Lying in the chalky soil, amid the dark roots, was a prone figure, dressed in what Bert, the invasion expert, knew was a dark blue German naval uniform. On his feet was a pair of fine, laced, leather ankle-boots. On the soles was the reverse of the pattern they had been hunting, with the P the right way round. It was also obvious to Bert that the man was quite dead. His face had been badly burned and there was congealed blood on his clothes. It was his first dead body. He determined to note the date.

The Tweedy Man explained patiently that the P and the lightning strikes told him that the boots were from the town of Pirmasens, centre of the German shoe trade, and manufactured by a company called Pessen. Then he sent him off to fetch one of the soldiers.

When he returned, the Tweedy Man ducked out of the hollow, brushed himself down, and told the soldier that this had been the second-in-command of the Zeppelin, that he hailed from Bremen and that his high-quality boots, belt and other leatherwork suggested that he was from a wealthy family, as they were not standard naval issue. Residues and burns on his hands suggested it was he who lit the charge to destroy the stranded craft.

Injured in the subsequent explosion, and fearing he would slow his friends down in their futile attempts to evade capture, he had walked, dragging one foot behind him, away from the burning dirigible, then had fallen on his hands and knees and crawled several hundred yards, leaving tell-tale tracks, droplets of blood and flakes of burned skin, to hide in this hollow, where he had expired at some-time shortly after midnight.

Having made sure the dumbfounded soldier had all that straight in his head, the Tweedy Man thanked Bert, explained how he had known he was a Boy Scout, and left him with his shilling and a very odd sentiment. 'It seems, young Bert, that man cannot live by bees alone after all.' And then he strode off, his legs covering the ground with the speed and spring Bert remembered from his first encounter with the strange man.

THIRTY-SIX

They were battling in the dark, fighting a spectre with no shape or form, with no idea what it might be vulnerable to. Watson felt as if had been transported back to the Middle Ages, facing up to disease and pestilence armed only with primitive herbal medicines and superstitious spells.

De Griffon leaned over the bed and vomited noisily into the steel bucket. As he swung back Mrs Gregson wiped his mouth and placed the rubber oxygen mask back on. He was still fitting, but less often. They had purged him, with syrup of ipecac as an emetic and compound powder of glycyrrhiza plus Rochelle salts as laxatives, to try and eliminate whatever toxins were in his body. Guaiacol anti-pyretic had been administered to bring the temperature down. Although he hadn't yet turned blue − his pallor, though, was distinctly grey − his pulse was wildly erratic and the fits caused the facial muscles to spasm towards that awful grin.

Watson was close to his wits' end.

'I'm going to change his blood,' he said as the patient lapsed back into quiescence.

'Change it?' asked Mrs Gregson.

'Total body transfusion.'

'Good Lord. Isn't that dangerous?' asked Mrs Gregson.

Watson didn't answer. There was only one he could give: yes it is. But so was doing nothing.

They had managed to get de Griffon back to the CCS by hijacking the lorry that had arrived towing the mobile bathhouse. For one tense moment the Leigh Pals thought he intended to take the entire rig, trailer and all, and there was a hint of mutiny in the air. Watson had let Platt disconnect the bathing machine before Mrs Gregson had commandeered the Dennis and driven it at reckless speed to get back to the transfusion tent.

Now Watson took a sample of blood from de Griffon's ear and smeared it onto a porcelain dish. He intended to make a cross-match with his own blood.

'I can't think of anything else. If it's a poison, then cleansing the blood should work. Some members of the royal family have it done on a regular basis. For their blood disorder.'

'Over how long a period?'

Watson smiled at the pertinence of the question. 'At least twenty-four hours.'

'How long have we got?'

He shrugged. 'Less than that I would wager.'

'And isn't there a shock to the body?'

'In a weakened state there can be acute dilation of the heart when the myocardium is shocked. The more blood we put in, the harder the heart will have to work. So we'll have to drain him a little as we infuse.'

Watson waited for an objection, but none came. In truth, he was at the boundary of his knowledge here. Transfusion was a young science, one forged, and forged quickly, in the heat of battle.

Watson pricked his own finger and put a few drops into a suspension of sodium citrate solution in a test tube, which he held up and shook vigorously.

'You are going to give him your blood?'

'I can spare a couple of pints. Can I take a sample of yours?'

She held out her finger and he used a lancet to collect some of hers into a citrate solution.

'I'm group II,' she said. 'Oh, hold on . . .'

Mrs Gregson removed the oxygen mask from de Griffon and stepped back as he rolled and vomited again, bringing up a trail of green slime that she wiped away. 'I think we've got his stomach emptied.'

The captain muttered something unintelligible and slumped back. His forehead still glistened with fever. Mrs Gregson busied herself changing the bedpan arrangement in the window of quiescence. By the time she returned, Watson had finished the agglutination tests. 'I think we have a universal recipient.'

Mrs Gregson rolled up her sleeve. 'In which case . . . And once I've done I'll go and get Miss Pippery.'

'Thank you.' He began to pull the dressing off his arm. Might as well use the old incision. 'And thank you for getting the information on Hornby. What made you decide to do that?'

'Didn't you get my note?'

His hand automatically went to his trouser pocket and he pulled out the creased envelope that Staff Nurse Jennings had given him. 'I'm sorry.' He went to rip it open.

'Don't bother. It just says I'll placate Sister Spence by going back to Bailleul. But while I am there I'll try and access the records of the man I saw with the same symptoms.'

'Did you have difficulty doing that?'

'Not really.' A fleeting expression suggested otherwise. 'I might have bent the rules a little. Which means I might have put myself in a bit of difficulty if I ever go back there. There is someone who I am sure now feels there is a score to settle.'

'Mrs Gregson, I wouldn't have expected—'

'Oh, I haven't done anything too rash. I haven't promised my body or anything.' She said this with an unsettling little grin, as if she had considered it. 'Just got on the wrong side of someone. I'll think of a way out of it.'

The captain groaned and twisted, as if trying to cast the sheets and blanket off. Mrs Gregson laid a cold compress on his forehead and the distress subsided. 'You've checked his body for marks?'

She nodded. 'Nothing out of the ordinary. He bites his nails.'

'As long as it's not his toenails.'

They both laughed at the absurdity of the comment.

'And it said nothing about any marks on Hornby's body?'

'No. But then again, it rather played down the facial spasm and the hands, too.'

'If nobody was looking for the numerals . . .'

'That's why I stole that piece of paper from the file.'

Watson didn't quite follow. 'You took it to show that he shared a regiment with Shipobottom.'

'Not that one. This one. I ripped out part of a second page. It has the number of Hornby's burial plot at the Bailleul hospital cemetery.'

'Mrs Gregson, are you suggesting what I think you are suggesting?'

'I should imagine so.' She kept a steady gaze and an even tone to her voice, as if what she was about to say was the most natural thing in the world. 'We're going to have to dig up Private Edward Hornby.'

Metcalf was pacing the ground outside the transfusion tent when Staff Nurse Jennings found him. He had no trench coat on and the drizzle had soaked the upper part of his tunic.

'Lieutenant, you'll be wearing a hole in the ground. And if you carry on getting wet like that, we'll be putting you in it. Are you waiting to see the captain?'

He waved an arm at the transfusion tent.

'Yes, but Major Watson sent me away with a flea in my ear,' the young man said petulantly. 'Asked me to write down my movements for the past two days. Which I suspect is a ruse to get me out of his hair.'

'Do you know who Major Watson is?'

Metcalf shook his head. 'No. Should I?'

'Possibly not. But trust me, he knows what he is doing. Come with me.' She grabbed his elbow and steered him back up towards the Big House. On the way she passed Sister Spence, who eyed her suspiciously. 'Staff Nurse Jennings.'

She inclined her head at Metcalf. 'Shock, Sister. Sweet tea.'

'Of course. You don't have to stay and watch him drink it, mind.'

'No, Sister. I am on surgical in fifteen.'

'Fine. There is some mail for you. Nurse Cummins has it at the office.'

'Thank you.'

She steered him towards the refreshment station, an open-sided tent staffed by orderlies who kept two large urns of stewed tea – far too strong for her liking – on the go day and night. She sat Metcalf down and fetched him a mug with three sugars.

'I've only got a few minutes,' she said. 'I wasn't fibbing to Sister Spence.'

He took a sip of the tea. 'Thank you. You're very kind.'

'The captain is in good hands.' She gave an outline of Watson's past, as far as she knew it. 'So you see, Major Watson is a very capable man.'

This seemed to cut little ice with Metcalf. The Afghan War was a long time ago and he had little time for detective stories. 'He'll need to be. Anything happens to Captain de Griffon, I would imagine there would be hell to pay.'

'Oh? Why is that?'

'Well, he's recently . . .' Metcalf hesitated, wondering if he was speaking out of turn, '. . . recently discovered he is the new Lord Stanwood.'

'And that makes a difference, does it?' Jennings asked.

'I should say so. The family will want to know what happened here.'

'I think we would like to know, too. There was a time, Lieutenant Metcalf, when having a Lord Stanwood here would have made us all agog. Most of us had never seen an earl or a duke or even a sir.' She shook her head. 'But when you've seen the Earl of Croftford with his insides on display or Sir William Tennant contemplating life without knees, or anything below them, you soon lose any notion that they are somehow different.' She gave a sigh. 'Goodness, listen to me, I sound like Mrs Gregson.'

'What does Mrs Gregson sound like?' he asked, although, having had a taste of her conversation, he felt he had a good idea.

'Well, she has — had — rather strong views on those things. On inherited privilege and such matters.' Strong enough to support anarchy and murder at one time, she recalled. Or only at one time? It was probably worth mentioning to Dr Watson what she knew of his VAD's past. Although could that be misconstrued as spreading malicious gossip? Mrs Gregson's chequered history might have nothing at all to do with current events. She would ponder on it. She had mail to collect, patients to care for, and there was always a chance he might think her meddlesome. Or just another nurse with an axe to grind against VADs.

'You should do what Major Watson says. Write everything down, from getting out of bed yesterday to seeing the captain taken ill.'

'But why? What good will that do?'

'You were here yesterday, correct?' she asked.

'Yes. I was with Mrs Gregson and Miss Pippery. And visiting the men, of course.'

'Of course. But you saw Shipobottom?'

'I did. I visited him first thing, and again before I left when he was being taken for his transfusion.'

'And then, today, you were with Captain de Griffon when he began to show the same symptoms.'

He slammed his tea down, slopping some onto the table. 'Look here, what are you driving at?'

Just what Major Watson will be, she thought. She stood. 'Nothing at all. But if I were you, Lieutenant, I'd get writing. You seem to have acquired the habit of being in the wrong place at the wrong time.'

THIRTY-SEVEN

Watson awoke with a start, his mind struggling to make sense of where he was or what time it was. He was lying, still fully clothed, on one of the cot-beds. In the lamplight he could see Mrs Gregson on one of the others, sitting upright, with Miss Pippery curled next to her, eyes tight shut. The older woman was stroking the young VAD's hair, slowly and tenderly. She smiled when she saw Watson was awake.

He helped himself to some water and looked at his watch. It was almost midnight. The last he remembered was a visit from Torrance and more cross words with the major. Then, another infusion of blood and feeling light-headed. Staff Nurse Jennings had come, he recalled, although he couldn't say whether she volunteered blood or not. The tent swam a little with the effort of remembering. 'I'm sorry—' he began.

Mrs Gregson shook her head. 'I'd have woken you if anything happened. You looked all done.'

He moved stiffly, feeling his age, over across to where de Griffon lay. He no longer had the oxygen mask on, his face looked serene, his breathing was steady. Watson gingerly checked the pulse. It was nicely robust.

'I think you saved him,' said Mrs Gregson.

'I think *we* saved him. I'll need to question him about how this started, once he is strong enough. And I should get his sample to a laboratory.' Watson had saved some of the blood extracted from de Griffon for analysis.

'All that can wait. You look dreadful. You gave too much blood.'

It was probably true. He was certainly fatigued and the room felt as if he were on some ocean liner, rolling gently in a swell. 'You did the same.'

She threw him a look that, without any need for vocalizing, told him she was younger and fitter than he. 'I'll wake up Alice — Miss Pippery — in a while or so and I'll get some sleep myself. But you go back to your room, now. That's a VAD order. The other thing can wait.'

'The other thing?' he asked groggily.

She mimed digging with a shovel.

He shook his head. 'Mrs Gregson, I am many things, but I'm not a grave robber. We'll have to go through proper channels.'

She raised an eyebrow to show what she thought of those. 'Go to bed. Now. Shoo.'

Too weary to argue, he thanked her, picked up his tunic and walked out into the dank night.

Well done, Watson, said the imposter in his head.

Yet, even knowing it was fraudulent, the return of the voice gave him some comfort. As he took one leaden step after another up the hill, his collar turned up to the wind, he wondered how his life might have turned out without that fateful meeting in the chemical laboratory of St Bart's. It was one of those forks in the road that litter everybody's life. That one had hinged on a chance conversation with Stamford, his former dresser from Bart's, at the Criterion Bar. What would he have become if their paths had never crossed and Stamford hadn't engineered a meeting with a man who had 'a passion for definite and exact knowledge'? And if that man hadn't already secured lodgings in Baker Street?

He would have become a quotidian GP, he supposed, like one of those he had bought his several practices from over the years, fingers stained with silver nitrate from burning warts, iodine from treating cuts and burns and nicotine from the endless cigarettes a long surgery demanded, his shoulders hunched from too many bedside visits, the hours spent peering over dying men and expectant mothers.

No, he'd take the way the world had turned out for him over the past few decades. Even if the final act wasn't the one he had been anticipating. But then, he thought as he heard the low, pitiful moans of a delirious soldier issue from one of the tents, who could have anticipated all this?

In answer, there came only the low grumble of assault guns from the south.

THURSDAY

THIRTY-EIGHT

The rejuvenating power of sleep once more worked its wonder, dragging Watson back from what had been a yawning abyss of despair when he had laid his head on the pillow. His mood was lifted further by the discovery of a pair of thick socks at the foot of his bed. They had been hand-knitted. He remembered what Churchill had said. The way to win a soldier's heart and mind was through clean socks.

He was already up and dressed when Brindle arrived with tea and he was again busy writing down his own account of what had happened over the last forty-eight hours. Watson hoped that putting things down in logical order might present some sort of solution, but no new insight was granted him. The link, if it was a link, suggested that all the victims had come from the same regiment, indeed the same company, although this Hornby was from a different platoon.

As he supped his tea, his mind drifted off to what, exactly, Mrs Gregson had promised in order to establish Hornby's identity. He knew his moral standards were formed in another century, but nevertheless he felt uneasy. It was true that widows were not expected to have the same level of decorum as an unmarried woman – he certainly did not feel as defensive towards Mrs Gregson as Staff Nurse Jennings or Miss Pippery – but he hoped she hadn't compromised herself for his sake. Or, the sake of the investigation he should say.

On whose authority are you investigating?

It was the stentorian tones of Major Torrance invading his thoughts this time. And the major was right. Once he had a full set of facts, he had to involve the Military Police. He would do so that very day. And he would have to tell Mrs Gregson that exhuming Hornby's body without official sanction – did that include the permission of the next of kin he wondered? – was out of the question. But first, he had a few small chores to perform.

He scooped up the mahogany box containing the Colt .45 and went along to Caspar Myles's room. There was no reply. He hesitated before turning the handle on the primitive latch system – the monastery had clearly not believed in keys or privacy – and entered the room. The curtains were still drawn and he pulled them back to let in some of the grey morning light.

The bed, as far as he could tell, had not been slept in. It was possible that Dr Myles had bedded down in the wards – that was not unusual if there was a patient that needed a careful watch.

And then, plucked from his memory apparently at random, came a phrase. '*And I told Dr Myles I would not even contemplate a dinner this evening without a chaperone.*'

There it was: *this evening.* Somehow the timing had failed to register or his ageing brain had not had the wherewithal to hang on to it.

Myles had asked her to dinner the previous evening, she had nominated Watson as chaperone and come to find him at the transfusion tent. He, of course, had clearly been in no position to come along anywhere. So she had . . . what?

He hurried out of the room, slamming the door behind him, and went down to the transfusion tent, where he found de Griffon sitting up in bed, a smile on his face and a mug of tea in his hand. He and Mrs Gregson were giggling about something, but stifled the laughter when they saw Watson, and the concern distorting his features.

'Morning, Captain,' he said. 'Feeling better?'

'To be frank, I didn't expect to be feeling anything. I owe you a debt of thanks, Major Watson, as Mrs Gregson here was just explaining.'

'Mrs Gregson and Miss Pippery played their parts. I'd like to ask you some questions, if you feel strong enough, Captain.' De Griffon nodded. 'And Mrs Gregson, I wonder if I could ask you a small favour. Do you think you could locate Staff Nurse Jennings for me?'

Mrs Gregson, clearly suspecting a ruse to exclude her from the session, hesitated. She wanted, and deserved, answers as much as the major.

'It's important,' Watson said, with a grimness that convinced her it wasn't mere subterfuge.

'Very well.'

'Oh, by the way, my feet are lovely and warm,' he said, to try and lighten the mood.

'I'm pleased to hear it.'

'New socks,' he explained.

'Congratulations,' she said, as if baffled.

Watson still had the Colt box in his hand and he laid it down on a spare bed. Before he began the questions, Watson took the captain's temperature and pulse. He appeared to be entirely back to normal.

'You were lucky.'

'Lucky to have you two,' de Griffon said.

'Mrs Gregson seems to have got over any objection to you and your family.'

'Really, we capitalists are not so bad once you get to know us, Major. I think she was confusing my family history with the current generation. My father is dead, my brother is dead. I have spent time with the men of Leigh. I have seen what fine fellows they are on the whole. Rough and ready perhaps, but salt of the earth. Look at Platt, the sergeant. One of twelve children, of whom four survived. You know when the children died, they couldn't afford to bury them? The hearses up there have little compartments at the front, so a child could be buried with an adult, any adult, to defray the cost.'

Watson nodded. He had seen plenty of child deaths in his time: scarlet fever, diphtheria, consumption, polio. He knew what a burden the burial could be on a family that could barely afford one meal a day.

'His mother died of TB when he was twelve, which is when he started doing split days – morning at school, afternoon at the mill. Father was a drunkard, by all accounts, so it was Platt who raised his brothers, starting full time at the mill at fourteen. The lives we made those people lead . . . I tell you, I intend to be a very different kind of owner if God spares me this war.'

'I am pleased to hear it. But first, we have to establish who or what did this to you. Whether one of your salt-of-the-earth is not quite as benevolent as you think. You were poisoned, you know. Just like Shipobottom.'

De Griffon looked grave. 'Even I worked that out for myself, Major. But I can't imagine who in my company would want to kill me. You have to remember, Major Watson, that I never had any dealings with Leigh. The mills were the business of my brother and my father. I was being groomed to look after the estates. But with them both gone, well, it changes things.'

'One of which is that you are now Lord Stanwood?'

'I am, but I'm not about to shout about that. The "de" in de Griffon is bad enough. If I called attention to my new status, why, they'd be wondering if they should call me Captain, Sir or your lordship. Do they tug at their forelock? Take their caps off? No, that's something to address later, if I get through this. And if I don't, there is a young cousin who will inherit. So please, do not use the title.'

'Of course. But you'll continue with the family business? With the cotton?'

'We shall have to see. Major, I have never even visited our Satanic Mills, except for once when I was young, paraded through the spinning rooms like . . . well, I blush to think of it. Like some visiting prince. All I really remember is the sparks off the steel caps on the women's clogs as they walked down the cobbled streets. Fascinated me. But it's not my town. Everything I know about Platt, for instance, I know from talking with him or keeping my ears open. Not first-hand.'

'But someone could have a grudge against the whole family? In the same way Mrs Gregson reacted badly to the de Griffon name.'

'It's feasible. Although let me assure you, the de Griffons weren't the worst of the owners by a long chalk. Some would say that we've been enlightened for decades.'

'Except for unions.'

'With respect, we were no different from the other mills, as far as I know. From this distance, it looks like unreasonable behaviour, but you underestimate the threat the owners felt from organized labour. It seemed likely they could lose everything. But it's different now. Most mills have unions. Including ours. Look, even if there was a vendetta against my family, why kill Shipobottom?'

'Did Shipobottom work at your mill?'

'Yes. One of them. And his father before him. But as spinners. Regular folk, you might say. Not bosses. Not even overseers.'

'And Hornby?'

'Eddie Hornby? Yes, I believe he was a Blackstone lad, too. He wasn't in my company. And he was gassed, I believe. Not poisoned.'

'That's not necessarily true. Mrs Gregson recalled that, in death, Hornby's face reminded her of poor Shipobottom. And Mrs Gregson checked: there was no record at Bailleul of any gas attack victims from this section of the line. How could he have been exposed?'

The captain bit his lip.

'What is it?

'The thing is, Major, C Company have been put under the command of Lieutenant-Colonel Charles Foulkes. Do you know what that means?'

Watson shook his head. 'I am afraid I don't.'

De Griffon scratched at his forehead. 'This is all rather difficult. Foulkes has been raising Special Companies for each section of the line.'

'Special in what way?'

He laughed at the absurdity of it all. 'I'm not allowed to tell you. The full title is BSGC, but nobody is allowed to say the "G" word.'

'Gas?'

'I didn't say that. Any soldier mentioning it is likely to find themselves strapped to a gun limber.' This was Field Punishment Number One, being left tied to the wheel of a gun carriage with no food or water for a specified period, often in atrocious weather. 'So you'll hear the words "special measures" a great deal, or "accessories" or some such euphemism.'

'But we've used gas before,' objected Watson. 'At Loos.'

'Yes. In so-called "retaliation". But the powers that be don't want the scale of our offensive preparations known. How can we decry the beastly Hun for its barbaric methods when we are preparing to do the same? If not worse?'

Watson rubbed his forehead like a magic lamp. No genie of clarity appeared, however. 'So these symptoms could be caused by accidental exposure to gas?'

'Certainly in Hornby's instance, because he was in charge of one of the special measures dumps at Burnt-Out Lodge, as we call it. It's the next farm along from Suffolk. How Shipobottom and I could have been exposed is another matter.'

Watson fetched himself some water while he considered this. Had he been barking up the wrong tree? Had he made a fool of himself insisting there was murder — or in de Griffon's case attempted murder — here? It was well known that both sides were busy creating ever more hideous ways to kill and maim. There were anonymous men in hidden installations all across Europe whose jobs were the perfection of death in all its forms. The Germans had certainly used cyanide formulations to cause heart problems. But, he reminded himself, there was no gas yet invented that he knew of that could scratch Roman numerals in a man's skin. Or had he been wrong about those marks and read too much into a couple of scratches?

He remembered Burnt-Out Lodge. It was next to the field of mules, the place with the sentries on the tower, covering all the approaches. So it was gas that needed protecting.

'Have you ever drunk from the well at the farm?'

'No. Early on the Germans threw some dead livestock down there. I know what you are thinking – it is contaminated, but not by gas.'

Watson instantly dismissed that train of thought. 'Captain, when you left me with Shipobottom's body, did you go straight back to Suffolk Farm?'

'No. Why do you ask?'

'I need to establish what you ate or drank or came into contact with prior to your attack.'

'Well, I was going to ride back immediately – I brought Lord Lockie, my best horse, over – but I was intercepted by Caspar Myles. He invited me for a drink.'

'Why would Dr Myles do that?'

The captain shrugged to show it was perfectly routine. 'Well, we'd never actually met before, but he is a friend of the family.'

'Myles?' asked Watson, unable to hide his surprise, 'A friend of the de Griffons?'

'Yes. I know he doesn't sound like a Southerner, but his family is big in American cotton. To be honest, I suspect they were Yankee carpetbaggers at the end of the civil war, who grabbed themselves a few choice plantations. So, the Myleses and the de Griffons have been doing business for, oh, half a century.'

'And you had a drink with him?'

'Several, in fact there was a lot of gossip to catch up on. Look, you don't really think—'

Watson raised a hand to prevent any futile speculation. 'I don't know what to think at this juncture.'

Mrs Gregson returned, alone. 'I couldn't find Staff Nurse

Jennings, Major. I did find Sister Spence, who was a little, um, surprised to see me back. Although furious might be a better description. I am to vacate the premises at once. However, she did manage to squeeze out of her pursed lips that Staff Nurse Jennings apparently took the several days' leave owing to her last night. Sister Spence didn't seem best pleased about her behaviour.'

Watson didn't like the sound of this one little bit. The American and Jennings absent at the same time pointed in a direction he didn't care for. Watson turned back to de Griffon. 'Has Caspar Myles ever visited the mills?'

'In Leigh? Yes, as a matter of fact, a few years ago, before he decided to pursue medicine. Major Watson, you are scaring me now. Are you saying my having a drink with Caspar Myles—'

'Did Myles say anything about where he might be going today?'

De Griffon furrowed his brow trying to remember. 'No, but he did moan a great deal about the British. Apparently we are a terribly stuffy bunch with no sense of fun. Said he missed the company of Americans and had a mind to go and visit his old chums at the All-Harvard Volunteers sometime soon.'

'Mrs Gregson, will you please write down every movement that Captain de Griffon here made after leaving Dr Myles. I just need to look into something.'

'What about Sister Spence? She told me to go and never darken her wards again.'

Watson had already steeled himself to tackle bigger foes than a razor-tongued sister. 'Leave her to me.'

Watson found Torrance's adjutant, Captain Symonds, in the main house, in a small anteroom next to the major's office. He barged in and kicked the door closed behind him. Symonds looked up, his pen frozen in the act of countersigning an order.

'I am afraid Major Torrance is rather busy this morning, Major,' he began, once he had recovered from his shock at such a rude entry.

'It's not the major I want to see, Symonds, it's you.'

'Me?'

'What had Dr Myles done to disgrace himself?' he asked bluntly.

'I'm sorry . . .'

'When we first met, you were rather keen to steer the conversation away from Dr Myles and the fact he had come here under a cloud.'

'He's a fine doctor—'

Watson brought a fist down on the desk and an inkpot toppled over, bleeding a blue-black pool over some papers. Symonds leaped to his feet with an oath and grabbed a sheaf of blotters. 'Major, for crying out loud. These are important documents.'

Watson swept them off the desk with one brisk movement of his arm. Symonds looked aghast. In fact, he looked as if he would like to convene a firing squad there and then. 'This is an outrage. Major Torrance said he thought the balance of your mind was disturbed—'

'It is,' Watson agreed, enjoying the look of discomfort on Symonds's face. 'It is disturbed at how you people can be so complacent. So he is a fine doctor. I hear tell Dr Crippen's patients spoke highly of him, too. I am sure somewhere there were people who thought Jack the Ripper was a first-class surgeon, such a pity about his other little hobby. Now, what did Myles do?'

'Oh, for God's sake, there was some unpleasant personal business.'

Watson leaped on the mealy-mouthed word like a big cat onto the back of a gazelle. 'Unpleasant? Unpleasant? What on earth does that mean exactly?'

'I don't know. We didn't ask for details. The chap was in a bit of trouble. His commanding officer asked if we'd like a doctor, no questions asked. Well, we had to check whether there was any professional incompetence. It turned out there was an incident with a nurse. But you know what these girls are like around doctors. No, perhaps a man your age doesn't. But I have seen them at work. Bag a doctor and the whole war has been worthwhile to them. If they can't get a doctor, an officer will do just as nicely.'

Watson felt like taking a leaf from Holmes's pugilistic handbook and striking the man full on the chin with a left hook, but instead he took a moment to recover his composure. He was still suffering from having donated a fair percentage of his blood volume, and his head was thumping wildly. The last thing he needed was to find himself on a ward, having fainted or worse. 'Where are the All-Harvard Volunteers based?'

'Major Watson, if you are going to stir up trouble—'

'I am not going to stir anything that isn't there already. We have a man who nearly died last night, poisoned by an unknown hand or agent, plus two who did expire, and we have a missing nurse and a lost American doctor with what Scotland Yard would call "form". And everything points to them being connected. I just want to know where the Americans that foisted Myles upon you are.'

Symonds took a deep breath, considering whether to answer this madman. In the end, he concluded it was the easiest way to get rid of him. 'The Harvards are attached to a French base hospital, just southwest of Armentières. A village called Nieppe, across the border.'

'Right. Thank you.'

'I shall have to report this to Major Torrance,' said Symonds to Watson's back as he left. Watson glanced over his shoulder and gave the man a parting glare. He was surprised to find that he had enjoyed his little moment of madness. He should burst his stays more often.

And he wasn't worried about Torrance; he had other matters on his mind. Firstly, he had to send a cable to his old friend Dr Anwar back in Egypt. Then, he had two things to collect from the transfusion tent. One was a sample of de Griffon's blood. The French base hospitals had excellent haematology labs, the country being a great believer in the analysis of bodily fluids of every description. The second was the Colt .45 that Myles had presented to Watson, doubtless never thinking his own gun might be used against him.

THIRTY-NINE

He sat in a café in the Grand Square, unable to comprehend the beauty of the buildings. It did not make sense. Here were medieval façades full of elaborate carvings and ornate statues, inlaid with gems and layered with gold, and they were intact. Not a single bullet hole. No shrapnel marks. Ears, noses, fingers, all were present and correct – the stone cherubs and saints appeared untouched and untroubled by war.

It was the same with the people. He was used to seeing faces disfigured with fear, drooping with exhaustion and caked with filth. Here the men and women were clean, composed and calm. True, some of the braver civilians glanced from under their umbrellas at him and his fellow Germans with suspicion or hostility as they hurried by the café where he sat behind the glass windows. But apart from that, with their faces showing little trace of tension, their behaviour positively carefree, clothes neat, clean and pressed, their worries everyday and mundane, he couldn't help but resent them. Bloch had arrived from a degraded world, where the ramparts of civilization had not only been breached, but pissed on. Perhaps coming to Brussels so soon had been a mistake. He wasn't healed. Even the quiet was unnerving. It felt odd to admit it, but he missed the noise of the guns.

Bloch ordered a schnapps to go with his coffee, his ragged nerves making him ignore the resolve that said he must be clear-headed when he saw Hilde. Of course, she might not come. Might not have got the telegram. Or been able to get a train. Although those visiting wounded relatives or loved ones at or near the front were apparently given priority on the railways. *Please let her come*, he pleaded with nobody in particular. *Please.*

He looked around the café. He was the most junior in rank, but he wasn't worried about that. Lux had provided him with one of the élite stormtrooper uniforms, which gave him a status well above any of the local *Leutnants* and *Kapitäns* with their fat-arse desk jobs. With the bandage on his face – he noticed that, like the local statuary, very few of the officers bore any signs of combat – and his new outfit, he could affect a swagger that had even the Belgian waiter being attentive.

One of the officers, a *Rittmeister* in the transport corps, caught him staring at his raucous little group of penpushers and fixed him with a challenging stare. He had a bony, haughty face, and one cheekbone sported the kind of duelling scar that Bloch always thought was probably self-inflicted – a nasty shaving accident rather than an affair of honour. Bloch met the man's gaze, held it, and threw back his schnapps without wavering. The *Rittmeister* scowled and turned back to his friends and their beers. He said something that caused a ripple of laughter. Bloch imagined the man in the cross hairs of the Mauser he had been promised, wondering what the new *Spitzgeschoss mit Stahlkern* ammunition might do to his skull.

'Ernst?'

Taken by surprise, he almost upset the table when he leaped to his feet. It was Hilde, but a slightly thinner, paler version of the one he remembered, and dressed in black, as if a widow.

He reached towards her cheek and brushed it with his calloused fingers. It was the softest thing he had ever felt. A tightness grew in his chest and he felt close to tears. The beauty of the square had overwhelmed him, the sight of Hilde, Dresden-fragile, dressed in mourning clothes, was almost too much. It was as if she had come to his funeral.

'Sit down, please,' he said, signalling for more coffee.

'Ernst. Your face . . . are you all right? You didn't say in your telegram you were hurt.'

He touched it, as if he had forgotten all about it. 'It's nothing. I mean it will heal. It looks bad now. The doctors were worried you might run screaming when you saw me.'

She touched his hand and he put his other over it to lock it in place, fearing it might be a fleeting touch.

'Of course not. You still look perfectly fine.' She took a breath and the next sentences came out in an unseemly rush. 'Mother did not want me to come. Karl is dead. We buried him just last week. He was shot down. He survived, but his wounds were . . . The plane caught fire when it crashed, just behind our lines. Soldiers ran to him, but . . .' She closed her eyes, unable to continue.

'I'm sorry. He was a good boy.'

'A boy, yes. We are still mourning him. Mother thought it inappropriate for me to come. My father said that to deprive you, a fighting hero, of my company was a disgrace.'

Bloch gave a hollow laugh. 'Your father was on my side?'

'He was.'

'The man who once called me a country bumpkin?' It was where he had first met Hilde, out in the countryside, two hiking clubs camping on adjacent hilltops in the lovely, endless summer of 1911. 'I'm shocked.'

She looked pained. 'The war has changed everything. Even Father.'

He nodded. 'How is it at home?'

'Well, there are shortages, of course. It's not so bad for us, because . . .'

Because your family owns a department store, he almost finished for her.

'And you? Is it awful out there? I watch the newsreels every week.'

Which newsreels? he wondered. He had never seen an official cameraman at the front. Rumour had it the authorities restaged battles somewhere away from the real fighting with actors, to show the clean, pristine flower of German manhood overwhelming the filthy, rat-like French and cowardly British. Certainly, the footage he had seen at the mobile cinemas in the reserve areas bore little resemblance to his life, to the hours out on that blasted plain of no man's land or living like a troglodyte in concrete bunkers.

'Ernst?'

'I'm sorry,' he said, snapping back to the present.

'I asked you what it was like. Do you have friends? Comrades?'

He fiddled with his fresh coffee. 'There's my spot—' He didn't want to explain what a spotter did. She knew he was a marksman, that was all. 'There's . . . it's difficult to say.'

'Have you been in battles? Your letters never mention anything.'

'Not as such. Skirmishes, I suppose. The letters are censored, you know. For security.'

'I'm not sure Karl's were. He used to describe the thrill of flying. The joy of being up in an empty sky. Then the attacks on barrage balloons, the excitement and terror of the dogfights—'

'It's different,' Bloch interrupted. It wasn't hard to look up from the mud and envy the flyers. And they had little tactical information to give away in letters. As well as something almost admirable, noble to write about. There was nothing noble in his little corner of the war.

He remembered what one of the other snipers had said when he returned from leave: *They don't understand back home. Can't understand. Unless you have been in the trenches, it is impossible to believe what it is like. Don't waste your breath.*

'The war on the ground, I mean. Can we walk?' He stood, without warning, and put too much money down. 'Get some air?'

'It's raining, Ernst.'

'Not much. You have an umbrella. I have a raincoat.'

'If we must.'

The *Rittmeister* looked over at him, then his eyes switched to Hilde as she straightened her dress. They went up and down her body, slowly, taking in every inch. The mourning outfit did little to deter his lasciviousness.

Bloch had made the first step towards the man when he felt Hilde's hand on his elbow. 'Ernst. Please. What's wrong?'

They quickly left the café and crossed the square, heading towards the town hall. 'Ernst, please slow down. Is everything all right? You seem so tense. Like a wire stretched taut.'

Of course everything isn't all right, he wanted to say. Nothing will ever be all right again. 'Of course everything is all right, now you are here. I'm sorry. That man, the way he looked at you, it just . . . I'm not used to having women around and now I have, I find I don't want to share you. With anyone.'

'You don't have to.'

He found himself blurting out his thoughts. 'Can you stay? Tonight? We can have dinner. Be together.' He realized how that sounded. 'What I mean to say, you can stay in a women's hostel if we can find one.'

A heartbreaking shake of the head followed. 'I promised I'd be back. It was hard enough for them to let me come without a chaperone. I practically had to swear on a Bible I wouldn't . . . I'm so sorry.'

'I understand. I shouldn't have asked.' He fought hard to keep an irrational anger out of his voice. What did he expect? This was Hilde, not some red-light tart.

'You should. You should say what you think. What would you like to do now, Ernst?'

He thought for a moment and wiped the drizzle from his eyes. 'I'd like to walk. In silence. No questions. Then I'd like an early dinner, just looking at you. Then I'll put you on the train. And then you can forget me if you wish.'

'Ernst . . . ?'

He put a finger to her lips. 'No questions.'

'On one condition.'

'What's that?'

'You come under the umbrella.'

He had put her on the nine o'clock train. She had insisted that there be no steam-wreathed tearful platform goodbye, no watching forlornly as the train chugged out. So they had kissed, briefly, and he walked out of the station without a backward glance, back to his *estaminet-pension*, feeling surprisingly light-hearted. He had a quick drink in the bar downstairs, even though he had drunk enough for one night at the meal. He smiled at the barmaid, and made small talk with the corporal next to him. They both agreed that a strange inversion had taken place. That this town, the bar, the hotel, this was the dreamworld. The trenches, the filthy, sodden, rat-infested trenches, they seemed more real than anything else now. It would be a relief to get back, away from all the play-acting, back to where people understood.

On his way upstairs, he asked for some hot water to be sent up, then went to his room and undressed slowly, not begrudging the sounds of merriment he could hear from below. They had hardly spoken the whole evening, but she had made sure it was a comfortable silence, full of placating gestures. Letting him unwind in his own time. He loved her for that. It had been good for his soul. If only because it reminded him he had one. But, as the corporal had said, it had just been a little, comforting dream.

He put on the cheap cotton robe he had bought at the market when the water came, answering the knock with a few coins for the girl. He saw the jug first. Then Hilde, holding it.

The noise he made barely counted as speech.

'There's been a train crash,' she said.

'What? Oh my God. When? Are you all right?'

'Or a derailment. Or a sudden movement of troops causing delays. Perhaps a strike by Belgian train drivers. Or conductors. An act of God has brought the railways to a halt.' She gave a smile that caused his heart to race. 'Don't worry, Ernst, I'll have thought of something by morning.'

She pushed past him to enter the room. She had alighted the train when he left, followed him from the station, watched him from the street perhaps, bribed the maid, planned all this. His Hilde. The girl he had dismissed as just a passing dream.

FRIDAY

FORTY

As a major, Watson could always request or commandeer a seat on a military transport, and there was no shortage of that on the roads of Flanders or Northern France. However, he wanted to be independent of others for this trip. It was de Griffon who came up with the solution – he should borrow Lord Lockie for the ride to the hospital at Nieppe. The horse, he said, could do with the outing and ten miles there and back was as nothing to him, the captain promised. Watson wasn't so sure it would be as nothing to his buttocks, but he accepted the offer.

So he found himself back at Suffolk Farm, now full of idling lorries, waiting to take the Leigh Pals back up the line to the relief trenches, and then, after a few days, back to the front proper. Watson was in the gloomy interior of one of the two stone barns, with Sergeant Platt helping him saddle a bay gelding with a white blaze down its face. It was short in the leg, wide in the forehead and cautious about the old man who wanted to ride him. But Watson knew that bedside manner and stable manner were closely related and, over the course of fifteen minutes, with lots of soft whispers and several tasty bribes, he won Lord Lockie round. De Griffon had told him the horse was oddly proportioned – he hadn't inherited the looks or grace of his father, an Eastern England point-to-point champion – but, once settled, he was tough and trustworthy.

While they blanketed, bridled and saddled the horse, Watson asked Platt to tell him more about the Leigh Pals. Although he knew the rough details from Egypt, it was worth hearing a more complete picture to try to establish why anyone would target its members. He asked the sergeant to speak slowly and clearly, so he could turn the account into the Queen's English with relative ease.

'You knows about the Pals, reet? The idea be'ind them?' Watson nodded. 'Spread all over the north like a measles rash, it did. Dunno whose idea it was, but someone said that men should enlist wit' their muckers and workies. It were Liverpool first, I thinks.'

Watson knew he was right. It had been Lord Derby who suggested raising a force of entirely local men in the city. The patriotic drive, and the use of friends to chivvy each other along, was a clever way to avoid introducing an unpopular conscription.

'Then Salford got a Pals, Accrington, Sheffield. We heard there was taxi drivers' and footballers' battalions in London, an' trammen in Glasgow. So's our MP demanded to know why there wasn't a Leigh Pals, when them Germans was bricking up Belgian mines with Belgians in them, and setting fire t'mills with women and children still at looms, like. So he set up a raising committee. An' we said – cotton is an important cloth for t'war. Who'll do the work if we gin over there? Wives and daughters, they said. Oh, aye, and when they can get the women for farthings, what happens when we come back? And who'd feed our childer then? Well, most of them mill owners, and t'mine owners, too, says they'd pay six shillings to a wife a week and a tanner a child. Some even said ten bob for a family, no questions asked. Happen what swung it was, they said we men'd 'ave our jobs back after the war at old rates or better. That the women were temporary, like. Plus you know, when we enlisted we got the King's shilling, then a guinea a week for training. That was a lot o' brass. And, honest, for most of us it were a break from t'mills when all were said and done. Aye, so many of us turned up at the Hippodrome recruiting drive, they ran out of khaki. Wore civvies for the first few months, we did. Wi' army boots. Right shite they were, pardon me, Major. Some o' the boot makers made a pretty penny out of givin' us riffraff boots that fell apart after one drill. Lumber, they was. Them mullocks should have been shot, I reckon. War profiteering that were. Anyways, we trained at Conwy in Wales and Catterick, and had us some fine times, and then we went to Egypt for more clompin', before we came here. We thunk it'd all be a six-month adventure. A bit of a mank, like.'

Six months and a bit of a lark, Watson translated. 'And remind me, every man in the battalion is from Leigh?'

'No, no.'Twern't like some of the bigger towns with slums, where they just emptied folk out. We didn't have enough for a whole battalion, us. No. A Company, them of us what you did your blood tests on, we're all Leigh, so is most of C. But B is Bolton blokes, and D is Bolton and a lot of Wigan men, n' all. Some of the officers're from Liverpool and Manchester, as ye know. Some, like Captain de Griffon, had links to the area. He'll be all right now, will he? The captain?'

'I hope so.'

'And you dunno who did this to him?'

'Who or what, Sergeant, no. Tell me, what do you think of him? De Griffon? Just between us, man to man.'

'I think he's a fine fella, sir. Had no hesitation in promoting me. Happen he might see me worth when I get 'ome, too.'

If, Watson automatically corrected. If you get home.

'And 'e's got some gumption, too; won't ask a man to do anything he won't do 'isself. Not like some officers. If you don't mind me sayin'.'

'Not at all. Any particular officers in mind?'

'Not really.'

'Lieutenant Metcalf?'

Platt's eyes went to his boots. 'I couldn't talk out of turn, sir.'

'One more thing, Platt: could you get me a list of which particular mills each man worked at?'

'Aye, I reckon.'

Watson put a foot in the stirrup and, with a helping push from Platt, hauled himself into the saddle. Lord Lockie sidestepped a little and shook his head, but stayed calm. Watson leaned down. 'Sorry, one more thought . . . how many mills do the de Griffons own in town?'

'Three outright. The B-Stones they are called. Blackstone, Bankstone and Bradstone Mills.'

'Right. Just the names of the men who worked at those three for now. And do it discreetly, if you can.'

'Oh, I know most of 'em already, don't you worry. 'Tain't a big place, Leigh.' He adjusted the stirrups. 'You want a nip of brandy, sir, keep you warm?' He tapped his pocket.

'No, thank you, Platt.'

'Reet you are. There. You be all reet now.' He gave Lord Lockie's rump a light slap and Watson ducked under the barn lintel as the horse clopped out onto the cobbles, with the doctor wondering when was the last time he'd been foolish enough to get on a strange horse. And, later, how he came to ask all the wrong questions.

After Watson had left to fetch Lord Lockie, de Griffon felt well enough to sit up and try to take a few steps. His head was still prone to attacks of vertigo and when he stood, his legs felt unable to carry his body. He asked Miss Pippery to support him while he walked the length of the tent. He found he needed to grip her arm harder than he had imagined.

'He's quite a character, your Major Watson,' de Griffon said as he plonked one foot down after another.

'Yes, he is,' agreed Miss Pippery. 'A lovely man.'

'But should he be galloping around like this? Literally, I mean, now he has Lord Lockie. At his age? He's not a young man.'

'I suppose you can't break the habit of a lifetime.'

'How do you mean?'

Miss Pippery recounted what Mrs Gregson had told her.

'You mean he's that Watson? Oh my Lord. I never . . .' He shook his head, smiling to himself. 'Well, gosh, it's quite a privilege to have him investigate your case. If only the great detective were here as well. Soon solve it then, eh?'

'Oh, no, that's not likely, sir. Mrs Gregson said there'd been a,' she lowered her voice to a stage whisper, 'falling out.'

'Really? That's a crying shame. Still, it's all terribly exciting. Right, here we are.' They reached the exit of the tent, and he looked outside for a second. 'Looks like more damned rain. Excuse my language. We're due back in the line soon. The water table is so high here, you live and sleep in water. So, shall we try going back to the bed again? Oh, Cecil, there you are!'

De Griffon bent down and ruffled the back of his dog's neck. The animal gave a bark of greeting and began to pant excitedly.

'Why is he called Cecil?'

'After Cecil Rhodes. Another great explorer. All over the place, every day. Eh, Cecil?'

The dog yapped a reply.

'Miss Pippery, do you think you could get me a pen and paper? My company is due to return to the reserves imminently. I need to remind Lieutenant Metcalf of a few things before I can rejoin them.'

'That might be a few days.'

'Nonsense. I can feel my dancing legs coming back. Although don't think I am in any hurry to leave you lovely ladies behind.'

Miss Pippery blushed.

'Sorry. Didn't mean to be crass. As I said the other day, it's just that— Ah, Mrs Gregson, hello there.'

Mrs Gregson gave a brief smile, as fleeting as a lightning strike, 'Sister Spence says, thanks to Major Watson's representations, I can stay on for a few days, just as long as I do nothing more medical than serve tea.'

'Well, that's something,' said Miss Pippery, hesitantly.

'And only to the men. Not the officers.'

'That's a shame,' said de Griffon, as he pulled himself back on the bed. 'Can Miss Pippery here still do me a brew?'

'I think the rules only apply to me. Miss Pippery is all yours.'

De Griffon gave Miss Pippery a wink. 'So, Mrs Gregson, I hear tell you are from Manchester?'

'Cheshire,' she corrected. 'But my father worked in Manchester for a good few years when we were young.'

'And you, Miss Pippery? The name's Old English, I believe.'

Miss Pippery nodded, pleased someone had noticed. 'It is. Or so my father drummed into us.'

'And how did you two meet?' he asked. 'Come on. Sister Spence isn't here now.'

'Motor-cycling,' said Miss Pippery slowly, in case he was one of those who considered it an unladylike pursuit. 'My brother was a keen motor-cyclist, you see, and so was Mrs Gregson's. Both did time trials and hill climbs. I used to go along to watch at first.'

'Miss Pippery's parents will tell you I corrupted her to a world of leather, oil and grease.'

'Sounds rather splendid. I love motor cycles.'

'Do you?' asked Miss Pippery.

'Yes, I have a Sunbeam at home. A lovely machine. Perhaps all three of us could go riding. One day.'

Miss Pippery beamed at the thought.

'Look, about that paper,' he said. 'If it's not too much trouble.'

'Oh, of course not. I'll fetch you some.'

After she had left, Mrs Gregson said: 'Please don't.'

'Don't what?'

'Lead her on so. Miss Pippery might be able to change a spark plug, but she's not as worldly as some. She's almost ten years younger than me—'

His eyebrows shot up. 'Good Lord, you wouldn't have thought—'

'There you go again. Turn off the charm. Or at least turn the wick down a little, Captain.'

Cecil jumped on the bed with a frisky yelp and de Griffon

caught the look of disapproval and pushed him off. 'I'll send him back soon. He's the only visitor from my company I've had so far. Watson told me Metcalf came, but he sent him away. You haven't seen the lieutenant? No, probably trying to recruit more nurses for his damned dance. Look, I'm not toying with Miss Pippery. It's just . . . just it makes a change from all that relentlessly male company. It's all football, fags, and — excuse me — another word beginning with "f" with the lads.' His mouth turned down at the sides in an exaggerated grimace at his uncouthness. 'If you know what I mean?'

'I think I do.'

'Frollicking, let's say. I don't share their attitude to women, Mrs Gregson.'

'I should hope not.'

'Nor, as I said, my family's. Nothing like that strike-breaking of the last century will happen again on my watch. Terrible business.'

'What became of the ringleaders? My father used to talk about two women who were the main instigators?'

'The Trueloves. Bess and Anne. My father talked of them, too. They disappeared after the strike collapsed. Bess told the women to go back to work. There were rumours she'd been paid off.'

'And had she?'

He shook his head. 'Father always said not. Not a penny. Change of heart, he said. Then they disappeared. Nothing sinister. But there was bad feeling among the women after that speech by Bess. Some believed the rumours that they'd been promised money. The sisters moved to London and then abroad, so I heard.' His eyes lost focus for a second, thinking back on events a quarter of a century ago, before he was even born.

'There we are,' he said eventually. 'What do you think Major Watson hopes to find today?'

'I think Major Watson is a little confused at the moment.'

'How so?'

Mrs Gregson pursed her lips. De Griffon wasn't certain whether it was in disapproval or not, but there was certainly a buzz of wasp-ishness in it. 'Major Watson's not entirely sure whether he is being a detective or a knight in shining armour.'

'I don't quite follow.'

'He has gone off to save the virtue of Staff Nurse Jennings. And . . .'

She gave a little snort of a laugh.

'What is it?'

'Nothing, I have to go before Sister catches me in here with you.'

But there had been something. A little spike in her heart. And it was funny. Hilarious. And ridiculous, she thought. Just for a moment there, she'd actually been jealous of Jennings having her very own white knight.

FORTY-ONE

Wallace McCrae was a ruddy-faced, fiercely beetle-browed man somewhere in his forties, with ginger hair and pale eyes. He was sitting behind his desk, fingers interlocked, listening intently to Watson, who was pacing in front of him, explaining exactly why he had ridden over from Suffolk Farm to visit the American volunteers.

'Therefore,' Watson concluded, 'as he seems not to be here——'

'We have not seen Caspar Myles for some time, no,' agreed McCrae in a deep baritone.

'I really need to know what, exactly, occurred to cause him to leave this hospital and the Harvard Volunteers.'

McCrae began fiddling with the Notre-Dame paperweight on his desk. The gloomy room, the doctor's office, was on the third floor of what had once been an old mental asylum. The original patients had been rehoused, shipped south, out of danger. Now it specialized in the treatment of fractures, with an X-ray machine installed by Madame Curie herself. 'Much as I appreciate the situation, I'm not sure I can tell you everything. There are reputations at stake.'

Watson didn't give two hoots for reputations. 'There might be lives at stake.'

'I can't say I condone what Myles did.'

Watson stopped pacing, horrified. 'I should think not.'

'Then again, he's a red-blooded man.'

'Where I come from, that's no excuse.'

'That's as maybe. I'm from Chicago, Major Watson. Not the subtlest place on God's earth. Hog Butcher to the World. And proud of it. So am I. My father made his money in meatpacking. Enough to send me to Harvard. My grandfather, mind, was from Dundee. One of the Scots who came over to build Chicago. Both of them believed that there were times when men's baser instincts take over. That there is a natural justice—'

'And the nurse in question? How would she feel about "natural justice"?'

'Might agree also.'

Watson gave a snort of impatience. 'I don't believe this. A nurse is raped—'

'Almost raped,' McCrae corrected.

Watson was pleased he didn't have Mrs Gregson with him. The resultant explosion might have knocked the earth off its axis.

'A serious assault, then.'

'Two serious assaults, in fact.'

Watson could not believe his ears. 'Myles is a habitual rapist?'

McCrae's brows beetled together even more. His nose twitched as if he had just detected a bad smell. 'Myles? He's no rapist.'

Watson threw his arms in the air. 'Then for pity's sake, McCrae, tell me what he is!'

'He's a complicated fellow.'

'So it appears.'

'He is one of those chaps who, on the surface, has it all. Good looks, wealth, fine manners. Sense of humour. Well-connected family. But there are areas where the edifice cracks. He is surprisingly crass sometimes, especially where women are concerned. His approach can be, let me see, flat-footed. If you get my drift.'

Watson thought of Myles's attempts to find out if Watson had any designs on Staff Nurse Jennings. 'I do.'

'There was a nurse, a very good one, called Amelia Wilkes. One of the Connecticut Wilkeses. Very nice. Very pretty. We all knew that Caspar was sweet on her. Well, there was a dance. And two fellows thought it would be funny to make Myles jealous. First by dancing with her. Then by disappearing with her. Doctor, I am ashamed to say this, but much alcohol was consumed. The two fellows became boisterous. To be frank, they tried to force themselves on Nurse Wilkes. She resisted. One of them . . .' He repositioned himself in the chair. 'One of them slapped her to try and gain some compliance. The other ripped her dress. It was at that point that Caspar Myles found them.'

Watson was seized by the terrible feeling he had misjudged the man. 'And?'

'And, as I say, I can't condone what he did. But part of me admires him. He waded in. One of the two men ran away, although not until his nose was broken by Myles. The other decided to put up his fists. Myles doesn't look like a boxer. And the Harvard Athletic Committee does not recognize it as an official varsity sport. But perhaps you know that Teddy Roosevelt boxed on campus? No? Well, Caspar Myles did, too, and with some success. He pounded this guy. And pounded. And pounded. Until all three of them, the nurse included, were drenched in his blood. That was how I found them.'

'Good Lord.'

'Quite. The man he attacked was the son of a very generous benefactor of the Longwood facility. The medical school. And Myles's parents are not without influence.'

'And Nurse Wilkes . . . ?'

'Was actually unharmed, physically. In fact, she still works here. But the man that Caspar had beaten, well, we operated on the face, but he'll never be handsome again.' Watson remembered Myles's right hand. Holmes would have known what it was: broken knuckles that had not healed well. 'There were those who thought Myles had over-reacted. Mostly friends of the man he had assaulted. It was agreed that Caspar would leave the Volunteers, at least for the time being. I knew the British were short of doctors, and that there was a CCS nearby. I told Torrance a version of the truth.'

'One that suggested he was a rapist?'

'That he'd been indiscreet with a nurse. I don't have to tell you that most men would see that as the nurse's fault.'

'Shame on you,' Watson said.

McCrae shrugged, unabashed by the criticism. 'Perhaps. We shipped the injured boy back home. The story was he had been injured when the hospital was shelled. We left it to him to embellish the details.'

'He's probably a war hero.'

McCrae made a noise a little like laughter. 'Knowing the young man in question, I don't doubt it.'

Watson finally sat down in the chair and let out a long, slow breath. 'Thank you for being so frank with me.'

'In retrospect, I might have done things differently. But it's done.

As I say, in Chicago, we would have said he did the right thing. Have you been?'

'To Chicago?' Holmes had, of course, during the Von Bork affair. 'No, we once had some dealings with . . .'

The thought tailed off. McCrae waited and then prompted: 'Now, would you like to explain what this is all about?'

'Yes. I just . . . Chicago, it reminded me of something, but I'm blowed if I can recall what. But yes, I can give you the basics.' Watson, after requesting McCrae's discretion on the matter, gave him an outline of the death of Hornby, Shipobottom and the near-murder, as he believed it to be, of de Griffon.

'Peculiar,' McCrae said when he had finished. 'But my instinct would be gas. We've had a few cases of a new one that Fritz is using. It's not like chlorine, doesn't act as an irritant, so you don't cough. Which means it gets inside your lungs quicker. Some say it smells like a meadow that's been freshly cut, others like silage. But, this is the strange thing, men report they are fine until one, two, even three days later. Then their lungs stop working.'

'What's it called?'

'We haven't had a chance to name it yet. Did you bring any blood samples, by the way? From the victim?'

'I did. There is citrated blood with the lab.' He unfolded the batch number the laboratory assistant had given him.

'Fine. You want to leave that with me? If it throws up anything, I'll get a message to you. You'll be at the CCS?'

He put the docket on the desk. 'For the foreseeable—'

Chicago!

'You OK, Major?'

'Yes. No.' Watson's collar suddenly felt very tight. *Chicago*, that was the key. 'I just remembered what your home town meant to me.' He stood, suddenly anxious to be on his way. 'I have to go. Apologies.'

'Right. Listen, be careful who you talk to about gas. It's a mighty sensitive area right now. Unless you have friends in high places, they'll stonewall you.'

'I do,' said Watson, gathering up his cap.

'Do what?'

'Have friends in high places.'

FORTY-TWO

The sharpshooter moved through the woods as silently as was humanly possible. The ground underneath was sodden and slimy, which, although hampering his progress, helped deaden the sound of his steps. The rain had left the trees shedding water with a steady pit-pat, like a leaky tap. His ears were attuned for a sudden burst, a spray of water, evidence of a disturbed branch, which could well indicate an enemy being careless.

He was dressed in the latest sniper outfit, loose fitting and coloured with a mottled pattern of green and brown. On his head was a hood, decorated with a corona of twigs and leaves. He thought it made him look like a ball of mistletoe or a swollen scarecrow. The hood restricted vision, made breathing hard and would slow down any attempt to slip on a gas mask. He had already made a note of five improvements that could be made to the outfit.

There was a burst of birdsong, a jarring sound these days, and he stopped at a crouch, close to a tree trunk, to make sure it was a genuine chorus and not the enemy communicating. It was. No guns thumping, the rain gone, and the birds singing. It might have been a day to enjoy, if he wasn't intent on killing.

His target was Churchill's so-called reserve HQ, which had been christened Maison 1875. His advanced HQ, Laurence Farm, had been badly hit by the surprise bombardment and was undergoing repairs.

The trees were thinning now and he could see the building, a rather impressive four-square manor house, standing behind what had once been a ploughed field, now dotted with shell craters, each with its own stagnant pool in the bottom.

With rifle held across his body, he threaded through a stand of saplings, some of which showed artillery damage, from shredded branches to shards of shrapnel that protruded from the slender trunks, like dull, metallic bracket fungi.

He felt exposed among the slender young trees, but there were some mature ones, also showing war scars, to his left. He moved towards them, stopping every few yards. The hood also amplified the wearer's breathing, which meant it was hard to pick up on extraneous or threatening sounds from the outside world. They should cut ear holes. He licked his lips. Fear dried the mouth. Always.

Two more steps and he froze, knees bent. There were figures, some distance beyond the edge of the wood, deep in conversation. Three men, each coddled in heavy coats and scarves, wreathed in smoke from their cigars. The centre one, unmistakable even at that distance, was Churchill. He smiled to himself under the sacking. Don't rush it. Target acquisition and recognition was two-thirds of the process. Still at a crouch he crabbed through the undergrowth, trying to frame a perfect, clear shot. At the same time, he kept a watch for any patrol that might discover him.

With a slow, steady movement, he raised the rifle and sighted.

Another step to the side, leaning against a tree trunk that had lost its upper crown trunk to a shell burst. He put the A.PX scope to his eye.

Target acquired. Kill imminent.

The point of a bayonet pricked his neck.

'Ow,' he protested.

'You're did, so you are, mae son,' said the tree in a broad Scots accent.

Corporal Leith ripped off the sniper's hood and put his fingers to his throat. His fingertips showed a red smear. 'You cut me, you Jock madman.'

His fellow fusilier stepped from within the elaborate, hollowed-out trunk of the fake trunk and pulled off his own hood. 'Aye, an' you'd get worse from a Hun.'

'It's a fuckin' exercise, you daft cunt.'

'Oi,' said the treeman, waving the bayonet. 'Wha' you call me?'

A whistle blew, marking the end of the manoeuvre. The two men relaxed and, after a moment, punched each other on the shoulder. The treeman even gave something that could be interpreted as an apology for his over-enthusiasm. The sniper took out a field dressing and mopped up the trickle of blood staining his collar.

Watson, flanked by Churchill and his aide-de-camp Captain Edmund Hakewill-Smith, the young officer who had blown the whistle, watched as a dozen men emerged from the battered Ploegsteert woods, all outlandishly dressed in various outfits of deception.

'What do you think, Watson?' asked Churchill. 'Not quite Savile Row. But the finest that the *Section de Camouflage* in Marne can supply. They are working on fake heads for us, too. Stick up above the parapet, draw fire. Might get m'self one for the House. Eh?'

'Impressive,' said Watson, as a soldier appeared to emerge from a tree trunk, like a wood-goblin sprung to life.

'The trees are remarkable,' said Churchill, who was clearly enjoying himself. 'Metal skin, with wood and papier-mâché over them. Fool anyone at close range.' He tossed away the stub of his cigar. 'Hake, can you debrief the men? The major has something he wants to ask me.' He turned back to Watson. 'Isn't that right?'

'It is, sir.'

While Hakewill-Smith gathered the men, corralling them into place with his sharp South African bark, they began the walk back to Maison 1875, where Watson had stabled his horse.

'I know it looks like playing silly buggers, all this dressing as trees, but we have to take the fight to the Germans. All this Big Push nonsense that Haig spouts about is just that – nonsense. They haven't grasped one simple fact. If you send over a hundred thousand shells on one sector, then the Germans bloody well know where you are coming across. Might as well send them a telegram: *Hope you don't mind, Fritz, thought we'd try and take the Wytschaete Ridge tomorrow.* Madness. The war has become too static. As I told you at Somerset, we need small, mobile units, to tackle their snipers, take out their machine gunners, take prisoners. There should be no such thing as no man's land. It must be our man's land.'

He turned and looked back at the soldiers, huddled around Hakewill-Smith. 'Hence the training. I'll whittle them down to six or seven men. An élite squad. Tough little Scots, mostly. We'll be out there within a day or two, sniper hunting. We will own no man's land.' He tossed aside his now expired cigar.

Churchill fetched a bullet from his pocket. 'When you told me about the tower and the sniper, I was sceptical, Watson. Very sceptical. What you called logic, I thought was guesswork. But that was one hell of a wound in the sentry. So we searched the rubble of the church. We found a Mauser and a large number of these.' He held the steel-and-brass projectile between thumb and index finger. 'I have sent several to the Royal Small Arms Factory for analysis. But we fired a round through the Mauser. Remarkable effect. If we could duplicate that explosive power for shells . . .'

'You'd copy it?'

'Of course. Illegal as bullets, maybe, but scaled up . . . That's not to say I won't complain about the fact it breaches the Geneva Convention. Although I intend to grab myself a few more snipers first, see if this is common issue by the Hun.'

'You? Surely you won't go out there?

Churchill stopped walking, put the bullet away and took another cigar from his top pocket, which he shoved into the corner of his mouth. 'Why do people keep asking me that? I'll be back in London one of these days. Perhaps in the Cabinet once more. I don't want them saying that Winston spent his time at the front shuttling between the bordellos of Armentières and the wine cellars of Bordeaux. I don't want them to think that the man who can order an attack on the Dardanelles is too cowardly to get out there and show some real leadership.'

He screwed his face into a grimace. Watson could see why he had a reputation as a tricky customer and a hothead, out for personal glory. In this case, though, it appeared there was the need for a kind of redemption, a purging of the soul, too. Those men slaughtered on the beaches at Gallipoli would weigh heavy on any man's mind, no matter what degree of bravado he presented to the world.

'Even so, sir——'

'What?'

Watson realized he had displeased Churchill. He wanted an admiring slap on the back. Not reservations about the wisdom of chasing around with men half his age.

'It's your decision.'

'Glad you think so.'

This was an argument he wasn't going to win. 'When we met previously you mentioned something about a case that might be of interest.'

'Ah.' Churchill brightened. 'Yes. Is that why you are here?'

'No. But if you care to give me details, I will think on it.'

'Not much to tell. I told you, *The Case of the Man Who Died Twice*. It was a distant cousin of Clementine's. A subaltern. Roddy Blunt. Deserted his post under fire. Left his platoon to be overrun. All of whom fought to the last, I might add. Not one left standing. Well, there was no option but to court-martial him. Excuse me.' He turned his back to the wind and lit the cigar. 'There have been grumblings about differential treatment of men and officers. Disproportionate amount of death sentences for other ranks is what they say. What they don't take into account is that any fleeing junior officer is likely to get shot by his commanding officer out of hand.' Churchill's piggish eyes narrowed conspiratorially. 'Happens more than you think. So, there's a court martial and before Clemmie hears of it, he's been shot at dawn. Quite right too.'

'Seems very straightforward,' Watson said, knowing there was more to come.

'Ah,' said Churchill, his bad mood now completely forgotten. 'I said it was called *The Case of the Man Who Died Twice*, didn't I?'

'I believe you did.'

'The execution was some months ago. Four weeks back, a body turned up in Wiltshire. Under a hedgerow, where he had been living rough like some gypsy. It was identified as Roddy Blunt.'

'And how long had he been dead?'

'No more than two days.'

Watson fetched his cigarettes and lit one. He and Churchill turned back and looked over the uneven field, towards the scattered farmhouses that formed the Royal Scots Fusiliers' reserve positions, and the marks of distant trenches – coils of wire and posts for the most part – where two armies were literally keeping their heads down. In the very far distance there was a speck ascending slowly into the sky. A German observation balloon.

'Curious,' said Watson at last.

'Have you any thoughts?'

He smoked on for a while, watching a distant biplane of indeterminate nationality. Dark puffs of ack-ack explosions bracketed it for a while, until it gained height and was lost to the clouds. 'Where in Wiltshire?'

'Idmiston.'

Watson smoked on, revelling in the moment. 'Then I do believe I have a solution.'

'Really?' Churchill asked.

'But first, I would like to ask a favour.'

Churchill narrowed just one eye this time. 'Ever thought of going into politics, Major Watson?'

'I can't say I have,' he replied.

'Pity. It's only blackmail with stricter rules. So what is this favour?'

Watson explained the deaths and the possibility that poison gas might be involved. He was concerned, he said, about the secrecy that surrounded the whole project. Churchill listened patiently.

'Well, between you and me, Watson, if I go back to Westminster, I suspect it will be as Minister of Munitions. The gas will be mine to control. Not that I have any objection in principle. But in the meantime, I can give you a letter asking for all co-operations as you are investigating on my behalf. Not worth the paper it's printed on, of course, but the Churchill name might still have some currency.'

The man knew damned well it did. 'I am sure it has considerable weight. Thank you.'

The observation plane he had seen earlier now dropped from its cloud cover and began circling the observation balloon. It was too far away to see the details, but the gas-filled envelope began to descend quickly, as it was frantically winched in. He imagined the observer raking it with bullets from his Lewis gun as it went. Having been suspended under such a canopy, even if only for a few brief minutes, he felt an affinity with the horribly exposed observers.

'You have time for a brandy before you go?'

Watson looked at his wristwatch and the sun, already beginning to fall, and the temperature along with it. 'A quick one, perhaps.'

Churchill slapped him on the back. 'Excellent. And the solution to my problem?'

'Before I took the opportunity to come out here to preach the gospel of blood transfusion, I was offered a position on the home front. At a place called Porton. It is where the War Department Experimental Ground is based. My role would be to investigate the effects of poison gas on soldiers and possible protective measures and antidotes. I am afraid I refused because I suspected such work might involve human guinea pigs. And besides, I wanted to be closer to the front.'

The dull crump of an explosion reached them, and they turned to see a dark column spiralling up into the sky. A trench mortar at work.

'Although perhaps not this close. Sir, what if a soldier, under a death sentence, is given an alternative? You can live, but you have to help with top-secret war work. It will involve changing identity, not getting in touch with your family. At the end of the war, some cover story will be released to say that you were acting under the Defence of the Realm Act, and that the story of you being shot was bogus.'

Churchill looked doubtful. 'That is all very Buchan-ish.'

Watson continued with his conjecture. 'But once you are at the Experimental Ground, you realize the truth. You will be experimented on—'

'By your own side?'

'The man was a coward,' Watson said, playing devil's advocate. 'Deserved to be shot. You said so yourself.'

'Shot, yes. Tortured, no. But really. The British wouldn't do such things.'

'I am afraid there are scientists who would. Scientists for whom the ends always justify the means. Men who are certain they will not be answering to any higher power for their actions. I should imagine that he escaped and was hunted. He died at Idmiston, not far from Porton, hiding under a hedgerow. Exposure, I would wager, exacerbated by any effects from the chemicals.'

Churchill had gone quite puce. He puffed on his cigar, releasing a plume of smoke. 'How can you be certain?'

'It's just a theory. But it fits the facts.'

'It sounds impossible.'

'No. When you have eliminated the impossible, whatever else remains, however unlikely, must be the truth. Is it possible he died twice? No. So who would have use of a "dead" man in Wiltshire? The scientists who need live bodies to test their theories.'

'If this outrage is true . . .' Churchill's jowls wobbled as he shook his head.

'As Minister of Munitions, you'd be able to find out.'

More furious puffing. 'I will, Watson, I will.' They had reached the house, and both men returned the salute of the sentry. 'Come, there's that brandy.'

'And my letter,' Watson reminded him.

'Yes, and your damned letter.'

Watson paused as a thought struck him. 'And one other thing.'

'What's that?'

'Can you get me the post-mortem notes from Wiltshire?'

Churchill waved the cigar as if it were a magic wand. 'I'm sure I can. Why?'

'I want to know if Blunt had turned blue.'

FORTY-THREE

Those who saw the figure of Dr Watson racing through the hospital grounds turned and watched, some in admiration at his turn of speed, others in concern for the man's heart. It was thumping in his chest, that was true, but not all of that was from his exertions.

Sister Spence, who was standing with a cup of tea outside her tent, attempted to check his progress. 'Major Watson—' she began, but he didn't slow his pace.

'Later, Sister,' he managed to gasp. 'I have some most urgent business.'

Watson didn't catch her reply.

He took the steps up to the Big House two and three at a time, marvelling at his burst of energy. He might pay for it later, but he didn't care. If he was right, this would be worth a few aches and pains.

He burst into the room, grabbed the magazine he had been sent and collapsed back on the bed, the air rasping in his throat and his heart pounding at double-time. It was a few seconds before he could pick up a pencil and begin.

My years of investigations as a consulting detective revealed nothing in the criminal annals that has been quite so baffling or exciting as trying to decipher the behaviour of the humble honeybee, specifically how information is distributed around the hive. Yet during the past three years, my colleague and companion, Thomas Patrick, and I have made considerable progress in this area.

Despite the best efforts in the last century of august apiarists such as Leon Alberti and Auguste Kerckhoffs, the mechanism by which a foraging worker bee conveys information to its fellows remains a mystery. Every year brings new theories, as regular readers of this journal can testify. After reading the works of von Frisch (*Zoologische Jahrbüch*, copies of which, despite the hostilities that exist between our two countries, are still imported by several learned institutions, including the Zoological Society of London), we installed glass windows into several of our hives, the better to observe events normally hidden from human eyes. Round-the-clock observations were made and records kept. Where the bee had come from – direction, type of flowers visited – was noted where possible. Any abdominal movement sketched. The direction of the 'dance' indicated. Several of the bees were marked with dabs of paint to help distinguish individuals. On several occasions field trips were made to try to observe where the bees from our hives were foraging. Notable

Watson couldn't wait any longer. Along the top of the page, he wrote down the sequence of letters he had circled.

My Dear Watson

A blast of euphoria coursed through him. He looked at the phrase again.

My Dear Watson

Three words that told him there was no Thomas Patrick, no new colleague and friend. He found he was on his feet, doing a little jig, as if he had the knees of a man forty years younger.

Tommy Patrick was the villain in Chicago who had created the Dancing Men code. Alberti and Kerckhoffs weren't apiarists – they were cryptographers. And the code used in the article was one of the simplest in the annals of ciphers, yet his blithering idiot's eyes had not recognized it, nor the clues that the article was a device to deliver a message to Watson. It was McCrae's mention of Chicago that had caused the synapses in his brain to finally fire properly. To appreciate that Holmes was up to his old tricks.

With shaking hands Watson set about ringing the other letters, until he had an entire missive from his old friend. He read through it, twice, and felt his eyes sting. He was tired, he supposed. Soon, his body would start protesting about his sprint through the hospital grounds and his impetuous dancing. It had been another long and eventful day and there was a lot more to do before the cloak of night allowed the war to restart in earnest. He blew his nose.

After he had finished the code, he quickly wrote out the longest, most expensive telegram he had ever composed and went in search of Miss Pippery to send it for him. Anyone observing the man who bowled down the stone steps and burst out into the gloom of late afternoon might have thought he had taken some kind of stimulant, or found an elixir that could roll back biological time by a decade or two. There was a hint of weightlessness about Watson, as if the gravity around him had been turned down a notch or two. With nary a creak of the knees he bent and scooped up Cecil, de Griffon's Jack Russell, and, with the dog yapping under his arm, he picked up the pace, aware he had to give his body some respect now, walked briskly to the transfusion tent.

FORTY-FOUR

Corporal Percy Lewis considered himself a lucky man. True, he was cold, his feet ached, his puttees were too tight, and rain was dripping off his steel helmet into the gap between collar and neck. Yet, guard duty was preferable to being ten miles to the east, where the men he had served with before being seconded to the BSGC were about to re-enter the front-line trenches for another four days of alternating boredom and fear. The only constant up there was discomfort, and it was of a different magnitude from a cape that didn't keep out all the water.

Lewis had been lucky before. He had been sent home poorly from the four p.m. shift at the Connolly Pit when it fired. He'd only just reached home and was preparing to go and sleep off whatever was ailing him when there came a knocking at the door. Smoke was coming out of the shaft, the neighbours said. He had rushed to the pithead and the women were gathering for their terrible vigil. Of course, he'd volunteered for the rescue party, but it was three hours before the fires were put out and it was safe to send a cage down. There were three survivors. They buried the thirty-six dead in two communal trenches. His father and two brothers among them. He swore he would never go down a pit again. So he'd joined the army.

He was also lucky to have survived the conflict for this long. Only a handful of his original Old Contemptibles had come through unscathed. Most of those who had landed with him at Le Havre existed only as faded faces in his mind's eye, slowly merging into each other, to become one single entity. And now, just when there was talk of another big push coming, he had been taken out of the front line for guard duty. Perhaps it was his age: nearly forty. Maybe someone thought he'd done his bit, that one day his luck might just run out.

The rain gave one last violent burst and then faded to nothing. Lewis gave a little shake to flick the water from his clothes.

'Rider approaching!' The voice came from above. Reggie Smillings, a Durham lad, also from a mining family.

Lewis raised a hand to show he had heard and stepped out from the meagre shelter the stone-capped pillar had provided to position himself in the centre of the iron gates that gave access to the grounds of Burnt-Out Lodge.

The rider came out of the thickening dusk and down the approach road at a steady trot, slowly resolving from a blurred, indistinct shape, to an officer on a horse, to a major on a rather fine steed. And not a young major, either. Certainly not one of those schoolboy officers, the one-pip wonders, who still needed help wiping their arses. Lewis felt a touch of butterflies, wondering what sending a senior member of the brass meant. Were they being recalled to go back to the front?

'Sir!' he shouted when the mounted officer was within hailing distance. 'I'll have to ask you to stop there. This facility is out of bounds to all but authorized personnel.'

The officer made no sign of acknowledgement. He pulled the horse to a halt, dismounted, and tied his mount to a makeshift hitching post, stroking the face and saying something softly in its ear. He turned, flicked the rain from his cape and approached Lewis.

'Corporal. I wonder if I might see your commanding officer?'

'Sorry, Major,' he said in a Lanky accent not so broad as it had once been. 'The unit's bin moved to the front. Just a couple of us left to guard the site.' He glanced up at Smillings. 'Four privates, a lance corporal an' me.'

'Which makes you the senior person here,' Watson said brightly.

'I don't know about that,' Lewis said cautiously. He'd never liked too much responsibility. Never wanted to proceed as far as sergeant. He was happy where he was, anonymous enough, but not sitting at the bottom of the heap.

'I assume all the, um, special armaments have been moved up as well?'

Lewis put an index finger under his collar, releasing another trickle of icy water. 'I am not allowed to discuss such things, sir.'

Watson hesitated. He knew that his sponsor was a double-edged sword. The Hero of Sidney Street; the Butcher of Gallipoli. Which would the corporal recognize? 'I have here a letter,' he said at last, extracting it from his pocket and displaying it with a flourish. 'Which gives me permission to inspect these and any other grounds where I believe there to be a medical issue.'

'Medical?'

'The material we are dealing with is designed to hurt, maim and kill. I need to ensure they only hurt, main and kill the enemy.'

'Ain't heard of no accidents here. Besides, there's only—' He caught himself.

'Corporal. If I have to ride all the way back to Colonel Churchill to tell him that I have been obstructed—'

'There's only one small dump left. Everything else has gone for'ard.'

'May I see?'

Watson held up the letter again as a reminder of his authority. Lewis read it once more. '. . . *are required to offer all consideration and assistance in all matters pertaining to* . . .'

It wasn't so much a request as an instruction. Even the signature, aggressively scrawled across the lower half of the page, had a bullying tone. Was this, Lewis wondered, the moment when his luck ran out? A decision either way could have fearful ramifications.

'Come with me, sir,' Lewis said eventually, turning to unlatch the gate with heavy steps and an even heavier heart.

Burnt-Out Lodge had been chosen, Lewis explained, because, although the upper building had been severely damaged, there were extensive cellars that were intact. It was below ground that the 'special armaments' were stored. It was, he explained, a wise precaution to guard against air raids, which might cause casualties over a wide area if a dump were hit.

Lewis led Watson down mossy stone steps to double steel doors that had replaced the original wooden ones. These were kept closed with a bolt that was provided with a hasp for a lock, although none was fitted.

'Do we need any sort of protection?' Watson asked, as Lewis swung the door back. 'Against the gas?'

Lewis flinched at the three-letter word. 'Not really. You get the odd sniff now and then, stingy eyes, mebbe, but nothing too bad.' He reached in and flicked a switch for the electric lights. There was a low hum and several false starts before light flooded the place. He pointed to a rack on the wall, lined with hypo helmets and emergency packs of gauze soaked in anti-gas chemicals. 'Anything happens, you just grab one of those quick.'

Watson stepped into the subterranean space, its vaulted ceiling supported by sugar-twist pillars. Beneath his feet was an uneven, stone-flagged floor. It was cold, damp and mostly empty, save for a small hillock of something at one side, covered with a tarpaulin.

'May I?' asked Watson.

'Aye. But be careful how you lift it.'

Watson did as instructed, removed the stones that weighted down the edges of the covering and gingerly rolled it back. Underneath was a series of canisters, each shaped like a steel cigar, with a valve arrangement at one end. Each of them had a lengthy rubber tube, coiled like a tendril, emerging from the neck, just above the valve wheel. The cylinders were marked with a skull and cross bones on the side, stencilled in white, with a prominent red star beneath it. Watson felt something grab at his throat even as he looked at them. 'Is this the only dump?'

'Only one with anything left, I reckon.'

'Where were the others?'

'Wherever there was a decent cellar. Dotted about, they were. But emptied now.'

'Then why are these still here?' Watson asked Lewis, pulling the cover back over the pile.

'Old stock.'

'It loses potency?' A blank expression greeted him. Watson rephrased. 'Does it become less effective over time?"

Lewis unslung his rifle. He'd already compromised himself; he reckoned he could do no more harm. 'With these you build a trench, bury the cylinder in sandbags, run the tube up onto no man's land, wait till wind blows in t'right direction and open t'valves. And then, run. 'Cause if that wind changes . . . The new stocks, them's not cylinders at all, but they call 'em projectiles. Well, designed to be fired at enemy from some sort of trench mortar. So at least ye know it's goin' to right side of lines.'

He gave a laugh. Watson didn't feel able to join in. The whole concept of chemical warfare was anathema to him.

'What's in these exactly?'

'Chlorine.'

'And the new ones?'

Lewis shrugged, as if he didn't quite grasp what he was being asked.

'What type of marking do the new projectiles have? The same red star?'

'Reckon.'

'Have you ever had any cylinders here with different markings? Symbols or letters or colours?' Watson knew from laboratory work that there were internationally accepted codes that denoted various gases.

'Not so I've seen, sir.'

Chlorine was a horrible vapour, an irritant that burned the eyes and stripped out the lung lining, causing victims to drown in the leaking fluid. But it didn't turn people blue nor bring on *Risus sardonicus*. Whatever hideous new methods of poisoning were being deployed at Burnt-Out Lodge, they weren't the source of the poison that killed Edward Hornby, Geoffrey Shipobottom and almost did for Robinson de Griffon.

FORTY-FIVE

Night was setting in as Watson reached the barn at Suffolk Farm. The lorry parks he passed were alive with lights and idling engines; the munitions trucks rattled along the narrow-gauge tramways that crisscrossed the countryside, and everywhere men were on the march. The crunch of hobnails would have filled the air but for the blasts of the guns that had started up, their muzzle flashes scorching the base of the low clouds.

Suffolk Farm was deserted, the only sign of habitation the detritus left behind by the Pals – bully beef cans, piles of carelessly thrown tea leaves, rain-sodden newspapers and magazines, a few broken and useless piece of equipment – and a brief sighting of Cecil, who raced a few circuits around the yard before sprinting off.

'Hello?' Watson shouted. There was normally a farmer around, the man who would have let out his property (five francs for an officer, one for a regular soldier), a Madame and some kids. This one appeared deserted. 'Anybody there?'

Watson dismounted, reached down and picked up several large, dangerously sharp shards of earthenware that were littering the yard. They had once been part of a container marked SRD, the mysterious organization – Supply Reserve Depot or Special Rations Department, depending on whom you believed – that managed to deliver rum to every corner of the conflict. It was the remains of one of the jugs that the tots arrived in. He tossed the pieces onto the big rubbish pile adjacent to the stone horse trough. Another unit would doubtless be in the next day, complain about the state the billet had been left in, clean it up and then, as was the way of the world, leave it similarly strewn with detritus when they abandoned it. Lord Lockie pulled him over to the trough near the midden of garbage, bent his head and drank.

The bay gelding had done exceptionally well, riding dozens of miles without any complaint, and appeared to have more to give. Watson, on the other hand, was almost spent. He felt somewhat deflated, his bones excessively heavy. The sudden elation he had felt when he discovered the coded message in the magazine had been deflated by fatigue and a gnawing sense of failure. He could not help feel that, had Holmes been with him, he would have seen wide avenues to explore where Watson only saw culs-de-sac, discovered connections when all Watson could sense was a scatter-pattern of unrelated incidents, spread like buckshot across the fabric of the case. He was, he concluded, only half a detective. Perhaps less.

But, he reminded himself, half a Holmes was better than none. He had met successful policemen at Scotland Yard who were a fraction of that. But so far he had established one fact: Caspar Myles was a far more decent man than he suspected. Though perhaps hot-headed and clumsy around women, he was no molester. Quite the opposite. Which posed the question: where had he taken Staff Nurse Jennings?

No, it didn't, he reminded himself. It wasn't any of his business. His sole concern, he told himself, had been for Staff Nurse Jennings's safety. If she was safe, even if she was perhaps behaving foolishly, then he really should close the matter.

Is that all you are worried about? Her safety?

He wasn't going to justify that with a reply, he decided.

But you like her.

Of course I—

Ha. His conscious was trying to tell him his concern for the girl was distracting him away from the real matter in hand. Of course I like her. He had always enjoyed the company of intelligent, independent women. He even appreciated Mrs Gregson, although there was a wild streak in there that any man of his generation would find unsettling. It was fine when it was harnessed for good, such as the retrieving of the burial records of Hornby, but he suspected—

And speaking of Hornby. And Shipobottom. And de Griffon.

Yes, yes, enough of women. Back to murder. So, he was now as certain as he could be that gas had not played a role in this case, unless Churchill found otherwise from the Wiltshire death. Had he been right about that? It was possible he had maligned British scientists.

Watson pulled open the door to the nearest stone barn and lit one of the lanterns in the doorway. He wrinkled his nose at the acrid smell of ammonia and worse. Some of the men had decided to use at least one of the stalls as a latrine. These were people, he reminded himself, who often made do with earth closets at home. A pile of clean straw might seem rather tempting to them. They could have used some chloride of lime, however, to soften the stink.

He took the light and walked Lord Lockie to a stall at the far end, away from the odiferous area. Hanging up the lantern, he began to untack, starting with the nose lash to release bridle. He didn't bother with a rope harness; Lord Lockie was glad to be home and wasn't going to give him any trouble.

As he unbuckled the girth, he thought about how marvellous it would feel to be going back to Baker Street. To a steaming cocoa from Mrs Hudson. A hot bath and soaking to the sound of a violin seeping through the closed door. A good whisky waiting on a side-table. One of their landlady's fine pies for supper. Perhaps an unexpected knock at the door . . .

Stop torturing yourself, Watson admonished. There are a million men crouched in trenches all across Europe, pining for home comforts and old friends. You have considerably less right to them than they. He was an old man sliding into the past rather than facing his inevitable future. He had seen it happen to many of his patients, that yearning for a golden age that had never really existed, at least not in the prelapsian version that memory presented. It was true in this case. He had always exaggerated Holmes's ability on the violin. It could be maddeningly caterwauling at times. The pies, mind, really were delicious.

Watson chuckled to himself as he heaved off the saddle and its pad, and placed it on the stall divider. Then he draped a fresh mantle over the horse's back. Lord Lockie gave a little shudder of pleasure at the touch of the cool blanket and Watson stepped back as the animal emptied his capacious bladder. Watson fetched oats and water for the horse while he waited for the stream to weaken. He had just started to search for some brushes, when he heard the barn door slam in the wind. At least, he thought it was the wind. But it was a clever breeze that could lift up a beam of wood and re-bar the door from the outside.

'Hello?' he shouted, his voice strangely deadened by the stone and wood that surrounded him. The flat, empty timbre of the word made his heart beat a little faster. It sounded like it had come from another place, the dream world he had just been indulging in.

'Who's that?' he asked. 'Lewis? Is that you?' Why would it be Corporal Lewis? Because he had asked where he was going next and Watson had told him. Using footpaths, Burnt-Out Lodge was only a short walk across two fields.

Watson took a step towards the now-closed double doors when he saw something snake underneath them, whiplashing as it came. It was a hose. Perhaps, he thought, the stable was to be sluiced. Then it gave a twitch and a jolt, as if given an electric shock. A shushing noise issued from the open end, followed by a foul white-green cloud that blossomed rapidly, like the bloom of a flower speeded up by a cine camera. Watson instinctively took a step back and put a hand to his mouth. It was the hiss of chlorine gas.

FORTY-SIX

'See?' Robinson de Griffon cried triumphantly. 'See this?'

He was pacing up and down the tent at double speed, his arms pumping, legs straight out and stiff. Cecil followed him, snapping at his heels.

'And this!'

The captain began to hop, alternating one leg with another, pyjama bottoms flapping. He looked so ludicrous that Mrs Gregson had to laugh. 'Can you stop now? One of us will burst an organ.'

He collapsed onto the bed, a smile on his face, his chest heaving. 'I am well enough to be discharged,' he said at last.

'Major Watson ought to have the last say in that,' said Mrs Gregson. 'And I have to go and serve tea. Would you like some? As long as you don't tell Sister its provenance.'

'Mrs Gregson, have a heart. I can't rely on Major Watson. Lord knows where he is off gallivanting to now.'

She had to agree. He had come in with Cecil under his arm, his eyes wild with excitement, almost feverish, she would have said. He had asked Captain de Griffon a few questions about poison gas, and then declared his intention to visit Burnt-Out Lodge. He had also mentioned something about Winston Churchill and sending Miss Pippery off with a telegram. He had been babbling, as if a whole clutch of sentences were trying to get out of his mouth at once. Mrs Gregson wondered if his brain had scrambled into dementia or, rather unkindly, if he had been at the morphia. The calm, reassuring gentleman doctor she knew seemed to have deserted, leaving a voluble Mr Hyde in his place.

'Look, my whole company has pulled out,' said de Griffon, in measured tones. 'All gone up to the front for another stint. I really need to be with them. There are young, frightened men in their ranks who, strange as it may sound, look to me for guidance. I'm not a professional soldier. Not that long ago I was an idiot subaltern. But my job is to lead the men by showing them the correct way to behave, both in and out of combat. If they think their officer is shirking—'

'Nobody can think that,' she objected. 'Not after what you have been through.'

He shook his head ruefully. 'Mrs Gregson, I wouldn't be the first officer to find a creative way out of this madness. But upon my return to England, if God spares me, I will take up my role as Lord Stanwood.'

'You are Lord Stanwood?'

'Both my father and brother are dead. My mother lives in that great house all alone but for a cook, a single maid, and Harry the chauffeur. Who is not the man he was. My job will be to return Flitcham to the house it was before my father took ill, and to make sure the mills are ready for the peacetime economy. A great many of the lads in my unit will be my employees. They'll want their jobs back. Imagine if they lose all respect for me, for the family name. It's a recipe for disaster. One thing that is going to be very difficult when all this is over is getting back to normal, to bring back the old order. Dereliction of duty by me won't help.' He pushed back his hair from his forehead and Mrs Gregson thought he was really quite attractive when he was agitated.

'I didn't realize. That you'd lost . . . that you were now the head of the family.'

'Head of the wicked de Griffons.'

'I didn't say that . . .'

'I think you did. But I promise. After the war, no more wickedness. I know I said I wanted the old order back, but it will never be quite the same. Good Lord, how many lords have shared a trench or a shellhole with their men, watched them die, carried them from . . . ? What I mean is, I can't see them as faceless pawns on a board after this. Ever. Nor will I ever think of women in quite the same way.'

'I'm pleased to hear it, Lord Stanwood.'

'Good Lord, no, not here. That's for the future. Robinson, please.'

'I think that might have to wait a while longer, too,' boomed Sister Spence. She had slid in behind them, unseen and unheard. 'I thought I told you not to fraternize with the officers, Mrs Gregson.'

'Sister, this is all my fault. I sent for Mrs Gregson. I needed to know how Major Watson's investigation was proceeding. Please, if you are going to shout at anyone, shout at me.'

Sister Spence tutted at the thought. 'I knew having VADs would turn the place upside down. What with Field Marshal Haig on the way—'

'Sir Douglas won't be here long,' said de Griffon. 'Not in any hospital. I hear he doesn't like to see the end result of his grand schemes.' He winked. 'Better to think of them as faceless pawns on a board, eh, Mrs Gregson?'

The VAD wondered how he could possibly know this about Haig, but for once she kept quiet.

'So, there we are,' de Griffon announced, as if a mutual decision had been reached. 'I'm going to get dressed now and I'd appreciate it if neither of you lovely ladies stood in my way. I'll answer to Major Watson for my actions. Oh, and one last thing, Mrs Gregson.'

'Yes?'

'I wouldn't mind that tea before I go.'

Watson's first thought was to grab a wooden hay rake and push the belching hose back under the door. He scooped one off the wall and advanced on the cloud, but already, in less than a minute, the sickly-coloured fog was so thick he could hardly see the point of origin. He held his breath, turned his head away and sent the wooden implement into the mist, jabbing like an ineffectual prizefighter.

The amorphous monster, however, struck back and within an instant Watson's eyes were aflame as the chemicals attacked his conjunctivae. It was like having oil of vitriol flung in his face. He squeezed his lids shut as tightly as he could and retreated towards Lord Lockie. The horse could now smell the pungent gas and he began to shake his head and snort violently.

Think, Watson. Think, man.

He looked around the solid, stone barn, but the only windows were piercings high up by the roof line. There was no hayloft to clamber up to. At the end of each stall divider, upright wooden beams, fat and square, ran from the floor to the open rafters and tie beams. No doubt the roof tiles could be penetrated, if only he could reach them. But they were twenty-five feet away.

Now he began coughing for real as the first of the corrosive molecules attacked his upper airways. He looked down. Tendrils of the whiteish gas were curling at his feet and slowly climbing his leg. Very slowly. The straw was rippling in places as rats and mice scurried away from the danger.

Heavier than air.

The phrase leaped into his head. Chlorine gas was heavier than air. He had to get higher. He put a foot on a crossbeam and heaved himself up onto a stall divider, clinging on to one of the vertical supports. Could he shimmy up that? Unlikely. If he did, would he be able to lift the tiles? Nearly every building he had seen hereabouts had lost part of its roof, but here it was maddeningly intact.

'Help!' he tried to yell, but that just ended in a terrible hacking. Now, though, even coughing was beyond him. He was choking. His throat was constricting. He fumbled a handkerchief from his trouser pocket, folded it and held it to his mouth and nose.

Lord Lockie was stamping, thumping the ground and making strange barking noises. He reared up, and Watson's perch shook under him as the hoofs thumped down. The horse did it again, his calls of distress louder. There were equine nose plugs, anti-gas hoods and goggles in sporadic use along the front, but Watson could recall no evidence of them in the stable. Man and beast were in this together.

What was the antidote to chlorine gas? What did they soak those hypo helmets in? Calcium hypochlorite and glycerine. No help. But there was another possibility. The first anti-chlorine pads were impregnated with urine. The ammonia in the urine had a delaying effect on the gas. But, as he balanced precariously on the divide, he thought of the impossibility of trying to successfully soak his handkerchief in his own urine. Tricky to balance. And would his bladder comply? But perhaps there was no alternative except to try. He had to buy himself some time. With a free hand he reached down for his buttons.

Lord Lockie reared up in the stall to his full height, his teeth exposed and head blurred as he tried to shake off the terrible burning that was afflicting him. His whole body quivered in pain and he flung himself against the side of the stall. There was a terrible crack and the wood underneath Watson twisted and splintered. He managed to hang on to the upright with one leg waving free. Then, the thrashing head caught the doctor a full blow on his flank. Watson found himself in mid-air, arms flailing, falling head first into a swirl of billowing green vapour, a series of gaseous arms that appeared to reach up to welcome him into their embrace.

FORTY-SEVEN

The cottage was as cluttered as ever. Not only with newspapers of every stripe, dating back ten years or more (he would get around to preparing and filing cuttings one day, he promised himself) but also the apparatus and materials for chemical experiments long forgotten or abandoned. There were also boxes of proprietary medicines, a complete set of the *Illustrated London News* and other periodicals stretching back forty years or more, four pipe racks, with an assortment of occupants, not one but two violin cases – although only one actually contained an instrument – and the evidence of recent meals, in the form of uncleared trays.

Still, the girl was due in the next day. At least the crumbs and half-eaten chops would be disposed of, even if the rest was beyond her. As it was him. This was, he thought, truly the end of days. The flashes of inspiration at the Zeppelin had been welcome, but an anomaly. All too often his waking hours were spent existing in a fog of half-remembered intentions.

He knew his faculties were dimmed. Had known it from the moment when his intellect had first failed him. No, failed was too strong a word. There had been blanks in his thought process, infinitesimal little moments where his brain had thought of . . . nothing. He doubted anyone would notice even now. But he knew they were there. It was like a conductor homing in on a horn player who was a fraction of a second behind the metre or a mechanic hearing the tiniest misfire of an engine. Most people wouldn't be able to detect anything wrong, but a specialist could. And his brain had always been his special instrument.

Pride had stopped him telling even Watson that this was the real reason for his retirement. He had not wanted to see out his days with diminishing powers. Better to pretend the bees were the sole attraction.

He was sitting in front of the fire, wrapped in a woollen shawl, contemplating tea, when there came a knock at the door. He was always careful to leave a path through the accumulations of his bachelorhood, but the ease that the fire gave his joints was terribly difficult to abandon. Still, a second persistent knock sealed matters and he creaked to his feet.

'One moment!' he tried to shout, his voice, about as forceful as a rustle from the dried leaves that lay on his lawn, letting him down again. He cleared his throat and filled his chest with air on the third strike of the knocker. 'Have some patience! I am coming.'

The latch resisted his first groping efforts, and when it broke free, the door flew open in his hand. The startled telegraph boy took a step back when he saw the sallow, unshaven face, the white hair that needed a good trim and the yellowing teeth that populated the smile. He confirmed that the old man was the intended recipient, presented the telegram and, once it had been removed from his grip, he turned to go.

'Just a moment, young Hargreaves,' the old man said.

The lad froze before spinning to face the doorway once more. 'Sir?'

'Your mother is a fine seamstress,' he said. It wasn't a question.

'Yes, sir. She is.'

He pointed to the boy's name, elaborately stitched above the pocket of his red jacket. Both it and the trousers had been well tailored for the lad, but the stitching was the real clue to the mother's proficiency with a needle. 'That's Bulgarian embroidery. Haven't seen that in an age. Hold on.' From the fluff and debris in his waistcoat pocket he fetched a sixpence and handed it to the boy. 'Here. At least it's not bad news,' he said, holding up the telegram.

'Yes, sir.' Young Hargreaves, too, could tell from the bulk of the message that it wasn't one of those terse bringers of terrible grief that were often his lot to deliver. It had taken some getting used to, how his mere appearance in a lane could cause a ripple of fear through the households. A *red-coated harbinger of misery*, one of them had called him. Young as he was, he sometimes felt like death itself, stalking the land, a stealer of innocent young souls. 'Lot of bad news about.'

'A lot,' the old man agreed with a sage nod, as if he understood his burden. 'Off you go, Hargreaves.'

'Thank you, sir.'

He watched the boy remount his red bicycle and pedal off back to the post office where, no doubt, there were more grim tidings waiting to be distributed.

The old man went back inside, slamming the door behind him and taking his place back at the fireside. Even the brief exposure to the outside had numbed his fingers. He had noticed it when he had been preparing the hives for overwintering. His circulation simply wasn't what it had been. He rubbed his hands together before opening the envelope of the telegram.

He read it carefully. As he did so, he felt like an engine starting up. He read it again, and now the pistons were pumping, the valves nicely oiled. His cranium hummed with power. A warmth other than that from the coals and seasoned wood in his grate spread through him. He stroked his chin. My goodness, he needed a shave. And perhaps a haircut. Simpson & Son in the High Street would fit him in. Not quite Truefitt, but highly serviceable.

A third read of the staccato message, and now a plan formed. What he would wear, where he would go, what approach to take when he got there. Well done, Watson, for cracking the code. Although it was schoolboy-simple. Still, it had been easier for his pride for him to dress it up like that, eking out the apology for his boorish behaviour one letter at a time, than put the whole thing down in one solid *mea culpa*. And how had Watson rewarded him for his deviance?

Why, perfectly.

He stood with a speed that made his head swim. He steadied himself and bounded over the piles of newspapers to stand before the bowing shelves of the bookcase where, for the first time in many a month, he reached for his Bradshaw. His fingers had almost touched it when he felt a snapping sensation in his back. What felt like a jet of liquid pain shot down his thigh and he felt his right leg wobble and collapse completely, sending a fragile old man sprawling across the stone-flagged floor.

FORTY-EIGHT

Bloch was convinced he was in trouble when he was intercepted by Lux's driver at the railhead. He was late and the driver was obviously irritated. Bloch intended to blame this on the heavy military traffic that delayed civilian trains. In fact, it was because he had stopped off near the railway station in Brussels for a tattoo. It was very simple: a black, gothic-styled 'H' on his left shoulder. If anyone saw it, he would claim it stood for *Heimat*: homeland. He knew otherwise.

The taciturn young man would give him no information other than the fact Lux wanted to see him at once. And that he had been waiting at the station for two hours. He pointed to the front seat of the Mercedes Torpedo. He clearly didn't want Bloch mistaken for an officer. They drove northwest, away from the front lines and the Ypres salient, into the Belgian countryside. Bloch decided not to apologize for his lateness. Not to a mere driver.

Where was he taking him? To another hare-brained scheme, no doubt. Perhaps Intelligence had another clue as to Churchill's whereabouts. Lux, Bloch was certain, was not a man to let a near-miss stand. The thought of crossing over again made him feel sick, but he fought it. He wasn't ready to sacrifice the afterglow of a night with Hilde just yet. He shuffled Lux and the Englishman to the back of his mind.

For the first few kilometres the roads were crammed with DAAG transports and horse-drawn carts ferrying troops from their reserves places up to the front. Engineers were also at work creating a fresh crop of *Feldbahn* narrow-gauge railways, for moving men and munitions, the tracks scything across fields where need be. However, soon the traffic thinned, and the countryside, although denuded of colour by the poor weather, began to take on its usual peacetime appearance. Only the scowls that the occasional local threw their way as they drove through villages, and the German flags flying from town halls, suggested anything other than rural normality.

After around fifty kilometres the driver turned the Torpedo off the main road, heading for hillier country, covered with thick strands of naked, deciduous trees. It was a welcome change of scenery after the monotonous flatness of the journey so far.

Where the route passed through a cutting, there was a roadblock, manned by three serious-looking sentries who inspected papers and questioned the driver. Another two kilometres on, at the edge of the forest, was a more substantial barrier, a thick striped pole spanning a punctuation in a three-metre-high fence, which was topped by coils of barbed wire. This looked serious, thought Bloch. A prison?

An echo of his original anxiety tweaked his guts.

A twisting track led through the telegraph-pole-straight trees to a clearing, where six brand-new single-storey huts stood. Chimney smoke was rising from the nearest of them. There was also a group of field tents and, outside one of them, drinking coffee, stood Lux, wrapped in a greatcoat. The driver took the Torpedo close to him and pulled to a stop. Lux waited while the vehicle made a series of shudders and creaks before finally coming to a full halt with a sigh of relief.

'Bloch. There you are!' said Lux with what sounded dangerously like bonhomie.

'I'm sorry I was late—'

'Don't worry about that. Here, let me get you some coffee.' He signalled to one of the orderlies in the open-sided mess tent. 'Schneider, take the car round the back. I won't be needing it again.' He turned back to Bloch. 'How was the furlough?'

'Good, thank you.'

'You'd almost think this was real.' He handed Bloch his tin mug of ersatz coffee. 'Did you see that girl of yours?' He smiled when he saw the expression on Bloch's face. 'As your senior officer, who do you think censors your letters and cables? Hilde, is it? Did you see her?'

'I did, sir.'

'All well?'

Bloch couldn't help himself. He smiled. 'Very well, sir.'

'Excellent.' Lux winked, slapped him on the back and then eased him out of the way as the Torpedo drove off.

Bloch was beginning to feel very uncomfortable. A jovial Lux was about as endearing, and convincing, as a wolf inviting you to drop in for tea and cake. The coffee was surprisingly good, though.

'Manfred!' Lux shouted to a figure that had emerged from the nearest hut.

The gold lace around the collar and cuff told him that Manfred was an *Etatmässige Feldwebel*, although as he approached Bloch could see no regimental or regional insignia on the staff sergeant's uniform.

There was usually some sort of heraldic device to indicate the senior NCO's allegiance. Manfred waddled slightly, thanks to an enormous stomach that gave him a low centre of gravity, and a patch covered his right eye. As he got closer, Bloch could see the skin of his face had a strange, glazed quality, the shiny surface peppered with tiny black dots, and one side of his mouth was pulled down, as if by a palsy. He saluted Lux, who returned the greeting.

'Manfred, this is the man I was telling you about. Unteroffizier Bloch, der Speiss Manfred Loewenhardt,' said Lux, using the casual term for a senior sergeant.

Loewenhardt grabbed Bloch's hand. 'You are the young man who nearly got Churchill, yes? And only failed because of our own artillery!' He began to laugh in the way that some Berliners – the accent was unmistakable – were driven to find humour in every situation. 'Bad luck. But I know all about that, eh?'

He grabbed Bloch's arm, spun him round and the three walked towards the edge of the clearing and the beginning of the forest. 'I always have to tell people about my eye. Get it out of the way.' The mouth drooped even more on certain syllables, slurring them. Bloch leaned in to make sure he caught every word. 'I was testing a new rifle. Austrian. And new ammunition. Breech blow back. Bolt took the eye. The phosphorus powder burned my face. Shrapnel severed a nerve in my face. I learned to shoot with my left eye, but they said my sniping days were over. So now, I teach people how to do what I can no longer do myself. Like a eunuch at a gigolo academy.' More raucous laughter followed this.

'Manfred has been running a sniping school in Hesse,' said Lux, more soberly. 'He kindly agreed to come here and set this up with me.'

'A sniping school?' Bloch asked. He'd had no such luxury. With him there was no theory or practice, just learning on the job. And if you weren't a good student . . .

'And we want it to be *the* sniping school,' said Lux. 'We only have a few candidates at the moment. But soon there will be fifty at a time. Each training for two weeks. Even with a failure rate of twenty per cent, we will be feeding more than a thousand snipers a year into our sector.'

'A thousand snipers as good as you,' added Loewenhardt.

They were walking deeper into the forest now, bare branches above them crisscrossing the darkening sky, a multihued mulch of leaves beneath their feet. 'Why are you telling me this?'

Lux stopped. 'About here, I think.'

'Lothar!' shouted Loewenhardt.

The ground to Bloch's immediate right trembled, as if there was a local earthquake, and then came an enormous, yawning upheaval. From the detritus of leaf, soil and twigs, a young boy emerged, holding a rifle with a scope.

'Jäger Lothar Breuchtal. This is Unteroffizier Ernst Bloch.'

The kid held out a grubby hand. Bloch took it. 'I have heard a lot about you, Unteroffizier Bloch.'

Bloch looked at the carefully made leaf-litter netting that the young man had camouflaged himself with. 'Very impressive cover.'

'Thank you, *Unteroffizier*.'

'*Jäger?*' Bloch asked Lux.

'A new rank for snipers. Equivalent to a corporal.'

'And Lothar is our best *Jäger*. Never play hide-and-seek with him!' laughed Loewenhardt.

Bloch wasn't certain what was going on. He looked to Lux for help.

'We would like you here as a teacher. In concealment, target acquisition and evasion techniques. You aren't the best shot we have. Close, but not quite. However, you are the finest at operating out there.' He pointed back towards the lines.

'Young Lothar looks pretty skilled at camouflage to me.'

'Ah,' said Lux. 'But there is one thing he is missing. What's that, Breuchtal?'

'I haven't killed enough Tommies, sir. Unlike the *Unteroffizier*.'

Lux raised his eyebrows at Bloch. 'See?'

'No, sir. I don't,' he confessed.

'No tutor can hope to have respect unless he has been out there and lived through what he is teaching. Manfred here has clearly paid his dues. You too, almost. You would move here as a *Feldwebel*, with potential to move up to *Vizefeldwebel*, and perhaps *Degenfähnrich*.'

That was effectively a cadet officer. Play his cards right and he could rise to a field commission. To go home, having finished the war as a *Leutnant* would be quite something for a country boy. That would impress Hilde's father. One thing puzzled him. 'What do you mean by "almost" paid my dues, sir?'

'Lothar is to take over your sector. And your spotter. Schaeffer, isn't it? But I'd like you to break him in. Show him the ropes. Just for a week or so. You know every crater and tree stump out there.'

The import of what he was saying finally hit home and for a second Bloch felt the world shift below his feet. No more trenches, no more mud-filled depressions, no more shunning by his fellow troops, no more days in concrete bunkers without daylight, no more shooting unwary officers through the head. Lux was offering him warmth, safety, status and prospects.

'It would be a pleasure to teach him what little I know. And to take a position here.'

The three men beamed at him.

'Wonderful. We will do great things here, Bloch. Just one more tour out there,' said Lux, directing him back towards the huts. 'And you're home and dry.'

FORTY-NINE

The first inkling that something was amiss was when Mrs Gregson saw the monster in the headlamp of the motor cycle. As they entered the farm courtyard, the creature staggered out of the twilight and into the beam, and then ducked away. She was so shocked at the apparition that the front wheel of the bike wobbled, and she felt they must go over.

'Stop!' cried de Griffon from over her shoulder, and she managed to skid the bike to a halt on the cobbles. The captain was off in one quick hop, grabbed her by the shoulders and flung her to the hard ground. The bike crashed down beside her and stalled.

'Stay still,' he instructed. 'Keep your head covered.'

She did as she was told, using her arms as a shield, trying to recall what she had seen of the being. A hideously featureless face, apart from two prominent, bulbous eyes and a kind of trunk where the nose and mouth should have been.

'Stop right there!' she heard de Griffon yell from behind. 'You there.'

There came an incoherent reply.

'Don't be a fool, man. Put down the rifle.'

Another muffled sound was followed by two sharp reports from de Griffon's revolver that made her start. There was a third shot, and a sound like a sack of coal or potatoes being dropped.

'It's all right,' de Griffon said. 'Oh, my good God. Hold on, stay there. Please.'

The alarm – no, sheer panic – in his voice made her jump to her feet. She wasn't going to lie there whimpering.

The captain was illuminated by the fading, tallow beam of the motor cycle. To his right was a prostrate form; the creature, she assumed, rifle at his side, arms spread akimbo. She was too distant to see any wounds, but was in no doubt that de Griffon had shot him. The captain was bent over a gas cylinder that lay in front of one of the barns, frantically turning a small hand wheel.

'Stay back, Georgina!' he shouted and began to cough. 'For God's sake, stay away.'

She could smell petrol. The tank of the fallen bike was leaking through the cap and she heaved it up, training the headlamp on de Griffon as he rolled the cylinder away, bringing a length of tubing with it. Mrs Gregson pulled the motor cycle onto its stand and ran across the cobbles towards the barn, but as she drew level with the farm's well, de Griffon again waved frantically and warned her to stay put.

He lifted the bar across the double doors, flung them back and retreated as fast as he could from the billowing cloud that rolled out.

'It's gas!' he shouted over his shoulder. 'Cover your mouth—'

His words were knocked clear out of him. Head thrown back in pain, trailing streamers of green fumes like a horse from hell, Lord

Lockie burst from the folds of smoke and barrelled into de Griffon. The captain tried to keep his balance, but his feet went from under him and he slithered along the cobbles.

'The major!' she shouted. 'Dr Wat—'

De Griffon began to cough and heave, and even at that remove, Mrs Gregson felt the first stinging attacks by the vile substance burning her nose and eyes. She pulled the collar of her coat to her mouth to create a barrier.

De Griffon was up again now, clawing frantically at the face of the dead man, when another living thing emerged from the gas rolling out of the barn. He was staggering, and holding a cloth pressed flat against his entire face. He careered around blindly, one arm outstretched, and appeared to crash into the horse trough, but at that point he threw away the handkerchief and plunged his head into the water, submerging it to his shoulders.

De Griffon was before her, holding up something that smelled disgusting. 'Put this on. Now!'

It was a gas mask. One of the new respirators she had heard about but not seen. That was what the creature had been. A man in a respirator. She slipped the suffocating rubber and canvas contraption over her head. It was damp with a dead man's breath, the mica eyepieces were fogged up and one was cracked. But at least the gas wasn't scratching at her throat now.

'Get the major clear,' de Griffon instructed. 'Out of the farm. On the bike.'

'Wha'boutoo?' Her words came as if she was underwater.

'What?'

She tried to enunciate more clearly. 'What about you?'

'I have something to do. I'll be all right, now go.'

Mrs Gregson walked back over to the parked bike, straddled it and, to her relief, it rumbled into life on the second kick. She opened the throttle just enough to take her alongside Major Watson. He put his dripping head on her shoulder, his chest heaving.

'Can you get on?'

A nod was all the wheezing doctor could summon, but he managed to throw a leg over the pillion.

They both watched, frozen, as de Griffon walked over to Lord Lockie. The horse's legs had buckled from under him, his breath was coming hard and the flanks were glistening with sweat. As he approached, Lockie shook his head and gave a pitiful neigh. Then, with a ground-shaking impact that felt like it reverberated for several seconds, he keeled over. The hoofs began to paw the air, as if he were still trying to race away from this terrible place. A piercing whine escaped from foam-flecked lips.

De Griffon stood watching for a second, but even that was a cruel hesitation. He knew what he had to do. He stepped forward, raised the revolver, took careful, merciful aim, and pulled the trigger. Lord Lockie gave one almighty thrash and lay still.

As the motor bike growled and popped out of the farm gate, Cecil ran past it, his little legs pumping, tongue hanging from the side of his mouth.

De Griffon picked up the dog and put his cheek to its muzzle, walking away as quickly as he could, his eyes streaming with tears that weren't entirely due to the chlorine still swirling around the farmyard.

FIFTY

Mrs Cartwright stepped out of the motor taxi and turned back to her son. 'You stay there, boy. All right?'

She knew the driver had instructions to wait and take her back home. The extravagance of it was unbelievable. She couldn't imagine how much this round trip was costing. Still, it had piqued her curiosity.

The cottage before her was decidedly modest. It was not at all the home that she had imagined, the house of a man who could lavish pounds on taxi fares. There was smoke coming from the chimney, the glow of light in the window, even though it wasn't yet dark. But they could be gloomy, these old places. The door, she noted, could do with a lick of paint and nobody had blacked the doorstep in months.

She glanced back at Bert, who waved her on. She raised the knocker and let it drop and almost instantly came an imperious command. 'Enter!'

The door was unlocked. She stepped into a room that smelled of tobacco, woodsmoke and mildew. It was piled high with boxes.

There was a fire in the hearth, but her eyes were drawn to the chimneybreast where multiple pieces of paper had been thumb-tacked into the rough plaster. In some cases lengths of cotton had been stretched between the pieces of paper. Most of them had but one thing written on them. A person's name.

'Ah, Mrs Cartwright. How kind of you to come. Forgive me for not getting up.'

He was lying on a slightly raised wooden platform on the floor, just in front of the sofa. He was dressed in a red smoking jacket and loose-fitting trousers, with oriental-patterned slippers on his feet. Next to him was the paraphernalia for his pipe, a bottle of whisky, a bottle of tablets, several notebooks, a jar of pencils and several mounds of shavings where they had been sharpened. There was also a tottering stack of books that looked ready to collapse at any moment. 'I have to do this for several hours a day, so the doctor says. I have damaged my back, Mrs Cartwright. At a most inconvenient time.'

'I'm sorry to hear it,' she said, looking around at the stacks of boxes that held yet more books and magazines. It was likely where the smell of mildew was coming from.

'Please make yourself at home. Did young Fredericks find you all right?'

'Young Fredericks', the cab driver, was sixty if he was a day. But that was younger than the man lying prone in front of her. He was clearly in some pain, as his features were drawn and every so often he winced. 'I would offer you some tea or coffee, but . . .'

'Shall I make some?'

'Would you mind? My girl has been today, but that was some time ago. It's all laid out.'

As she busied herself in the kitchen, which was simply one end of the main room, a step down, she said: 'My Bert has told me about you, sir.'

'And he has told me about you and your sterling work in the munitions factory.'

'Has he?'

'He has. Your Bert is a smart boy, you know. And better, keen as mustard. You must be very proud.'

She nodded. 'I hope all this is over before he is of an age to serve.' She hesitated. 'Does that sound terribly unpatriotic?'

'Not at all,' he said. 'Not at all. Now, Bert has already been of assistance to me.'

'With the Zeppelin? Full of it he was.'

'The Zeppelin, indeed. Well, Mrs Cartwright, not to put too fine a point on it, I need him now. I need his wit, his passion and most of all I need his youth,'

Mrs Cartwright stopped what she was doing and walked back over to where he lay, so she could look him in the eye. 'And what exactly do you mean by that, sir?'

She was no woman of the world, she knew, but she had heard of things that went on in London with young lads. And this man was a Londoner.

'I mean, I need a strong back. Someone who can fetch my books from that shelf up there. Answer the telephone without taking an age to cross the room.'

She looked around the room. There was no telephone.

'Which will be installed presently.' He had pulled strings at Mycroft's former department, trading shamelessly on old connections and the now-faint echoes of his success in the Von Bork case. It had worked. The Post Office's six-month or longer wait for connection to an exchange had magically disappeared. The cost, however, remained astronomically high.

'And someone,' Holmes continued, 'who can help me with that wall.' He caught her confused expression. 'It is a visualization of my methods. I find it helps these days. I need to add items to it ten, fifteen times an hour, often more. Even when I am up and about, it takes me some considerable time each day. Bert can read and write, I assume?'

'Like a dream. He'll be good enough for the Civil Service exam, mark my words. But—'

'I am a detective, Mrs Cartwright. A retired detective who has been given the opportunity for one last hurrah. I shall be honest, I am used to having a companion, a sounding board. I find I miss that. Then there were my Irregulars. Also no longer available. Being a solitary detective is a lonely path, Mrs Cartwright. Of course, I will pay for his services.'

'I haven't said yes as yet,' she retorted.

'No. True. We can discuss that over the tea now the kettle has boiled. I can get references if you wish. From the police. There must be someone at Scotland Yard who remembers me. Sometimes Bert might have to stay over – there is a boxroom I can have made comfortable – or even travel. At other times, Fredericks can pick him up and deliver him home.'

Mrs Cartwright had returned to the kitchen to make the tea. 'He's at school,' she said over her shoulder.

'Ah. I can assure you, Mrs Cartwright, he will receive an education with me no school in the land can hope to match. But I will speak to his headmaster and ensure I cover any areas he might miss.

But I hope to keep his absences to a minimum. I think after school and weekends might suffice.'

'If I were to agree, when would you want him to start as your apprentice?'

Apprentice? Nobody had mentioned that word. But it would do as well as any other description. *Bert Cartwright, Detective's Apprentice*. It had a ring to it. 'Why right away, Mrs Cartwright. Right away. This very evening.' He lowered his voice, revelling in the drama of the moment. 'I believe there are lives at stake even as we speak.'

FIFTY-ONE

The sentry at the gate of the East Anglian CCS watched the single headlamp heading down the rutted lane towards him with rising alarm. Was it an ambulance with one light out? If so it was travelling at a real lickspittle. Judging from the way the beam was bouncing, the lad behind the wheel wasn't slowing for potholes, nor keeping to the duckboards that had been laid. Then he heard the thin note of the engine. It was a motor cycle. Which made the speed even more reckless. Could really damage something, haring along like that.

As the noise and the yellow orb grew, he unslung his rifle. He had to keep up the formalities. He placed it at hip height, assumed an aggressive, bayonet-thrust position and set his jaw. It remained set until the moment he realized the bike didn't intend to stop.

He nimbly hopped aside and caught a glimpse of the rider, face set in a grimace, a mass of curls streaming from her head, and the lolling figure behind on the pillion. It was Mrs Gregson. Everyone knew her and that red hair, and her strange motor-cycling clothes.

'Stop! Who goes there?' he shouted ineffectually at the taillight.

From the pocket of his greatcoat he took out the official CCS whistle – designed to alert staff of an ambulance convoy and gave three long blasts. Then he hesitated. Should he run after the bike rider and remonstrate or stay at his post? He had never heard of anyone being shot for not running after a mad motor-cyclist. He had, however, heard tell of those who had been shot for deserting their sentry duty. He blew three more times on the whistle. That should cover his back.

Mrs Gregson drove straight to the transfusion tent, where she knew an oxygen cylinder was still set up from the treatment of de Griffon. She killed the bike engine and kicked down the stand.

'Major, just stay still,' she said, as she dismounted. She tried to prop him up, but he flopped, as if deboned. 'Major, can you hear—'

'Mrs Gregson . . . oh, for goodness' sake. Is it you alone? Not a convoy?'

Sister Spence, judging by the dressing gown tied tightly around her and her brushed hair, had been preparing for bed. Mrs Gregson could see other figures moving towards them, some dressing as they came.

'Just me, Sister. Major Watson has been gassed.'

'Gassed? But how? Why? By whom?'

All very good questions. None of which she could answer. 'Can you give me a hand?'

Watson was leaning against her, his full weight pressing on her chest. Sister Spence came around the bike and took one of his arms, but as she did so he twisted and almost fell. Then he began to retch.

'Hold on, Sister.'

Mrs Gregson crouched down and came up beneath Watson as he

pitched forward, her shoulder meeting his waist. He jackknifed across her, steadied by Sister Spence.

'There'll be a stretcher in a minute.'

'We might not have a minute.' She straightened up, staggered a little and felt Sister Spence's support. She carried him into the transfusion tent, each step wobblier than the last and pitched him onto the nearest bed.

'Heavier than he looks,' she said, one arm on the bedspread.

'What kind of gas?'

'Chlorine. He'll need oxygen. Over there.'

For a second Mrs Gregson thought Sister Spence was going to object to being ordered around, but she gave a curt nod and went to fetch the trolley.

'Oh my goodness!' Miss Pippery, unable to decide who looked more shocking, Watson or her friend. 'George, are you all right?' Her eyes went down to Watson. 'Is——'

'Alice,' Mrs Gregson said calmly, 'his eyes need irrigating. And his mouth. It's poison gas.'

Mrs Gregson watched approvingly as she, too, snapped into action. Other medical staff arrived, including Major Torrance, and soon Watson was being attended to by half a dozen willing hands, including Nurse Jennings.

'How can I help?' she asked as she entered the tent.

'What are you doing here?' Mrs Gregson replied.

'I work here.'

'Not for the past few days.'

Jennings prickled. 'Twenty-four hours, I think you'll find.'

'He's been worried sick.'

'Who has?'

The nurse's eyes flicked towards the bed holding Major Watson.

You have to be cleverer than that, Georgina.

'Dr Myles,' she said. 'Very concerned about you.'

Jennings looked puzzled. 'I don't see why. Is he here?'

'Don't you know?'

'No. What are you talking about, Mrs Gregson? Have you been at the ether?'

'No. Have you been at Dr Myles?'

Jennings's eyes narrowed suspiciously. She knew better than to cross swords with this woman. The Red She-Devil was capable of anything. 'I haven't seen anything of Dr Myles since I left the CCS.'

'My apologies, I . . . a misunderstanding.'

Watson began to retch again. Jennings pulled off his oxygen mask. 'We'll need another oxygen cylinder. This one is nearly empty. Shall I organize one?'

'If you would,' said Mrs Gregson, unsure why everyone was suddenly doing her bidding.

After Jennings had departed to find an orderly, Mrs Gregson walked over to where they had slung Watson's tunic, reached into the pocket and brought out his magnifying glass. In the dim light she read the inscription on the handle. It was so tiny, she almost needed a second glass to decipher it.

To my all-seeing eye, my steadfast companion and my infallible conscience, with my eternal gratitude, S.H.

She backed slowly out of the tent. For the moment those tending to Dr Watson didn't notice. Only Alice looked up and a quick shake of the head warned her not to draw attention to the exit. If Mrs Gregson stayed, someone would start quizzing her about what had happened at the farm. She didn't have enough answers yet. She had to go and fetch de Griffon, bring him back for a check-up. And, now Watson was incapacitated, she had to carry on his work. Mrs Gregson slipped the magnifying glass into her pocket, feeling as if a baton had been passed on.

SATURDAY–MONDAY

FIFTY-TWO

Watson knew that he had been sedated, but there was little he could do about it. The chemicals had him. He had tried to break out from the stupor, but he felt like a diver trying to rise from the deep, only to find that someone had placed a translucent but impenetrable sheet just beneath the surface of the water. He could make out what was going on – vaguely – but was unable to join in because of this glass ceiling. The effort so exhausted him, he eventually floated back down into the dark depths. At some point he became aware of various people standing over him and struggled to put a name to the rippling features. Sister Spence. Torrance. Mrs Gregson. De Griffon, too. Miss Pippery. Another face joined the throng that he almost recognized, but he couldn't quite place.

Words drifted through the barrier as well. *De Griffon*, he heard. *Lord Lockie*. That poor animal. *Gas*. On the mention of this he felt his throat close again and he struggled to breathe.

He remembered being on his face in the stall, having fallen to the floor. The stench and attack of the gas was overwhelming. He had held his breath for as long as possible. He had pressed his nose to the floor, pushed through the straw and almost gagged on the smell of urine.

Urine. Ammonia.

In between the stalls were gullies full of the stuff, from both horse and man, great pools of it. He had forsaken all pretence at dignity and soaked his handkerchief in Lord Lockie's still warm fluids, and placed the cloth over his face, even his eyes. It was disgusting in a different way from the gas, but as far as he knew, nobody ever died from exposure to horse piss.

It had been, at best, a temporary measure and he had no idea how long he had lain there before he had heard the motor bike and the gunshots. When de Griffon had opened the door Watson had herded out the poor, suffering horse ahead of him, as grateful thanks for saving him. Too late for the poor beast, though.

There was one question he needed answering above all others. One he wanted to burst back into real life for. One he had asked Mrs Gregson before his collapse at the CCS, but apparently she had no more of a clue than he.

Who had been under the gas mask?

A delirium took hold. Above the waves that swamped him he could see Staff Nurse Jennings. And Caspar Myles? No, he was nowhere to be seen. Just Staff Nurse Jennings leaning in, her face lit by the smile that reminded him of Mary . . . or was it Emily? No, Mary. The smile playing across her face, so soothing. She said something, but the words came out slow and fat and then floated off, like balloons.

He tried to reply, but he could tell by the vibrations along his own jawbones that the words were ill formed and clumsy. He tried to warn her, about throwing her life away on Caspar, about dishonouring herself.

But where was honour now? The morals he had lived by as a grown man, the rules that had been his waymarks in a journey across three monarchs, had all been blasted apart like the ground of Flanders.

He dreaded to think what fate awaited England after the war. *A cleaner, better, stronger land.* Did anyone still believe that? It was just one of the stories, the fairy tales we have told ourselves.

Your Country Needs You. It'll All Be Over by Christmas. God Is on Our Side. The Germans Bayonet Babies and Rape Nuns. The Sun Will Never Set on the British Empire. There Is a Corner of a Foreign Field That Is Forever England. It's a Long Way To Tipperary.

No, hold on, that last one was true. He tried to laugh, but couldn't. Did I tell you, Staff Nurse Jennings, that we are friends again? No? Well, I think we are. Holmes, I'm talking about. We'd been through too much to throw it all away on a spat.

My Dear Watson,

I pray this finds you well. I have thought long and hard about what to say in this letter. How to express the anguish I felt, and still feel, at the manner of our parting and the anxiety every time I hear the news from France.

It was a peculiar way to get in touch, but it was perhaps the single most cheering message he had ever received. What would he make of the reply? Would he realize it, too, was a coded message? No great outpourings, just the snippets of a puzzle. It said one thing: forget that silly disagreement. This is business as usual. *What do you make of this, Holmes?*

The game's . . . no, the game has changed, transmuted, evolved. Everything had. He just hoped his old friend hadn't.

FIFTY-THREE

Rain billowed across the graveyard, rippling like sheets of chain mail, making the rows of wooden crosses seem even more baleful than usual. The light was fading now, and the two people standing at the graveside were shivering, although not all of that was due to the plummeting temperature and the rain seeping into their greatcoats.

An ambulance was parked nearby, as close as they could get to the grave. It contained the coffin of Sergeant Geoffrey Shipobottom, awaiting interment. But first, there was another coffin to examine.

'You are sure about this?' asked Brindle, a globule of rain hanging expectantly on the end of his nose, his long face a picture of misery. 'It's rather a lot of laws to break in one day.'

Mrs Gregson looked around the Bailleul cemetery. There was hardly another soul in sight. This section of the burial grounds was full; it had burst its boundaries. New burials were happening in adjacent plots. A few solitary figures walked between the rows some hundreds of yards away, searching for a name or number. Relatives, probably, or comrades. They paid the pair no heed, being locked in another time and place.

'Just count yourself lucky,' she said, 'that they don't do mass graves here.' She pointed to the name on the cross. Edward Walter Hornby. 'And it's one man, one plot.'

The cover story for their spot of exhuming had been clever, Brindle had to admit. Mrs Gregson had told the gatekeepers that she had permission to bury Terence Hornby with his brother Edward. She even had documents saying as much. But there was no Terence Hornby. Shipobottom was playing that role. She had promised Brindle that she had written to Shipobottom's parents with the plot number and location on it. She was adamant that any subterfuge would be undone. The driver had chosen to believe her.

'Well,' said Brindle in his best plummy tones. 'I suppose we'd best get to it.'

Mrs Gregson hesitated. The confidence she had felt the previous day had evaporated overnight. She had forced herself to go through with this, to recruit Brindle, to convince him to meet her with the ambulance and the body and to start digging. It was, she had said, a matter of life and death. But at this particular moment, it felt more about death than life. That was a real body down there.

Mrs Gregson made a tentative stab with the blade of her shovel and was surprised when it slid into the soil. She looked up at Brindle.

'Still loose from the burial, I would imagine.' He put his own spade into the plot and lifted a dome of dark earth. Then a thought struck him. 'Is it true the hair and nails still grow after death?'

Mrs Gregson didn't know for sure. 'I don't think so. No. Unlikely.' She carried on excavating. 'You've seen enough bodies, surely?'

'Fresh meat, mostly,' he said. 'And a lot of skeletons. We did do some work with bodies at St Martins, but they'd been embalmed. Death studies, as opposed to life studies.'

'How peculiar.'

'It made some sense. You didn't have to pay the cadavers by the hour.'

'No, I suppose not.'

'They were like wax, shiny and unnatural. What will he look like when we open the coffin? Hornby?'

'I have no idea.' She leaned on the spade. 'Not at his best, I suspect. But he's probably past caring.'

Brindle laughed.

'What's funny?' she asked.

'You are.'

'How do you mean?'

But he just shook his head and then bent to the digging. Mrs Gregson copied his rhythm and was soon sweating under the layers of heavy clothes she was wearing. The rain meant her hair began to stick to her forehead and cheeks, so she had to keep blowing or brushing it out of the way. Soon her face was filthy.

'There's another thing we haven't thought of, Mrs Gregson,' said Brindle when they were down about two feet.

'What's that?' she gasped, glad of the chance to rest.

'He was a big boy, that Shipobottom. It took four of us to get him into the ambulance. There's just you and me. It's going to be a struggle to get him in this grave.'

She looked over at the vehicle. It suddenly seemed a long way away. 'You'll think of something.'

Brindle hit a solid surface first, shallower than he had expected, certainly not six feet deep. So digging up Shipobottom again wasn't going to be a problem. He would be close to the surface.

As dusk approached, they redoubled their efforts, shifting earth at a healthy lick. Soon enough, they had exposed the simple square wooden coffin. Nothing fancy, she thought.

Brindle passed her a screwdriver. 'Me?' she asked. 'You want me to do it?'

'I'll hold the flashlight.'

'How gentlemanly of you.'

The lid eased off after three digs and twists with the screwdriver. It looked as if the army were economizing in nails too. As she levered the top up, the box seemed to belch the vilest of smells. She staggered backwards, against the edge of their earthworks. Brindle let out a groan, found his handkerchief and pressed it against his nose.

Mrs Gregson waited for the attack of nausea to subside. If she was going to be sick, she'd be sick. She found her own handkerchief, ripped it in half and screwed one portion into each nostril. This wasn't the time to worry about appearances.

'There's flashlights over there,' said Brindle with some alarm. 'Looks like a foot patrol. They must be closing up the cemetery.'

'Don't worry about that.'

'Mrs Gregson, I don't want to be in some stockade for grave robbing.'

'We are not robbing.'

'Molesting then.'

'I'll molest you with the sharp edge of this spade in a minute,' she said. It didn't sound as if she was joking. 'I need a light here, Brindle.'

His whining gave her courage, and she pushed the coffin lid up, holding her breath as she felt another waft of noxious gas brush over her face.

This must be the worst time to do this, she realized. In another few weeks all the decomposition would have been completed and the flesh and organs mostly liquefied. Here, the digestion was in full swing, hence the stink.

'I hope this is worth it,' she said to herself as she flipped open the canvas sheet that covered him. There was the sound of scuttling.

Hornby was naked under the shroud. The hands, she noticed, were still curled to claws. Despite herself, she looked at the face. The eyes had been pushed forward from the sockets. There were tiny creatures, bright red in the torch beam, running over the clouded, sightless hemispheres. The tongue, startlingly black, had been forced between the teeth. The skin had shrunk hard onto the skull. But, she noticed with relief, the skin was still intact over the upper body. A vile colour, perhaps, but intact.

She took out the magnifying glass and began to look at the blue-grey covering of his torso, examining the throat and chest, trying to ignore the red mites and other scavengers. Three, she reminded herself. You are looking for the numeral three. A series of slashes. Something regular, artificial.

Sure enough, the skin had split here and there, but in ragged lines. There was nothing that looked like a knife or a scalpel mark.

'They're getting closer. The guards.' Brindle sounded frightened.

Mrs Gregson swore vigorously, which made her feel better. 'Just a minute. I'm rushing it as it is.'

'I'm bloody rushing you,' said Brindle. 'They're coming right for us.'

She stood up, away from the coffin, and took in a lungful of rela-tively sweet air then, as if about to dive for pearls at some great depth, plunged in again. She waved her arms to direct the beam that Brindle controlled. The rain was hissing on Hornby's taut skin and she risked brushing away the film of surface water. A piece of Hornby's outer flesh the size of a dinner plate came away on her fingers. She tried to shake it off, but it seemed glued tight. 'Oh, Jesus.'

She could hear voices now. It was hopeless. So much for playing the great detective-ess.

She scraped the pancake of skin off on the side of the coffin and replaced the lid. She stood on it, hoping that might push some of the fixings into place and then scrambled up the side of the grave.

'Aye, aye. What's going on here?'

There were two of them, dressed in oilskins and helmets, but, judging by their ages, not front-line soldiers.

'I slipped in. Sorry. Gosh, that wasn't nice. Look, we've been asked by the family to make sure that these two brothers are buried together. As a personal favour. And, well . . .' She wiped the rain off her face.

'You can't just come here and do your own digging,' one of them said.

'No. I can see that now.' She reached into her coat pocket and brought out a flask. 'I need a drink after that tumble. Anyone? Filthy night ahead by the look of it.'

The two newcomers shrugged in unison. She moved round the hole in the ground and handed them the rum. She had intended it as a gift for Brindle, a thank you for joining her, but needs must, she supposed.

As they drank she took the flashlight off the driver and waved it at the ambulance. 'The thing is, we'd be awfully grateful if you could help us get the coffin in here.' She swung the flashlight down into Hornby's grave. She heard Brindle give a little gasp. Her efforts to reseal the coffin had dislodged some of the clumps of soil that had clung to it. There, in the beam of light, as clear as if they had been recently scored, were three deep single grooves in the lid, capped and underscored by lighter strokes. The Roman numeral for three.

FIFTY-FOUR

'This Mrs Gregson is an interesting one,' the old man said, handing an old copy of the *Pall Mall Gazette* to Bert. 'Have a read. Then do you think you could snip that out and put it on our wall?'

The space above the fireplace now reminded Bert of a spider's web, an intricate pattern of threads spiralling out from the centre. Or dual centres, he should say. And the spider, he had to admit, looked to be intoxicated, as wobbly as his father on Christmas Day. But even though it looked to be a confusing jumble, Mr Holmes, as he called him, seemed to hold every piece of information in his head, too.

Having spent the day on his plank, the former detective was spending an evening on the sofa, although propped up ramrod straight by cushions. They had enjoyed a dinner of bangers and mash cooked by 'the girl', who was far from being as young as that name suggested, Bert thought. Now, they were talking over the case. Thrillingly, he was treated as an adult in these sessions, with no subject — sex or war or politics — out of bounds. Bert did occasionally offer opinions and sometimes his employer reacted as if he were surprised Bert was in the room. Or could speak at all.

But at times like this, when his opinion was sought, he relished the fact that his mother had allowed him to come and assist. Although her permission was granted only after she had insisted on scrubbing the place to her standards (she clearly didn't think much of 'the girl'), blacking the front doorstep and putting fresh sheets on the narrow bed shoehorned into the boxroom. Before his first overnight visit she had taken Bert aside and said: 'Even if he is a bit funny, he isn't likely to cause you too much trouble with that back of is, is he?'

'Well?' he asked when Bert had finished and was neatly clipping the piece with the long-bladed scissors that Mr Holmes had designated for the task.

'It is obvious she has criminal tendencies from this article,' said Bert, using a term he had heard the old man use. 'And is quite ruthless. And political. So could she be the murderer?'

'We can't rule anyone out at this stage. Watson has given me the *dramatis personae*, but little in the way of stage directions.' He pointed at the centre of his web. 'I think the answer lies in one or both of those places.' There were two names written at the heart of the construction on the wall. One was 'Leigh' and the other was 'Flitcham'.

'We shall have to see where Mrs Gregson was born or brought up, to see if she has links with either area. There might be more on her trial in *The Times*.' He indicated a stack of boxes hitherto untouched by Bert. 'Which we have back until 1905. But there is something we should look at closely now, Bert, before we call it a night.'

'What's that?'

Mr Holmes pointed to the top shelf of the bookcase behind him. 'The red volume, please, Bert.'

Bert clambered up the bookcase and fetched the tome the old

man had indicated. He read the gold-lettering on the spine and said it out loud, '*Who's Who*?'

'The very same.'

Ten minutes later he asked for a run of *The Times*, covering dates almost a year previously. Having located what he wanted, he asked Bert to fetch his Bradshaw railway timetable.

It was, he said, bad back or no, about time they made a 'house call', whatever that was.

FIFTY-FIVE

When Watson emerged from his drug-induced exile, it was as if he had been launched from the seabed like a projectile. One minute he was admiring the luminescent blobs floating around him, giant versions of the tadpoles that swam across his retinae in bright sunlight, the next he was propelled from this warm, enervating soup into a harsh reality. It was like a bucket of cold water to the face and, for a few seconds, he kicked against it.

'Major Watson, calm yourself.'

'Can't speak, can't speak,' he gasped.

'Hold on, let me take this off.'

He sucked at the air while his tumbled senses realigned themselves. Slowly, his brain began to tick off a checklist, as if going through an inventory of goods.

He was in the transfusion tent. Electric lights had been installed, hence the brightness. He had been wearing an oxygen mask. That really was Staff Nurse Jennings. His throat was terribly parched.

'Can I have some water?' he croaked.

'Of course.' Staff Nurse Jennings slid a hand under his head and tilted it while she put the glass to his lips. It tasted marvellous, like fine Islay or cognac. But he knew that was always a reaction to finding yourself, against all better judgements, alive. For a few precious moments the nervous system was capable of heightened responses, as if under the influence of some opiate, before they calmed down, back to normality. This was probably why his neck was tingling to Staff Nurse Jennings's touch.

'What are you doing here?' he demanded.

She spoke softly, as if to a child. 'Me? I work here, Major. At the Casualty Clearing Station.'

'I know that. But you'd gone. With Myles . . .'

Staff Nurse Jennings laughed. Why was everyone trying to pair her off with Myles? 'I'm sorry, Major Watson. The sedatives haven't worn off.'

'Dinner! You wanted me to accompany you . . .'

'Dinner?' She furrowed her brow, before she realized what he was referring to. 'Oh, yes. That's right. But then I had news that my brother was in Boulogne. He was at a hospital there, awaiting transport. Sister Spence kindly let me go to him, but on condition I didn't shout about it. I don't think she wanted anyone to think she'd gone soft.'

Brother. Yes, Sister Spence would feel sympathy for a nurse with an injured brother. Had she not lost her own to a 'relapse'? But he could see she might not want others to know she had a tender spot in her iron soul.

'But what of Myles?'

'I have no idea. Is that why Mrs Gregson was questioning me about him? On your behalf?' She sounded extremely annoyed.

'Not at my behest. Mrs Gregson is her own woman.'

'You can say that again,' she said. She bit her lip, as if she wanted to add more.

'And, forgive me, about Caspar Myles . . . ?'

Jennings shrugged. 'There was talk of him going back to his unit.'

'He hasn't.'

'Oh.' She looked thoughtful. 'But by all accounts he did clear out without a by-your-leave to Major Torrance. Who is none too pleased with him. More water?'

'Thank you.'

After another sip, Watson lay back on the pillow and licked his lips. 'Do you knit, Staff Nurse Jennings?'

'Knit? Yes. But not for a while. Not much time for it over here. Why, what do you need?'

He waved the subject away. 'How long have I been here?'

'Since just before I returned. The best part of three days. You missed Field Marshal Haig. Mind you, most of us did.' What a storm in a teacup that turned out to be. Although it was a storm captured by cine cameras for the newsreels.

'Three days!' Watson threw back his blankets.

'Stop that! You are lucky to be here at all,' interrupted Miss Pippery. 'George carried you in over her shoulder and virtually demanded the entire CCS stop what it was doing and tend to you.'

'I must thank her,' said Watson.

'She's not here,' said Jennings. 'Gone back to take up other duties at Bailleul.'

Watson frowned. There was a reason she had not wanted to go back there. Something about having burned her bridges. 'And Captain de Griffon?'

'With his men once more.'

'I need to . . .' He could feel a fatigue building. 'I need to find out something. There was a man there. The one who locked me in the barn . . . set off the gas . . . the dead man. '

'Yes, well, I think you had better ask the Military Police about that,' said Staff Nurse Jennings. 'They have been here once, asking questions, but asked to be notified when you were strong enough to answer any. Are you?' Watson nodded. 'In that case I shall send a message to the Military Police barracks at Camar. Tell them Major Watson will be well enough to answer questions later on today.'

'Very well,' said Miss Pippery. 'To whom shall I address it?'

Jennings hesitated. 'I suppose you'd better contact Lieutenant Gregson.'

'Gregson?' Watson asked. It was a common enough name, but even so. 'Any relation to Mrs Gregson?'

Jennings shrugged, but in a way that suggested she knew more than she was letting on. 'I think you'd better ask her that, Major.'

MONDAY–TUESDAY

FIFTY-SIX

Lady Stanwood stood in a first-floor window and studied the driveway of Flitcham, impatient for the stranger's arrival. The grounds she inspected looked far better than they had at the time of her husband's passing. True, the death of old Tommy Turner had been a blow. Some said the old gardener should never have come back, once all the groundstaff had volunteered *en masse* to serve. That being out in the cold and wet with his gang of novices had taken him off. Lady Stanwood believed it had been the loss of his two grandsons within three days of each other at Ypres that had accelerated his end.

Oh, how she wanted this war to end. Then she could get on with her plans. As it was, she felt frozen into inertia by it. Like, she supposed, every other mother in the land, dreading that little red demon on the crimson bicycle, with his sackful of sorrows. Surely it couldn't go on much longer?

Yet conscription had been announced, which suggested that there was some way to go yet before they defeated Germany. And now there was a request for her to hand over parts of the hall to the Canadians for the rehabilitation of the wounded. She could see no reason to refuse. The place was too large for her now, especially with a denuded staff.

The Albion turned tentatively into the driveway, brushing close to the gatehouse, and began making a stately, albeit somewhat jerky, progress between the limes. It was, she hoped, carrying providence. She moved back from the window, not wanting to be seen by her visitor.

The voice on the telephone had been tremulous, suggesting an older man. But the words had carried the force of youth. He had read the obituary of her husband in *The Times*, he had spoken to Dr Kibble – whom he stressed was the soul of discretion – and this man was convinced that Lord Stanwood had died what he called an 'unnatural' death.

She caught sight of herself in one of the gilded mirrors. Time and worry had blurred her features. The years of fretting over poor Bimmy, as she called her husband, slipping away into a terrifying dementia. And now the constant, gnawing concern over Robinson, the new Lord Stanwood. Would he ever get to take his seat in the Lords? Would he ever be half the man his father was?

An 'unnatural' death. It was certainly that. Which was why she had agreed to see this man.

She watched the chauffeur get out and limp round to open the rear door. The road accident that had broken Legge's limbs and scarred his face had been a godsend. Nobody would ask about why he wasn't serving now. It had saved his life. She waited for the newcomer to emerge from the vehicle. It was a shock when the person who emerged turned out to be a *boy*.

But no, there was another figure, struggling to get out. First came a stout walking stick, followed by the long, spindly fingers of the free hand, which the boy took. The man shuffled to the edge of the seat and, with assistance from Legge, struggled upright.

He stood for a few moments, the effort having taken something from him.

He was even older than she had imagined on the telephone. Stooped and frail. Who at that age gallivanted about the country in taxicabs and on trains? However, it suggested to her that whatever this man had to say, he believed it important. Why else put himself to what was clearly a great deal of trouble?

Lady Stanwood watched as he positioned himself between the boy and his stick and began a slow but stately progress towards the hall. It was his back that troubled him, she could tell from the tiny steps he took. After a few yards he stopped and used his walking stick to point at the oleanders. Legge nodded the answer to his question, whatever it was.

The man bent down, cautiously, and whispered something in the lad's ear, then the strange entourage continued on its way towards the house. She had arranged for Mrs Talbot and Mr Steen the butler to greet him. She herself would be in the library when he entered. Time to take position.

She had misgivings now. Had she done the right thing? Bimmy's death had been terrible to behold, but nothing this ancient crock could say would bring him back now. She would listen politely and send him on his way. After all, her primary concern – her only concern now – was to make sure Robinson de Griffon, Lord Stanwood, survived this war to enjoy his inheritance.

FIFTY-SEVEN

Ernst Bloch heard the rasp of the Mercedes engines and looked up at the sky. A flight of Albatros two-seaters burst out from behind the trees, almost low enough to do some impromptu pollarding with their undercarriages. They had taken off from the airfield to the east of the sniper camp. As they wobbled overhead, wings dipping in the crosswind, he could see the racks of hand-bombs sitting on the fuselage next to the observer. They were on a combined spotting and bombing mission over enemy lines.

Once they had spiralled into a climb to gain altitude, he went back to the trestle table in front of him, on which was laid a captured British SMLE rifle attached to a peculiar contraption. It was known as a periscope rifle. Such was the accuracy of Bloch and his counterparts, it appeared the British had been forced to adopt this remote firing device.

The rifle was more or less standard. Not as accurate as the Mauser, but with a very good action that made for a rate of fire the German weapon could not match. However, it had been modified with a long brass tube housing the telescopic sights, which fed into a prismatic device. That formed into a box periscope, with, some 50 centimetres below the rifle, the eyepiece. It meant that a Tommy could poke the gun over the parapet and line up a target without showing himself. There was even a lever device for pulling the trigger remotely.

Lux had asked him to evaluate the weapon. He had seen similar devices from Kahles. This model, the inscription told him, was made by E. R. Watts and Son of Camberwell Road, London.

Well, he would tell Lux, he wouldn't order any sights from Mr Watts. The system was ingenious, but calibrating it for accurate fire would be a nightmare. It was hard enough to make sure a standard telescopic sight was properly set up. This was too complex for anything other than random fire in the general direction of the enemy. Still, he thought, he could give it to young Lothar Breuchtal to try on the range. A whole day of tests. Don't come back until you have hit six bulls in a row. That would keep him out of his hair.

Bloch lit a cigarette and stared up at the circling specks of the biplanes. They formed up into three separate wings and moved off to the west.

Lothar was getting under his skin. He was like a young puppy, or perhaps a cousin that idolizes his older relative. There was no escape from him. Bloch might even be on the latrine and Lothar would come and plonk himself down next to him and start with the questions. What sights did he prefer? Goerz or Kahles? And why? How important was crosswind? How often should you recalibrate a scope? What were the British trench loopholes made of? How did he rate the penetrating power of the Krupp ammunition versus the *S.m.K.*?

On and on it went. Much as he had enjoyed helping devise the school curriculum with Loewenhardt, he couldn't wait for no man's land, where the rule was enforced silence. Perhaps Lothar would explode like a landmine with the effort of staying quiet. They would find out soon enough.

He could see the lad coming towards him now, one hand held on his cap to stop it blowing away, the other holding a piece of paper, a smile on his face.

Bloch puffed on the cigarette and kept his features neutral.

'Unteroffizier Bloch!'

He remained impassive in the face of the grinning ball of enthusiasm heading his way.

The boy stopped before him, breathless and flushed.

'Orders from Lux. The British have just moved in an untried unit to the front line in our sector.'

'Our' sector. He liked that. Kid hadn't even seen it yet.

'What are they called?'

'Part of . . .' he looked at the paper, '. . . the Lancashire Fusiliers. The Leigh Friends.'

Bloch nodded, dropped his cigarette on the floor and ground it out. 'Chums' was a more accurate translation. Well, he thought, whatever they called themselves, they wouldn't be chums for much longer. Not living ones, anyway.

FIFTY-EIGHT

Watson had just read the telegram from Egypt and was digesting the contents when Lieutenant Tobias Gregson arrived. The major had been anticipating this all morning. Staff Nurse Jennings had suggested that the man must be a relation of Mrs Gregson, but Watson had assured her this was unlikely, once he had discovered the man's Christian name. He knew Tobias Gregson of old. He must be almost the same age as Watson, certainly no more than ten years younger – what a gap in age and experience that had seemed at the time.

Miss Pippery ushered the policeman into the transfusion tent where, in the absence of any major offensives or hate bombardments, Watson was still the only patient. 'Major Watson, sir,' Gregson said, as he took off his red cap.

Watson was confounded. The man was thirty years junior to the chap he had expected. He had a young, unlined face and a handsome black moustache. His eyes were bright and unclouded, with dark hair swept back from the beginnings of a widow's peak. This was certainly not the Tobias Gregson he had once known.

'Lieutenant Tobias Gregson of the Military Foot Police,

Investigations Division. Are you all right, sir?' He glanced at the VAD. 'I can come back.'

'No, no. Miss Pippery, some water, please.' He took the glass and gulped. 'And tea? Lieutenant?'

'Splendid, yes.' He waited until they were alone. 'How are you, sir?'

'Well,' said Watson. 'They tell me every day from now on I should treat as bonus. I've won the tontine. Lucky to be alive.'

'We are all pleased you are, Major.' He unbuttoned his top pocket and took out a notebook. He adopted a more formal tone. 'I am here to investigate the exact circumstances that led to the death of a soldier at Suffolk Farm.'

'Which soldier?'

'And also, I am afraid, to evaluate your role in the proceedings.'

'Why afraid?'

Lieutenant Gregson sighed. 'My superiors feel that you should have involved the RMP earlier, sir.'

'Do they? And been laughed at?'

The policeman shook his head in a grave manner. 'We take this very seriously.'

'Only now there has been a casualty you can't blame on blood transfusion.'

He looked puzzled. 'You've lost me there, sir.'

'Pull up that chair, Lieutenant.' The policeman did so and Watson gave a quick recap of the deaths of Hornby and Shipobottom, and the near-demise of de Griffon.

'I see,' he said in a manner that suggested he had no such insight.

'And had I suggested that in the midst of the carnage of the Western Front, someone was taking the time to murder fellow soldiers, I would have been given short shrift. I get the distinct impression you MPs are more concerned with AWOLs, desertions and traffic control than actual crime.'

Gregson looked offended by the slur. 'That's primarily the mounted division. At the beginning of 1915 twenty of us were seconded from Scotland Yard—'

'You're from the Yard?'

'Yes, sir.'

Now he was really confused. 'I knew a Tobias Gregson. Of the Yard.'

'I know, sir. He told me all about you. My father.'

'Really?' He couldn't help feeling a warm glow at such a connection to his old life. 'Holmes always said he was the best of the Scotland Yarders.'

Gregson nodded, then added with a twinkle, 'He also said that wasn't actually saying all that much.'

Watson, who had been the real author of that comment, said, 'Nonsense. We always liked him. How is he?'

'He passed away just before war broke out.'

'I'm sorry to hear that.'

'Yes. Although in a way, a blessing. He would have hated,' Gregson waved his notebook around the ward, 'all this. All this noble sacrifice, as they call it. He would even hate me being here. But I must get back to the matter in hand.'

'You can begin by telling me the identity of the man shot by Captain de Griffon.'

The lieutenant flipped a few pages in the book. 'It was a sergeant. Man called Platt.'

'Platt?' Watson almost shouted the name.

'You'd met, apparently.'

'Yes, he helped me saddle poor Lord Lockie. The horse that had to be put down. Why on earth . . . ?'

'We think the reason he killed Sergeant Shipobottom was to take his place. Promotion.'

'Promotion? And de Griffon? The man who promoted him?'

'Perhaps he was afraid the captain would change his mind. Or discover the murder. He also had a written undertaking from de Griffon that he would have a position as a tackler in the mills once hostilities had ceased. It's some kind of overlooker, by all accounts.'

Watson grunted his assent. 'Oversees the looms, I believe.'

'Well, with the captain out of the way, I have no doubt that the family would have honoured the appointment.'

Watson didn't feel the usual excitement that came when a solution presented itself. Instead, he heard the swirl of waters being muddied. 'And me? Why try to kill me?'

'Perhaps you were getting close to the truth.'

It wouldn't do. Wouldn't do at all. 'Not to that truth, Lieutenant. That truth wasn't even a twinkle in my eye.'

The tea arrived. Watson was glad of the interruption. The whole business didn't make any kind of sense to him. There was an inevitability about, an elegance to, the correct interpretation of a series of events. He had seen it time and time again, a golden thread running through a Gordian knot of dead ends and diversions. Not in this case. 'You've spoken to de Griffon?'

'Yes. Something of a broken man, sir,' said Gregson.

'After shooting Platt? Understandable.'

A slight raise of the eyebrow. 'After shooting the horse, I think.'

'Ahh. Of course,' said Watson. 'So, will the Military Police take action against de Griffon for the killing? Of the soldier, not the horse.' Although with the British Army, one could never be sure. Sometimes there were more tears shed over one dead pony than a thousand slaughtered men.

Gregson shook his head. 'Good officers are in short supply. He acted in self-defence. And to rescue you. We are assuming the balance of Sergeant Platt's mind was disturbed.'

Watson picked up the telegram and handed it to the policeman. 'Read that.'

'Sugar?' Miss Pippery asked.

'Two please,' said Gregson, as he read. 'I don't understand.'

'My friend Anwar in Egypt. A doctor who helped me with the transfusion experiments. I asked him to investigate the death of a captain in Egypt. Leverton. He died sometime after I left the country.'

'Cyanosis,' the policeman read.

'A blue colour to the skin.'

'Thank you. Terrible grin. Spastic limbs . . .'

'And?'

'A roman numeral carved on one arm. Post mortem.'

'Which numeral?' Watson prompted.

'The number two.'

'Two. Which suggests this man was the second victim. If Platt was the murderer, this little spree began back in Egypt. Perhaps before. We still have no idea who number one might be. You'll need a motive to explain all that. A promotion to sergeant and the promise of a foreman's position just won't do.'

'You don't suspect who number one might be?'

'No. And we aren't certain yet that Hornby is three.'

'And could you be mistaken about Shipobottom's mark?'

'I could be mistaken about a great many things. But I'm sure that was a number four on Shipobottom, not random scratches.'

'And Captain de Griffon . . . if he was a potential victim?'

'He should have a "V", a Roman five. But remember, Shipobottom's marks were post mortem. The poisoner might have intended to score de Griffon once the toxins had done their work.'

'I see.' Gregson looked thoughtful. 'Does that not suggest the murderer might be someone who would know he would have access to the body?'

'Such as?' Watson asked.

'A doctor. A nurse.'

'An orderly, a stretcher-bearer or a gravedigger,' Watson completed. Talking of which, where was Brindle? he wondered. 'Possibly. We don't tend to guard our dead as well as we might, though.'

'Thank you,' the policeman said to Miss Pippery as she handed him the tea. He took a sip and smiled. 'Perfect.'

'Sir, I hope you don't mind me interrupting, but we have a Mrs Gregson here. Or did have until recently,' said Miss Pippery.

'I have interviewed her. At Bailleul hospital.'

Miss Pippery glanced at Watson. Her cheeks were glowing red with embarrassment. 'We were wondering if she was a relative. Of yours.'

'We' were wondering? Watson began a gentle admonishment. 'Miss Pippery, I'm not sure this is appropriate—'

'That's perfectly all right,' Gregson said. 'The answer is no, not really.'

'Oh,' said Miss Pippery. 'Right, I'll leave you to it—'

Watson spotted the evasion. 'Not really? What is she then?'

The policeman swallowed hard and squirmed a little in the

canvas chair. 'Wife. Ex-wife, to be perfectly frank. We were divorced some years ago.'

Miss Pippery's eyes grew to saucer size and her hand went to her mouth. She gave a small gasp of dismay. 'But she told me . . .'

Gregson waited for her to finish the sentence. But Miss Pippery was unable to. 'Divorced? From George?'

'Georgina, yes. I am afraid so,' he confirmed.

Miss Pippery turned and ran from the tent, leaving only the dying echo of a sob behind her.

'Tricky subject. Divorce,' said Watson. 'Mrs Gregson told me she was a widow, too.' What had she said? *In my experience nobody seems too concerned about the honour of an aging widow.* He had naturally assumed she was referring to herself. But he hadn't pursued it, not wanting to open old wounds.

'I can't blame her,' said Gregson, running a hand through his hair. 'There's still a stigma.' He glanced over his shoulder at the departed Miss Pippery. 'Your nurse seemed rather upset by the news.'

'Miss Pippery is a Catholic. At least I assume so by her cross,' explained Watson. 'She might be modern in some ways. But perhaps not divorce.'

'I never wanted it, Major. I had no choice. Georgina was, is, a headstrong woman.'

'Headstrong enough to save my life. If de Griffon hadn't inveigled upon her to give him a lift to Suffolk Farm to collect Lord Lockie . . .'

'Yes, quite.' He paused. 'Georgina joined the suffragettes in late 1906, perhaps early '07. Just as I was making progress in my career at Scotland Yard. I blame myself. I couldn't pay her my full attention. A policeman's hours . . . Well, she got up to mischief. She couldn't see how untenable the situation was for me. Always being arrested, civil disobedience and what have you. And then there was the trial. The last straw. I was told in no uncertain terms that if I wanted to remain a policeman, I would have to separate myself from her. Which I did.'

'Trial?'

'At the Old Bailey. You probably remember it. The Sutton Courtenay Outrage. '

It rang an ominous bell, but it was around the time he had been so wrapped up in the death of Emily, he had hardly picked up a newspaper. It was more a sensation than a clear memory, a prickling of the skin. 'What was she on trial for?' Watson asked, dreading the answer.

'Attempted murder.'

'Of whom?'

'The Prime Minister.'

FIFTY-NINE

THE *PALL MALL GAZETTE*

THE OUTRAGE AT SUTTON COURTENAY: VERDICT IN

At the Central Criminal Court, yesterday, before Mr Justice Bankes and a jury, Mrs Georgina Gregson, thirty, was placed on her trial charged with having set fire to the summer house (by the use of a specially constructed 'arson' or 'Orsini' bomb) at The Wharf, Sutton Courtenay, knowing full well that the Prime Minister, The Right Hon. H. H. Asquith was within, which resulted in a charge of attempted murder. Mr Bodkin and Mr Travers Humphreys prosecuted; Mr Langdon, KC, and Mr E. D. Muir appeared for the defence.

Despite testimony of good character from Mrs Carter-Tate and Mrs Gregson's husband, Inspector Tobias Gregson, a member of Scotland Yard's élite CID squad, Mrs Gregson was found guilty.

Mr Justice Bankes, in summing up, said that 'not very long ago it would have been unthinkable that a well-educated, well-brought-up young woman could have committed a crime like this. Not long ago one would have heard appeals to juries to acquit her on the grounds that it was unthinkable she could have committed such a crime. But, unfortunately, women as a class have forfeited any presumption in their favour of that kind. As a consequence it is impossible to approach these cases from the standpoint from which they would have been approached only a few years ago. It was open to the accused to give some explanation, but she has not done so, and the suggestion of her counsel that she is wholly innocent when traces of mercury of fulminate were found in her home and on her clothes was rightly dismissed by the jury.'

The judge went on to call her alibi for the night in question 'laughably thin' and to praise the anonymous individual who had 'tipped off' detectives that Mrs Gregson was one of the perpetrators.

The prisoner then proceeded to read a long statement in which she denied the jurisdiction of the Court, contending that women should be on the jury.

The Judge: 'I have listened to what you have had to say, and my duty is to pass sentence upon you. It is no desire of mine to lecture you, but I am provoked by what you said to say this, and this only: The statement you have made seems to me to indicate that you have lost all sense of the consequence of what you are doing. You do not seem to realize the loss and injury and anxiety that such acts as yours cause to all classes – not only to the rich but to the poor and struggling; not only to men but to women. You talk about man-made law as if that was the only law that ought to govern people's actions. You must have heard of another law which says: "Ye shall do unto others as ye would that they should do unto you." That is the law you are breaking.'

The judge also said that her unwillingness to give up her co-conspirators would count against her. Mrs Gregson was sentenced to ten years with hard labour. She immediately announced her intention to go on hunger strike.

SIXTY

Watson waited until the policeman finished explaining the case and the coverage of it by the newspapers and periodicals. 'I remember it, vaguely. Bad business. Did the women's cause no good at all.'

'Georgina, or the Red She-Devil as the lower papers liked to call her, had a hard time of it in Holloway. You have to bear that in mind when she is being . . . prickly. The force-feeding, the humiliating searches, the attacks, they took their toll.'

'Attacks?'

'A policeman's wife in prison? It was one of the reasons I divorced her. She could deny being a copper's missus then. Of course, too stubborn to change her name.'

'Only one of the reasons?' Watson asked gently.

'Don't judge me too harshly, Major.' From the depths of his wallet he produced a small newspaper cutting. 'You might not have seen this.'

It was two paragraphs long. It described how 'new evidence' had come to light that suggested that Mrs Gregson had been wrongly convicted. She was freed on appeal. In a statement she said she was glad justice had been done and swore to promote the cause of women's rights through peaceful means. What was she looking forward to most? A bath in private and a ride on a very fast motor cycle.

'The trials and the convictions get all the fanfare,' said Gregson, 'the aftermath very little. I still meet people who remember the Red She-Devil, but not that she was acquitted. It's why I carry this around.'

'I must confess this second act of the drama passed me by completely,' said Watson. 'But if she didn't . . . ?'

'It was to frame her, Major. The Women's Freedom League, which Georgina supported, believed in civil unrest and disobedience, but not some of the extreme anarchist acts that the Women's Social and Political Union and others indulged in. Nor the harrying and physical assaults on politicians that were commonplace.'

Watson nodded. He recalled that Churchill had been laid into with a riding crop by the suffragette Theresa Garnett. He had not pressed charges, merely saying that he had sworn to treat his horse more humanely in future after feeling the bite of a whip.

'Well, the guerillists of the WSPU were losing influence to the WFL, and they decided to tar them with the same brush. They planted the bomb, having lured Georgina to a false meeting, and left materials that implicated her in our cellar. It took me a long time to prove that she had gone to the deserted hall for a fictitious meeting and could not have planted the bomb.'

'You continued the investigation?'

'She was my wife,' Gregson said softly.

But you did divorce her, Watson thought. Still, the man at least had the decency to carry on trying to clear her name. He should be given credit for his tenacity. 'And relations now with Mrs Gregson?'

'Cordial,' he said with regret. 'Little more than cordial. After her release she moved from London, to where she enjoyed rather less notoriety.'

'But still didn't change her name?'

'No. She was an innocent woman, she said. With nothing to hide.'

Except a husband, it seemed. 'Still, interesting. That a militant suffragette should be part and parcel of the events here.'

Gregson looked as if he had been slapped. 'You're not suggesting—'

'No.' Watson shook his head vigorously. 'No. Not unless Mrs Gregson was in Egypt within the past year.'

'Not that I am aware of.'

'There is something here that is making me uncomfortable. Something not quite right.' Watson slumped back on his pillow, drained by the effort of thinking, and of groping in the dark for tenuous connections. 'I'm not quite on top form, Inspector—'

'Lieutenant,' Gregson corrected.

'Sorry. I can see your father in you now, you know. We were a little cruel to the policemen. Not just your father. Poor Lestrade. And to Inspector Gregory. I'm sorry. It was just a little game.'

'Major Watson, let me tell you, he used to huff and puff, but secretly he was pleased as Punch to be included in your stories. Proud, even. I should let you rest now. I will be back to continue our discussion.'

'Thank you. Can you send Miss Pippery back in? If she feels up to it?'

Watson's eyes were closed when Miss Pippery returned to the tent and she was about to tiptoe out when he spoke. 'Don't think too badly of her.'

Miss Pippery fingered the cross on the chain she had taken out from her collar. 'I'll try not to, but *divorce*.' She said it in the way she might have said 'cockroaches' or 'spiders', and with an accompanying shudder. 'Perhaps I should have guessed. My parents never liked her, you know.'

'Well, forgive me, Miss Pippery, but I do. Like her, I mean.'

Her face was a picture of distaste. 'But—'

'Thirty years ago, I might have thought like you. I hope not, but I had views then at odds with those I hold now. But there are also mitigating circumstances at play here. Powerful ones. I suggest you write and ask her to explain herself.'

'I couldn't.'

'Write to her at the hospital.'

'I already have. I have told her that we can never be friends again.'

'So soon? You haven't posted it?'

'There was a messenger leaving for Bailleul. I scribbled a note—'

'No!' the vehemence with which he pronounced the word brought on a coughing fit. He groped for the water and took a gulp. 'You foolish girl. Trust me on this one thing if no other. You let that stand, from the other end of your life you'll look back with nothing but regret. She's your friend, and that is not something to be tossed away lightly. You get in touch with her.' He found himself wagging a finger. 'God, if He is anything like the God we think we know, will forgive you.'

'And her? You think He will forgive her?'

'Yes. God will forgive her. But will He forgive you if you drive a schism between two friends?'

'How do you mean?'

'We are born alone and die alone. In between we have the chance to make precious few connections to other men and women. It is a human imperative to find someone, be it friend or lover, that we can take succour from and offer it in return. Look at those men in the trenches. To them, the comradeship forged out there might turn out to be the most important bond they will ever know. Because, one day, only someone who has been through this at their side will understand, really understand them.'

He took another drink of water. 'It's a messy business sometimes. Husbands and wives divorce, friends become enemies, love cools. But we are driven to try again. And again. You are wounded because Mrs Gregson lied to you. So am I. You feel deceived, betrayed. Put those feelings aside for a moment. Tell me about Mrs Gregson.'

Miss Pippery began to fiddle with her cross again. 'Well, let me see . . .'

'Put the cross away. Not the divorcee. The Mrs Gregson you love.'

'Love?' she repeated, as if it was the first time she had heard the word.

'Don't you?'

'I . . .' She squeezed the cross and tucked it down her neckline. 'I love that she has this, this skin that seems thicker than everybody else's. That she is always ready to try something new. That she isn't cowed by authority. I love that she defends me.'

'You love that you can call her your friend. You love that she chose you to be her friend. It makes you proud,' he said, remembering what Gregson had said about his father. 'Doesn't it?'

Miss Pippery nodded, suddenly feeling foolish and naked before this man. 'It does. I'll never be her, but she certainly made me appreciate what I am. What I could be. But how do you know—'

'I just do. Call it the wisdom of years. But don't try to count how many years. Now go. Write to your friend again. Tell her you have reconsidered and that you now know this changes nothing.'

She gave a smile and left at a half-run. 'Thank you, Dr Watson.'

Major, he corrected. Although it was nice to hear the old honorific in front of his name. Dr Watson. It still had a good, solid ring to it. Just like old times.

He closed those lids again, felt himself slide away, reaching out to embrace sleep, but the growing, comforting darkness was rudely penetrated by the shrill whistle of a falling bomb.

SIXTY-ONE

Winston Churchill had not slept for a whole day and night. Neither had the six men in front of him, now all standing in a surprisingly erect line considering the fatigue they must be feeling. All were dressed in dark colours, their faces streaked with black dubbing, although the dark circles under their eyes were the soldiers' own. They were arranged in front of Plug Street forest, where they had spent twelve hours on exhausting manoeuvres.

Churchill began to walk up and down before them, tramping his way through the gluey film of mud covering the field. It would rain soon, he thought. These men deserved hot drinks, a warm meal and a good stiff brandy. He would keep this brief.

'I'd like to offer my congratulations, gentlemen,' he began, his voice coarser than usual. 'You have earned the admiration of your officers. And soon you will win the gratitude of the nation.'

He cleared his throat. 'We are not from the same background.' It hardly needed saying. He was the product of unbelievable privilege and patronage; most of the men were the rough-arsed offspring of the tenements or coarse country boys. 'Nor the same branch of the services. As you discovered on my first day.'

There was a chortle. He had tried to drill the battalion on his arrival, but had used arcane and confusing cavalry commands from his South African days. That had not gone well. It had taken him some time to win their confidence, but he was certain he had it now.

'Yet we find ourselves here, in the same boat, as it were. Facing an enemy who seems to know more about us than we do about them. That has to change. Our job . . .'

He looked back towards his HQ. Two young adjutants were struggling over the uneven earth, holding a large wooden packing case by its rope handles.

'Our task,' Churchill continued, 'is to reverse that imbalance. To go out and capture as many of the enemy as we can and turn them over to our finest minds for interrogation. To help weed out any spies in the area. You are the ones chosen for this. You must turn to your task with vigour.' He paused and took a breath. Time to turn the volume up. 'We have all lost friends and colleagues. Two officers out of five in my mess have gone. Now, though, we must look forward. Do not look back. Gather afresh in your hearts and spirit all the energies of your youth. Bend anew together for a supreme effort over the coming weeks. The times are harsh, the need is dire, the agony of the British Empire seemingly infinite.' He now affected a bulldog growl. 'But the might of Britain will prove irresistible. She will prevail. We are the vanguard of the Allied cause and we must march forward as one man.'

He noticed, with no small pleasure, that his chosen six were standing even straighter than before. Major-General Furse, his commanding officer, had admonished him for the 'softness' of his approach. There had been no extended field punishments and no executions since he had taken command. But he was convinced that there were better ways to inspire the men than being a martinet. Lead by example, for instance.

The junior officers, annoyed at having to act as coolies to the men, dropped the packing case at the side of Churchill. 'Sir!'

He looked at the two boys. The battalion had suffered appalling losses at Loos before his arrival. Two-thirds of the officers were new. Polite Scottish lads – often only just at regulation height – with a spirit well removed from the legendary belligerence of their countrymen. William Wallace would have little use for them. Churchill's job would be to change that. 'Take off the lid.'

The pair struggled with their clasp knives and eventually managed to lever off the top planks. They peered inside. 'Step back, gentlemen, please,' Churchill instructed. 'These are not for the likes of you.'

He reached into the case and extracted a piece of dense, hard wood one foot long. 'A billy club,' he said, dropping it to the ground. 'Old police issue, I suspect.' Now he pulled out a shorter version, which swelled at one end. 'Scotland Yard's finest. Truncheon.' He dropped that, too. 'Ah, now, a lathi, used for cane fighting. Not heavy enough for our needs. Now this, a jungle club.' He held up a club with a paddle-shaped head. 'From Burma, I believe.'

Churchill stepped back. 'Gentlemen, I appealed to my friends and acquaintances in the House for any batons or clubs that might be used in close combat. Souvenirs and the like, which might serve our purpose.' He had also appealed for some decent beef, champagne and Rioja, but he wasn't going to mention that. 'There are axes and knobkerries, too. I am sure you will find something to your liking in here. Help yourselves.'

Churchill picked up the police truncheon from the ground. It was chipped and gnarled from use. It must have been fifty years old or more. He slapped it into the palm of his hand. Yes, that would do nicely. 'I've got mine,' he said, as the six men rifled through the weapons. He swished it through the air, miming concussing an unsuspecting Fritz.

'You're nae goin' out, are you, sir?' asked one of the subalterns, a chubby-faced lad of nineteen. 'On the raids?'

Churchill pointed the bulbous end of the truncheon at him and narrowed his eyes. 'Not a word, lad. Not to anyone. And especially not within earshot of Major-General Furse. If Clemmie finds out, I'll be blaming you, and I'll have you strung up from one of yon trees.'

The young man looked so horrified, Churchill burst out laughing.

'Sir. Colonel.'

It was a corporal from his HQ, breathless from the run over such sticky ground.

'Yes, what is it?' Churchill asked, his good mood evaporating as quickly as it had arrived.

'Telephone call, sir.'

That might be news from GHQ at St Omer of Haig's impending inspection of the entire Guards Division, of which Churchill's battalion formed part. It was the final part of his inspection before Haig's anticipated promotion. He wasn't particularly keen on a visit; on his arrival in France Haig had been cordial, but not much more. Churchill was well known to be a supporter of Sir

John French, a man whose star was falling rapidly to earth. 'Who is it?'

The corporal looked at the paper in his hand. 'I was to say it's a Mr Sherlock Holmes, sir.'

SIXTY-TWO

Watson, with a hastily recruited dressing gown thrown over pyjamas, ran out into confusion and cacophony. Above him there was an agitated flock of German biplanes, the black crosses livid on the underside of the lower wings. They were turning and diving like the bees at the entrance to one of Holmes's hives. Their target was clearly the lorry park to the east of the CCS, and already thick columns of oily smoke were rising, fusing together into one bulbous black cloud. It looked as if a giant insect out of H. G. Wells's imagination was bestriding the countryside.

Around him came the pop-pop of small-arms fire. The pack store, a locked wooden hut where soldiers' kit was stored, had been wrenched open. It appeared that every patient who was mobile had grabbed a rifle from it, burst out into the open and was taking aim at the Albatroses. The rapidity of the fire reminded him that when they first encountered the BEF in France, the Germans were convinced the British had machine guns. He could see, just over the treeline, the very upper dormer windows of the monastery, which had been thrown open. Men were leaning out, shooting revolvers futilely but magnificently into the sky. A handful had made the slate roof, and they, too, were taking pot shots.

Watson felt a real surge of pride at this group of men scattered across the CCS, many bandaged, some on crutches, others who had crawled from their beds, all determined not to let the marauders have it all their own way.

Even as he peered into the sky, one of the aggressors faltered, falling slightly. He gave a hoarse cheer.

It was only as it performed a twisting acrobatic that Watson realized the aircraft was not hit. The pilot had noticed the pinpricks being aimed its way. It was like a big dog suddenly becoming aware that it had fleas. Now it was going to scratch.

With a flip that Watson thought might rip the wings off the biplane, it flattened out and headed straight for the CCS. Now the hornet-like buzzing of its engine stood out from the general mêlée of sound. Behind the propeller, lights winked, like semaphore signals: interrupter machine guns, synchronized to fire through the propellers. Watson watched, as frozen as any statue, as a dust devil swirled across the grounds of the hospital and churned its way through a group of patients who were left collapsed in its wake.

Still the others fired, and the angry machine banked, turned and started another run, the nose winking again, the angry engine note singing in his ears.

'For God's sake, sir, get down.'

Brindle, his driver, was sprinting towards him, his long limbs splaying as he did so, and launched himself into a rugby tackle on Watson just as the ground exploded around them.

He hit Watson full force amidships and the pair of them crashed down into the mud. The air was punched out of Watson's lungs and a sharp stab in his side told him a rib might have gone.

As the plane soared overhead he could hear the popping of the guns above the screaming engine. The prop wash engulfed the entwined pair in wet leaves. A Humber ambulance's petrol tank ignited at the entrance, the vehicle bucking as it was lifted in the air by the explosion. It came down and split into two, broke-backed.

At a signal none of those on the ground could discern, the attackers all broke off the assault in the same instant. A last bomb was tossed, detonating with a loud crump, and the planes regrouped, their buzzing diminishing as they deserted the scene, wings wagging in the aerial equivalent of a loud guffaw. It was little consolation that one of them was trailing an oily plume and appeared to be losing height.

Around him more fuel tanks exploded, and the air filled with black specks and an acrid, rubbery stink. With some difficulty Watson rolled Brindle off him. 'You all right?'

'Leg,' he said groggily.

Watson scrambled to his knees. A bullet had severed something significant in the driver's thigh and blood was pumping from the wound like claret from an uncorked cask.

He could see panic rising in Brindle's eyes at the size of the pool forming on the ground beneath him. The colour fled from his cheeks, leaving a grey pallor.

'I'm going to die.'

'Yes, you are,' said Watson, taking the cord from his dressing gown. 'Just not today.' He carefully positioned the tourniquet and pulled it tight until the flow reduced to a trickle.

'One thing we've got a lot of, Brindle, old chap,' he said calmly, 'is spare blood.'

A shadow fell over his face and he stood, feeling a catch in his ribcage as he did so. Something had gone in there, all right. Sister Spence was a few feet away and she looked down at his sodden pyjamas, darkened with blood, in some alarm. 'Not mine,' he assured her, pointing to his driver.

Sister instructed two stretcher-bearers to load up Brindle.

'He needs a transfusion,' said Watson. 'I'll prepare the tent. Have you seen Miss Pippery?'

'You'd better come with me,' said a stony-faced Sister Spence.

She was lying on a cot-bed in one of the bell tents. Someone, perhaps one of the several nurses that surrounded her, had cut open the top of her uniform. It had revealed a mound of pink froth. The foaming mass looked like an aerated blancmange, but, along with the sickly whistle coming from her chest, it confirmed that Miss Pippery was dying.

The nurses parted and Watson kneeled down, ignoring another protest from his ribcage. He gripped her left hand. In the right she was holding her cross.

'I'm not scared,' she said in a whisper.

'No, of course you're not.'

'You believe me, don't you?' she implored.

'Yes.'

'Have they sent for the padre?'

He glanced over his shoulder. Sister Spence, her face a pale mask, nodded.

'Morphine?' he mouthed at Sister.

Another inclination of the head.

'He's on his way,' Watson confirmed to Miss Pippery.

She tried to take a deep breath, but more bubbles appeared and there was that hideous whoosh of free air. 'I'll prepare the way,' she said.

'For what?'

'For Mrs Gregson. I'll tell God she is a good woman. Her work over here. She should be judged on that. Not . . . not the other things.'

He squeezed harder. 'I'm sure she will be grateful.'

'Don't mock me.'

He leaned in closer. 'I wouldn't do that.'

'Will you tell her?'

Watson was painfully aware he had no saliva. He tried to keep his voice normal. 'Of course.'

'I'm sorry.'

'For what?' he asked, puzzled. 'It's not your fault.'

'For lying.'

Lying, had she said? Or dying? Watson stroked her forehead. 'It doesn't matter now.'

'I told you I never left the sergeant alone in the transfusion tent. But I did. Just for a second. Well . . . a few minutes. Lieutenant Metcalf asked me outside for a chat. About . . .'

He waited, letting her marshal her fading reserves. There was blood on her lips now. He used the sleeve on his jacket to dab the pink flecks away.

'. . . my foxtrot.'

There was commotion behind him. The RC padre had arrived. Watson stood to give him room. He bent down to catch her words as her lips moved.

'Very persuasive. The lieutenant is. And Captain de Griffon. Charming. Very nice. For a toff. Who knew they could be so . . . so normal? I'm sorry. About leaving the sergeant. I thought I would get into trouble. Be sent away.'

'None of that matters now, Alice.'

A cloud of pain crossed her features. The shock of the bullet's impact was wearing off quickly. Her stunned nerves were coming alive once again. Even the chemical blanket of morphia couldn't hold back the pain. She, too, realized what was to come. 'Would you go now, Major? And leave me with the padre?'

'Of course.'

Watson gave a final squeeze of her hand, turned and walked out into the late afternoon drizzle, turned his face to the sky and, with the water stinging his face and merging with his tears, silently raged at heaven and all its monstrous works.

Watson had the luxury of one of the giant beer vats to himself. Filled with hot, soapy water up to his chest, he sat on one of the wooden blocks that had been sunk into the enormous half-barrel. He was not in tip-top shape. If he were a racehorse, he'd either be withdrawn from the race or face Lord Lockie's fate. His body ached from neck to ankle, his knee throbbed and his left ribcage had a livid purple bruise on it and was tender to the touch. He needed it strapping.

After leaving Miss Pippery, he had seen to Brindle and his transfusion and then assisted with the other casualties until Torrance had ordered him away. By that time his pyjamas and dressing gown had been soaked in blood, rain, saline and more blood. He had given them to the orderly for burning.

Only now, in the gloom of the old beer cellar, did he think about Miss Pippery. Mrs Gregson was with her now, inconsolable. Would she blame Watson for her death? After all, in the midst of all this, he himself had delivered a murder. He had brought Miss Pippery up into the firing line. A stab of guilt, a physical punch to the stomach, made him groan, before logic reasserted itself. It wasn't his fault.

No?

No. Just this bloody war.

He turned his head as the door opened and Major Torrance entered. He looked in need of medical attention himself. His white coat, worn over his uniform, was almost as soiled as Watson's pyjamas had been. His face was drawn and pallid.

'I am sorry to interrupt, Major Watson.'

'There's plenty of room in here,' he said.

The man smiled and shook his head. 'Not yet. Apparently our phone lines are down thanks to that air raid. I have a message for you. Marked Most Urgent.'

'From whom?'

Torrance tried not to sound impressed as he raised the envelope. 'Winston Churchill.'

'Hand me a towel, would you?'

The major passed one across, along with the note. Watson dried his hands and ripped at the gummed flap. It was a single sheet of paper. Churchill, it said, had received a call and there was a message from Mr Sherlock Holmes. 'What is it?'

'I'm not sure,' said Watson.

He handed it across and watched Torrance's face as he read it and took in the implications.

'It explains a lot,' said Watson.

'But not quite everything. You should finish drying yourself and come with me to the morgue.'

*   *   *

The young American doctor had been blown to pieces. One leg was missing and most of a hip, leaving a huge crimson wound, from which part of his entrails poked. The left arm was amputated above the elbow. The right hand was present but was detached from the wrist. Tendons poked from the severed surfaces like cut electrical wires. His face showed the disfiguring ripples of blast damage. But there was enough left for Watson to tell that, at one time, the eyes had been bulging and that the face carried a distorted grin.

Watson took all this in and asked the morgue attendant to draw the sheet back over and cover the remains of Caspar Myles. He desperately wanted a cigarette to mask the smell of death all around him.

'Well?' asked Torrance.

'All these injuries are post mortem,' Watson said.

'True. A bomb from the air raid appears to have unearthed one of the mass graves. He was blown to the surface. At least, most of him was. The blast also ripped open the blanket he had been put into. An orderly recognized the body.'

'He never left the CCS then,' Watson said.

'It seems not.'

Watson pondered for a second. 'He was murdered and buried sometime after he left the Shipobottom tent.' It was a devious place to dispose of a body; just one more blanket-wrapped corpse among many.

'And it looks like this *Risus sardonicus*,' offered Torrance.

'Oh, it is.'

'So, forgive me. What does this mean?'

'It means we know who the murderer is,' said Watson.

SIXTY-THREE

Lieutenant Metcalf moved along the fire trench, fighting for grip on the slimy duckboards, past the gas alarm stations and the snipers, the observers with their periscopes and the machine-gun crews in their raised strongholds. He kept his head down, below the sandbagged parapet. The water table was high here and the trenches relatively shallow. Sandbags and wooden planks were used to give the excavations extra depth, but even so, it was far too easy to expose yourself to enemy fire for his liking.

He found Tugman, Farrar and Moulton together, as always, in a sodden funk hole, looking miserable as they chewed on their hard tack biscuits.

'Don't get up,' he said, even though they had shown no inclination to do so.

'No hot breakfast this morning, sir,' said young Moulton.

'No, so I heard,' said Metcalf, who had enjoyed a meal cooked by their batman in a rather spacious dugout. 'The supply column didn't get through. They'll be here this evening.'

'Funny how we got more bullets through, though,' said Tugman, indicating a new ammunition box.

'Tugman, a word, please,' Metcalf said.

The corporal struggled to his feet and stepped out of the alcove into the body of the trench. Metcalf indicated they should move along, out of earshot of the others. They turned the corner of the trench and halted at a small redoubt, excavated to protrude a little way into no man's land as a forward observation post. At the far end a box periscope, unmanned, had been nailed to an upright plank of wood.

Metcalf offered the corporal a cigarette, which he took. 'Tugman, I know we don't always get on or see eye to eye, although I confess I have no idea why.'

Tugman lit his cigarette and didn't offer an answer.

'Well, Captain de Griffon and I were talking, and we were saying that, despite that, you are the most senior and capable of the men.'

Senior? Well, he was thirty-five, which made him an old 'un for a Pal. 'Go on.'

'Well, with Shipobottom and Platt gone—'

Tugman began a laugh that turned into a hacking cough.

'You all right, Corporal?'

'Blimey. You're not offering me an extra stripe are you, Lieutenant?'

Metcalf didn't like the tone one bit. 'As a matter of fact, we are.'

'Must be mad,' Tugman muttered.

'I beg your pardon, Corporal?'

'I said it makes me sad, sir.'

'What does?'

Tugman puffed on the cigarette. 'To have to turn you down.'

Metcalf put a foot on the firestep. 'And why would you do that?'

'Because the last two who got that stripe ended up dead, that's why. Permission to speak freely, sir.'

'Granted.'

'The men is frightened. They ain't stupid, not a bit of it. Someone killed Shippy, then Platt tries to kill a fuckin' major and gets shot for his trouble. We all saw Captain de Griffon rolling around in agony; lucky to be alive he is, I reckon.' He pointed over into no man's land. 'When we signed up for this, we thought we knew who the enemy was. Over there. Fritz. The Hun. But who's the enemy now? Time was you could stand on that firestep and at least know your back was covered. Not now, though. The enemy might be the bloke next to you, the one bringing the tea, even your lieutenant.'

'Don't be ridiculous.'

They both heard what sounded like a ragged volley of gunfire.

Tugman shrugged. 'I'm just sayin'. You were in with the captain when he took queer, like. You tell me what's goin' on?'

'I have no more idea than the next man. But the Military Police are investigating.'

Tugman curled his lip at the mention of the despised 'cherry-knobs'.

'So "no" is your final answer?'

Tugman nodded and said something, his words drowned out by the roar of a misfiring engine. A crippled German plane came low over their heads, trailing oily smoke as it tried to maintain enough height to reach its own lines. That's what the shooting had been. Pot shots from trenches further back.

Without thinking, Metcalf unbuttoned his holster and raised his revolver to have a pop at the now vanished plane. He levered himself up on the firestep. As he did so, Tugman heard the faintest of metallic pings and Metcalf stepped back.

He turned to stare at Tugman, a dazed expression on his face. 'Damn,' he said softly.

A curtain of blood oozed down his forehead towards his eyes and his knees buckled. The revolver clattered onto the firestep and bounced off into the sludge. As the young officer collapsed onto the duckboard, Tugman stepped back to give him room to fall, looking down at the neatly drilled hole in the Brodie helmet that clearly showed where the sniper's bullet had entered Lieutenant Metcalf's skull.

SIXTY-FOUR

After they had said their goodbyes to Miss Pippery and she had been removed to the mortuary, Sister Spence had invited them to her tent for her special brew of hot chocolate with rum.

Mrs Gregson, uneasy at the truce that had apparently been declared between them, said very little as Watson, forced to address an audience despite the sombre occasion, told them what he thought was the most likely explanation for the events they had all witnessed.

'Mrs Gregson here found three marks on Hornby's coffin,' said Watson as he took a sip of the invigorating drink.

'I shan't ask how,' said Sister Spence, handing her a mug.

'Thank you,' said Mrs Gregson, her voice thin after all the crying she had done at poor Alice's side.

'Which means that the murderer couldn't get to the body, so had to do the next best thing. Mark the box that Hornby was to be buried in.'

'Why?' asked Sister Spence. 'Why mark the bodies?'

'I don't know,' Watson admitted. 'One thing at a time. This is the next step.'

He passed Sister Spence part of the message from Holmes, which she in turn handed to Mrs Gregson. 'Lord Stanwood was victim number one in the sequence,' she read.

'Stanwood, Leverton, Hornby, Shipobottom, numbers one to four,' Watson added.

'And Captain de Griffon, potentially five,' said Sister Spence.

'No,' Watson said, giving her the second section of the telephone message.

Captain de Griffon is an imposter.

'My goodness,' the sister said, showing it to Mrs Gregson. 'How can this be?'

'The murderer was, is, de Griffon, or someone pretending to be him. Right under my nose.' He balled a fist and swept it through the air, as if striking an invisible table.

'Our nose,' Mrs Gregson corrected. 'We were all fooled.' She thought for a moment. 'But he saved your life. From the gas.'

'I've thought of that. Was he saving my life? Or was he trying to save his horse?'

'Save his horse?' Mrs Gregson asked. 'He shot his horse, remember?'

'Or was it to silence Sergeant Platt?' continued Watson. 'Perhaps he wanted to put Platt in the frame so we would think this was all over. That we had our murderer.' The sergeant was hardly the shiniest button in the box; Watson was certain it would have been easy for a charmer like de Griffon to subvert him to his cause.

'But de Griffon nearly died himself. I saw him. You saw him. The fits.'

'Mrs Gregson, I think we are dealing with a man of many parts. What if he knows just how much of this toxin is fatal? What if he diluted the dose?'

'But his fever. The pulse.'

'Bah,' said Watson. 'How blind could I be? The pallor, the palpitations. Chewing cordite would do that. A mix of his poison and the propellant would be enough to blur the symptoms. And a fit is easily imitated. You don't have to be Edmund Kean to do that.'

'A risky strategy,' she said.

'And killing your own men isn't? Don't imagine we are necessarily dealing with a rational mind here.'

'Hmm.' Sister conceded the point but went on gnawing at the bone of doubt. 'How on earth could he have arranged the gassing? He was here, man, in this station.'

Watson had considered that. 'Cecil.'

'Cecil?'

'The dog. I would wager anything you will find his collar contains a sleeve or similar for messages. It was how he would communicate with Platt. So he could be here and tell Platt to take me out of the picture.' He thought for a moment. 'In fact, Platt offered me a tot of rum at one point, just when I had mounted Lord Lockie.' He shivered at the thought of what might have happened had he accepted. 'The gas was the second attempt on my life, perhaps.'

'But why all the deaths?' asked Mrs Gregson. 'What links them? And why would he kill Myles? He's not on your little list.'

Watson already had a theory about that, but he knew enough not to blurt it all out at once. He could see that he had already strained their credulity. 'We'll just have to ask de Griffon.'

'The Leigh Pals have pulled out of Suffolk Farm,' said Sister Spence. 'So he's at the front.'

Watson pinched the bridge of his nose. Gassed, shot at, bombed, saddled with cracked bones he may be, but he had to summon up some more reserves. He had to see this through. By himself, for once.

'Then that's where I'll have to go.'

SIXTY-FIVE

The old man was dozing when the mine detonated. He knew from experience that you didn't so much hear the explosions as feel them. Such was the amount of TNT packed into the tunnels under the enemy's lines – for the mine could be either German or British, he had no way of telling – that it caused a ripple in the earth. And the resultant wave was so powerful it spread out from Belgium, travelling under the Channel and causing the windows of his cottage on the South Downs to rattle and the building to creak alarmingly. It also set up a powerful resonance of fearfulness in his body. His friend was out there, in the very place where whole swathes of the countryside – and any living things upon it – were swallowed into vast craters. Men were turned to dust in an instant. The thought made him feel nauseous.

He had been resting in his chair in front of the dying embers of his fire. The effort of travelling to Flitcham had depleted his shallow reserves of energy. He had been snoozing off and on for the best part of two days. But the unease generated by the mine meant he wouldn't be able to sleep for a few hours now. He looked at the clock. Time for some hot chocolate. And a small brandy, perhaps. He would have to get it himself. He had given Bert a few days off. It would take at least that before he had the strength for his next visit, all the way up north to Leigh.

He felt a second vibration through his feet, like an aftershock.

Strange, he thought, they usually detonated the mines first thing in the morning. Just before dawn was the preferred time. Of course, accidents did happen. They always did with high explosives. He looked down at the book he had been reading when he had nodded off. *The American Civil War*. The technique of burrowing under enemy lines and creating a huge subterranean bomb had been perfected in that conflict.

And something else relevant to Watson's predicament had also played its part. In certain Confederate states, he had read, if a man was conscripted, he could nominate a willing replacement to go in his stead. These doppelgängers had to be roughly the same age and physical fitness, and they were often paid by rich landowners to avoid their sons having to go into battle. It was like nominating a 'champion' to fight in your place. If they survived, the champions would come home to wealth and land. If, of course, the South won. It was a double gamble – being alive and on the winning side – but many thought it worth the risk, as they would end up serving anyway.

Something similar had happened at the Flitcham estate, he was certain. He had been somewhat disquieted by Legge when the young man had picked him up at the station. For a long-serving chauffeur, he had been quite an appalling driver. And his conversation was strange, his speech almost childish. But it was when he had seen Legge and Lady Stanwood together that his suspicions had been truly aroused. What the French neurologist, psychologist and author Henri Reclerc called 'The Silent Language' had positively screamed whenever they were near each other. Reclerc had studied non-verbal signs and signals that could be used to determine the relationship between people. It had proved very useful in the detective's work: more than once, people pretending to be brother and sister had revealed themselves as lovers by a simple analysis of gestures.

It was obvious by applying Reclerc's methods that theirs was no servant-mistress situation. There was an unspoken familiarity between the lady and the driver. Lovers? he had wondered. Was that why Lord Stanwood had been done away with? He had sought out Dr Kibble, who had described the symptoms of Stanwood's long, slow death that echoed many of the details that Watson had described in his communication. And, Kibble had agreed, at the end he had turned blue, with a facial expression he could barely bring himself to describe. The patriarch had been poisoned. Was it so that Lady Stanwood and the dim-witted chauffeur could carry on their illicit tryst?

No, not lovers, he corrected. The bond was different. He could see it in her eyes, a mix of warmth and selfless concern. And in the driver's willingness to please. This was not predicated on anything as base or transient as sex. This was a maternal link. The chauffeur, Harry Legge, was Lady Stanwood's son. He was, in fact, Robinson de Griffon. The new Lord Stanwood. And he was sitting out the war as the family chauffeur. Which had meant the man over in France, the man Watson was chasing, had to be an imposter.

SIXTY-SIX

After much searching, Major Watson found Staff Nurse Jennings in the small chapel around the back of the Big House. It had been kept consecrated, for use in the Sunday services that were compulsory for all ranks who were mobile. It was often full and an overspill Communion or blessing was held in a marquee next door.

Jennings was busy lighting candles. 'We are having a memorial service,' she said, when Watson entered.

Miss Pippery wasn't the only staff member that the East Anglian had lost that day. Two orderlies had died and a QA nurse was hovering on the brink of the next world, not expected to make it through till the following day. Plus there was poor old Caspar Myles to be commemorated.

'Non-denominational,' she added.

'Good. Staff Nurse Jennings, I came to say goodbye and thank you.'

She stopped what she was doing and turned to face him. 'You're leaving?'

'For the time being. I have to help arrest the man who murdered

Shipobottom and the others. I would imagine I will have to spend time helping formulate the case against him.'

She waited, a mix of apprehension and curiosity written across her features.

'It's Captain de Griffon.'

She clearly wasn't expecting this revelation. 'Lord Stanwood? But—'

'He isn't Lord Stanwood. We've all been taken in.'

'You are certain?'

'As I can be at this moment.'

She shook her head at this. 'For a while I thought it might be Lieutenant Metcalf. Then Mrs Gregson. She had a history, you know.'

'I know. Her ex-husband told me.'

'God forgive me, I think part of me hoped it would be her,' she confessed.

Watson was shocked. 'Why on earth would you hope that?'

She moved to a pew and sat down, head bowed. Watson came and stood next to her.

'That's not a nice thing to say.'

She looked up, her eyes glistening. 'Nice? Oh, Major, it's wicked. Very wicked. But, women like Mrs Gregson . . . I don't know, they make the rest of us seem so pale, so feeble.'

He sat down next to her. 'I have known men like that.'

She put her head on his shoulder, exhausted. 'I'm sorry if I caused you concern when I left to see my brother. I thought you were being over-protective.'

'I was. I am. It's a curse. But I am not sorry. I speak as one who will remember you as a friend for the rest of my days. Although, of course, I might have fewer days left than most here.'

It was meant to be a jest about his age, but the church now seemed very chill indeed.

'Don't say that. Please.'

'I have to go. I have some business to attend to before I leave.'

Jennings sat up and straightened her clothing. 'Where are you really going?'

'As I said. To the front. I'm going to try to find out why a man would adopt a whole new identity and then, in the midst of war, set about murdering his own side.'

'You don't know?'

'I know the answer must lie in Leigh. In the mills. The owner dead, workers dead. I suspect something terrible happened there. And whatever it was, this is where it came home to roost.'

SIXTY-SEVEN

Come hear the story of two sisters, sisters
good and true,
They worked the reels in Lancashire,
and only wanted their due.

They asked for men and women to be treated the same, to be
treated all alike,
And if that was not to be, they
promised a bitter strike.

Well, you won't strike, you cannot strike, you will not strike, said the boss,
For the Lord will hear of it, and it'll surely
be your loss.

Oh, we can strike, we will strike,
we are ready to fight
And you can tell the Lord Stanwood,
his mill will close tonight.

And if the looms stop turning, he said, stop for even for one day
If I know Lord Stanwood, you'll be the ones to pay.

And a tackler standing by and hearing
what was said,
He swore Lord Stanwood he would know, before the sun was set.

And in his hurry to carry the news,
he bent his breast and ran,
And when he came to the broad millstream, he took off his shoes
and he swam.

And the next day the engines were all quiet, the looms were very
still
And be sure that no cotton was going to come out of that mill.

The same pay for the same work, the women marched and
shouted,
But the men who knew the Lord, a good ending they doubted.

And the first message came that if they called off this strike, ended
their charade,
Then the Lord would make sure that the sisters, they'd be richly paid.

But we cannot leave the other girls, we cannot leave them that way,
For we are honourable women, not ones to betray.

And after four more days, another note it came
Would the sisters meet with the bosses, before they all went lame?

But come alone, it said, and come to the woods at dusk
For the Lord himself will come along, for meet with you he must.

And so the two sisters went after sundown, they went down to the
    woods,
Only to find no Lord, but seven men in hoods.

And they grabbed the sisters hard and rough
And threw them to the ground.
We'll teach you to strike, they said, and they began to pass them
    round.

Well, the older she pleaded and begged and made them a promise
    fair
If they spared her little sister, she would be their mare.

And so while little Bess watched the seven, gagged so she couldn't
    shout,
They took their pleasures with the older girl, till no man was left out.

And by the time they had finished with her, there was madness in
    her eyes
And they left the sisters in the grove, deaf to their terrible cries.

And if we hear of any of this again, even hear your very name,
We'll be back for little Bess, and she will get the same.

And to make sure they remembered, remembered what they had
    done,

They carved their number on Annie's skin,

A stroke for each man who committed the sin.

And so the sisters left the mills, left with a terrible curse

And a promise to come back one day and do their very worst.

This is the true story of two sisters, sisters brave and true,

They worked the reels in Lancashire, and now they'll give their due.

The captain finished singing and cleared his throat, trying to hide the emotion. It always made him choke up.

'Do you know that song, Corporal Tugman?' de Griffon asked his temporary batman, who was polishing the captain's boots. Sunderland, his regular servant, had been taken ill. He had asked Tugman to stand in, for the usual fifteen shillings a week, until Sunderland returned. He was not, though, to be excused from other duties in the same way as a proper servant usually was. And no more mention of being promoted to sergeant.

'Not in that version, sir,' the man replied brusquely.

They were in one of the officers' dugouts, an L-shaped sandbag and plank room — the ceiling supported by four impressive timber props — which successive occupants had tried to make homely, despite the instructions from high command that any creature comforts might erode the 'offensive spirit'.

There was a gramophone, although only two records were left intact to play on it and most of the centre was taken up by a make-shift billiard table, created from a cut-down door. On the walls were some theatre posters, framed poems, a tester with 'Home Sweet Home' and an arrow pointing to the left stitched on it, some

Old Bill cartoons and a selection of purloined street signs from local towns and villages. Pride of place was a meticulously painted crest of Uppingham School, executed by an old boy, probably dead by now. On a low, homemade table sat a stack of tatty magazines – mostly *Bystander* and *Punch*. There were books, too: well-thumbed and often mildewed copies of Homer and Horace, Henty and Kipling.

The dugout smelled of lamp and stove fumes, cigarette and pipe smoke, damp socks and chloride of lime from the latrines, but it was relatively dry and, apart from the occasional rat incursion, comfortable. It would be his home for a week, although by the next day he would be sharing it with several other officers – there were four bunks in the shorter section of the 'L' – as fresh units arrived. Still, most of his men were spending the night in rubber-lined funk holes or standing up to their ankles in water and mud in the forward trenches. And poor Metcalf was in a wooden box, awaiting the gravediggers' attentions.

'You don't care for the song?'

'I don't, sir. No.' His eyes remained fixed on the leather he was buffing. 'Not that version. Begging your pardon.'

'Which version do you know?'

'It's about a lady who sleeps with a commoner. And it's Lord Darnell in the version I heard. Not Stanwood, sir.' He shook his head in dismay. 'I mean, that's your brother.'

'Yes, just a little personal joke there.'

'Right, sir,' he said, not amused.

'They were real, you know.'

'Who?'

'The two sisters in the song. Pass me my cigarettes, will you?

Thank you. Anne and Bess Truelove. She had a baby, Anne. But her mind was gone. They had marked her, you know? Cut a number in her skin, to show how many had taken her. Of course it sent her over the edge. Seeing that every day. The child was brought up by Bess. In Italy. Where nobody knew their story.'

'There,' said Tugman, not really listening, giving one last rub on the boots. 'Bloomin' shame to go out there and ruin them.'

'Terrible shame to get killed in unpolished boots, Corporal. Just won't do.'

'Sir?' It didn't do to talk about such things.

'Looking forward to tonight? Chance to do something other than a bit of spit and polish? Get one back for the lieutenant?'

'I am,' said Tugman, without conviction. He didn't want to think on the death of Metcalf, the hideous randomness of it. 'Good of you to choose me, sir.'

De Griffon looked at his wristwatch. An hour or so to go. 'Well, that's a fine job, Tugman. I think a drink is in order.'

Tugman looked doubtful. Rum rations were issued at stand-to, just after dawn or before going over the bags.

'Come on, I know it's not morning, but it'll keep the cold out. Gets mighty chilly out there in dead man's land.'

Tugman looked uneasy. He wasn't sure what had got into the captain. It wasn't like him to be maudlin. But it got them all in the end, the feeling that the end might be nigh. Some men even foresaw their own death, in gory detail. And it came to pass, just as they had described. Had the captain been cursed with a dream or a vision? Some premonition or a prediction, like poor old Shippy. 'You mean no man's, sir.'

'Of course I do.'

De Griffon took out his hip flask, poured a shot for Tugman and handed it over.

'You not having one, sir?'

'In a while, Corporal,' de Griffon said with a smile as Tugman threw it back. 'In a while.'

SIXTY-EIGHT

Watson was seething by the time he reached the concrete loading apron of the overhead railway. He was enraged at the way the nocturnal army had sprung into life at sunset, spilling out onto the roads its battalions of marching soldiers, details loaded with precious water destined for the trenches, ration orderlies humping dixies of hot stew, and the convoys of lorries and carts moving men from rest to reserve and active and back again, all of which contrived to block his way to the front. Going into that mêlée would require the determination and stamina of a spawning salmon.

He was mad at the idiots who had managed to misdirect a whole company, who were now jamming the roads trying to find the correct village.

He was angry at the German airmen for wasting an innocent, harmless life. Miss Pippery deserved to die old, with many grandchildren to mourn her.

He was irritated with Tobias Gregson who, apparently, was on a suicide watch for a man condemned to be shot at dawn and could not help with an arrest till morning.

And with a Major Tyler, who had agreed to place de Griffon under close arrest. His incredulity, however, was apparent even down the crackly field telephone line. He would detain the captain but not release him to an outside party until someone had explained the situation fully to him.

Watson, though, was mostly furious with himself, for not being able to solve completely the conundrum that de Griffon presented. It was within his grasp, he was sure, if he just knew which pieces of information to hold on to and which to discard.

He hauled himself off the motor cycle and looked up at the sky. No rain, thank goodness, but a three-quarter moon playing hide-and-seek with an archipelago of clouds. There would be little or no wind down in the trenches, but the subterranean system could be bitterly cold and damp, so he had swapped his Aquascutum for a British Warm greatcoat.

'Will you be all right, Major?' Mrs Gregson asked, turning off the machine.

'Yes. I'll sit with him till your . . . until Lieutenant Gregson comes to place him under formal arrest. Perhaps I can get some answers from him before that.'

'Do you have enough to arrest him? For the Military Police to charge him?'

A good question. Watson had enough circumstantial evidence of murder; but nothing he would bring to the Bailey with confidence. There was a trail of death in de Griffon's wake, going all the way back to England, that much was certain. But how to link it to de Griffon's coat-tails?

'I hope so. At least until we can piece everything together. I'd best get on.'

The overhead railway was a system for delivering the wounded on stretchers from one of the forward dressing stations. It was actually more like a cable car than a rail system, with the platforms for loading the injured hanging from a steel cable that ran around giant drums and was fed through a series of pulleys en route. Most of the carriage system was sunk into a trench, to protect the wounded from further injury by shrapnel. Some of these systems worked by hand cranking, others by gravity or steam; this one ran on electricity. It was, Torrance had suggested, like a latter-day Roman road – the straightest, fastest way for a solitary officer to get near the front without too many tiresome questions or delays on crowded roads and circumventing hundreds of yards of zigzagged trenches.

There were two sappers in charge of the railway and, standing idle, half a dozen ambulances and their drivers, ready to ferry the wounded when and if they arrived. Most of the men were sleeping in the cab, heads cushioned on arms folded across the wheel. A couple, however, knowing they were well out of sniper range, were smoking with open abandon.

'Here,' said Mrs Gregson, handing him an armband. 'Put this on.' He slid the white band with a Red Cross symbol on it over the sleeve of his greatcoat. 'That'll explain quicker than any words why you are up there. Are you certain you should go?'

'Try and stop me.'

He was shocked when she stepped forward and threw her arms around him, clamping him tight. His damaged rib protested and he tried not to flinch. 'I could, you know. I could stop you. If I really wanted to. We've already lost Alice.'

Her body began to quiver, and he put his own arms around her back, the Dunhill leathers creaking as he did so. Her torso was shaking and her breath was hot against his neck. There were tears, too.

'The padre told me Alice knew. About the divorce. It's . . . difficult to accept that she must have died hating me.'

'No.' With a studied deliberateness Watson untangled her arms from his body. He made a mental note to intercept the letter than Miss Pippery had written in haste. Mrs Gregson must not see it. 'That's not true. There was an initial shock when she discovered—'

'That I had lied to her.'

'A necessary deception. I've indulged in a few of those in my time. She didn't die angry, Mrs Gregson. You shouldn't think that. She spoke to me, she understood, I promise you. Now, I have to leave before de Griffon charms Major Tyler into letting him go. And you crack another of my ribs.'

'Sorry.' A big sniff. 'Back to being a grown-up.'

She took off a glove, and wiped her eyes, giving her bravest smile. Their breaths pooled and mingled in the chill air. He was aware of the sappers watching. They could be two lovers parting. Ridiculous, he knew, but the thought cheered him. He leaned in and kissed her forehead, as chastely as he could. 'I shall be back tomorrow.'

A distant rat-tat of machine-gun fire sounded, way south, towards Churchill's HQ. A Very flare arced up, burning like a lonely firework. There was a ragged volley of shots, then silence and blackness once more.

A vast darkness lay over the land ahead, cloaking three enormous armies, and men drawn from across the globe, all preparing for more killing and maiming. A locomotive's whistle hooted a desolate warning, but Watson couldn't tell from which side of the lines it came. It didn't matter; it sounded lonely and scared, whichever army it served. It was like despair made tangible. As if in response to the sounds of war, an enthusiastic nightingale started up – his lusty song doubtless a result of trying to compete with the guns – reminding everyone who could hear that the natural world was still out there, and fighting back, despite man's best efforts to annihilate it completely from this part of the earth.

'Be safe, Major.'

'Just in case, I've left some letters—'

She put a finger to his mouth. It felt incredibly warm against his chilled lips. 'Shush. They'll be there when you get back.'

She removed the digit, leaving a tingling afterglow. 'They are on the washstand in my room. Just the two.'

'I can guess who gets one.'

'You don't have to think too hard,' he admitted. Holmes would want to know he had a good crack at finishing the case.

'You can rip it up when you get back. Tell him yourself. And the second?'

'It's for you.'

'Me? Why—'

'No, it's your turn to be quiet. There're a few favours in there, Mrs Gregson. I can't think of a better person to ask.'

Mrs Gregson's mouth worked but no word came. What kind of favours? Is that all there was? She oscillated between disappointment in the workaday explanation and relief that there might not be more in there, no matter how small. But in the end, she simply felt touched. She reached up and put a hand to his cheek. He didn't recoil.

'Then you can do me a favour in return.'

'What's that?'

'Call me Georgina.'

He tried to answer, but there it was again. The finger to the lips. 'Next time we meet will do just fine, Major Watson. Now go.'

She watched him walk to the hut where sappers sat, show his armband and point east, towards the front. There was a moment's discussion before the men shrugged and got to work. The pair strapped a stretcher between two of the hanging supports, which were shaped like upside down 'L's, and stood back to let him on. Watson clambered aboard stiffly, although she could tell he was making an effort to seem sprightly. One of the sappers threw a switch, there came the whine of a motor and, after a single jerk to overcome the machinery's inertia, the cable began to run, taking a prone Watson up towards the hostilities.

As its solitary occupant rattled and clanked off into the darkness and the cable descended into the dark slit of the protecting trench, Mrs Gregson shuddered. As if someone had walked over her grave, as the saying went. Major Watson was a remarkable man. She wished she had known him when he was younger. She remounted the bike and kick-started it to life, unable to shake the terrible sense of fore-boding that had descended upon her.

SIXTY-NINE

The first crater they came to was rank, the water in the bottom slimy and green. Even in the weak moonlight, they could see gas bubbles forming. Something was decomposing beneath the surface. Man or beast, it wasn't clear. A rat the size and shape of a rugby ball was scurrying around the edges of the fetid pool.

'Best push on,' said de Griffon quietly.

Private Farrar looked longingly over his shoulder, back to the tumbled wire of his own lines.

'Come on there, Farrar,' said de Griffon in hushed tones. 'Think about the leave this'll earn you if we come back with a live one.'

'Sir.' The voice that came from the blackened face was tiny and devoid of any enthusiasm. The deal they had struck earlier no longer seemed such a bargain, out here in no man's land. At any second, they knew the sky could burst into revealing light and machine guns spit in their direction. The sense of vulnerability had tightened their sphincters and loosened their bladders. Farrar thought he might vomit.

'Now,' hissed de Griffon, waving them on with his revolver. 'Let's be going.'

They slithered through the icy mud to the next depression in the ground and rolled into it. It was then that Tugman had his first seizure. 'Jes...' he started. De Griffon's hand clamped over his mouth.

'For God's sake, man,' said de Griffon. 'You trying to get us killed?'

But Tugman had begun to thrash, he held his hands up, which were bending into claw shapes and apparently causing him fierce agony as they did so. His eyes, wide with fear, coupled with the boot polish on the face made him look like a music-hall minstrel.

'What the fuck's the matter with him?' Moulton, a boy of barely eighteen, asked in a terrified hiss.

Tugman began to groan and his feet lashed out, as if he were cycling. De Griffon grabbed the ankles.

'Look, you two, I want you to move over there to...' He took off his cap and risked poking his head above the rim of the crater. Steel helmets were avoided: there was a danger of them clashing, and any metallic noise was a magnet for enemy fire. '... that fallen tree there. See it? Good cover. Just watch for trip wires or booby traps, OK? I'll take Tugman back and join you shortly.'

'Shouldn't we all go?'

'Don't get windy on me. You two go on.'

The two younger men looked doubtful. They exchanged glances. De Griffon pointed his revolver at the pair. 'Now. If we go back empty-handed now, we'll be strapped to gun limbers by dawn.'

The two men knew that, whereas they might face such a fate, it was unlikely the captain would suffer Field Punishment Number One. The blame for any failure would fall onto them, the lowest of the low.

''Ow you gonna get 'im back, sir?'

'How do you think? Over my shoulders. I'll be back before you know it. Now move.'

He watched the pair take their rifles and move off as if Satan himself was at their backsides. He laughed to himself at that. Satan was at their backsides, if only they knew it.

De Griffon turned his attention to Tugman. From his belt pack he took out the billiard ball he had purloined from the dugout. Then he put his gloved fingers in Tugman's mouth, forced the teeth apart and rammed the ivory sphere home. With his cravat, he fashioned a gag, which went around Tugman's head and fastened at the front. When the soldier struggled he punched him.

He leaned in very close, his lips next to the left side of Tugman's head, his breath warm and cloying in his ear. 'Now, let's see how that holds up.'

He withdrew the man's short trench-raid knife from its sheath and plunged it up to the hilt into Tugman's thigh. His body arced in a spasm of agony, but hardly any sound came from the mouth. Tears welled out, skittering over the layer of boot polish on his cheeks.

'Good enough.'

Machine-gun fire, some way to the south. *Dat-dat-dat*. Some other poor bastards out there, no doubt.

'It was the rum, of course. The poison usually takes an hour or so to have an effect. You had quite a dose. So we haven't got long. I'm going to tell you a story. Ready?' He twisted the knife handle and Tugman thrashed. 'Ready? Good. Then I'll begin.'

'What do you mean, he's gone?' Watson demanded.

Major Tyler shrugged. They were in the dugout recently vacated by de Griffon. Watson lifted a cigarette end from the makeshift tin ashtray. It was still warm to the touch. 'He can't have been gone very long. Why didn't you detain him?'

'As soon as I got your message, I tried to call the forward trenches,' said Tyler, a remarkably young man for his rank, who spoke with the merest hint of Lanky burr. 'But the Germans have severed the telephone lines. Absolute bloody fiasco. Engineers trying to sort them out now. So, I sent young Fairley here to put him into custody.' He indicated a fresh-faced fop of a subaltern who was wearing a fashionable Yeltra trench coat and a pair of Harrods War Comfort knee-high boots. He was having trouble complying with the King's Regulation that stated the upper lip must not be shaved. What was under his nose could hardly be described as a moustache. 'But de Griffon had already left on a grab mission.'

'A what?' Watson asked.

'To grab one of the enemy. More, if possible. We need to know why they have such good Intelligence about our movements. Patrols like that go out quite often. Volunteers. Which are in short supply. So, when de Griffon offered . . .'

They paused as a trench mortar round detonated nearby, dislodging dust, sand and straw from the roof of the bunker.

'That's just to stop us sleeping,' said Tyler. 'A way of keeping us disoriented. So, you can reckon on Captain de Griffon being back by dawn.'

No, he couldn't, thought Watson. 'His name isn't de Griffon.'

'So you said. Really, it's quite a story you have there, Major Watson.'

He had to agree with that. 'It is. I assume he hasn't gone out on this patrol alone?'

'No, of course not,' said Tyler. 'Lieutenant Fairley, do we know the make up of the raiding party?'

'Sir,' said the subaltern in his high, fluting voice. It was as if it hadn't broken yet. 'Quite a small one. Just the four. The captain, Corporal Tugman and Privates Farrar and Moulton.'

Watson groaned.

'What is it? Do you know these men?' Tyler asked.

'Not at all. Not personally. But I tell you, when he comes back, if he comes back, he'll be alone.'

'What do you mean?'

Watson ignored him. 'Lieutenant Fairley, how did they get out into no man's land?'

'Through a newly dug sap, sir. Engineers do the dig after dark. They run out under wire. Only good for a night or two before some Fritz sneaks over and lobs a concentrated charge in. That's six stick grenades tied together. We do the same with theirs, mind, with Mills bombs. Up until then, there's a ladder, up you pop and there you are. The famous no man's land. If you want to be out there, that is. I've done it a few times. That's enough for me, I can tell you.' He giggled and cast an anxious eye at Tyler, but his commanding officer didn't react to the admission.

'Can you show me?' Watson asked.

'I suppose so, yes, sir.'

As Fairley pulled the gas curtain aside, a tardy thought struck Tyler. 'Major Watson?'

'Yes?'

'One thing.'

The ground shook and heaved beneath them and for a moment Watson felt giddy. His ears popped as he opened his mouth to speak.

'That's a mine detonating,' said Tyler, brushing off his shoulders the debris that had fallen from the ceiling. 'I know it felt near but it could be hundreds of miles away.'

Watson had heard that British miners were tunnelling under the German lines and vice versa, the idea being to blow each other to kingdom come with no warning. 'You were going to ask me something?'

'Oh, yes,' said Tyler. 'If de Griffon isn't his real name. What is?'

SEVENTY

'I've had a lot of names in my time. I was Harry Legge for a while. Fond of that one. That could have been a good life. Nice cars, willing maids who didn't mind a bit of upsie-daisy. I even did the cook, the old bat, just to keep her happy. Very popular man was Harry Legge. Thing is, I was there to get rid of Stanwood. Arthur de Griffon. Bimmy, as they called him. Now, originally I intended to go and do it quick. But then, I thought, why not make him suffer? After all, my mother suffered for years and years, didn't she? I was having fun in the house. Real fun. So I poisoned him nice and slow. You don't get the strange grin if you administer it over time. That only happens when you are in a hurry. Like here. Do you know what it is? This poison? My auntie discovered it when we were in Italy. The Sardinians used to use it for the ritual killing of the elders, people who had outlived their usefulness. Are you listening, Tugman?'

He tweaked the handle of the bayonet and the eyes popped back open. Tugman nodded.

'It's an extract of the water dropwort. Latin name *Oenanthe crocata*. Although Aunt Bess added her own little twist. Oleander, such a pretty flower, so lethal. Then, to cause the fitting, an extract of *nux vomica*. The three alkaloids together . . . well, I don't have to tell you. Ah, the shitting the pants. Whoo, what a stink. That's the oleander. I used a little more of that in your tincture. So, once the old man died . . . he was one of the hooded men in the Trolley Woods, wasn't he? Although my Aunt Bess told me the song is wrong. It happened in the spinning room. No matter. Seven men in hoods took one young, frightened woman while the other was forced to watch. When they had finished they scratched seven lines on her breasts, one for each of them. Anyway, the old man finally died. I think it was the effort of trying to tell the doctor that I'd done it. Like with you, I waited until he had lost the power of everything till I whispered in his ear who I was. That's the important thing. You have to know why you are dying. Otherwise, where is the justice? Where is the satisfaction?'

De Griffon unscrewed the lid of his hip flask and took a swallow. 'No, don't worry. This is the good stuff. Two flasks, you see. Just have to be careful to remember which is which. So, where was I? Yes, the old man expires, horribly, and then an opportunity presents itself. The son, Charles, whom I had no issue with, was killed not far from here. Lady Stanwood is bereft. They'll be coming for Robinson next. Well, they would be if he wasn't soft in the head. But nobody knew that. The shame of his being a simpleton had been kept from all but a few family members and loyal staff. He was harmless but, as you might say, daft as a brush. So Harry Legge had an idea. The de Griffons could pull a lot of strings up north. Harry would volunteer for the Leigh Pals as Robinson de Griffon. Over two years, he'd learned how to act posh. It was easy.' Well, a slight exaggeration. It had taken a while to create the hard carapace of privilege that members of such families developed from birth. 'And the Pals – all the men from the mills. There was a good chance I'd be able to get a few of the hooded men. I knew their names by now, of course. 'Cause some of them boasted about it. Wasn't hard to discover who had been there under the canvas sacks.

'So, Lady Stanwood would put it about that Harry had been injured – and badly scarred – rolling a car on the estate. And Robinson was going up north, where nobody knew him, to volunteer. He'd been there only once, as a child. At the end of the war, we were to swap back, and Harry gets a big fat stack of cash for his troubles. Nice cottage on the estate. Worked perfectly. It was a shame about Caspar Myles. Old friend of the family. I got cocky. Thought it amusing to carry on the deception. After a chat, though, he knew something was wrong. I made a few errors, apparently. I could see he was puzzled. So, I invited him to come for a drink. Whisky and water dropwort. Well, time moves on. I see I have to draw things to a conclusion.'

A rattling was coming from Tugman's throat, squeezing its way past the billiard ball and the gag. The first grand mal took hold and his back arched.

'You must have been what, Corporal, fifteen or sixteen when they told you they were going to teach those Trueloves a lesson? That you'd be one of the seven who violated poor Anne Truelove just for asking for the same money as the men. She lost her mind, you know. Never really spoke again. But she didn't lose the baby. Bess saw to that. Bess, whom Anne had nobly saved from the same fate. Let you all have your way, while the little sister watched. Aunt Bess used to tell me that story over and over again. She's dead now. But I promised her I would find the seven and make them suffer. I know, you're thinking that young Moulton and Farrar, they weren't there. No, but their fathers were, weren't they? One of them's gone now and the other has the Monday fever, the brown lung. But imagine what Moulton's mother and Farrar's parents will feel when they get a letter from me, describing how their sons died whimpering cowards? And how I'll tell the whole town. I will take their names and make them laughing stocks. Don't worry, I'll be telling Farrar and Moulton all this before they die. In fact, their first symptoms should be occurring now. I'd best go.'

With some difficulty he pulled the blade free of the flesh, ignoring the blood that pulsed out in its wake. He took Tugman's hand and, using the point of the blade, etched a roman numeral on it. Five. Just two to go and he could rest easy. He rooted in Tugman's top pocket and found what he was looking for. 'Cigarette?'

He masked the flame and the glowing tip while he lit it, and then forced the Woodbine into the corner of Tugman's mouth. The corporal began to shake his head. Trying to dislodge it. But Johnny Truelove grabbed him by the waist and, staying low himself, lifted him clear of the edge of the shell hole.

The bullet came within two seconds, a small thump as it entered the skull, and Tugman slumped down dead.

'Just like Lieutenant Metcalf. Give him my best.'

Truelove extinguished the cigarette and waited for a few minutes before he scrambled out of the shell hole and propelled himself on his belly towards the two men sheltering behind a fallen tree.

Ernst Bloch swore under his breath and broke cover. He crabbed over to where Schaeffer, his spotter, and Lothar were lying under their netting. 'You fucking idiot,' he hissed.

'What do you mean?' asked Lothar. 'That was a clean shot.'

Bloch put himself in the younger man's face. 'That was a ruse. Or something. Who lights a cigarette in no man's land? Only someone who wants to commit suicide. Let's move, now.'

'Why?'

'Before a grenade drops on our heads. Never trust an easy shot. It might even have been a dummy head. Even if it wasn't, I'd wager it wasn't an officer.'

Lothar mumbled to himself. Perhaps not an officer, but a good clean kill. And not easy, not without that fancy night sight that Bloch had. The sharpshooter, he thought, was just jealous. Still, he had been warned at the sniper school about dummy bodies out on no man's land and a host of little deceptions to lull you into revealing your hiding place. Best be cautious. It was how you stayed alive, they said. 'All right, do we go back or take up new positions?'

Bloch watched as thicker clouds shrouded the moon. The night was still young. And something, ruse or not, was happening out there. 'New positions.'

SEVENTY-ONE

Watson was standing on the filthy wooden ladder, looking out over no man's land, when he saw the briefest muzzle flash. For a second, he thought he was dead, having taken a step too far. He fell back into the wet, newly excavated sap, and slipped onto the duckboard that covered the bottom. His hand sank into the yellowish mud that caked everything as he tried to steady himself. As it went in he felt something hard to his touch. Bones. They were everywhere, glistening and protruding from the walls. This wasn't a trench; it was an open-topped ossuary.

With some effort, Watson extracted his hand from his glove, then recovered the glove itself and shook the glutinous clumps from it. 'You all right, sir?' Fairley asked, shining his blackout torch with its slit-like aperture onto him.

'Yes. Fine,' Watson said, feeling anything but. There was a gurgling at his feet. Freezing water was seeping into the trench. Soon it would be an ankle-deep slurry. And they hadn't been exaggerating about the stench of the front line or the size of the rats. He swore you could have saddled some of the ones he had seen darting from the water or scurrying along the duckboards.

'Sniper,' Fairley said with a frown. 'That was a Mauser, I believe. They might be having a little trouble out there.'

Watson struggled upright and brushed himself down. 'More than you can imagine.'

'I can imagine a great deal out there,' he said, with a slight tremor in his fluting voice. Watson realized just how very young he was. 'The army can train you for almost everything. Except what it's like to be frightened day and night.'

He said it without self-pity. It was, Watson knew, absolutely true, fear was a long-term, almost subliminal companion on any front line. Watson was touched he would dare to confide such a thing to him. 'Rugby was it, Lieutenant?' This was a wild guess.

'Winchester, sir.'

'Very good. Always reassuring to have a Wykehamist at your back,' Watson said.

The lad brightened at that. Complimenting his old school was a surefire way to gain a subaltern's trust.

It was icily cold in the trench, but Watson shrugged off his great-coat and handed it to the lieutenant. He didn't need the bulky item restricting his ease of movement out there.

Fairley took it with a puzzled expression. 'What are you doing, sir?'

Watson unclipped the top of his holster and took out the Colt .45 automatic that poor old Caspar Myles had presented to him. He pressed the button and dropped the magazine. Full. But he had no spare. Seven rounds would have to suffice. 'Going to try and stop him, Lieutenant.'

'The captain? Stop him doing what?'

'Murdering any more people.'

Fairley looked taken aback. 'Are you serious, sir?'

Watson realized how ridiculous he must look to the youngster. An old man about to go 'over the bags' and charge into one of the most lethal few yards of ground on the planet. A flutter of fear began in his stomach, as if a small bird were trapped in there. 'Completely.'

'Right.' The lieutenant folded the greatcoat in the crook of his left arm. 'If you must go, sir . . .'

'I must.'

With his free hand, Fairley scooped a fistful of wet soil from the sides of the excavation and smeared it all over Watson's face.

'In the absence of a balaclava.' He stepped back and examined his handiwork. 'That'll give you a fighting chance.'

'Thank you, Lieutenant.'

'And keep your gloves on. Hands show up out there, too. And hold on.'

Fairley disappeared for a second, leaving Watson shivering in the brutal cold radiating from the excavated earth and the water ascending his legs in increments. At least, he hoped that's what the shivering was from.

Fairley returned with a Very flare pistol.

'No, really,' Watson said, balking at the size of the barrel.

The lieutenant unbuttoned the major's tunic and shoved it inside. 'Take it from one who spent a whole night and day out there once. Hiding among the dead men. There's a red flare in it. Not white. In this section of the line, red means "Man fallen. Come and get me." You fire that, someone'll try and reach you. At least we'll know you are alive and out there.'

'Thank you, Fairley.' He held out his hand. 'I'll try not to be that much trouble.'

Fairley took the hand. 'That would be jolly kind, sir. I wish I had a tot to give you. Helps no end.'

The last thing Watson wanted was alcohol. 'I'll manage.'

The lieutenant looked over his shoulder. 'Go on, sir, there's someone coming. Probably wondering who is raiding the sap supply locker. They might not be as accommodating as me about the flare, sir. Might think you've taken leave of your senses.'

Watson put a foot on the first rung of the ladder and waited until the moon was masked. The jittery bird in his stomach had returned to its perch and a strange calmness had come over him. 'They might be right, young Fairley. They might be right.'

As if in agreement, lighting up the blackness behind him and cracking open the sky, the British guns began firing.

SEVENTY-TWO

De Griffon almost ran headlong into Moulton coming the opposite way. Any noise of their progress across the mud was masked by the new barrage, and both had taken the chance to make rapid progress on all fours.

'Sir,' Moulton gasped as they confronted each other in the gloom. 'Thank God. Farrar's got it.'

'Got what?'

'Whatever the others had. What you had. He's . . .' he pointed back over his shoulder. 'I'm going to get help.'

'Good.' He grabbed the boy's arm. 'Just a second. What about you? Are you all right?'

'Yes. It hasn't got me.' He made to leave. De Griffon pulled his arm back and stabbed him through the neck with the trench knife. The boy's gurgles were lost to the rolling thunder of the Allied guns and the whistles of shells overhead.

'I'm beginning to think you didn't drink the rum. Probably spat it out. Teetotal, are you? Oh, well.' He pulled out the blade, feeling the serrations catch on bone, and slit the soldier's throat open. There was nothing but anguish and confusion in the lad's expression. Not an iota of understanding. Pity. It was telling them why they were dying that he had enjoyed most.

Lord Stanwood had been the most satisfying, because he had eked it out for so long. Leverton, too. But out here, apart from Tugman, they had been rather rushed affairs. Perhaps he could stretch out the pleasure with Farrar. 'Your father, that's why I am doing this. The sins of the father avenged by the actions of a son. Say hello to him when you see him in hell. Tell him Anne Truelove's boy did this.'

He waited until the light went out in Moulton's eyes, before he tossed him onto his back. With the tip of the blade he scratched the next number in the sequence on the lad's unlined forehead. Six. One more to go.

De Griffon realized his own uniform was caked in both mud and still-warm blood. There were spots of blood on his face, too. Still, it was going to back up the story he would bring home of fierce hand-to-hand fighting, out here in the dead man's land. Right, he thought, one more to go and it was all over. No, two more. Once he dispatched Farrar, there was another person to get rid of. It would be time to retire Robinson de Griffon, the trickiest murder of all.

SEVENTY-THREE

Watson couldn't tell how many guns were firing. Twelve? Twenty? A hundred? The detonations rolled into each other, creating a single unrelenting roar, like a giant traction engine running rough. Behind him, the clouds' bellies spat and sparkled from muzzle flashes, above him shells whistled, hummed and screamed. Ahead there was the steely-blue flash of high explosive, the jaundiced glare of lyddite or the invisible 'woolly bears' of shrapnel bursts.

The noise invaded his brain and rattled around it, scouring every corner. It became the sole inhabitant of the cranium, like a giant, booming cuckoo taking over the nest. Nothing else could live in there. It blanked out any rational thoughts, froze the limbs, made you want to find a hole, curl up and lie in it. But Watson didn't have that option. He pressed on.

Holmes would have been proud of him, he thought. A few yards from the sap, he located the fresh squiggles in the mud of four bodies crawling forward. Sometimes they had been on their stomachs; at other places they had raised onto all fours and, later, he found one place where they had sprinted at a crouch.

Despite the trampled and sodden soil, it wasn't too difficult to follow the route the quartet had taken, especially as his eyes adjusted. The disturbed earth here was a palimpsest waiting to be read: he had to ignore all but the topmost writings.

Within a few minutes, Watson came to the first shell hole, but there were no signs of occupation by any of the men that he could discern. The boot, knee, elbow and hand marks all skirted it. The rancid smell that stung his nostrils was enough to make him sympathetic to their decision to move along.

From there, he was punished for his smugness by losing the traces. While the noise continued to build — was it two hundred guns now? — and batter his senses, he grew increasingly desperate, aware that he could get himself seriously disoriented and lost. The tarry blackness was almost total and he could feel his sense of direction deserting him. He took several steps, then retraced them, before setting off again. Don't just blunder about, he told himself. He could easily find himself snagged on the wire. Next stop, a muddy grave or a POW camp. More likely the former.

Watson crouched down into the mud, hoping for some sign to help him regain his bearings.

It wasn't until he saw the ivory white of a dead man's hand in the pale glow of the newly emerged moon that he realized he had picked up the trail again. Aware that the pitiless light made him vulnerable, he slithered down the wall of the crater, his feet dipping into the icy pool that filled the bottom. The high, officer's boots saved him from a bad case of wet socks, but his toes chilled in an instant.

Watson examined the body as best he could under the circumstances, easing the makeshift gag down. The expression of terror, the hideous grin, that was there, but in the bleached moonlight he couldn't tell if the man had the equally distinctive blue tinge. Cause of death, a bullet through the skull. Plus there was a nasty penetrating thigh wound that appeared to have pierced the femoral artery. This man was dead three times over.

A heavy shell growled over and fell close by, showering him with earth. They were pulverizing the wire and the trenches on the far side. Was there a big push coming? Or was this a bluff? Certainly there had been no evidence of preparations for going 'over the bags' that he had seen. Major Tyler had been far too relaxed; Lieutenant Fairley, too. By all accounts you could cut the atmosphere with a blunt bayonet on the eve of an attack. It was possible Churchill had had his wish and there was an assault coming, but in a sector where the British hadn't signalled their intentions to the Germans.

But any move would come at first light. There were hours to go before that. Smoke from the explosions was beginning to haze the moon, and the light level was fading once more. He could smell the acrid mix of ammonia, picric acid and volatile toluene leaching over from the enemy lines. Some gunners had switched to air burst shells, and stabs of red, white and green burned his retinae as they detonated.

There was a thump nearby, heavy enough to register through his body. A dud, burying itself into the soil. Watson tried to keep his composure, not to let the screaming in his head overwhelm him. Men suffered under this for days, weeks on end.

And it sends them mad, he thought.

If he could just lie down and put his fingers in his ears till it was over. Then he could continue. But part of him knew that if he did bury himself close to the dead man, he would never get up again.

Watson holstered his gun, pushed himself into a crouch and

cleared the edge of the depression, running fast. A star shell had gone up, some miles distant, it was true, but its capricious, incandescent beauty was throwing incidental light in his direction. He had a shadow now, not a good companion. Then it was gone and darkness wrapped him again. There were flashes on his eyes. He shouldn't have looked at the star burst. Get lower, he instructed himself. Give me another shell hole. I'll stay there. I'm too old for—

His feet were taken from under him and Watson sprawled forward. As he hit the ground he felt the rib go properly, even imagined he heard a crack. A lance of hot pain flared along his side. He let out an oath, but had enough sense to stay still while he took stock.

Had he been hit? No, the pain came after he fell. What had he fallen over? He inched his head around, trying to make sense of the dark shapes behind him. Again, pale skin betrayed what he was looking at.

Another body had tripped him, this one looking up to the heavens, gaping as if he had two mouths. De Griffon had killed two of the men. There must be another out there. Was he too late? Think, man, think, what would you do if you wanted to kill your comrades?

The first dead man had the alkaloid contortion about the face. This one, as far as he could tell, had not. Had he poisoned some before coming out here? It was probable the toxin took some time to begin its insidious work. Of course, he might have offered them a tot before they came out here. And this one? Perhaps some were immune; perhaps he was teetotal. Oh, for God's sake, switch off that infernal—

The guns fell silent. His ears buzzed in the aftermath, the sudden silence seemingly as loud as the howitzers and cannons.

Then, above the hum emanating from his distressed eardrums,

came another sound. A voice, carried like the smoke on the breeze, so soft he had to strain to catch the words.

'. . . your father was one of them. The seven hooded . . . And so, you see, I am come back to exact revenge for little Anne Truelove. I am Johnny . . . called . . . dropwort. And oleander. Almost there now . . . smile. The sardonic smile . . . the old in Sardinia.'

Even in snatches, he could hear the deep, corrosive malice in the words. By peering in the blackness, aided by a splinter of moonlight, he could just about make out the speaker. An inky shape, darker than his surroundings, as if no light could leave his body. He was hunched against what appeared to be a fallen tree and, sitting up against the trunk, his last victim, the speech he was making suggesting the poor lad was already poisoned. The sardonic smile, the last spasm of death, would be on its way. He couldn't be saved out here, no matter what.

Watson reached for his holster and almost cried out. The rib was on fire. It felt as if it had been coated in phosphorus and ignited. He squeezed his eyes shut and let them fill with tears. His breathing was alarmingly shallow now. He was panting like a dog. Any attempt to fill his lungs caused a stabbing through his chest and into his heart. He tried again for the holster, managing to get his finger on the pistol. It was bitterly cold, but sweat was prickling on his forehead.

It took an age, but eventually he had the gun. Safety off. When he looked up, the dark shape of de Griffon had begun to move. The other man slumped, dead. You bastard, de Griffon, he thought. Could he raise the gun? A grunt escaped from him and he saw de Griffon freeze, momentarily, and drop to the ground. It had been louder than he thought.

Should he call out? Tell de Griffon to surrender? That the game was up? No, that would be madness. A child could overpower Watson now. No, it was to be a silent execution. But firing the shot would also give him away. Any sniper out there might home in on him. But it had to be done. Fire the shot and sprint for the cover of the log.

Sprint? Who did he think he was fooling?

The murderer was passing within a few yards of him now, the man's attention solely focused on getting back to the Allied lines. Watson pulled back the slide to chamber a round. The snick sounded like a thunderclap.

The figure froze. It turned towards him, like a hunting dog sniffing the air for an elusive scent.

The pistol was heavy in Watson's hand, the aim none too steady. The pain had dried his throat. Squeeze. The man has killed seven times. No, eight. Myles, remember Myles. Watson had to be judge and jury.

You aren't a judge. Or a jury.

He was right. Watson couldn't fire. Not without a warning. Nor would his hand stay still. The jigging fore sight traced the fleeing silhouette, until the night swallowed it. Watson slumped back, allowing himself another groan. A pulse of guilt and shame passed through him. He lacked the moral fibre for such an act.

The murderer had him now and he moved towards him. Watson thrust the gun forward.

'Fire that and we are both dead,' hissed de Griffon.

'You are coming back with me.'

De Griffon moved in. He could hear the pain in Watson's ragged breathing. He was a spent force. 'You aren't going anywhere, old man.'

He moved like a snake, twisting the pistol from Watson's grip, dropping the magazine. He flung the clip far away. There was a distant plop of water. Watson imagined hidden eyes swivelling towards the sound. De Griffon placed the now useless Colt on the ground at his feet.

'Why?' Watson asked. 'Why the murders?'

De Griffon shook his head. He had no intention of giving Watson chapter and verse. He was done with that. And why should he give anything to this boorish doctor? The one who had made such a fuss about Shipobottom, who had forced him into that painful charade of fitting at the farm and drained him of blood, who meant the final act of his drama had to be rushed. No, he owed him nothing. Except perhaps a swifter end than the others. De Griffon dropped almost on top of Watson, close enough for the doctor to see the wild gleam in his eyes. 'You'll die out here never knowing.'

He was fumbling for his knife when they heard the crack of a rifle, and the captain's head whipped around. There was no whistle or sigh of the bullet, but neither man could be certain they − or their voices − weren't the target. De Griffon spun, crouched once more and took off, zigzagging back towards the lines.

As soon as de Griffon had taken the first few steps, Watson reached and picked up the Colt. The effort set off a screaming in his head and one of the ribs popped.

But he had the gun and it wasn't entirely useless: there was still one in the spout. You had to eject the cartridge to unload it properly. One round was enough for what he wanted. He could just make out the beast-like shape, darting this way and that. He could drop de Griffon now. Shoot him in the back. He closed his eyes for a second, as if considering it. When he opened them again, the blackness had swallowed the murderer once more.

Don't fret. You were never a cold-blooded killer, Watson. But there is another option.

What's that, Holmes? he asked, knowing he was losing his grip on reality. Had the rib penetrated a lung? Was he bleeding to death? His body was oscillating between hot and cold with worrying rapidity as the earth drained his body heat. He shivered. This was no place for an old man. Or any living thing. *What are you saying?*

Let the gods of war decide. You'll be giving him more of a chance than he gave any of his victims.

The gods of war? What on earth do you mean? he asked.

No answer came, but the chattering of his teeth.

As he lay there, feeling delirium cloud his reason, Watson ran the phrase over and over in his mind. *Gods of war.* Ridiculous. Or was it? Perhaps he did appreciate what his spectral friend was suggesting. He was just shying away from it.

He unbuttoned his tunic, but as he did so he moved position and felt the ground shift beneath him in an undulating wave. He kicked backwards but he only sank deeper into the malevolent mud. As it sucked at his back he remembered Great Grimpen Mire. A flash of panic ripped through him, that the earth might swallow him, envelop him in its grasp until it filled his nose and mouth with semolina-like sludge. He would be just another corpse swallowed by this death strip. Food for rats and carrion. He began to thrash, the viscous soil around him making a horrible slurping noise, as if the poisoned ground was greedy for another body.

Now he had to try hard not to cry out as he felt the needle-sharp cold seep through his clothing. One leg had disappeared into the earth altogether, the boot filling with a runny mix of mud and icy water. Watson now knew he was lying on a place where a spring or a stream came to the surface, further liquefying the already fluid mud. He could pull the limb free, but knew he must lose boot and sock. The rest of him was being squeezed, as if by a watery vice, pressing against those damaged ribs. No man's land was determined to keep him, to never let him go. He stopped struggling, knowing it was only hastening his eventual immersion.

He put a fist into his mouth and yelled into it. This wasn't how he envisaged going. He was here to help the dying, not to join them.

His spine felt it first. Something unyielding, solid. Beneath the freezing slime there was . . . what? An erratic boulder, deposited by a glacier millions of years ago? A body, perhaps? A horse or a man? A lost howitzer or humble tractor? Or simple bedrock? He had no way of knowing for sure what it was now firmly beneath his buttocks, but he gave thanks as it slowed his progress, anchoring him, so that he was only half buried.

He moved his arms and his free leg. Yes, his progress towards the bowels of this Flanders field had been arrested.

So braced, Watson used his teeth to take the glove off his left hand, folded the leather in his mouth and clamped down with all his might. He bit harder and harder, until the ache in the jaw almost matched that of his ribs. He felt a tooth give.

With his right arm, he finished unbuttoning the tunic and reached in for the Very flare pistol, the one that had caused further damage to his ribcage when he had stumbled and fallen. The glove masked his grunts of pain as he extracted it. Gently does it, he admonished himself. Conserve your energy for this one last task.

With studied concentration on the required muscles, Watson raised the pistol to the sky. His side was on fire and tears squeezed from his eyes unbidden. He closed them and pulled the trigger, releasing the charge. The recoil jerked him against his subterranean anchorage, but whatever it was held fast. He dropped the pistol and opened his eyes. He watched the trail of fire streak away from him, arcing towards the friendly lines, then hesitate and begin to fall, where it blossomed into a bright red sphere.

Mars, he thought to himself. God of War.

Beneath the hellish fire, picked out for a few moments, was the scuttling shape of de Griffon, who looked up at the glow in horror. Like a judgement from above, it had sought and found the guilty man.

From over to his left, some many yards distant, Watson heard the crack of not one but two rifles. De Griffon stood upright, as if he was ready to run forward, but as the flare fizzled, the desperate sprint became a stumble. As the exhausted red ball fell to earth and died in the mud of no man's land, so did Johnny Truelove.

SEVENTY-FOUR

Ernst Bloch knew the flare would bring out Tommies to try to rescue the stricken soldier. Although he was certain that it had been his headshot that killed the unfortunate man who had been bathed in its glare, he magnanimously ceded the kill to Lothar. It would have taken him to that magic thirty, but now he was leaving this strange life, it didn't seem to matter.

The flare had damaged his night vision and, even with the new scope, he couldn't actually make out the exact position of the man who had launched it. There were several possibilities he could see, humps and lumps in the night, but none moved and it wasn't worth wasting a bullet on an inanimate object. Whoever it was would probably expire out there anyway. Only the desperate launched a red flare.

Minutes passed, the slow beat of life out there.

'I have movement.' It was Schaeffer. 'Dead ahead.'

'On my instruction,' said Bloch to Lothar.

'Yes.'

Bloch used the night sight to scan the area just ahead of the enemy wire. Some of the smoke from the bombardment had cleared and the moon was strengthening. Yes, there was something there. Gone now. Wait. He needed a starburst, but there was no way of communicating that back to his lines. Perhaps that was something they ought to experiment with.

There it was again. A very unusual outline.

'Target acquired,' Lothar said.

God, his eyes must be good. 'On my instruction,' Bloch repeated. 'It is my call.'

Now he could see the shape clearly. He looked for any sign of an officer. No, not a cap . . . that was . . . out here? How could it be?

'I'm taking the shot.'

'No,' he said, louder than intended, and pushed Lothar's shoulder.

The rifle gave a crack and the bullet whined off uselessly into the sky.

'What the hell . . . ?'

'It's a woman.'

'A what?' Lothar asked.

'I would recognize that headgear anywhere.'

'Ssh,' warned Schaeffer.

'Well, if it's a woman, it's a fucking British bitch, isn't it?'

'We agreed not to shoot them. They are the Women of Pervyse. It's a gentleman's agreement.'

That made the boy laugh. There were no gentlemen out in no man's land. 'What the bloody hell is a woman doing out there?'

'I saw one near here the other day.' She had helped patch him up, in fact, along with the elderly doctor.

Lothar lay back down and resighted. 'That's your agreement. This is my patch now.'

'Stop, that's an order.'

'A woman? Out there? You're mad.' He adjusted the focus and took a deep breath. 'Target acquired.'

'Let him, Ernst,' said Schaeffer softly. 'You could be mistaken. And he's right. This is ours now.'

A few moments passed while the boy's rifle barrel tracked a few centimetres to the right. He had her. 'I am taking the shot.'

Bloch knew he was going to have to stop him, somehow. He turned to extract his knife from its sheath. That is when he caught a movement of black ghosts in the corner of his eye.

The hardwood club rang off Lothar's skull and, before he could react, something equally heavy struck Bloch. His vision exploded into spinning galaxies and his limbs turned to lead. He was unable to react as his arms were rapidly bound together and a rag of some description pushed into his mouth.

He shook his head to clear it, trying to make sense of what was happening. Five, perhaps six men, dressed head to toe in black, were circling around the three Germans. Schaeffer and Lothar still lay sprawled on the ground close by, totally out of it. One of the raiders picked up the two sniping rifles and slung them over his shoulder.

They'll have the new night sight, he thought. *Lux will kill me.*

'Right, back the way we came,' said a low, growling voice. 'But we just need the one, I'm afraid. And if we leave them be, these two will be back out here again tomorrow.'

The scream from Bloch's throat dashed itself against the gag filling his mouth as one of the wraiths stepped forward and drove a bayonet through his two prostrate comrades, one after the other, like sticking pigs. He squeezed his eyes shut as he was hauled to his feet and half-dragged, half-carried west, towards the British lines.

Bloch didn't know it yet, but Churchill's new team of trench raiders had just grabbed their first prisoner.

EPILOGUE

The journey that took Watson to this place, standing at the rail of the HS *Arundel Castle*, had been an interminable one. After time at the CCS for an X-ray and bandaging – two broken ribs, one cracked – he had been moved onto an ambulance train. On the scale of things, it was a mild wound. But everyone knew the damage went deeper. That the sheet-drenching nightmares of drowning in mud weren't abating. Hence his ticket home.

Thanks to being a medical man, an officer and one of the walking wounded, he had been given a berth in the staff car, the old First Class compartment. He earned his bunk by helping with general medical duties where he could. His heavily strapped ribs made lifting impossible, but he could administer medicine, reapply mustard plaster dressings and offer comforting words. It was the latter, more often than not, that the broken and smashed soldiers needed.

It took three hours to load on the patients. The coaches had been converted to take racks of stretchers and the patients were warned they might be there for up to sixteen hours. It was, he was told, a French train, not a 'khaki' as they called the English rolling stock.

These were preferable because they didn't have the central corridor like the khakis, which meant easier access to the men.

Despite the depressing catalogue of injuries, amputations and disabilities – nearly all of them life-changing – the atmosphere during entraining was surprisingly buoyant. These were men who knew, no matter what was in store at the other end of the journey, they would never again have to go back to those trenches. It was a feeling he could empathize with.

The train to Boulogne had taken just over ten hours. The journey was a series of spurts, crawls and shunts. It proceeded through the countryside at little more than a walking pace for some of the time, the rhythm of the rails just gentle enough to act as a lullaby for those who could sleep. Soon enough there would be a squeal of brakes and a halt. A ripple of apprehension would run through the carriages if the stop were too long. These men wanted to be *away* from the front, the further the better.

On occasion the train moved backwards, from whence it had come, and apprehension turned to panic for some of the wounded. The nurses moved along the swaying carriages, telling anyone who would listen they were probably reversing for a troop train. Ambulance trains were fourth in the transit pecking order – men, ammunition and food had priority on the tracks.

Getting men up to the front, bringing the food to feed them and the bullets to kill other men were, apparently, more important than recovering those who had already been through the mincer. On the other hand, if the stop was at one of the stations, gaunt-faced locals appeared like wraiths from the dark, offering water, alcohol, coffee and precious fruit for the wounded men, not caring if the train held British Tommies or French *poilus*.

A jerk and the train would move again, speeding up to perhaps ten or twelve miles an hour to make up lost time. Watson had been amazed at the nurses who cared for the men. They were half medical staff, half acrobats. They could clamber up a bunk and hold on against the swaying while adjusting splints, applying fomentations, changing dressings, offering tea or Bovril. All in a strange hazy half-light caused by the veiled lights.

Once on his trip the lamps were extinguished altogether and the darkness beyond the windows was cut by the flashes of an air raid. Still, the train chuffed on its sinuous way, every tortured mile taking the soldiers closer to Blighty.

At Boulogne an army of stretcher-bearers and orderlies had appeared to take off the wounded, while the exhausted medical staff began to scrub the carriages, ready for the return journey and another load. Would these people ever get the recognition they deserved, Watson had wondered. But he knew the answer. Nobody would be striking an Ambulance Train Service Medal in the foreseeable future.

Then, another delay. They had waited overnight in the port for the ambulance ship to set sail. There was talk of U-boat activity in the Channel. A troop ship had been sunk off Poole. A legitimate target, but nobody was in any doubt that the days of the Red Cross being given free passage were gone. The Hospital Ship *Pride of Lancaster* had been lost to a mine off Dover. So the wounded piled up on the quayside; more serious cases were taken to 2AGH, the huge Australian-staffed hospital on the cliff tops.

As the darkness fell the air had thickened about them and the temperature plummeted. It felt as if ice crystals were about to form and blankets were distributed to the stretcher cases. After all the rain, a cold snap had descended across Benelux and Northern France. Watson had thought of the men in those trenches, their fingers and lips blue, their feet immersed in icy water. More trench foot and frostbite. Even if there were no more action in their section, the East Anglian CCS would have its work cut out now winter was well and truly here.

Watson had spent the night in a tent at the officers' transit compound, sleeping on a Wolseley camp bed, with twenty-odd others and two pet greyhounds. Breakfast was egg and tinned sausages. Eventually, at mid-morning, the all-clear was given and they began to embark the 450 patients onto the *Arundel*, taking up every conceivable inch of deck space. Just after midday it steamed out of Boulogne, en route, although on a meandering zigzag course, for Folkestone.

It was drizzling and misty in the Channel and visibility was poor. This, said some old hands, made it equally difficult for the marauding submarines to find them as it was for the captain to spot a periscope. Watson wasn't so sure, but the rumour lifted the spirits of men huddled under tarpaulins and greatcoats. Mugs of tea, the universal panacea, were dispensed in an endless stream.

They were lucky in that the *Arundel* was a proper Channel steamer; many ships that did the crossing were converted pleasure craft or river ferries, like the Mersey ones. They rolled and wallowed in the gentlest of seas and the decks became awash with vomit. The *Arundel*, however, felt good and solid, piercing the swell rather than bobbing over the top.

Watson helped with mundane tasks, one eye on the grey sea that surrounded the ship, imagining the white line of a torpedo heading for them. But once they were half-way, he began to hope they might make it after all. As the scale of the evasive manoeuvres diminished, and it was obvious the captain was running for home, he took his place at the rail and allowed himself a cigarette, even though drawing the smoke too deeply hurt his ribs. He was out of his own brand; an orderly at the quayside had slipped him a pack of White Cloud, but the tobacco was coarse and nasty, rasping the throat.

At the transit camp he'd managed to buy forty of Fortnum's own Virginian Special from a young subaltern, an Old Etonian, who was returning home without most of his right arm. 'My smoking hand,' as he put it. 'Can't get used to using the left. Keep missing my mouth.'

Watson had told him the new prosthetics could be ordered with a built-in cigarette holder, which cheered him up no end.

Watson had hoped for a sudden unveiling of the coast, to see the brightly lit uplands of Great Britain, something to make his weary heart soar, but the capricious weather denied him this. Still, he could smell it now on the breeze, the scent of the land, as well as the pungent mix of oil, steam and fish from the docks. But it was a very British stench.

'There you are. You'll catch your death up here.'

He'd known she was on board, but had spent her time on the train, at the quay and on the boat tending the most seriously wounded, so they had seen little of each other since leaving the CCS.

'I'll be fine. What on earth have you got there?'

She was holding a large, painted cast-iron, very French cockerel.

'It's a present for someone. I bought it off one of the patients,' said Mrs Gregson.

He looked at it. 'It's quite spectacularly ugly,' he said.

'Isn't it just?' she said with a wide grin. 'But then so is the man I'm sending it to.' She smiled at the thought of the note she would include with it when she sent Lang his very own cock. Childish, but she also knew it was the kind of juvenile, smutty humour that might placate him. After all, she might end up having to deal with him again one day. She didn't need any residual anger or suspicion on his part.

'Will you stop in Folkestone?' he asked her. 'It's getting late now.'

'I'll see what the formalities are. Lots of paperwork I should imagine.'

'If I can help with that, as a doctor, please ask.'

'Thank you. I would like to travel up there with her as soon as I can. Get it over with. And get back to France.'

'You'll return?' he asked, surprised.

She nodded firmly, as if there was no doubt. 'I shall.' She pointed at the metal cockerel. 'Hence this peace offering. I'll put in a request once I've seen the Pipperys. If they'll even entertain me.'

Mrs Gregson was determined to face Miss Pippery's parents. She feared, however, that they would blame her for their daughter's death. Without Mrs Gregson, there would have been no motor-cycle club or weekend hill climbs, no volunteering for nursing duties as soon as war broke out. The great adventure had ended, like so many, with a German bullet. On the other hand, someone had to tell them about how the shy, self-effacing girl had comforted dying men, helped repair wrecked bodies and, in the early days, defied snipers to extract the wounded men from what would become no man's land.

'You're returning their daughter to them. Of course they'll see you. And you are a link to Alice's final days. I can't tell you how important that will be to them. Don't be surprised if they adopt you.'

He was serious, but she brushed it aside. 'I'm not sure I make a good orphan. Even if they don't invite me in, I can hand over her things. There's some unfinished letters.' Mrs Gregson cleared her throat and sniffed. 'She talks about you in them.'

'Me?'

'You. It's always the quiet ones. She thought it was hilarious that you suspected everyone of knitting those socks but her. I think Alice was a little goofy for you.'

Watson hooted so hard his ribs hurt again. He didn't know the expression, but it was clear what she meant. 'Oh, really, Mrs Gregson.'

She had given up trying to get him to call her Georgina. On the few occasions he had tried, he had rolled the word around his mouth like a gobstopper before he could bring himself to utter it. Even then, it never sat easy. She was beginning to wonder if he had called his wives 'Mrs Watson'.

'Oh, don't be so surprised, Major,' she said. 'You have a certain something. For an older man.'

He let his smile fade into an exaggerated grimace. 'It was all going so well until that last part.'

Mrs Gregson took a position next to him on the rail and slid close. 'It's not so bad, getting old.'

'Isn't it?'

'Not when you consider the alternative.'

Her eyes gave an involuntary flick down to the deck. Miss Alice Pippery's coffin was below, in the hold. Goodness knows what strings her family had pulled to have the body returned to them. It was very rare that anyone other than a very high-ranking officer or a member of the nobility was repatriated. A few dozen had made the crossing to rest under the earth of home; hundreds of thousands were interred where they had fallen, from labourer to lord, an equality in death that had been denied in life.

'That is true.'

'Did you hear that young Lieutenant Fairley is to be awarded the Military Cross?' she asked.

This was a new award since his day, introduced in 1914, for warrant officers and commissioned officers below the rank of major. 'I did. For rescuing me, apparently. Brave lad.'

Even braver when Watson discovered that Fairley really had been trapped out there once, wounded and pinned under a dead colleague, for several days; hence his aversion to no man's land. It made his feat of excavating Watson from the lethal gloop that had almost engulfed him and carrying him back to safety even more remarkable.

'And for making a fool of himself with my scarf.' She shook her head at the embarrassing memory. 'I don't know what I was thinking.'

'You were thinking it might just save his life. Which it did.'

Mrs Gregson had followed Watson along the overhead railway, and almost caught up with him several times. However, the presence of a woman had caused consternation among the men and she had been delayed several times by over-zealous and over-protective junior officers. Only the force of her personality, the sharp edge of her tongue and agreeing to hide her hair under a steel helmet had got her to Major Tyler and Lieutenant Fairley.

When Fairley saw the flare and determined to go out to get Watson, Mrs Gregson had persuaded him to don the green bandana and her topcoat. It had kept her safe out there, once upon a time, she insisted. Young Fairley, who had a healthy regard for the vagaries of no man's land, and a superstitious streak just as wide as it, had agreed to the unusual garb. He'd dressed up as worse during high jinks in the mess, so he said.

'He asked to keep the scarf, you know,' said Mrs Gregson. 'Claimed it had brought him luck. That he would carry it with him for the rest of the war.'

'I hope it works for him.' The phrase 'rest of the war' had a chilling ring. Who knew how long this madness would endure?

'Did you hear from your friend Mr Holmes?'

'Not yet.' He had cabled Holmes to tell him that, judging by what he had overheard out in no man's land, and from talking to Mrs Gregson, the key to the de Griffon case lay with the Truelove sisters. They were, apparently, legendary in suffragette circles for standing up to mill owners for equal pay, rights and promotion. But something had mysteriously made them flee the fight. And he had clearly heard 'de Griffon' call himself 'Johnny Truelove'. A son, perhaps, out to revenge a mother and an aunt. But for what?

Holmes had replied he would be travelling to Leigh armed with the information and looking for that answer. 'He will be disappointed in me, I fear, for losing the one man who could provide every answer.'

'We've been through this, Major. You identified the killer. Nobody could have expected more.'

Watson gave a small, dissatisfied grunt. There had obviously been seven names on Truelove's list. Seven potential victims. The man had got them all. And poor Caspar Myles. Truelove died knowing he had won, after a fashion. Which meant Watson had lost. *Nobody could have expected more?* Well, one man would have. A lot better.

'At least you came back alive.'

'I murdered him, didn't I? De Griffon. I didn't pull the trigger. Couldn't do it. But by pinpointing him with that flare . . .'

She put a hand on his forearm and squeezed. 'John, please.' She hoped the use of his Christian name might make him listen for once. 'You were just signalling for help. How were you to know there was a German sniper out there?'

Because there is always a German sniper out there, he thought. They hadn't found Truelove's body, although in truth nobody had looked very hard. It was possible that he was at the bottom of a shell hole, slowly rotting into mulch, or been blown to wet dust by a shell. Plenty of others had suffered such fates.

The ship's horn sounded – a deep, confident blast that caused a shiver of pleasure in him – and he became aware of the propellers churning water. The hull of the ship juddered. They were slowing. Folkestone was ahead. The constellation of following gulls screeched their encouragement. A sudden sense of relief was palpable throughout the ship, as if all, including the vessel, had been holding their collective breath. They were safe from the U-boats at last.

'Will you ever go back?' Mrs Gregson asked.

He looked towards France, but a milky veil had been dropped over the Channel. He imagined he could smell the fortifications, though, and the vile taste that came with it made his stomach perform somersaults. Churchill had asked him to return. His interrogation of a captured sniper had convinced him that there was a spy network operating around Plug Street, communicating details of troop movements. He wanted Watson to investigate. But Watson had recommended he hand it over to Tobias Gregson. However, he had a feeling Churchill wasn't finished with him yet. The man seemed to trust, even like him, now his suppositions about Porton had turned out to be correct.

'I don't know, is the honest answer. I'd be more than happy never to stand in a damned trench again. Excuse my language. Or see no man's land.'

He had thought of it as a river when he had first spied it from the balloon, snaking its poisoned course across Europe. Now he knew it was nothing so benign; it was a raw, bleeding wound in the flesh of the earth, made and sustained by deranged men. One day soon, perhaps, it would scab over, but a full healing would take a lot longer than the time he had left in this world. Generations, perhaps. No, he didn't want to lay eyes on that again.

'On the other hand,' he continued, 'there is a terrible guilt at leaving our young men out there, fighting in those conditions. They need doctors. They need blood. No matter what you think of this war, they'll need blood.' He shook his head at the thought of the desperate transfusions, the hasty surgery, the number of maimed to come. Not to mention the bountiful crop of white crosses sprouting from the earth of Northern France and Belgium. Young men like Fairley were being cut down in droves.

A new general order had been issued that junior officers going into battle must dress like regular Tommies to stop them being targeted. Sticks, the badge of office, were prohibited during attacks. Watson doubted it would help. Snipers and machine gunners would still aim for the man with the revolver or the chap encouraging his platoon forward. But just thinking about the trenches gave him a hollow feeling, as if he had left some part of himself behind. Perhaps that was why men kept going back. To find the part of them that was missing when they were away from the front. Perhaps, of all the ailments they treated, war itself was the most virulent, insidious, strangely seductive disease.

'I don't know,' he repeated.

'Then where will you go when we dock?' she asked. 'London?'

He thought of smoke-filled lounges, crowded hotel lobbies, busy concert halls – would they still play Wagner or Beethoven at the Bechstein Hall now it had become the Wigmore? – and long lunches, of walks in Greenwich Park, the smell of the brewery along the river and of the tanneries when the wind blew from the northeast, the mournful honks of the lightermen in the fog, the view from the Observatory on a clear day. 'I intend to. I telegrammed my club from Boulogne, asking them to keep me a room.' He couldn't face his cold, empty house near his old practice in Queen Anne Street. Not yet. Not ever? In that precise second he decided to sell it and buy somewhere that wasn't suffused with the spirit of Emily. Perhaps he would move to rooms around the corner to Harley Street. Or even Baker . . .

'I still see their faces in my dreams sometimes,' Mrs Gregson confessed. She spoke quickly, as if she had been waiting to admit this for some time. 'Hornby, Shipobottom. Do you?'

'Sometimes,' he admitted. And that poor horse, too.

'Will you ever get to the bottom of everything that de Griffon did? And why?'

As they slid into the harbour, Watson imagined for a moment he saw a familiar figure, out on the breakwater, leaning on a heavy cane, watching intently as the ship slid into calmer waters. But that was impossible, as the movement of Channel traffic was highly classified. Nobody could possibly know he was on this boat at this time. No ordinary man, anyway.

'Major?'

He looked at her, holding her headdress as the wind whipped at her. 'Sorry. Miles away. I can't quote chapter and verse about de Griffon or Truelove just yet.'

When he turned his gaze back to the spray-lashed wall, the figure with the walking stick had disappeared.

'But I suspect there's someone who can.'

ACKNOWLEDGEMENTS

Dead Man's Land was inspired by Sherlock Holmes's suggestion, at the end of Sir Arthur Conan Doyle's *His Last Bow* (set in 1914), that Watson would return to his 'old service', which by that stage was called the Royal Army Medical Corps. What, I wondered, would a man of a certain age be able to do for the war effort? And how would he get along without his great friend?

My first and most heartfelt thanks go to Sue Light, whom I found through her blog This Intrepid Band (http://greatwarnurses.blogspot.com). It is a wonderful source of information about the medical services in WWI, especially the QA nurses. She kindly read an early draft of the book and made suggestions and corrections. Any errors remaining are mine alone (some by choice – she warned me not to have a VAD at the front). Very early on in our discussions about writing a WWI historical thriller, my editor, Maxine Hitchcock, came up with the idea of a detective in the trenches, and had the patience and tenacity to wait until I had worked out it had to be a doctor and a famous one at that. David Miller, my clear-headed agent, then pointed out that Dr Watson has been trademarked by the Conan Doyle Estate. So thanks to him and to Olivia Guest of Jonathan Clowes, which administers the estate. She listened while I pitched the idea over the telephone, and supported its progress through to permission being granted. Susan d'Arcy — as always — and Rob Follis gave early advice on the story and structure. Roger Johnson of The Sherlock Holmes Society of London (www.sherlock-holmes.co.uk) put me in touch with David Stuart Davies, who gave the manuscript a once-over for any Holmesian howlers (although any that remain are my responsibility, of course). I would also like to thank lifelong Sherlock Holmes fan Anders Peter Mejer (see www.anderspetermejer.com) in Copenhagen for his long-distance enthusiasm and guidance, and Maxine Hitchcock, once more, and Clare Hey for their exemplary (and diplomatic) work on plot, character and pace, and for believing in Dr Watson. Also I am very grateful to James Horobin and Kerr MacRae for sticking with me over the years.

There were many, many texts I consulted for the book's background, but if you want to know more about nursing in WWI, try *Women in the War Zone* by Anne Powell (The History Press), *The Roses of No Man's Land* by Lyn MacDonald (Penguin), *Elsi and Mairi Go to War* (Arrow) and *A Nurse at the Front* (IWM War Diaries/Simon & Schuster) by Edith Appleton, edited by Ruth Cowen. Plus, of course the first part of Vera Brittain's classic *Testament of Youth* (Virago) recounts her experiences as a VAD.

Robert Ryan

PROLOGUE

The orderlies carried the six bodies down the steps of the sunken ice house that lay half hidden in the grounds of the Suffolk stately home. The commanding officer of the 'special' unit that had displaced the owner and his retinue from the mansion stood at the bottom of the stairs, watching the orderlies manhandle the stiffening forms, grunting with the effort as they laid out the dead on the stone flags. Each of the deceased was tightly swaddled in a waxed groundsheet. They looked like latter-day mummies, the colonel thought grimly.

The officer lit a cigarette. There was a smell of decay in the air that the smoke would help mask. Not from the six bodies – these poor souls had been dead only a matter of hours – but from the ice house itself, part of which had doubled as hanging rooms for the estate's bag of venison, partridge and pheasants in the years before the outbreak of war. A persistent sharp, gamey tang tainted the atmosphere.

It would be high summer soon enough, and the colonel didn't want the dead men adding to the stink before they could be properly examined. Hence he directed the orderlies to move them to the coldest corner of the subterranean chamber. *Examined for what, though?*

The colonel tried to keep his jaw set and his face impassive as the orderlies neatened up the row of cadavers, moving the legs so they were absolutely parallel, as if this were some kind of Best Laid Corpse competition. Inside, though, his stomach was a bucket of eels. He had been entrusted with the secret project that was intended to bring a swift resolution to the war, to see it all over by Christmas 1916, to consign the horror of the trenches, the slaughter of the Somme, to a hideous but fading memory. Yet out there, in the grounds of the house, in front of generals and politicians and even minor bloody royalty, *this* had happened. Six dead, two others reduced to jibbering lunatics.

Oh, they had managed to cover it up as quickly and smoothly as possible, postponing the test for 'technical reasons', and the bodies were only removed once the viewing stands had been cleared of the dignitaries. Still, it was both an acute embarrassment and a serious setback. And a damn sight worse for six dead members of the Machine Gun Corps, he reminded himself. What on earth would he tell the next of kin? 'Died for King and Country' would have to do, wrapped in a bow of the usual platitudes.

The colonel's job now was to keep a lid on this, to get to the bottom of the deaths before someone decided to stop throwing good money – and men – after bad. To save the project at all cost. He dismissed the orderlies, warning them, on pain of the most severe punishments he could threaten, not to reveal or discuss anything they had seen that day. Exile, imprisonment and disgrace awaited those who betrayed his trust.

He smoked on, staring down at the shrouded forms for a few

minutes. The flickering oil lamps had turned the groundsheets a glossy, sickly yellow-green. The very colour he himself felt. He could taste bile in his mouth. The colonel tossed the remains of his cigarette onto the stone flags and ground it out with the toe of his boot. He did this rather longer than was necessary to extinguish it.

There was a polite cough behind him and he turned, wondering how long he had had company. It was the unit's intelligence officer, a deep frown corrugating his youthful brow.

'Yes?' the colonel demanded.

'Trenton just expired,' said the young man.

Seven, then.

Seven dead men in one afternoon. And then there was one. The colonel muttered a particularly fruity oath. 'Get him brought down here, quick as you like. Who was with him?'

'The new nurse.'

'Well, make sure she keeps her mouth shut. Let's be clear: I don't want anyone outside the main committee to know about this until we are certain what is behind it. I am not letting two years' worth of work go to waste because of an unfortunate —' He looked at the bodies and shivered. The perpetual chill of the ice house was penetrating his bones — 'accident,' he finished.

'But how do we find out what happened out there?' asked the intelligence officer, glancing over his shoulder.

'We have to hope the survivor talks.' The remaining man was the least affected by whatever malaise had struck the eight. He had settled into being merely comatose. 'Hitchcock, isn't it?' asked the colonel.

The younger man nodded. 'And if he doesn't talk?'

The colonel considered this for a moment. 'Then we'll find someone who will make him.'

PART ONE, 10–29 July 1916

ONE

The sound of the bell was an icicle plunged into his heart. At the first few notes, shivers racked his body and his pulse raced like a rodent's; a prickling sweat broke out, beading his forehead and wetting his palms. A sense of blind panic threatened to overwhelm him as the ringing grew in intensity and then abruptly stopped. The ominous silence that followed was somehow even more threatening.

The gas alarm.

Time to mask up. Major John H. Watson of the Royal Army Medical Corps stepped away from the young lad he had been patching up at the Regimental Aid Post and looked down beneath the trestle table. His gas mask case was not there. He had tripped over it too many times. He had hung it outside, he remembered, on the trench wall. If this was a genuine attack, he needed that mask.

The bell resumed its warning again, seemingly more urgent than before. He heard the bellow of the company sergeant major. 'Gas! Gas! Gas! Come on, lads, snap to it if you want to keep y'lungs on the inside where they belong.'

There was only one other patient in the dugout, and he didn't need a mask. He had breathed his last. The RAMC orderly next to the poor lad, who had been preparing the corpse for burial, was busy struggling with his own rubber and canvas respirator.

'Orderly, when you have done that, get a mask on this man too!' Watson shouted, indicating his own patient. 'It'll be with his rifle. I'm going to fetch my nosebag.'

Watson stepped out from the low-roofed aid station, his feet slithering for purchase on the slimy and worn duckboards. In front of him, on the opposite side of the trench, was a recess, where metal hooks had been screwed into the supporting timbers, forming a primitive open-air wardrobe. From the hooks hung a motley assortment of capes, caps, helmets and coats, but no gas masks.

A figure thumped into Watson and he was spun round, scrabbling to retain his footing. The man, a lieutenant, made goggle-eyed by his air purifier, apologized in a muffled voice and indicated that Watson should protect his face. The junior officer pointed upwards, towards the pale blue of the early morning sky. Like a sly fog, the first tendrils of greyish-green gas were creeping over the sandbags of the parapet. Watson felt his eyes prickle and sting.

Not again. Not chlorine gas again.

It was too late to run through the trenches hoping for a spare mask, so he turned to take whatever shelter the aid station could offer. As he did so, his left foot slipped off the duckboards. It plunged into the thick slime of the trench mud, a glutinous mass that had been festering for nigh on two years. It clasped his ankle and held him firm.

He uttered a crude curse, a bad habit he had picked up from the men. He tried to lift his foot free, but the grip only tightened and the suction pulled his leg deeper into the mire. He would have to lose the boot, a precious Trench Master, ten guineas the pair. *Don't worry about that now, man. Pull!* But the pressure of the ooze was too great to allow him even to wiggle his toes. He held his knee and yanked, but to no avail. The greedy sludge that had taken so many men had him tight.

The gas was rolling down the sides of the trench now, viscous and evil. The gas alarm bell sounded once again and didn't stop this time. Attack in progress. All across the front a cacophony of sirens, hooters, whistles and rattles joined in the warning. *Don't die here, not like this.* But by now he was holding onto the wall, watching the black filth creep further up his trapped leg, his desperate fingers leaving grooves on the rotten wood as he sought purchase.

He looked around for assistance, but every sensible soldier was taking cover. 'Help!' he yelled. The only answer was an imagined snide hiss from the poison drifting towards him. Watson closed his eyes, held his breath, and waited for the vapour to do its worst.

'Major Watson!'

The strident tones of the familiar and distinctly female voice snapped him from his reverie. He opened his eyes. Before him was the coal-grimed window of his surgery, and beyond that, Queen Anne Street, its features blanketed by an eerily unseasonal fog, the traffic reduced to a passing parade of ghostly silhouettes. He wasn't at the front. He hadn't seen, or smelled, a trench for months. Mud was no longer his constant companion and intractable enemy. It was another waking dream of the sort that had haunted him since his return from France.

He turned to Mrs Hobbs, his housekeeper, standing in the doorway to the hall, her face drawn even tighter than her bun.

'Major Watson, did you not hear the telephone?'

The telephone. Not a gas alarm.

She indicated over her shoulder to where the phone sat on its dedicated walnut telephonic table from Heal's. It was a piece of furniture that Mrs Hobbs had insisted was the only proper platform for the new instrument. Not that she actually liked using it herself; they had an agreement that Watson would normally pick up the receiver.

'No, I didn't. My apologies, Mrs Hobbs. Who was it?'

'Mr Holmes.' She said this with studied neutrality.

What again? Watson looked at the wall clock. It was three in the afternoon and already Holmes had telephoned him four – perhaps even five – times that day, on each occasion repeating some trivial news about having a new water tank fitted at his cottage or some such. Watson had to admit that, to his shame and chagrin, he had taken to drifting off while his friend rattled on about such inconsequential trivia. Especially if it involved bees.

'Is he still on the line?' Watson asked.

'I expect so. He said it was important. He did sound agitated, sir.'

It was always important. And he was always agitated. Watson glanced outside at the lazily eddying wall of fog, the phantom stench of chlorine still prickling his nose. The senses were no longer to be trusted these days. Neither, sadly, could his old companion be relied upon to make sense.

'If you would be so kind as to tell him I'm with a patient.'

Mrs Hobbs pursed her lips at the thought of uttering an untruth, and closed the door after her.

Watson sat down in his chair and opened the drawer containing a tin of Dr Hammond's Nerve and Brain Tablets, which the salesman had assured him cured men's 'special diseases' arising from war service. He replaced the tin unopened, lit a cigarette and felt the friendly smoke calm him. His statement to Mrs Hobbs had not been a total lie. He did have a patient for company. Himself.

A nagging little voice was hammering away inside, though, even as he enjoyed the tobacco warming his lungs. It was that Holmes telephone call. It was like the Retired Detective Who Cried Wolf.

What if one day it really was something important?

TWO

Miss Nora Pillbody had cycled for a good two miles through the Suffolk countryside before she realized exactly what had been niggling at her. The day had begun like any normal school-day morning. After a breakfast of porridge, she had loaded her basket with the work she had marked and corrected overnight, and set off from her cottage in plenty of time to take registration. As always, she wondered what excuses would deplete her class that morning – 'So-and-so isn't here, miss, because he needs to help with sheep shearing/haymaking/de-horning the calves/irrigating the potatoes.' There was always something happening on the land that took priority over mere learning.

Once out of the dead-end lane that housed her cottage, her route took her past Cyril Jefford's farm, skirted Marsham Wood, with its shy herd of roe deer, in a long, lazy loop, before she took the old drovers' track that pierced the Morlands' property. This cut a good half-mile off the journey, even if it was a bone-rattling surface, baked dry by the early summer sun. The Morlands had eight children, including three in her school class. With two older boys already in the army and one just eligible for conscription, it was a nervous time for the family. Miss Pillbody ducked through the shifting, pointillist clouds of midges blocking her way and found time to admire a flash of iridescent green dragonfly, and a Red Admiral warming its spread wings on a fence post. A sparrowhawk hovered expectantly above a cornfield, beady-eyed for potential prey.

She was a few hundred yards from the low, flint-built school-house when it hit her what had been amiss throughout that whole morning's ride. The children. There hadn't been any. Her ears had been full of the calls of skylarks and the rougher cadences of the rest-less crows, underpinned by the creaking and cracking of the wheat and the buzz of passing bees, but not the usual babble of conversa-tion as her pupils made their way to her schoolhouse.

She had not had to stop to tell Freddie Cox from flicking Ben Stone's ear, or coax poor cleft-lipped Sidney Drayton down from a tree as he indulged in his favourite pastime, spotting and logging the planes taking off and landing at the RFC aerodrome. Or chivy along the Branton sisters, three pretty, startlingly blonde siblings, a year between them in age, always with arms linked as if they were a single child facing the world. With their vile father, mind, it wasn't surpris-ing they needed a united front. Or what about lonely little Victoria Hanson, trudging down the road, feet dragging, trailing an air of melancholy behind her, all big sighs and even bigger eyes that appeared to be perpetually on the brink of leaking?

Where had all the children gone?

She felt a curdling in her stomach, as if she had eaten something unpleasant and her head swam with a sensation akin to vertigo. She had last felt this when the telegram about Arnold, her brother, had arrived. Her mother had passed the brown envelope to Miss Pillbody and she had handed it back, unwilling to be the first to read the news. In the end, they had opened it — and wept — in unison.

He had been nineteen, a full ten years younger than she, when a trench mortar dropped a shell on him, the baby of the family and, she realized much later, unexpected by her parents. But they had made out he was the son that, after three girls, they had always longed for. People said Nora and Arnold were very alike, but she couldn't see it. The grief of his death had chased her away from Chichester to the Suffolk countryside, to teaching the children of the estate and the surrounding villages, trying to blank out the war and what it was doing to millions of young men like Arnold.

It wasn't only the children who were absent. By now she should have seen a dozen or more people on the farms. In summer, Mrs Dottington always leaned on the gate after she had collected the eggs from her henhouses, enjoying the sun on her face. Old 'Zulu' Jenkins, veteran of the South African wars, ninety if he was a day, was normally out in the fields, helping – or just as often hindering – his son Johnnie. If not, he'd be sitting on a stump, taking a pipe. And then there were the nameless workers who would pause and doff a cap to her as she rode by.

All nowhere to be seen.

The area outside the schoolhouse was also empty of children, who by now would usually be playing marbles or jacks, or gossiping and sniping. An ad hoc game of boys' football or cricket, perhaps; hopscotch or skipping rhymes from the girls. But apart from a car she didn't recognize, parked across the entrance, the playground was deserted.

She dismounted from her bike, leaned it against the wall and examined the vehicle. She didn't know much about the various makes of car, but from its drab paintwork and stencilled numbers on the bonnet sides, even she could tell it was military in origin.

Miss Pillbody undid the ribbon under her chin and removed her hat before she stepped inside the little vestibule of the schoolhouse. 'Hello?' she asked tentatively. 'Who's there?'

'Come in, please,' came the reply. Inviting her into her own schoolhouse. The cheek of it.

She opened the door and stepped through into the classroom, chairs still up on desks from the previous night, the six times table chalked on the board, because she had promised her pupils they would be doing it again first thing.

There were two men in the room, one standing next to the blackboard, the other perched on the corner of her desk. The one on his feet was older, his moustache almost white, a corporal of the new Home Service Defence Forces, who were ubiquitous in the towns and villages of Suffolk and East Anglia. The one seated was an officer, as proclaimed by the gleam on his boots and the swagger stick in his hand. He was square of jaw and dark of moustache, probably a good few years younger than she. Striking-looking, she thought, but with a cruel aspect to his mouth and sharp blue eyes that shone with a glacial coolness. His top lip was a smidgeon too thin, she decided, for him to be entirely handsome, but he was certainly attractive. And, she suspected, he knew it. The officer and scooped off his cap stood as she crossed towards the pair.

'Miss Pillbody.'

So he had her name. 'You have the advantage of me, Lieutenant . . . ?'

'Booth. Lieutenant James Booth, from the Elveden Explosives Area.' His eyes ran over her, making her feel uncomfortable. 'I must say I was expecting someone older.'

She was in no mood for flirtatious flattery 'Where are my children, Lieutenant Booth?'

The grin faded to something more sombre. 'They won't be coming to school today, Miss Pillbody.'

'And why not?'

'In fact,' he said, the pink tip of his tongue touching his top lip for a second as he hesitated, 'they won't be coming to school for the foreseeable future, I am afraid.'

A multitude of possibilities rattled through her mind – were they recruiting children for the war? Was it a disease quarantine? Evacuation because of the Zeppelins? – but none made any sense. 'And why not?'

'I can't say. But we have extended the quarantine zone around Elveden. All the tenant farmers are being relocated for the duration and the children are going with them.'

'Duration of what?' she pressed. In fact, there was only one week of school left before the holidays, but she wasn't going to let that assuage her indignation.

'I can't say.'

She looked at his uniform, searching for regimental badges, but could spot none. Wasn't that unusual? She wished she had paid more attention to such matters. 'Who are you with, Lieutenant? Which regiment?'

A tight-lipped smile silently repeated his previous statement. Those chill eyes told her not to pursue the matter.

'These children need schooling, you know. A good proportion still can't read or write—'

'All that has been taken into consideration. They will be well looked after where they are going.'

'And where is that? No, don't tell me. You can't say.' She could feel anger rising in her, the sort that bubbled up when she had to deal with locals who told her that their young daughter was going to marry at sixteen and be a farmer's wife and had no need of any further schooling. 'You have no right to do this—'

'But I have,' said Booth, his manner suddenly abrupt. He reached into his top pocket and brought out a folded sheet of paper. 'I have every right under the Defence of the Realm Act. You actually live just outside the new exclusion zone, so you can keep your cottage, but after today you will not be allowed anywhere on the estate until further notice.'

'But—'

'And if you do set foot on the estate, or indeed mention anything that has happened to you today, or speak to any of the locals about this or any subsequent events, you will be prosecuted under this Act.' He unfurled the sheet of paper and shook it threateningly. 'I'm sorry we didn't reach you before you made the journey here, but there has been a lot to do. I suggest you return home to your cottage now. You will be compensated financially, of course, for loss of salary. Perhaps you should go back to your parents in Chichester. I am sure you can find a young man who will snap you up.'

She was furious at both the crass remark and the fact that he had been peering into her life. 'There is more to life than finding a young man.'

Booth raised an eyebrow.

'And there is no appeal against this?'

'None, I am afraid.' He put on his cap. The matter was closed.

He indicated to his driver they were leaving. 'Look on the bright side, Miss Pillbody. Your holiday has come a little early.'

She could think of nothing to say, although she wanted to stamp her foot and wail at him. 'Very well. But I intended to run summer art classes here—'

'Cancelled,' said Booth bluntly.

'And if I need anything from the schoolhouse at a later date?'

The lieutenant and his corporal exchanged glances. When he looked back at her she felt something icy on her neck and the hairs prickled to attention. 'I'd make sure you take everything you need today. If you come back here, Miss Pillbody, you will be shot on sight.